DADDY

Diane Martin

Nitram & Srewolf, Inc.

First Edition: March 2018

Cover Design by Denise Billups of Borel Graphics
Email: denise.billups@gmail.com

Book Layout and Design by Diane Martin

Edited by William & Diane Martin

The model on the cover is A'Dante Martin.
Email: dantemartin1111@gmail.com

United States ISBN Agency:
ISBN 10: 0-997576146
ISBN 13: 978-0-9975761-4-6

Disclaimer: This is a book of fiction and is not based on actual events. Any similarities to current events, characters, names, and locations are purely coincidental and based solely on the imagination of the author.

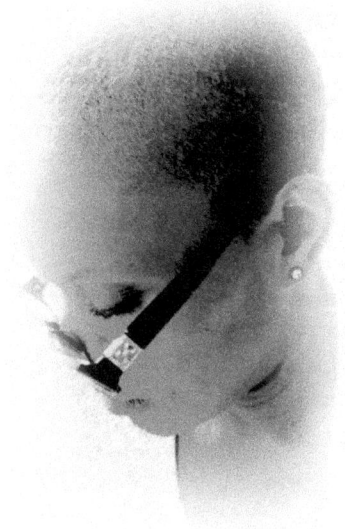

Thank you…
– Diane Martin

DEDICATED TO OUR DADDIES

DADDY BY DIANE MARTIN 5

"IT IS A MAN'S OWN MIND, NOT HIS ENEMY OR FOE, THAT LURES HIM TO EVIL WAYS."

- BUDDHA

8

PROLOGUE

My name is Paul. I'm the oldest of eight kids. If you look at my brothers and sisters, you can't really tell that we're related. If you saw us together, you would probably think that someone had either kidnapped us, or that someone was having a meeting with members of the United Nations. We were mixed with everything. I have a half-Asian sister, two half-white brothers, a half-Mexican-brother, one brother who was part Filipino, a sister who was part Puerto-Rican, another brother who was part Indian, and then there was me. I wasn't mixed as a result of anything that my mother did, but you could tell by my light grey eyes that somebody in my family tree got a visit in the middle of the night by somebody who was of the Caucasian-persuasion.

Being the oldest of eight, I was given the role of babysitter. It wasn't something that I wanted to do, but when your mama makes babies faster than *Ford* makes automobiles, then what do you do? And as soon as she made us, she tried to get rid of us like a wad of gum that was stuck to the bottom of her shoe. We were the shit residue on the toilet bowl that was her life and no amount of toilet paper would get rid of us. She didn't want to be bothered with us, but she had no choice, because we were the "link" to that government check that she got every month.

But she was mama, and nobody questioned mama. Even when I didn't understand why she did what she did or agreed with what she did, I did what she told me to do, because that's what kids are supposed to do. And I was so young. Too young to know that what my mama was doing to us was wrong, because I trusted her and as a child, that's what we do. We love and trust our mothers, unconditionally, even when they don't love us, and I learned that. It took some years, but I figured it out. She hated us so much that it oozed from her pores like pus from an infected wound and she didn't hide it. But as kids, we didn't know the difference between love and hate. All we knew was mama and we loved her, not realizing the suffering that it would cause us.

Our lives were so unstable. Other than the times that we stayed with my grandparents, she lugged us from one abandoned building to another. It was always so cold, so dark, and so dirty, and I was, always, so afraid and so hungry, and as a child, the only thing on my mind was when we were going to eat again and believe me, that was something that I had to think about a lot, because we didn't get to eat often. I remember the days when she'd left us with nothing, but the memories of the meals that we'd had days before. The younger ones would cry so loud. I used to cover my ears to silence the noise, but it was hard shutting out the sound of my own stomach growling.

And she left us – a lot. She used to wait until we were asleep to slip-out in the middle of the night, leaving us for days at a time. Then, out of the blue, she would pop-up, with bags of rotting fruit, molding bread, and spoiled lunchmeat that she fed to us until our bellies were full - only to turn around and leave us again. And this was our lives until the day it all came to a tragic end.

And it hurts so bad to even think about it. How would I've known that what was going to happen on that day was going to change our lives forever? Things started out so simple. We woke up and again, she was gone, but on this occasion, she'd left us in an abandoned building near a park. The kids were crying, so I decided that we should go to the park. It wasn't to play, but I knew that there would be food in the garbage cans and if we were lucky, we would find some. I just wanted to make them happy. I just wanted to stop the crying.

So, I led them all out of the house and across the street. We all held hands like we'd been taught in school and we made it across without incident. We walked around, searching the cans for whatever we could find, but we'd gotten there too late. The cans

DADDY BY DIANE MARTIN II

had already been ravaged by critters and the people who lived in the park. I looked across the park where I spotted a man sitting on a bench feeding the birds. I dragged the others over and we watched him, hungrily. At first, he acted like he didn't see us, but when he realized that we weren't going to leave until he shared his bread with us, he finally acknowledged us by saying, "Ain't y'all supposed to be in school somewhere?"

We shrugged our shoulders.

"Where's your mama?" he asked, next.

I shrugged and said, "I don't know."

He looked around for a second and said, "So, you're here by yourself?"

I looked at my brothers and sisters and said, "No…we are here together."

He stared at me for a second and said, "So, it's just y'all?"

"Yep…" I said, staring at the bread.

He smiled. "You want to feed the birds?"

Thinking for a second, I said, "Ummmmm, yeah…the birds…"

He began to break the bread into little pieces and handed it to us, but to his surprise, we didn't feed the birds. Instead, we, quickly, stuffed the bread into our mouths. Amused, he began to break the bread and toss the crumbs onto the ground. He smiled as he watched us fight the birds and each other for the food. After he ran out, he looked at us and said, "Well, that's it." He stood and began to walk away, but then turned and said, "Hey, I have more food at my house. Would you like some?"

Without hesitating, we all said, "Yes!!!!"

Then, a sad look came over his face. "I'm sorry, but I can only take one of you. How about this? What I will do is, take one of you, we will get the food, and then, we will bring it back to all of you."

Something about this didn't seem right, but we were so hungry. "Mister, I can't leave my brothers and sisters...I would get in trouble."

He looked at all of us like he was picking through a litter of puppies and said, "How about that one right there? He would be perfect."

I looked at my little brother and with the most trusting look in his eyes, he smiled and began to walk towards the man. The man held out his hand. "I promise, I will be right back."

"Okay..." I said, as I watched them walk away. "We gon' be right here waiting for you." I promised my brother.

As he walked away, he turned and waved at us.

"I promise...I'mma be right here," I said, trying more to convince myself than him.

The man shooed us away. "Fly away little birdies...go home." Then, he paused and smiled. "Don't worry. We'll be back...after he plays with my worm."

DADDY BY DIANE MARTIN 13

We both died that day.

CHAPTER I

It was May 11th, 1988 when it all began – the beginning of the end. They say that the way that you come into the world sets the stage for the rest of your life. If this is true, then I was doomed from the start. You see, I was the by-product of a one-night stand. As the story goes, she met some boy, developed a crush on him, and gave herself to him, but after he got what he wanted, he tossed her ass to the side like a used condom. She went on with her life, but he'd left something, behind, to remind her of him. She started to notice changes in her body, but she didn't tell anyone. At age 12, she probably didn't know what was happening to her body as I began to grow inside of her. I was told that she hid me from everyone until the day that she gave birth to me. I'm sure that my grandparents were shocked when they took her to the emergency room thinking that she was only having bad cramps and found out that I was the reason behind them.

While she was old enough to make a baby, she was too young to raise one, so I spent a lot of time with my grandmother – to the point where I thought of her as my mama and I saw my real mother as the stranger who slept down the hall from us. Her name was Betty and that's what I called her. She tried to make me call her mama, but I wouldn't. I refused to, because I hated her, and she knew it. In my head, I used to call her B.B. That stood for Bitter Betty or Bitter Bitch based on what day it was and how pissed-off she made me. When I was younger, I never truly understood my resentment towards her. I just knew that she was the enemy. She was the reason why my granny had no money to buy us toys. She was the reason why we barely had any food to eat and the reason why my granny cried at night, while waiting for her to come home.

Betty had some serious problems. By all accounts, Betty was fucked up. When she wasn't making babies, she was getting high or trying to find a way to get high. As a baby, I was unaware of how bad things were, but as I got older, it became clear how troubled she was. It was unfortunate, as a child, to have to watch someone who'd given birth to me – given me life – destroy her own. Sure, my grandparents tried to protect us from it, but it's hard to ignore someone who is hell-bent on killing herself. I never understood why she just wouldn't do it and get it over with – put us all out of our misery, but she was too evil for that. Betty wanted to take us all with her.

I will never forget, one day, while getting ready for school, I heard a loud crashing noise coming from the kitchen. I didn't pay it any attention, at first, because something was always crashing in our house. I actually turned the volume up on the TV to block out the noise. Several minutes had passed, before I grabbed the plastic grocery bag that I carried my books in and headed down the hallway. As I walked down the hall towards the kitchen, I noticed a pair of feet lying on the kitchen floor. I remember that I didn't rush into the room like someone else in the same position would have. Maybe it was because I had a suspicion that it was Betty that I didn't feel fear or panic. I was actually angry that this was happening to me. For a moment, I wanted to turn around and leave the room hoping that after a while she would get up and get out of my way, but then out of some morbid fascination, I decided to walk into the room.

When I walked in, I saw her stretched-out across the floor. Her body was jerking, violently. She was foaming at the mouth as her eyes rolled into the back of her head. I walked over and stood over her. As I watched her body twist and jerk across the floor, I couldn't help but wonder what she was thinking. Did she know that I was there staring at her? Did she know that I was watching her die? Suddenly, out of some weird sense of responsibility, I kneeled down next to her and grabbed her hand. I felt like if she was going to die, she shouldn't be alone. Her body continued to jerk until finally, there was nothing, but silence.

A sense of peace swept over me. She was gone and now, granny would be happy again, but as I stood to leave the room, all of a sudden, she gasped for air. Her eyes flew open as she reached out to grab my arm. Frightened, I stumbled backwards trying to get away from her, but she continued to reach out for me. She grabbed my leg. I began to kick my feet trying to release her grasp from around my ankle.

"Paul...Paul...." she said, gasping for air.

I pushed her hands away. As I stood to grab my books, she said, "Paul, go and get help." I looked at her and frowned. Angry and disappointed that she was still alive, I turned and left her lying on the kitchen floor.

The weird thing is, is that I never gave it a second thought. I went about my day as if nothing happened that morning and when I returned home from school, I walked into the kitchen hoping that she was still lying on the floor, but as I ventured further into the house, I found her. I walked into her bedroom to find her asleep in her bed with her crack-pipe lying next to her. As I turned to leave the room, I stepped on a floor board that creaked. She looked up. "Paul?"

I didn't respond. I was walking towards the door when she said, "I bet you wish I was dead?"

I looked at her, frowned, and said, "Yeah, if only wishes came true."

CHAPTER 2

I didn't know who my father was. She used to joke and say that she got pregnant from sitting on a dirty toilet seat. For some odd reason, she thought that we'd believe that and for a long time we did, until I began to notice all of the men that was coming in and out of her bedroom. I may have been young, but I understood that whatever my mama did in that room led to another brother or sister.

For a long time, I resented the fact that I didn't have a father to call my own. I mean, I had my granddaddy, but I would have loved to have known the man behind my existence. And don't get me wrong, granddaddies are great, but they are no substitute. Granddaddies can only do and give so much, before they get tired of you and start mumbling things like, "I wish somebody would come and pick you little motherfuckers up."

He was a tough old man who didn't take shit from nobody. When he spoke, you listened even though most of the things that he said made no sense. You see, he served in the military – Marines, I think. He was never too sure what war he was fighting and when he was fighting it. Based on what day you spoke to him it could easily change from Vietnam, to Iraq, or to the mean streets of Chicago. He lost his legs in the war, but again, based on what day you asked him about it, that story could change too. While the truth varied from day to day, one thing is for sure, is that whatever happened, to him, set the course for all of the events that followed.

He wasn't the type of man who held his tongue or someone who tipped-toed around your feelings. He said what he wanted to say, when he wanted to say it and if you were the sensitive type, then your feelings got hurt, a lot, and he didn't give a shit. He felt that it was his right to tell you what was on his mind and it was your privilege to listen to it - whether you wanted to or not.

"Boy, you don't know shit from Shinola…"
"What is Shinola, grand-daddy?"
"That's what we used to call a brand of shoe polish…cause of the shine that it used to leave on shoes…that's how Black men made a living, back in the day…shining shoes…"
"Oh…is that how you lost your legs?"
"No, dumbass. Does that make any sense? I told you a million times, I lost them saving those hostages. I don't know why you keep forgetting…it ain't like you got shit-else going on in that head of yours…"
"So, you saved some hostages?"

"I just said that…is there something wrong with your ears too? I told you…it was about a hundred of them…dragged them across enemy lines. Bullets were flying everywhere, but that didn't stop me…I crawled and dragged them all to safety."

"So, your legs were gone, already, and you dragged people to safety?"

"Why you think they gave me all of those medals?" He paused to answer his own question. "Cause, they ain't have shit-else better to do with them?"

To avoid getting a headache, I decided to change the subject. "So, why did you join the military, grand-daddy?" I asked.

"We didn't have no damn choice…you think a Black man could get away from going to war? Shiiiiiiiiiiittttt, Black men were hung for less…let a motherfucker say he ain't fighting in the war…his ass would be dead before he finished that sentence…you had a better chance running from a Nazi's bullet than running from a gad-damn noose."

"Maybe, I should go to the military," I said, proudly. "To be like you…"

He smacked me in the back of the head. "You got a gad-damn death wish? Your weak-ass wouldn't make it through the application process…"

I rubbed the back of my head and said, "I could…"

"Okay, let's see what you got…"

"Huh?"

"Get your ass on the floor and give me fifty…:"

I sat down on the floor and reached into my pocket. "I don't have the whole fifty, but I got a dime…"

He took the dime, put it into his pocket, leaned over, and smacked me in the head, again. "Your ass wouldn't know your butt from a hole in doughnut…"

Rubbing my head, I said, "A doughnut? I thought that it was a hole in a wall…"

"Talking to stupid people makes me hungry…" He paused and pointed at the floor. "Now, give me fifty pushups…"

I threw my hands in the air. "Ohhhhhhh…that's what you meant. Why didn't you say that?"

"Cause, you got to think on your feet, boy. You can't wait for somebody to fill-in the blanks for you…you gotta know…it could be the difference between life and death."

He raised his hand, but I ducked it, and rolled over on my stomach. He began to count. "1, 2, 3, 4, 5, 6, 7…"

After seven, I stopped to catch my breath.

He placed his hand to his ear. "Do you hear that?"

"Hear what?" I asked, sprawled out on the floor, holding my chest, and praying that I wasn't having a heart attack.

"That's failure, boy, calling your name…putting you in the military would be a lot like this conversation…a waste of damn time…instead of the military, you should learn how to style women's hair? That's a good role for somebody like you…"

I frowned. "Somebody like me? What are you trying to say, grand-daddy?"

"I'm not TRYING to say shit…I'm saying that you need to get your mind off of the military and ain't nothing wrong with you doing hair with the womens for the womens…that's all I'm saying. Just as long as you keep your manhood intact you'll do just fine."

I jumped up and wiped my hands on my clothes. "I'm not going to be nobody's hairdresser…" I threw my hand in the air to wave him off.

"You see…you see how you just did that?"

"Did what?"

"That thing with your wrist…"

I waved my hand again. "This?"

"Yeah…that there…you see all that 'flick' in your wrist?"

I didn't respond.

"Your ass will fit right in…get you some tight-ass pants. You know? Like the ones those dancers wear…make sure that they show all of your 'shit' and wear a shirt that's two sizes too little…the ladies like that…show a little chest hair too…you know, after you grow some and your ass will be rolling in the dough…"

Frustrated, I teased. "Well, maybe, I should just be a male stripper…how about that?"

He rubbed his chin as he looked me over. "Unless you grow an ass within the next five years, I don't see it happening…you wouldn't be able to feed yourself on that little shit that you got back there now…and don't get it twisted, some of those hairdressers are tough…have you seen them? They ain't to be messed with…fucking around with those chemicals, nagging-ass women, while standing on their feet all day…them some bad motherfuckers. Don't underestimate them…and they make good money too. Black women will sell their kids to keep that hair done."

"I'm going to prove to you that I can be tough too… watch…"

He frowned. "Well, don't hurt yourself trying to prove yourself…now, sashay your little ass down to the kitchen and see if your granny picked-up some doughnuts."

CHAPTER 3

He was always on high-alert. Waiting for someone or for something to happen. We were not sure who he was afraid of, but whoever it was or whatever it was, he was waiting for it. He spent every waking moment sitting in the window with a shotgun in one hand and a 45 in the other. You never wanted to walk up on our porch, uninvited, because you never knew what war he was fighting that day. You could easily go from friend to foe.

Only having an eighth-grade education, he couldn't help me with most of my homework. He became, easily, frustrated when asked for help, so I didn't ask him, but he taught me what he knew – war – to kill or be killed. He believed that everyone was going to die and how a man died, mattered. He always said, "You want to die like a man, son…not like some little bitch. And the only way to talk to a man, is with your gun. That's the only language a man understands." He was always giving me advice, but things could get quite confusing coming from my grand-daddy.

There were many days that I would wake-up to find him, sitting across the room, staring at me, waiting to administer what he called, "Breaking the Bolo." In other words, wake Paul up and mess with him 'cause he ain't got nothing better to do.

"Good morning, Rainbow," he said, as he came towards me.

I frowned. "Rainbow? Don't you mean 'sunshine'?" I asked, as I rubbed 'sleep' from my eyes.

He pulled the blanket off of me. "Get that 'pansy' shit out of here. No, grandson of mine is going to be called, 'Sunshine'…unless he got some suga' in his tank…you got some suga' in your tank, boy?"

I shook my head. "No, grand-daddy…there's no sugar in my tank, but you did call me a Rainbow, grand-daddy…" I said, trying to pull my blanket from his hands.

"And you're going to be a rainbow until I say you're not a rainbow…now, get your butt out of that bed and line up," he demanded.

I looked around the room. "Line up? Where? Huh?"

"Yes, boy…NUTS TO THE BUTT!!!" he instructed.

Scratching my head, I asked, "Nuts to whose butt, grand-daddy? And why am I putting my nuts on somebody else's butt. I don't know what y'all did in the military, but I ain't rubbing my nuts on nobody's butt…"

Frustrated, he said, "I ain't asking you to rub your nuts on nobody's butt…"

"Didn't you say, 'Nuts to the Butt'?"

"Yes, boy, but that's not what I meant."

"You did say, 'Nuts to the Butt', grand-daddy..." I confirmed.

"Will you stop talking about nuts and butts?" He asked, growing impatient.

"You brought 'em up..." I paused and looked him up and down. "You sure you ain't got no sugar in YOUR tank, grand-daddy?"

He laughed. "Ain't no suga' in this tank...that's for damn sure...yo' grandmamma can attest to that...nothing but salt in this tank..." He rubbed 'himself' and placed his hand against his nose. "It's salty right now..." He held his hand up to my face. "Wanna smell?"

"Ewwwwwwww..." I frowned and pushed his hand away.

"Boy, you know what you are?" he asked.

"Other than sleepy...frustrated...confused...what am I, grand-daddy?"

"You're a gad-damn oxygen thief...that's what YOU are..." he spewed.

I blinked, rapidly. "A what? Now, I'm stealing oxygen, grand-daddy? I thought that air was free..."

"That's not what that mean...it means that you talk too damn much, boy...that's what that mean...that's why you keep getting tacos..." he said.

Excitedly, I jumped up and looked around the room. "Tacos? Who got tacos?"

"Boy, if ignorance was a crime, they'd give you the chair...tacos is what they give you when you fail..."

"Oh…I like tacos…and all I have to do is fail to get them? What do a brotha' have to do to get a hamburger?"

Smack!!! I grabbed the back of my head and yelled, "What was that for?!!"

"For being a gad-damn smart-ass…I'm trying to keep you out of a tango uniform…"

"Tango uniform?" I asked, confused. "Grand-daddy, you're killing me."

"That's what I'm trying to prevent…"

"Grand-daddy, you got my head spinning…"

"Then, get yo' ass up." He grabbed my arm and tried to pull me out of the bed. "They gon' find you one day with your tits-up, boy…"

"Tits-up? Now, you want my tits up? I'm starting to worry 'bout you, grand-daddy."

Annoyed, he said, "Dead, boy…when you die, your tits face-up towards the ceiling…"

"Not always…you could die laying on your stomach…"

"You want me to kill you, so we can test my theory?"

"No…"

"Then, knees to the chest, boy…knees to the chest…"

I was going to ask him what that meant too but thought that I'd been slapped enough for one morning and decided to leave it alone.

"Now, let's get out into the yard before your grand-mama gets up. That woman can sho' work my nerves."

*Talk about somebody working somebody's nerves...*I thought to myself.

So, we went outside into the backyard where the sun was waiting for us. He looked at me and instructed. "Okay, boy...line 'em up."
I looked over at the other side of the yard where some cans were sitting. I walked over and began to line them up on the fence. Suddenly, I heard a popping sound and then, something whizzed passed my head. I grabbed my ear. Startled, I looked at him. "Granddaddy!!!"
He was pointing the gun at me. "You came real close to dying, today, boy. Now, get over here...we ain't got all day."
Asshole. I thought to myself. I sighed and walked towards him.
"I want to introduce you to my girlfriend."
"Who?" I asked, as I looked around the yard.
"Right here, boy...this right here is the only thing that I will ever cheat on your grandmamma with. My gun. Ain't she beautiful?"
"Ummmm, I guess..."
"Boy, this bitch is fine as hell and if you can't see it then you're blind as hell..."
"Okay..." I said, agreeing with him.
"Now, here...' He placed 'her' in my hand. "Hold her pussy."
I frowned and jumped back. "What?"

"The gun is the woman and the trigger is her pussy…keep up, boy."

I didn't wanna know why he called it that, but the look on his face told me that he was going to tell me anyway.

"Boy, the relationship between a man and his gun is special and sacred. When you're deployed…away from home…for months at a time…and they stick this thing in your hand and they tell you that this is your new best friend…when you're out there alone and it's just you and 'her' against the enemy…you can't worry about the pussy you got back at home because you don't know what that pussy is doing, but this one right here…she never left my side, boy…faithful 'til the end…and when I pulled her out…put my hands on her…put my finger on that pussy, I knew that somebody was 'bout to die…" He began to get a weird look on his face. "Just gives me so much pleasure…"

"Grand-daddy…do you want me to leave you alone with your 'pussy'?"

He snapped out of his trance and said, "I don't need to be alone with it. Now, hold this bitch…"

I looked at it. 'She' was absolutely beautiful. She was black like coal and warm to the touch. Something about holding 'her' made me tingle inside. I smiled.

Pleased, he said, "See what I told you…now, don't just hold her…you have to caress her…let her know that you're in control and she'll perform for you, boy…oh, yes…perform like crazy…now, go on… stroke her and see what happens…"

For a moment, I felt uncomfortable and confused. I wasn't quite sure, at that moment, what kind of lesson he was trying to teach me. Was I learning about guns or was I learning about sex?

He continued, "Now, hold 'her' up and place your finger on her clitoris…"

Confused, I looked at him. "Her what?"

He snatched the gun out of my hand. "Let me show you, boy…you see what I'm doing with my finger? You got to get your finger in there." He slid his finger in and out of the area where the trigger was. "You ain't gon' ever get or keep a girlfriend if you can't get this part down-pat. It's essential that you know what you're doing…now, here…" He handed the gun back to me. "Look at it…"

I held the gun up to my face and looked down the barrel.

"Do you see the pearl?"

"The who?" I asked.

"The prize, boy…can you see the prize?"

"The can? Yes, I can see it…"

"Now, stroke that pussy, boy…STROKE IT…" he instructed.

Moving my finger back and forth across the trigger, I said, "I'M STROKING IT, dang…"

"You act like you're scared of the pussy…"

"I'm not scared of it…"

"Then, pull the damn trigger…"

I looked at him. "Is this safe?"

"Boy, if you don't shoot that damn gun..." He was becoming frustrated. "If somebody catches a damn bullet, this time of the day, then he deserves it...asses should be at work anyway..."

I held the gun up, again. Stared down the barrel and without thinking, I pulled the trigger. I fell backwards onto the ground. When I was able to regain my composure, I looked up and noticed that all of the cans were still standing. Disappointed, I stood up and walked over to see where the bullet landed. As I got closer to the fence, I could hear somebody whining. I looked around and on the ground near a tree was a squirrel lying helplessly – crying – dying.

I walked over and kneeled down next to it. My grand-daddy came over.

"Ooooooooooo weeeeeeee...look what you did, boy. I told you to shoot the can and instead, you got us lunch. Bag that bitch and let's take it to yo' grand-mamma so she can skin it and cook it...boy, I tell ya'...we gon' eat...we gon' eat good."

"But it ain't dead, yet...he's suffering." I said.

He snatched the gun out of my hand, pointed it, and said, "The only way to stop the suffering is with a bullet...right...between...the...eyes...just point and ..." *Click. Pop!* He pulled the trigger, and suddenly, the crying stopped. "Simple...now, let's go...I wonder if we got some eggs. Squirrel sho' taste good with eggs..." he said, as he wheeled himself back to the house.

I picked the squirrel up by its tail and carried it out in front of me. As I looked at him, a wave of satisfaction swept over me. This was my first kill and it made my grand-daddy proud of me and I liked making him proud of me.

CHAPTER 4

I couldn't stop thinking about it – death. Until that moment, I never really considered it. It wasn't like no one or nothing, in my life, had ever died before. As kids, it just wasn't something that we ever had to deal with. My grandmother did everything that she could to protect us from it or at least protect us from the ugly side of it. We were never allowed to go to funerals, because she thought that dead bodies would give us bad dreams. If an animal died, we just woke-up one day, and found it gone. Sometimes, we had it for dinner or sometimes, it just disappeared like it never existed and we weren't allowed to talk about it. That was just the rule.

But after killing that squirrel, I started thinking about it. I started wondering things like, "Did the squirrel know that it was going to die that day and if it did, did it know how, and did it know why? And if it knew that it was going to die, would it had done anything differently that day or was it ready to just accept its fate?" And finally, "What was it thinking as my grandfather placed the barrel of the gun against his head, as he pulled the trigger, and as that bullet pierced his brain?" Of course, I wanted the answers, but unfortunately, the squirrel couldn't provide any. Even if he could, he couldn't, because he was dead.

And just like that, it was all over. His life as a squirrel ended. No more running up and down the tree in my backyard. No more gathering nuts for the winter. No more anything and no one cared to ask why. He was just gone and why? Because my grandfather decided that it was time for him to die and he had the power to do that – to decide if the squirrel could live or die. I'm not sure who gave him that power, but he had it. And on many occasions, he spoke about that power and how someone in our government gave him a gun and told him to shoot everybody who didn't love America and he did so without asking questions. Whether they were good or bad. Didn't matter. They had to die, and he did it with pride – killing men, women, and children, all because someone in our government told him to do so and they rewarded him for it. They gave him medals. He lost his legs, but they gave him medals. He lost his sanity, but they gave him medals and they, also, gave him a gun.

And he loves that gun. It is the only thing that really matters to him. Sure, he loves his family, but that gun gave him back what the war took from him. The war took away his childhood. The war took away his ability to take care of his family. The only thing that the war did not take was his life and his ability to use that gun. And on that day, my grandfather gave me that gun. And I held it - felt its coldness against my fingertips. It was a tool given to me like the one that the government had given to my grandfather. And I didn't understand it at first, but I realized that the gun was nothing. It is nothing, but steel without the likes of someone like my grandfather or someone like me standing behind it. And it was me, that day, with the power to give life or give death.

And for some odd reason, there was something beautiful in that squirrel's death - like a love story that I created in my mind. We weren't given a lifetime together. We were only given that moment. And how that moment became the defining moment of our lives. And as I watched his chest rise, as he took his last breath, I wondered if he knew how important he was to me becoming the man that I would soon grow up to be.

And something in me changed that day. I wasn't sure what it was, but I was no longer the little boy scared to hold a gun. I was no longer the little boy scared to pull a trigger. I was the little boy who was given the power to take a life – big or small – good or bad – I was, now, the powerful one.

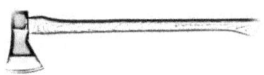

With each day came a new lesson. He was determined to make sure that I understood how much power I had and how it must be applied daily without hesitation or discretion. Today's lesson came while we were sitting on the porch, minding our own business, when two guys in a car drove passed and yelled, "Hey!" out of their car window.

Grand-daddy pulled his gun from his holster and pointed it at the car as it sped by. "Shit…they got away."

I looked up and said, "What 'cha doing, grand-daddy?"

"Did you know him?" he asked, looking down the barrel of his gun.

"No," I replied.

"Then, why do you care about what I'm doing?" He lowered his gun, shook his head, and said, "That's the damn problem with this world…"

"What is?" I asked.

"NIGGAS!!!" he replied.

"Niggas?" I asked.

"NIGGAS!!!!" he said, again, with emphasis.

"Why are niggas a problem, grand-daddy?"

"Cause that shit…that shit right there…" he said, pointing down the street. "Here we are…minding our own business…and some NIGGAS drive pass and shout 'Hey!' out of the gad-damn window…"

"Maybe they were trying to get our attention…"

"Or maybe, they were just being NIGGAS!" He said, becoming angry. "They didn't want shit. If they did, they wouldn't have kept driving. No, they did that shit to get on my damn nerves and you know what NIGGAS do and do well? They get on your damn nerves. That's what they do…if they didn't, they wouldn't be NIGGAS!!!" He was breathing so hard, I thought that he was going to pass-out. He slowed his breathing and continued, "If their asses had of slowed down, just a little, I would have put an end to that nigga-shit…"

"Why?" I asked. "They weren't doing anything wrong."

"Niggas never think that they are doing anything wrong until someone like me shows them the error of their ways." He paused and shook his head. "Motherfuckers should keep their 'Heys' to themselves…what if today, I was stressed-out…and it ain't like it ain't possible…I live with you motherfuckers…and he drove passed giving me the 'Hey' that set me over the edge…huh?" He twisted his mouth and continued, "He don't know me. I could work at a 'Hey' factory where motherfuckers don't do shit, but say 'Hey' all day and then, his dumbass pull that shit?"

"But you can't kill a man for saying 'Hey', grand-daddy."

"Why not? We killed men for less in the war…"

"But you're not fighting a war, grand-daddy…"

"But we are, son…it's a war against ignorance… Black, White, Yellow, Brown, Red, Beige, Green, Pink…whatever color they are…young…old… Niggas make me sick and they need to be stopped. They are a disease infecting this country and your grand-daddy got the cure, right here." He paused and placed his hand on his gun. "Let his ass drive pass here again hollering 'Hey' and see what happens. I'mma give him a shot in the ass that'll fix all that shit. Gon' be the last 'Hey' his ass ever say…the LAST motherfucking 'Hey'…"

As we sat there, looking out for niggas that he could shoot, I couldn't help but think about the things that he was saying to me. My grand-daddy was a man who'd survived the war and as a young boy who wanted to survive in this world, I felt that I had to listen to him and while I may forever question his "how", I can look into his eyes and understand his "why." Everything he did, he did for his family – both the good and the bad.

Chapter 5

He returned home a broken man – mentally, physically, and emotionally, but mostly, mentally. My grandmother said that he suffers from PTSD. That's when something traumatic happens to you and you find yourself stuck in a nightmare that never ends and most of the time, it was like that for him – like he was sleep-walking – talking about things that only made sense to him. It didn't help that he was already bat-shit crazy before he went in and if you add bat-shit crazy to PTSD, you get a man who's as unpredictable as the weather. Society, normally, locks these kinds of people up, but my grandmother said that a soldier who served his country deserves better than that. And that might be true, but while they were able to diagnose and treat his "crazy", we weren't always equipped to deal with it.

Beyond his craziness, he was an incredible man. My grand-daddy was born and raised in the South. He was a sharecropper's son who picked cotton from sun-up to sun-down. He didn't go to school much because work was more important than an education. He and my grandmother worked on the plantation together. It was during the harvest, that they met each other. He courted her for several months and it was during this time that she got pregnant with their first child. Their first child was a boy who was stillborn. They had their second child when they were only fourteen and married shortly thereafter. He was drafted into the war right after my grandmother got pregnant with her third child. He served one tour and returned home. It was then, that they left the south and any traces of his sanity. He tried fighting his demons with alcohol, but it's hard to keep them at bay when you barely have enough money for food and a house full of mouths to feed. So, his demons were left to run wild and wreak havoc on everything that he loved. The demons scared everyone else away. The only person willing to stay the course was my grandmother and his children.

And the "episodes" happened, frequently – almost, always ending with somebody getting hurt. One night, we were all asleep. It was hot outside, so we kept most of the windows open to cool off the house. It was late when I heard someone struggling. Then, there was a loud *thud!* I jumped out of bed and ran towards the noise. I walked in to find grand-daddy sitting on top of someone.
"Help me tie him up…" he instructed.
"What?" I asked, rubbing sleep from my eyes.

"Don't ask no dumb-ass questions, boy. We ain't got time for that. Now, find something to tie his ass up with before he wakes up."

"What did you do to him?" I asked, looking around the room. I found an extension cord and handed it to him.

"That's a dumbass question that I, specifically, asked you not to ask, but you're so damn hard-headed and need to know shit...and since it's not, clearly, evident...I knocked him, the fuck, out." He motioned for me to grab the man's hands.

I grabbed the man's hands and began to tie them together. "Grand-daddy, who is this?"

He shook his head and said, "Another damn question? You know, instead of tying him up with that cord, I can, easily, use it to answer your questions...how 'bout that?" He pointed at the man's feet. "Now, tie them up."

I did as I was told. After we made sure that the cord was tight, he said, "Now, help me back into my chair."

I wrapped his arm around my shoulder and helped him back into his wheelchair. Winded, he said, "Caught this motherfucker trying to rob us."

Stunned, I looked around the room. "Huh?"

"You heard me...he was trying to take our shit."

Confused, I looked around the room, again. "Are you sure, grand-daddy?"

He frowned. "He didn't come in here to watch me have sex with your grandmamma..."

"Ewwwwwww…" I said, trying to erase the image from my mind.

"Well, shit…that's exactly what I was doing…" he confirmed. "Tearing that ass up until this fool interrupted us."

"Ewwwwwwww…" I said, again. "You're going to give me nightmares, grand-daddy…"

"You think that I care about you having some gad-damn nightmares…I care more about this boil on my ass than I care about you and some damn nightmares." He began to pull down his pants, to show me the boil, but was interrupted when grandmother entered the room. She looked at us and then looked at the floor. She shook her head and proceeded to leave the room.

Trying to get the image of his boil and of them having sex out of my head, I looked around the room and said, "I find it hard to believe that he was trying to rob us…unless he came in here for spider webs…"

He pushed his wheelchair into the man's leg to wake him. The man began to come to.

"Huh? What?" the man mumbled.

"Well, let's ask him what he came in here for." My grandfather leaned over him and said, "What brings you into my house in the middle of the night…other than looking for an ass-whooping?"

The man struggled to turn over before saying, "Nothing…I wasn't looking for nothing…"

My grandfather squinted his eyes and said, "That's gon' look real good on your tombstone. This motherfucker died 'for nothing.' He sighed and continued, "Try again…"

The man hesitated for a second, but then said, "I came in here for the drugs…"

"What drugs?" I asked.

My grandfather laughed. "Now, that's some funny shit. You've been misinformed, son. We don't have any drugs. What we got is a drug ADDICT and you didn't have to break in here to get that motherfucker…you could have knocked, and I would have handed her to you."

"Clearly, I made a mistake…" the thief said.

"No doubt," my grand-daddy confirmed. "And you can't smoke the 'roaches' we got. You can try, but I don't think that you gon' get a buzz."

I shook my head. "So, what are you going to do with him?"

The man struggled to free himself.

My grandfather rolled his chair against his leg. "You might as well stop…you ain't gon' do shit but make yourself tired…might as well get comfortable." He paused for a second and looked around the room. "Did you climb through my window?"

Still struggling, he said, "I didn't climb into your window."

My grand-daddy folded his arms in front on his chest. "Really, now? Then, what happened? You were walking down the street, tripped, and landed in my living room? Huh?"

"Look, clearly there's no drugs here...I made a mistake," the man said.

"I said that shit already..." My grandfather paused and looked him over. Squinting his eyes, he continued, "With your lying ass...you weren't in here for no drugs. You trying to take my guns."

"You got guns? I didn't know that you had guns..." he said.

"Really? You stood outside of THIS house and thought to yourself, 'These motherfuckers look like they got drugs...' must have been the holes in the roof and the ripped-up screen on the screen door that gave us away..."

"No, wait...no..." he stuttered.

"But guns would make more sense. Cause, if poor people ain't got shit else, we got guns, right?"

"Look, just let me go..." the man begged.

My grand-daddy sighed and continued, "Sure and so that your night ain't a complete wash, why don't you take some of these damn kids with you?"

I frowned. "He ain't taking me nowhere."

"Your ass will be the first to go...keep talking shit."

I rolled my eyes and mumbled, "No way..."

He squinted. "There's room on that floor next to the dummy...you wanna join him?"

Ignoring him, I shook my head. "Grand-daddy, what are you going to do with him?"

"I'm going to kill him," he said, nonchalantly.

Shocked, me and the thief said, "YOU'RE WHAT?!!!"

My grandfather looked at him and confirmed, "Oh, you didn't hear me? Maybe, I need to talk slower. I'm…going…to…kill…you."

"Wait…what?" I asked.

"It's my God's-given-right. Eye for an Eye…that's what the Bible says…"

Confused, I said, "He didn't take your eye, grand-daddy."

The thief confirmed, nervously. "I ain't got no eyes…check my pockets…I promise."

My grand-daddy looked down at him and said, "Oh, but you do and I'm looking at 'em and I'm going to put a bullet right in the middle of 'em."

"Grand-daddy…nooooooo…" I begged.

The thief began to beg too. "Grand-daddy… nooooooo…"

"One, I ain't your grand-daddy. If I was, your ass wouldn't be breaking into nobody house in the middle of the night. Your ass would be sleep somewhere like that one right there." He looked in my direction and continued "…or reading a damn book. Second, you stole from me. Now, I get to steal from you."

Frightened, he said, "But I didn't take anything."

"You stole some of my damn sleep, but that ain't the story that I'm going to tell the police. I'm going to tell them that you broke in here, tried to rob me, tried to kill me, and I shot you in self-defense."

Struggling to free himself, he said, "You might be able to convince them that I tried to kill you, but that robbing shit is going to be a stretch…"

46

My grand-daddy pulled his gun and cocked it. "Look who's got jokes...the soon-to-be-dead-motherfucker on the floor..."

Without thinking, I jumped in front of the gun. "Grand-daddy...wait. Do you really want to do this?"

He pointed his gun. "He's gotta learn..."

"He can't learn nothing, dead, grand-daddy..."

"Yes, he can. While he's on his way to hell, he'll be thinking about the shit he did to get him there..."

"Come on, grand-daddy..." I begged.

He waved the gun in the air. "He will, also, learn that trespassing gets you a bullet to your head..." He aimed his gun. "Now, get out of the way, so that he can receive his lesson for the day."

The man closed his eyes. "Please...I'm sorry... please..."

Suddenly, I felt something warm under my feet. I looked down to find that the thief had wet himself. I jumped back.

My grandfather frowned. "And you pissed on my floor? On my floor? Oh, you are DEFINITELY dying today."

"Grand-daddy, don't kill him." I begged. Tears began to form in my eyes.

My grandfather looked at me. "Soft-ass...you willing to take a bullet for that piece of shit? Don't you ever jump in front of a gun for somebody like him."

"But he's...he's...he's..." I couldn't come-up with anything good to say about the man who'd just broke into our house.

He shook his head. "Somebody needs to teach these thugs the difference between right and wrong."

"I know, grand-daddy..." I continued, trying to reason with him. "But you will get his brains and guts all over the floor and grandma won't take too kindly to having to clean blood off of the floor."

"Shit, we already have to clean-up piss...it's just an extra 'wipe' to pick up the blood." he said.

"I know, but please..."

He paused for a moment to think about it. "You know, what? You're right...you're right...okay, untie him." I kneeled down to untie him.

"Oh, thank you...thank you...thank you..." he said, happily.

"Get out of my house," he demanded.

"Of course, I'm so sorry that I woke you. It'll never happen again." The man was walking towards the front door.

My grand-daddy frowned. "Where are you going?"

The man stopped. "I'm leaving..."

"Ummmm, front doors are for family and friends...we take the garbage out the back door."

We, both, followed him as he walked down the hallway. "This way?" he asked.

"Yes," he confirmed.

Just as the thief turned the door-knob, I heard a loud *POP!!!!!* I closed my eyes and placed my hands over my ears. The smell of gun powder filled the room. When the ringing stopped, I looked up to find the man lying on the floor. I ran over to his side.

"He shot me! He shot me!" he said, grabbing his back pocket. He lifted his hands to show me the blood that was covering them.

I looked over at my grandfather who was, now, smiling. "Boy, it's your lucky day. I was aiming at your head. It's a good thing that I didn't have my glasses on. Oh well, a bullet in the ass is just as good." He turned and began to roll his wheelchair down the hall. "Now, go and tell your friends. I don't want to have to shoot another one of you motherfuckers…" He waved his gun in the air. "Class is dismissed."

CHAPTER 6

We couldn't have friends over, because we didn't live in an environment where others felt comfortable. Plus, it was exhausting making excuses for the rats, roaches, and the addict down the hall and on top of those things, we had my grand-daddy to contend with. And when we weren't dealing with the episodes, we had his weird infatuation with his penis to contend with. Don't get me wrong, every boy and man has a close relationship with his "junk," but grand-daddy was obsessed with his. It was nothing to find him with his dick in his hand. If he wasn't playing with it, he was talking to it. At any random moment, he would just whip it out – at the kitchen table, as he was coming down the hall, and as he sat on the porch. And he wasn't embarrassed by it. What he couldn't understand was why we didn't do it. We tried to explain to him that in a normal society, folks weren't walking around whipping out their dicks, because they put people in jail for that kind of stuff, but he wasn't trying to hear it.

And they almost did. My grandmother hadn't left his side for more than five minutes, before he'd pulled "it" out and it wouldn't have been so bad if he hadn't have done it while a bunch of little girls were walking down the sidewalk. When the police arrived, he had a confused look on his face. He couldn't understand why they were there and when they told them that what he did was wrong. He told the police, "Well, they shouldn't have been looking. Nosey little asses got an eyeful, because they wanted to see it and believe me...it was an eyeful. They're the real freaks..." So, while my grandmother was trying to convince them not to lock him up, he yelled over her shoulder, "Kiss my ass!!!" and proceeded to whip that out too, so that they could see it and of course, kiss it...if they so desired. The only reason why they didn't swoop him up and throw him in a nuthouse, is because my grandmother showed them his military and medical papers that proved that he was "certifiable." So, they left him with just a warning – to keep it in his pants or else.

For a while, he was able to heed their warnings, but I guess a man can only keep his desires and his "crazy" in the "closet" for only so long. Then, one day, I caught him on the front porch doing his "business." He'd let-out a loud moan as his head fell back against his chair. As he was basking in his after-glow, I approached him.
"Grand-daddy!!!" I said, startling him like a child who'd just been caught with his hand in the cookie jar.

He jumped and pulled his gun. "What? Who? Where? How?" He said, stammering. When he realized that it was me, he said, "Booooooooooyyyyy, you gon' get your ass killed sneaking up on folks like that." He paused to wipe the sweat from his forehead and then, proceeded to put both "loaded weapons" back into their holsters.

I knew what he'd just finished doing, so to make him feel uncomfortable, I decided to ask him about it not realizing what I was setting myself up for. "What 'cha doing?"

Annoyed, he said, "None of your damn business…"

He wiped his hands on his pants.

"What were you doing with your ding-a-ling?" I asked.

"One, I'm a grown-ass man…we don't have ding-a-lings…" Frustrated, he continued, "And two, can't a man pleasure himself without motherfuckers asking him fifty questions?"

"Nope…" I said, being sarcastic.

"Well, he should be able to…"

"But if you do weird stuff, grand-daddy…"

"There ain't nothing weird 'bout a man taking care of his business."

"It's only your business when you keep it to yourself…when you do it in public, it becomes everybody's business…"

"And I don't have a problem with that. If folks want to look, who am I to deny them…"

"But grand-daddy…there's a time and place for that kinda of stuff…"

"And I chose this time and this place…what is wrong with that?"

"What's wrong is that you can't do that," I said.

"Who says that I can't?"

"Ummmmm…society…the police?" I said.

"Society can kiss my Black ass and so can the police…if their asses were fighting real crimes instead of worrying about what a man does with his dick, the world would be a better place…"

"But you can't do whatever you want to do with your …ummmm…whatchamacallit…"

"How can they tell me what to do with MY DICK while I'm on MY PROPERTY?"

"Because there's laws against that…"

"Okay…okay…so you say there's a law…right?"

Here we go. I thought to myself. "Right…" I answered, trying to see where he was taking this.

"Now, they say that it's indecent for me to relieve myself…in public, right?"

"Right…"

"Now, let's say that I was taking a piss…would that be indecent?"

"Yes…"

"Why?"

"Because…you're not supposed to do that in public either."

"But it doesn't become indecent until your nosey ass sees it…until then, it ain't a crime."

"Well…"

"And isn't that a natural function of the human body?"

"Yes…"

"Would you prefer that I piss on myself?"

"No…of course not…"

"Exactly…" He paused and continued, "And what about spitting? You can't get locked up for spitting…can you?"

"No, you can't…but…"

He interrupted. "Well, isn't that discrimination?"

"Huh? What?" I asked, confused.

"Why should spit be the only body fluid allowed to come from my body? Don't my other fluids have rights too?"

"Wait…what?" This conversation was becoming, both, weird and disgusting.

"Keep up, boy…we're talking about spitting…"

Trying to rein him back in, I said, "Like I was 'bout to say, grand-daddy…spitting is not a crime unless, you spit on somebody."

"EXACTLY!!!" He said. "And what I was doing…didn't get on anybody else, but me…as much as I would have loved it to…believe me…but it didn't."

"Ummmmm…but grand-daddy…"

He interrupted, again, "So, my point is…everybody should be able to cum and 'go' as they please as long as they don't cum and 'go' on nobody else…"

My head was spinning.

"The strange thing is…animals can have sex, spit, relieve themselves…do whatever…without people thinking twice about it. Matter of fact, animals can do all of that shit to humans and nobody even bats an eye." He huffed and continued, "Have you ever had a dog hump your leg?"

"No, I haven't…"

"It's an awful experience, but people think that shit is cute until a human turns the table on his ass and humps him back…THEN, they wanna start talking 'bout the dog's rights, but what about the human's right not to have their calf raped by some dog? Huh?"

"Ewwwwww…" I frowned.

"I'm just saying…"

"True, but we're not animals," I confirmed.

"Why? Because we wear clothes…'cause we go to work? 'Cause we live in houses? We are no different than animals. We love and protect our families like animals. We hunt like animals. We kill like animals. We eat animals…we are no different than a lion in the wilderness…"

I thought about what he was saying and said, "But it's what keeps us civilized…"

"What? Not pleasuring ourselves in public?"

"Yes…"

"Boy, you gon' have to come up with a stronger argument than that…have you seen how humans treat each other? Ain't shit civilized about that. And if keeping my hands off of my dick in public is what's keeping me a member of the human race, then cancel my subscription…'cause I'm gon' keep doing what I'm doing and if that makes me an animal then, ROAR, motherfucker, ROAR…" He grabbed "himself" and continued, "Now, get on out of here, so a man can finish what he was doing…in peace…" Before I walked away, he grabbed my arm. I looked down at it and frowned.

"And don't tell your grandmother."

CHAPTER 7

A nd over the next several months, the police became our best friends. One episode after another, they were at our house. They visited us more than anybody else on the block and our neighbors were drug dealers and crack-heads. One morning, I walked down the hall to find my grandmother standing in the front door, screaming at someone. "GET YOUR ASS IN HERE!!!" she demanded.

I walked to the door to look out.

"Go back in," she said. "You don't need to see this."

"See what?" I asked, rubbing my eyes. Quickly, it became clear what she didn't want me to see. Squinting my eyes, you could see him, butt-ass naked, lying in the bushes, covered in mud, grass, and leaves. I sighed. "Grandma, what is he doing?"

"He's hiding in the trenches..."

I twisted up my mouth before asking, "What trenches and why?"

She exhaled and shook her head. "He's hiding from the enemy."

"The enemy?" I asked, scratching my head. "What enemy? The gangbangers?"

She shook her head, "No…" She turned back towards him. "Bring your crazy ass in the house!!!"

He pulled out his gun and pointed it at the street. "I see youuuuuuuuu…"

I looked out towards the street. There was nothing there, but some papers being blown, back and forth, across the street. She grabbed me by the shoulders and turned me towards the hall. "Go get ready for school…I got this."

I turned and did as I was told. After I was ready, I walked out of the house. "Have a good day, grand-daddy," I said, waving my hand.

He crawled behind the bushes and said, "I think that we've blown our cover, soldiers…RETREAT!!! RETREAT!!!"

As I walked down the sidewalk, I could hear the police sirens in the distance.

The next episode involved us waking up to the smell of smoke. We followed the smell out into the backyard where we found him sitting next to a lit grill and throwing dollar bills into it. Trying not to startle him, I, carefully, asked him, "Grand-daddy…what are you doing?"

His eyes were glazed-over, and he seemed to be in a trance. I touched his arm. Slowly, he looked up at me. "He has to be punished…" he said, as he threw another dollar bill into the flames.

"Who, grand-daddy?"

"You know who, boy…"

My grandmother whispered in my ear – giving me the answer.

"The President?" I said, aloud.

"Yes," he confirmed.

"Why?"

"You know why, boy…"

My grandmother whispered in my ear, again.

"'Cause of your legs…?"

He became agitated. "That motherfucker took my legs."

"Sooooooooooooooooooo, you're burning money to punish him?"

With this wide-eyed look on his face, he said, "Damn right…I'm gon' kill him…"

"By burning money?"

"Yessssssssssss…I'm burning him."

"You're burning him?"

"Can't you see, boy? The root of all evil is money and whose face is on the money?" He tapped the side of his head and said, "Think, boy…think."

"Soooooooooooo, let me get this straight…" I began, but then stopped. Trying to get him to explain what the hell he was doing and why he was doing it, would make as much sense as me asking the face on the dollar bill why my grand-daddy was so mad at him and expecting an answer. It would be ridiculous, so we all turned and went back into the house. Everyone, but my grandmother who remained outside to make sure that he didn't hurt himself or burn the house down.

The other episode that stands out to me, was when he'd actually taken the mailman hostage. I'm not sure what set him off. Maybe, it had something to do with the mailman's uniform, but whatever it was, that mailman was going to die that day.

My grandfather was agitated all morning – going off about little things - like the fact that the sun was shining and that the birds were singing. "Will y'all shut those fucking birds up?!!!" And he went on like this for hours, until there was a knock on the door. He grabbed a kitchen knife and headed for the door. He opened the door and when the mailman extended his hand to give him the mail, my grandfather jumped out of his wheelchair and tackled him. He wrapped his arms around the man's neck and placed the knife against his chin.
"Help me!!!" he begged.
"Shut-up you, yellow, bastard," my grandfather demanded. He tried dragging the man inside of the house, but without his legs, it proved difficult. "You slimy, sneaky, bastard…I know why you're here."
I walked outside to find the man in a headlock. I looked over my shoulder and yelled, "Grandma, the mail is here and ummmmmmm, the mailman is too."
I could hear my grandmother's house-shoes smacking against the floor. "Well, bring the mail inside," she said.

I sighed and walked out onto the porch. I gathered the mail that was scattered all over the ground. I walked back in and handed it to her. "Here…"

She noticed that the door was still open. "Boy, go and close the door…"

"Okay, but should I leave grand-daddy out there?"

She walked towards the door. "Well, what is he doing?"

"Choking the mailman…" I said.

She dropped the mail and ran outside. "Let that man go…" She tried prying his arms from around his neck. "Let him go…you want to go to jail? They will put you in prison for assaulting a federal employee…"

"He's here to take me back…" my grandfather said.

"Let that man go, fool…it's too early for this shit." Finally, she was able to get his hands off of him. The man jumped up and ran down the street.

"Don't let him get away," My grand-daddy insisted.

My grandmother yelled, "I'm sorry!!!" She looked at the door and said, "Help me get him back into the house."

I did as I was told.

After that, they didn't leave our mail at the door, anymore. Most of the time, we found it on the curb or scattered around the front yard. Which was fine with my grandmother, because it was mostly bills anyway.

CHAPTER 8

As you may know by now, my grandmother was the complete opposite of my grandfather. If you saw my grandmother on the street, you would never know that she lived with a bunch of nuts. Outside, she carried herself with pride and dignity – never a hair out of place, but when she was at home it was easy to see the crack in her mirror of perfection. She had some issues and my grandfather was the least of them. Her biggest thorn in her side was her kids. My grandmother tried to raise them to be decent members of society. She was tired of struggling and just wanted for them to be able to take care of themselves. She was looking forward to a point where she could just sit back and enjoy what little life she had left. Sadly, things didn't turn out that way.

She had high expectations for her children. She wanted only the best for them. She had no idea that after all of the labor pains, all of the stretch marks, all of the diaper changings, all of the bottle feedings, and all of the sleepless nights, that she would end-up with a crackhead, a drug-dealer, an alcoholic, a cross-dresser, and the one that she considered a hoe. And that's how she described her kids. Well, maybe not the cross-dresser. She calls him a number of things. She was so disappointed in the paths that they had chosen in their lives that she refused to call them by their legal names and since she couldn't discipline them anymore, she thought that shaming them was the best way to get them to change - like "shaming the Devil". But it didn't work. The more she tried to push them in a direction that she thought was best for them, the more they resisted. They were going to live their own truth. Whether she liked it or not, but there was a price to pay and she made them pay it.

I remember a time, after one of my uncle's releases, and I say that because my uncle stayed in jail. As soon as he was released for one thing, he would, eventually, wind-up right back in there for another and it always had something to do with drugs. The last time, he was locked-up was for selling drugs to an undercover cop. He did a few years and when they released him, this time, my granny decided to throw him a little get together at the house. Now, mind you, we didn't have much, but she did what she could to try to bring us together. And it was the perfect day for it too. It was nice out, so no one could see the storm ahead.

We'd been waiting all day for his ride to arrive. She laid-out some drumsticks on the grill. At least, I think it was drumsticks. I did notice that we had less rats running around that day.

Before he got there, Betty and her sister had arrived. When they walked in, my grandmother embraced them. "If it isn't the crackhead and the hoe?"

They frowned. "I wish you wouldn't call me that."

"Then, change your life...until then, take your crackhead-ass in there and say 'Hi' to your daddy."

My mother huffed and walked out of the room.

My grandmother looked at my auntie and said, "What's up, hoe?"

My aunt shook her head. So, used to my grandmother's antics, she just said, "Hi mama..." and walked out of the room.

Soon the door opened. Everyone ran into the living room. We all jumped up. "Welcome back, Uncle Eddie...!!!" My Aunt Jasmine and Uncle John walked in behind him.

My grandfather came into the room. He reached up to hug him. "Welcome back, son..."

Everyone was hugging each other when my grandmother said, "Well, what do we have here? My three boys...the jail-bird, the whine-o, and Twinkle-toes." She reached up to wrap her arms around my uncle's neck. "Hide your purses everybody... Eddie's back."

We all shook our heads.

My aunt frowned and put her hands on her hips. "I'm not a boy and my name is not Twinkle-toes..."

My grandmother looked her up and down. You could tell, by the look on her face, that she'd been waiting for one of them to backtalk her all morning. Things

64

immediately took a turn for the worse. "Well, would you like for me to call you a fairy? Isn't that what they call your kind of people?"

"I want you to call me by my name," my aunt said.

"Okay, James," my grandmother said.

"That's not my name..." she said.

"That IS your damn name. I named you after your father. You're a damn junior...not this...this..."

My aunt interrupted. "It's Jasmine."

She waved her off. "Get out of here with that bullshit...your grandmother would crawl out of her grave, grab a switch off of that tree in the backyard and beat your ass, herself, if she knew you were running around here calling yourself, Jasmine..."

My aunt frowned and put her hands on her hips. "Like I said...Jasmine."

My granny looked at her. "Your Birth Certificate say James, damnit and that's what's going on your death certificate and your headstone...not no damn Jasmine...and your ass will be dressed in a suit and not a gad-damn dress. You came in this world a man and you gon' leave-up out of here the same way."

My aunt sighed.

My grandmother continued. "Shit, I was there when they cut that skin off of your little wee-wee. You still got a wee-wee, don't you?"

"Yes..." my aunt confirmed.

"Then, you're a damn man..."

Betty spoke, "Leave her alone, mama."

My grandmother gave her a look that indicated that my mother was messing with the wrong woman at the wrong time on the wrong day. "Stay in your lane, crackhead. You don't want none of this. I raised you. You can't raise me...don't you forget that." She pointed down the hallway and continued, "Ain't it some drugs in your room that needs smoking or snorting or whatever the hell it is that you do with that shit?"

Betty was about to respond when my little brother raised his hand. We all turned and looked at him. "I want to be a fairy. Can I be a fairy too?"

I pushed his hand down. "Believe me...you don't want to be a fairy."

"Well, why not?" he asked.

I frowned. "Because you can't be one."

Confused, he said, "But if auntie is a fairy, why can't I be one too? I like fairies..."

Finally, my uncle John responded. "Because fairies can fly and unless, your little butt got some magical shit going on that none of us are aware of...then you can't be a fairy."

My brother looked at my aunt and then looked at me. "Aunt Jasmine is magical and can fly?" Excitedly, he continued, "Auntie, please do some magic...could you? I like tricks."

My uncle John looked at my brother and said, "The dress is the trick, son...believe me."

My Uncle Eddie looked at my aunt. "Don't pay her no mind, Jasmine..."

Forgetting that there were kids in the room, my grandmother frowned, and said, "Don't pay who no mind? I'm not the confused one in the room. He's the one washing his ass every morning…seeing a dick and a set of balls and thinking that he's a damn woman. Because he throws a dress over it, don't make it disappear. That's some magical shit for your ass. Shit, Houdini ain't even that good at making things disappear." She took a deep breath and continued, "I would rather you just be gay. That's some shit I can understand. You got a dick and you like dicks. I understand that 'cause I like dicks too…but you running around chasing dicks in that dress is some damn nonsense. That's what it is, and motherfuckers get killed playing those kinds of games."

"You better love dicks…" my grandfather interrupted. "Can't have two of y'all running around here."

She frowned and continued, "But this dress shit is bullshit. No, son…never…you can chase and catch a dick in a pair of pants. Believe me…I know."

"I can wear whatever I want to wear…" my aunt said. My grandmother put her hand on her hip and said, "You know what? That dress should come with a period. Try that shit for seven days…try it for one day…and your ass would hurry-up and jump back on the other side of the fence. You want to wear a dress without the struggle that comes with it. That's what it is…"

My aunt interrupted her. "Whatever…but you know who else wore a dress?" Before my granny could answer, aunt Jasmine said, "Jesus."

We all dropped our heads and looked at the floor. We knew that aunt Jasmine had just crossed the line and there was no going back. You can mess with anybody, but you don't mess with Granny's Jesus.

Her false teeth shot out of her mouth and clear across the room. "Blasphemy!!!" my grandmother said.

Feeling like she had the upper-hand, my aunt said, "It's true. Every photo that we've seen of Him, He's wearing a dress. So, I'm not the only one throwing a dress over a set of balls."

My grandmother walked up to her. "Take that back."

"I won't…" She waved her hand in the air before placing it on her hip. She smacked her lips before continuing, "Folks like to ask, 'What would Jesus do?' Well, Jesus liked to wear dresses. That's what He liked to do."

"What did you say?" My grandmother asked, rolling up her sleeves.

Unconcerned about the imminent ass-whooping she was about to receive, she continued, "He could have been a transgender…maybe even a drag queen…"

"He wasn't having sex with no men…I bet 'cha…" my grandmother said, like a woman who, in another life, was the ground in which Jesus slept. So, she knew for a fact who He spent his nights with.

My aunt stuck her mouth out. "Who said I sleep with men? 'Cause I like dressing like a woman doesn't automatically mean I like sleeping with men."

"You damn right…'cause no self-respecting man is gon' sleep with a man in a dress. That's like buying a TV dinner with fried chicken on the box and he opens it and finds meatloaf…his mouth been watering for chicken, all day and now, he's looking at meatloaf…even if he decides to eat it, because it's all he got left, don't mean he stops wanting chicken… that's Science."

"That's bullshit…"

My grandmother squinted her eyes and asked, "Do you sleep with women?"

We all leaned-in to hear her answer.

My aunt looked around the room at all of our staring faces. "That's none of your business."

"You know, why? Ain't no self-respecting woman is gon' have sex with a man dressed in a dress…so, you're screwed on both ends."

My aunt frowned.

My grandmother shook her head. "You know what you are? You're a gad-damn oxymoron. Emphasis on the 'moron'."

My aunt walked up to her. "What did you call me?"

My grandmother stepped into her face. "You heard me…you think cause you walk-up on me, I'mma bite my tongue, Bitch…" She paused for a moment before continuing, "You can be called a 'bitch', right or is that some more 'selective' shit?"

My aunt began to suck her teeth.

My grandmother continued. "So, BITCH, I ain't scared of you. You will receive the same type of ass-whooping I would give to a woman…man…combo …whatever…you will never accuse me of discriminating."

"But you hate me,'" my aunt said.

"No, I don't…I love you. I don't love what you do and guess what? I ain't got to either. And I don't give a shit what other people say or do. But I do give a shit about what my kids do and I ain't gon' sit back and watch a SON of mine running around here perpetrating a fraud against humanity. It's fucking trickery…that's what it is. If my ass pretended to be a police officer on Halloween, the shit is cute, but let me pull that shit on any other day of the year…let me try to lock somebody up and you know what? A real police officer would put my impersonating-ass underneath a jail."

My aunt pulled her dress up to expose what she had on underneath. "Does this look fake to you?"

Everyone covered their eyes, but me. I wanted to see how she was able to tuck all of her man-parts into a thong.

My grandfather yelled. "Put that thang away before you fuck up these kids…you know that they ain't got no sense as it is…now, you gon' mess-up the little that they do have…!"

"Is there a dick hiding in those panties?" She shook her head. "Like putting lipstick on a pig…at the end of the day, it ain't nothing but a bucket of chitterlings that some woman put her mouth on."

Aunt Jasmine began to dance around the room, holding her dress up. "I might even have the surgery..."

"Surgery to do what? Cut your dick off?" She began to laugh. "Cause they cut your dick off won't make you no woman...I know a lot of motherfuckers... messing around with the wrong woman and ended-up getting their dicks cut off and you know what they are now? Dick-less...that's it...they ain't no more a woman than you are."

My aunt stopped and looked at my grandfather. "Like you castrated daddy..."

The next thing we heard was a loud smack. No one knew where the sound came from, but we looked up to find my aunt holding the side of her face.

Defending himself, he said, "Don't drag me into this shit...and by the way, I got all of mine and then some..."

My aunt was fuming. She took off her earrings and handed them to my uncle. "I will take your bullshit, but I ain't taking no ass-whooping from nobody..."

My grandmother's eyes grew wide. I knew that something bad was going to happen, but I didn't expect this. Without taking her eyes off of my aunt, my grandmother lifted her dress and stuck her hands in her underwear.

My grandfather said, "What the hell? Woman have you lost your mind…" He began to wave his arms. "Kids run…run…save yourselves!!!"

But we didn't move. We wanted to see what was going to happen next. The next thing we knew, my grandmother's hand came out of her underwear. She was waving something in the air. "I'm going to give you mine…since you will never get yours."

Confused, I asked, "A bloody diaper? Why would auntie want a bloody diaper?"

My grandfather yelled. "THAT'S IT!!!! DAMNIT, THAT'S ENOUGH. These kids don't need to see this shit!!"

"You got more stubble on your face than I got on my damn legs," my grandmother said, fixing her clothes. My aunt looked at her and said, "Shit, it looks like you got more stubble on your face than I got on my damn legs."

"Ooooooooooooo…" we all said.

My uncle Eddie picked up my grandmother's teeth and jumped between them. "Cut it out…y'all too old for this shit. Arguing ain't gon' change nothing."

Removing my uncle's hand, my aunt yelled, "SHO' AIN'T GON' CHANGE ME BACK INTO A MAN!!!" She turned to leave the house, but my granny wasn't done with her. She threw the bloody diaper and hit her in the back of the head. My aunt touched the back of her head and when she realized what she'd been hit with, she ran towards my grandmother. My uncle grabbed her.

"YOUR ASS AIN'T NEVER STOP BEING ONE!!" Grandmamma yelled as she put up her fists to defend herself. "You better get out of my face! No, let her ass go, so I can beat the 'man' back in her ass…"

They drugged my aunt outside. My grandmother picked the diaper off of the floor. The room fell quiet. Breaking the silence, my grandfather said, "Let me check your feet for shit…"

"Huh?" My grandmother said, lifting her foot and checking the bottom of it.

He laughed and said, "'Cause you put your foot all-up in that ass."

"I'm just tired of this shit…" she said. "Damn kids…"

My uncle Eddie grabbed my grandmother. Trying to change the subject, he said, "Hey mama…you want me to dispose of that while you go wash your hands?" He took the diaper from her.

She fixed her clothing and smiled like everything before that hug was a part of all of our imaginations. She signaled for all of us to join her in the backyard. We did so without mentioning the argument. We knew that trying to change her was a waste of time. It would be like trying to change her from Black to White. She was set in her ways and her way, no matter how wrong, was the right way. So, we all gave up and tried to enjoy the rest of the day.

And things calmed down. It was so nice to be together, once again. We were laughing and talking about old times. We were playing games, eating, and just enjoying ourselves when 'she' entered the backyard. "She" was a beautiful woman who looked like she'd just stepped out of a centerfold from *Jet Magazine*. She had on a mini-skirt that showed-off a pair of legs that were a mile long, a crop top that showed off her flat stomach, and sitting atop of it were a pair of breasts that were so big that it looked like she could end world hunger.

Everyone fell silent. My grandfather almost fell out of his wheelchair. My grandmother frowned. My uncle Eddie stood up. He took her hand. "I want you all to meet, Brandy."

My grand-daddy wiped the side of his mouth. "Can I get a sip of that Brandy…"

My grandmother cut her eyes in his direction. "You better sip on some damn water…"

My grandfather looked at her. "I've been sipping on water for more than thirty years. Ain't nothing wrong with me wanting something a little stronger… something intoxicating like a tall sexy-ass glass of Brandy."

My uncle Eddie laughed.

My grandmother stared at him, hard.

"Look all you want to. You don't control these eyes, woman…nor this mouth…"

She waved her fork at him. "Keep on…I'm going to hit you in the both of them…your eyes and your mouth."

My grandfather pulled out his gun. "I ain't scared of you, old lady. Bring your ass over here and see what happens...I'mma pierce those ears for you."

"My ears are already pierced," she confirmed.

"Well, I'll pierce 'em again," he retorted.

"And what you gon' do with her? With yo' no-legs having-ass..."

"You weren't saying that shit last night..." He slapped his chair. "Knocked the dust and cob-webs off of those bloomers. Surprised you're able to walk or talk...if you know what I mean." He winked at her.

My grandmother began to blush. "Ain't nobody asked you about all of that..."

"But if they do ask...you better tell 'em...you better tell 'em..."

My uncle began to kiss the woman on her cheek. Brandy giggled and whispered something in his ear.

"Ummmmm...mama...me and Brandy need to go in the house and 'talk' for a minute...:

My grandmother didn't even let him finish his sentence. "Oh no you won't...ain't no 'talking' going on in my house. Take your ass to a motel."

I guess that everyone knew what 'talking' meant except for me. "Awwwwww, come on, grandma. All he wants to do is 'talk.'"

She frowned. "Ain't nobody 'talking' in my house, but me, boy.

Confused, I said, "We can't talk in the house no more, granny?"

"Hell no...and you can start by not talking now..."

"Awwwwwww, man…" I said, pouting.

She frowned. "That counts as talking…"

Uncle Eddie and Brandy began to walk out of the yard. "Your uncle Eddie will be right back. Brandy has something she really needs to say to your uncle and your uncle reallllllllllyyyy needs to hear it."

My grandfather slapped his hand on his chair. "Go hear that shit, son and when you're done…come and tell your daddy what she had to say. It's been a long time since somebody, young, 'talked' to me."

My grandmother frowned. "Keep on…I'mma say something to your ass and it ain't gon' be anything that you wanna hear."

He waved her off. "Whatever…"

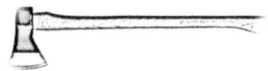

Everyone had gone home. It had been a long day, so I decided to sit out on the porch to watch the stars. Suddenly, a car pulled up and uncle Eddie jumped out. He walked up to the porch and sat down next to me. He looked up at the sky.

"The things that we take for granted," he said.

"Huh?" I asked.

"Stars…something as simple as being able to see the sky at night." He sighed. "It's been so long."

I looked down at my feet. "Uncle?" I began. "What's it like?"

He looked at me. "What's what like?"

"Jail?" I asked.

He exhaled and began. "It's a bad place…"

"I know that, but what's it like?"

He paused for a second. "You see this?" He pointed at the house. "To you…this is hell and to most people it is too. No one wants to live like this, but jail is a lot worse."

"It is?" I asked.

He nodded his head. "Can you imagine living in a box for ten years…being handcuffed, told what to do and when to do it…not being able to see your family…not being able to see the sky or the stars at night?" He paused for a minute and continued, "What I would have given for a hug from mama, a kiss on the cheek, a woman's leg wrapped around my waist, or for a sweet piece of ass…"

I smiled. "Is it sweet, uncle?"

"Sweeter than that candy that you love to put in your mouth, nephew, and better on your teeth."

I giggled.

"Look, you're going to be a man one day and you might as well learn it now…you don't want to be stuck in some "box" listening to some motherfucker beating his meat every night to some picture he got stuck on the wall…" He paused again. "You know what beating your meat is, right?"

I frowned. "Sure…that's how grand-daddy gets us dinner. He takes a shovel and he beats the meat…"

My uncle laughed. "There's so much that you have to learn."

"Will you teach me, uncle?"

He laughed and wrapped his arm around my shoulder. "Shit, I'm still trying to figure it out myself, but I can tell you this much, I ain't never going back. You hear me? Never…"

My uncle was right. He would never go back to prison again. A few months after his release, he was gunned-down during a drug deal. It was weird. After hearing about his death, I didn't feel sad or mad. I really didn't feel anything. I knew that I didn't want him to be caged like an animal, again, and if death was the only way that he was going to stay out of it, then I was glad that he was gone.

CHAPTER 9

T he next day, I was awakened to the sound of someone singing. Her voice was so beautiful. As I listened, I became confused because I wasn't used to waking up that way. I was used to someone cursing or waking up to things being thrown around the house, but not to singing. I was drawn to it. I got up and followed it down the hall to my grandmother's room. I listened outside of the door for a while before knocking. "Grandma?" I asked, as I turned the knob.

"Come in," she said.

Slowly, I opened the door. She had her back to me. I could tell by looking at her that she wasn't my grandmother. "Ummmm…excuse me. Do my grandma know that you're in her room?" I asked.

"No," she said, not looking at me.

I walked towards her, but every attempt to see her face was met with her turning her back to me.

"Excuse me…." I said, again. Frustrated, I grabbed her by the shoulder causing her wig to fall off.

She tried grabbing her hair, but it was too late. I recognized that haircut. Shocked and confused, I said, "Boy, what are you doing?"

He turned and looked at me. With his face covered in makeup, he said, "Playing dress-up like Uncle James."

My eyes began to blink rapidly. "Wait…what?"

"I'm playing dress-up…"

"What is wrong with you?" I asked.

"I'm just playing…" he said, again.

"Boy, you should never play like that…"

"Why not?"

"'Cause, you can't…it's either real or it isn't…" I said, pulling at the dress.

"What is?"

"This…" I said, pointing at what he had on. "People don't do this unless it's real…"

"Real what?" he asked, confused.

"Unless, you want to be a woman," I confirmed.

Trying to process what I'd just said, he said, "So, uncle really wants to be an auntie?"

I frowned. "YES! Do you think that folks go around playing like this? They are not playing…they get their butts kicked for this kind of stuff. Do you think that they would do this willingly…if it wasn't for real?"

Trying to understand what I was saying, he asked, "So Uncle James thinks that he's a woman…?"

"Yes, he believes it…"

"How can he?"

"I don't know…all I know is, is that you can't go around dressing like a woman unless you're serious." I pulled him towards the mirror. "Look at you…you can't come back from this. This image is locked into my mind…I can't erase this."

He pulled off the dress and handed it to me. "Don't give it to me…put it on the bed." Trying to avoid touching it, I threw my hands in the air, like it was hot and could burn my hands.

My grand-daddy heard us talking and came into the room. He looked at the both of us. "What is going on in here?" He came closer. "What the hell is that on your face?"

I didn't respond. I wanted to hear how he was going to explain this away, but before he could open his mouth, my grand-daddy said, "I go and fight a war, come back home to find out that we're still slaves, and now, this bullshit."

"But, grand-daddy…" he began.

"What the hell is going on with you, boy? Have you lost your damn mind? Well, you need to go and find it, 'cause something ain't right." He shook his head. "You want to get fucked in the ass? You want to suck a man's dick? You want a man's sweaty balls on your face? Tell me…'cause I need to know." He paused and placed his hands over his face like he was hoping that when he removed them he would find that this was all a bad dream, but it wasn't. "Lawd, Lawd, Lawd…I went months without seeing a woman… every day, there was nothing but men and NOT ONCE, did I imagine sucking a dick or having another man suck mine. Now, don't get me wrong. There were a lot of desperate nights…make a man want to do shit that he ain't got no business doing, but I was never that desperate. I would fuck a dog in the ass before I would fuck a man in the ass. Shit, a dog might bite you, but in the end, it is still a dog and you are still a man."

Our mouths fell open.

"How the hell do you think that we got by? When there was no woman, you fucked anything with a hole and that hole was not attached to no man. That way, when you came back home to your woman, you came back the way you left...I will never understand this 'other' shit."

My grandmother yelled from behind the bathroom door, "Don't forget that you're talking to kids..."

"Look who's talking...ain't you got an appointment with that toilet?"

"Ain't nobody asked you about me and no toilet..."

He yelled back, "That's why he got on your makeup and your good dress and wig..."

"Oh, hell no...beat his ass..."

My grand-daddy looked at me. "You heard her...beat his ass."

We looked at him and then, back, at each other. "Huh?" We both asked.

He backed out of the room. "You heard her. Now, let's go..."

For a moment, we both hesitated, but then we followed him out the back door. He turned to me and said, "I want you to beat his ass...or better yet, him

82

beat your ass...either way, is fine with me. Just as long as there's some ass-beating going on. I'll tell y'all when to stop."

I couldn't believe that this was real. "Grand-daddy, I'm bigger than him..."

"I don't give a shit...when your ass saw him in a dress, you should have been slapping lipstick off of his lips and getting eyeliner all over your fists. Instead, you're in there talking. Some shit don't deserve words...it deserves an ass-whooping."

"But he's my brother," I said.

"Are you sure?" he asked. "Look at his face...that motherfucker got on more rouge than a $2 whore..."

"Rouge?" my brother, asked.

"Shut your ass up? If you don't know what rouge is, then you shouldn't be putting it on...now, I don't have all day...let's get this over with."

We stood and looked at each other.

Becoming impatient, he said, "Don't make me pull out my gun."

"You will kill us, grand-daddy?" I asked.

"Damn right..."

"But he was just playing..."

"I'mma be playing too...when I shoot your ass." He pulled out his gun and sat it on his lap. "Whenever you're ready..."

Realizing that he was serious, I walked up to my brother, whispered the words 'I'm sorry' and proceeded to beat the shit out of him. He fell to the ground. I jumped on top of him. We wrestled back and forth, hitting each other. Blow after blow, we kept going. I thought that the fight would be easy because I was bigger, but my little brother was holding his own. For every punch that landed in his face, one landed in mine. This went on for about fifteen minutes, before we stopped. We were both covered in grass, dirt, and blood. Breathing heavily, I asked, "Is that enough?"

My grand-daddy looked at my brother. "You still feeling 'girly'?"

"No…" he confirmed, licking blood from his bottom lip.

"Then, yeah…that's enough." He turned to go into the house. "The next time, I'm just going to shoot you."

CHAPTER 10

W e were very poor. Being poor takes on a whole new meaning when you're the one experiencing it. It's sad to be born in the land of "milk and honey", only to be told that you can't have any. We moved 17 times in 18 years. We moved so much that we didn't bother unpacking our clothes – the little that we had. We lived in a community where every other building was abandoned and at any given time, one of those buildings became our home. Usually, the house had a million occupants – three adults, seven kids, and too many rats and roaches to count. The neighborhood was so scarce that if it wasn't for the rats and roaches, we didn't have anyone to play with. We've lived with them for so long that when one of them died, it felt like we'd just lost a family member and they were everywhere too. You couldn't walk without stepping on or tripping over one of them. All night long, you could hear them scurrying across the floor, scurrying across the walls - the crunching sound that the roaches made when you stepped on them – like cereal when you first put it into your mouth; their guts plastered all over the walls and floors like a crime scene.

DADDY BY DIANE MARTIN 85

And the noises never stopped. They slept in our beds with us. They crawled into our ears, in our noses, and in our mouths – they were everywhere. You couldn't pour a bowl of cereal without finding a roach floating in your milk. Speaking of milk, when the kids were put down to sleep, the rats would crawl into their beds and steal the bottles right out of their mouths and it wasn't limited to the babies' bottles. They used to bite our faces and nibble on our fingers and toes. It'd gotten so bad, that grand-daddy would lie awake at night, waiting for them in the dark, and when they came out to eat, he would grab a broom and bash their brains in. On those days, when he was able to kill a few, we knew that we could expect a good breakfast the next morning.

But there were many a day and many a night that we'd gone to bed hungry. I remember days when all we had was syrup and bread and we made sandwiches with it – breakfast, lunch, and dinner. We ate so much syrup that when it got hot, syrup seeped from our pores, and bees followed us to school. We wreaked of it and kids used to tease us about it. And when you're poor, kids can be cruel. They didn't care that we were miserable due to poverty and all of the shame that was attached to it and they didn't give a shit about finding ways to make sure that you never forgot about your situation. They used to crack jokes about how poor we were, and the jokes would be funny if they weren't so true and they weren't about us. They used to say things like, "Y'all are so poor, you can't even pay attention." Well, that was true. Kinda hard to pay attention when your stomach is eating itself. Or they would say, "Y'all are so poor, you can't even afford to go to the free clinic." And, again, they were right. We couldn't afford to go to the free clinic 'cause we didn't have car fare and the nearest clinic was several miles away. When we got sick, sleep was the cure. No matter what you were going through – the flu, a headache, a cold, the gout, high blood pressure, or diabetes. We took our asses to bed and prayed that we'd survived through the night.

We visited the food-pantries so much, you would have thought that we lived there. They gave us powdered milk, cheese, and beans. You can't imagine the effect that that stuff had on our stomachs. We were so stopped-up that we couldn't take a shit for days and when we did, it had to be outside, behind the house, because sometimes, we didn't have water to flush the toilets or toilet paper to wipe our butts with. Grass is what we used and there's nothing more embarrassing than having to squat in the bushes to take a "dump". The only people allowed to use the bathroom inside were our grandparents, because my grand-daddy had a hard time getting in and out of his wheelchair and my grandmamma felt old people shouldn't have to shit outside.

We couldn't take baths. My grandmother used to fill the bathroom sink with a couple cups of water from a pot that she kept on the stove. We used to take turns standing over the sink and washed the "important stuff." We couldn't do this every day, because most of the time we only had one bar of soap between all of us. We didn't have deodorant or toothpaste. We had baking soda. We brushed our teeth with it, we stuck it under our arms to keep the musty odors at bay, and on the days that we ran out of soap, we washed with it. We weren't allowed to play, because we weren't allowed to get dirty. We had two outfits that consisted of a pair of jeans that were ironed so much, they shined. It was a good thing that we were born right after each other, because then we could share clothes. God forbid if one of us had a growth-spurt. That would, definitely, mess up the rotation.

We all had one pair of shoes and we wore them until they tore up and when that happened, my grand-parents patched them up with duct tape and went over it with a permanent marker. And they used duct tape for everything – duct tape to patch holes in the walls, to fix window screens, to fix damage on the car, to fix our books, to patch-up "holey" mattresses, holey socks, to cover wounds, to fix a broken hand or foot, to keep us quiet - everything.

We were tripping over each other. Every time, you looked up, you were looking in somebody's face. You never had any privacy and it kept us all on edge, but we weren't the ones complaining. When you're a kid, you learn to deal with things that most grown folks would kill each other over – like something as simple as using the bathroom. It seemed like every time my grand-daddy had to use the bathroom, one of us would walk in on him. It wasn't like we weren't used to seeing him naked, but he was tired of seeing us.

"Every time, I come in here, I'm looking at one of y'all's faces. I'm starting to think that y'all like smelling my shit," he would say.

My grandmother always had a good comeback. "Clearly, you like smelling your own shit or your ass wouldn't be in there every five minutes."

Of course, he would tell her to go and fuck herself and the same thing would start all over five minutes later.

We never celebrated birthdays or any other holiday for that matter. Holidays came and went in our household like it was just another day. I would never forget the first year that I realized that it was my birthday. I woke up, screaming, "Yayyyyyyyyy, it's my birthday!" I jumped out of bed and ran down the hall, still screaming, "Yayyyyyyy, it's my birthday!" I startled my grand-daddy. He stopped me in my tracks. "Boy, you scared the daylights out of me. If you don't cut-out all of that damn noise…"

"But it's my birthday…" I acknowledged.

"So…" he said, raining on my parade.

I didn't expect that response. "Well, aren't we going to celebrate it?" I asked.

"You just did…," he huffed. "Making all of that damn noise…"

"Well, can I have a party?" I asked.

He frowned. "For what? For being born? That's funny…a party for being born…" He shook his head. "All you did was crawl out of somebody's butt. Somebody else did all of the work. I don't see them running around asking for a party…"

"But everybody else gets a party…"

"That's 'cause they're stupid…they buy food for one day…I got to figure out how I'm going to feed you every day…"

"But grand-daddy…"

"Grand-daddy, my ass…go in the room, thank God that you woke up this morning and stop making all of that noise…" He sighed. "A party 'cause you were born…shit, if that's the case, I want a party…a party for not knocking the shit out of your little ass for scaring the hell out of me."

The winters were brutal. Most winters, we didn't have heat. The electricity was the only thing that saved us. My grandmother would turn on the stove to heat up the house. I can still see the flames flickering on top of the stove and the heat rising from the oven door. I would lie awake at night to make sure that it didn't burn the house down. When we got dressed for school, we wore both of our outfits to keep from freezing to death. We never had gloves. We wore socks over our hands to keep them warm and they wrapped our feet in plastic bags, placed them inside of our shoes to keep the snow from getting in.

The interesting thing is, when you're born into this type of situation, you don't think it's abnormal. Sure, it's painful, but I grew up believing that everyone lived this way. Until, one day, I found out that they didn't. I felt betrayed – lied to. I became angry and with anger came the hatred for the people who put me in this situation. Then, there was the hatred for a society who turned a blind's-eye to my situation. It became the fire that kept me warm at night – the desire to make someone pay.

CHAPTER II

I couldn't understand why they didn't help us. I knew that my mother's brothers and sisters didn't like her, but why would they take that out on us? They heard our cries for help, but they acted like they didn't hear us. I used to think that they were afraid of us. Maybe they feared that if they came and got us, they wouldn't be able to get us to come back home or maybe, they were afraid that we would steal from them, but whatever it was, it wasn't enough to justify letting us suffer. We were kids and we needed them. But they came and went. I don't know why I thought that they were obligated to help us, but I always thought that that's what family is supposed to do – help each other. Clearly, I was wrong. It was easier for them to pretend to be blind and deaf to the same thing that they were subjected to as kids.

And they didn't hide their disdain for her. They treated her like shit and us like the "streaks" that was left behind after flushing it. Sure, they spoke to us, but they didn't really want to touch us. They acted like they'd been healed from poverty and touching us would only infect them with it again. When things were really bad, and after a lot of begging by my grandmother, one of them would come and get us for a few hours, but they took every precaution to make sure that we didn't bring any reminders with us.

I remember, one time, my Aunt Jasmine came to get us. It was during the summer when the water had been turned off. The city had received several phone calls that someone in our house kept unscrewing the fire hydrant. The city was threatening to impose fines on the perpetrator, so they sent us to stay with our Auntie Jasmine to keep me out of trouble. I knew that something was wrong when she came to pick us up. She jumped out of the car, frowning. Before we were allowed to get in the car, she made us remove all of our clothing. Except for our underwear. I thought that it was cool, because it was so hot that summer, so I didn't think twice about it. But there was something in the way that she handled our clothes and placed them in a garbage bag that made me realize that there was something else going on; something ugly. She picked them up like she was handling a dirty diaper and she kept them in that bag until she was ready to bring us home.

She did some other weird stuff too. I always thought that it was odd that she never brought her purse inside of our house and she never sat down. Most of her visits were spent standing up and she never left the house without checking her clothing, first. I used to think that she thought that she was better than us, but after staying with her for one day, I realized that her life wasn't as great as she led others to believe.

While we were visiting, she examined us to make sure that we weren't hiding anything in our underwear before she made us sit down, on the floor, in front of the TV to watch cartoons. After being there for a couple of hours, a few of us fell asleep. I was the only one that was still awake when I heard it. Someone was crying. At first, I tried ignoring it, but it got louder. As a kid, you learn that unless somebody calls your name, you don't move, but curiosity got the better of me. I walked down the hall to the sound and slowly opened the door. I walked in to find her standing on a chair with a rope in her hand. She was placing it around her neck when I interrupted her.

"Auntie?" I asked.

Startled, she looked down. "Why aren't you watching TV?" She removed the rope from around her throat.

I looked around the room. "I thought I heard someone crying…"

"Nope…no one crying in here…"

I walked over and sat on her bed. "What are you doing with the rope?"

She motioned for me to get off of her bed. "Oh, ummmm, I was going to hang something…"

"You?" I asked.

"No, of course not…"

"Then, what's that on your face?"

She wiped her tears and laughed. "I have allergies…"

I shrugged my shoulders and stood to leave the room. Over my shoulder, I heard her whisper, "You will never know what it's like…"

I turned and asked, "What…know what what's like?" She removed her wig. "What's it like…to…be me." "Gotta be easier than being me." She wiped her face on her sleeve; removing some of her makeup. I could see my uncle's face peering from underneath it. "I doubt it." She sat her wig in her lap and stared at it. "You know, what? Never-mind…go and lay down with the others. I'll be taking you home soon." As I turned to leave the room, I looked back to find her crying, again.

It was later, that I learned why she cried. She was different in a way that made everyone around her hate her. It was bad enough that most of society treated her like her lifestyle made her more crazy than human, but when her family did this, she had no one to turn to. My grandparents shunned her, and her sister became her enemy. In public, Betty pretended to like her, but behind closed doors, she talked about her like a dog. She called her things like, freak, homo, fag, and wished that terrible things would happen to her. She wanted Aunt Jasmine out of the picture – she wanted Uncle James back.

Aunt Jasmine was once the youngest of three boys. Betty was the oldest girl. When James was born, Betty "adopted" him as her own. My grandparents told me that she took care of him – loved him like she'd been the one to give birth to him. He was always with her. She dressed and fed him. She did everything, but when he got older, Betty started to notice that something wasn't "right." Uncle James used to sneak around the house – putting on her clothes and jewelry. They fought a lot over this. Betty didn't understand why my uncle wanted to wear women's clothing, so instead of allowing him to be himself, she beat him and when beatings didn't fix him, she turned her back on him.

And this hurt Betty. She felt betrayed by Uncle James. She didn't have a good relationship with my grand-daddy, so James was the first man that she ever loved and his decision to become a woman was like a slap in her face. She felt like a failure and every man after that suffered for it. Her pain was so deep that it led her to the "pipe." The pipe gave her back what she thought that her brother took from her. She stopped caring about everybody and everything. Even herself. Her need to fill the void that her brother's "illness", left inside of her, became the only thing that mattered to her.

And they grew to hate each other – one's hatred was for the woman who no longer wanted to be her little brother and the other's hatred was for a woman who was born a woman but took her role as a mother and as a daughter for granted. On the surface, you could see why they disliked each other, but there was something deeper going on. You could see it every time they were in the room together. There was an "uncomfortableness" that went far beyond the rivalry between two siblings. No, this was something else.

Chapter 12

She tried being a mother, but she wasn't good at it. It was after her and my grandmother had a falling-out that she decided, out of spite, to gather us all up and drag us, out, into the unknown. It looked like she had it all figured out, until we all got in the car. That's when shit went downhill and fast. After driving around for several hours, we started complaining about being hungry. She reached in her pocket and pulled out a box of breath mints and handed them to me. "Here," she said, "Share these with your brothers and sisters."

I looked at the box and frowned.

She returned the frown and said, "Look, it's all I got for now..."

I, slowly, took the box from her and said, "But we're hungry."

Frustrated, she asked, "Do you plan on doing that shit every day?"

"What?" I asked, confused.

"Eating..." she replied.

"People eat every day..." I said.

"If I'd known that shit, I would have left you little begging motherfuckers back with your grandmother." She searched her purse and found a small bag with white powder in it. "Here, eat some of this…"

"Is that drugs?" I said, holding the bag up.

"Yes…take some and give some to the others. It'll stop the hunger."

I handed it back to her. "But we want food…"

"And I want you to shut the fuck up…looks like neither one of us is going to get what we want."

I folded my arms in front of me. "I want to go home to mama…"

"That ain't your mama and this is your home…"

"A car?"

"Shit, it's better than nothing. There's motherfuckers sleeping on the street. You got windows, a roof over your head, a place to sleep, and heat…" She huffed and continued, "Shit, you could barely get heat in that place that you call home."

I began to cry like a baby.

"Shut up…" she demanded.

I cried louder.

"SHUT UP!!!"

I began to scream.

She slammed on the brakes; throwing me into the dashboard. When I bounced back, she hit me in the chest and said, "You little bitch…you UNGRATEFUL LITTLE BITCH! Get your ass out."

"What?" I said, trying to catch my breath.

"Get the fuck out of the car!" she demanded.

"For what?" I asked.

Scowling, she said, "Don't make me tell you again." When I refused, she threw the car in park, jumped out, and walked over to my side of the car. She opened the door and began to pull me out.

Kicking and screaming, I said, "Nooooo…STOP!!!!"

"Get out…you little shit," she insisted.

She dragged me to the back of the car and popped the trunk. "Get in…"

"What? No…wait…I'll be quiet."

"Too late…now, get your ass in the fucking trunk…a bitch can't think with your ass bitching and moaning. I haven't gotten high in the past 30 minutes and your little ass is fucking with my head…" She pushed me inside and the slammed the trunk's lid closed.

I started kicking and screaming. She jumped back in the car and said, "Any of you got something to say? There's room for a few more back there…" They didn't respond. She turned up the radio and pulled off. As I lay in the darkness, all I could think about were ways that I could hurt her. I balled-up my fist and began to pound it against the palm of my hand. With each strike, I could imagine myself hitting her in the face – beating her to the point that no one – not even my grand-daddy would recognize her. I wanted her to die. I didn't care how it happened, I just needed it to happen and soon.

Things only got worse when the car stopped. She must have forgotten that I was in the trunk because when she finally opened the hood, the sun was shining. She opened it and threw me a package of crackers. "Here's your breakfast…"

I adjusted my eyes to the light to look at it. My eyes darted back and forth between the crackers and her.

"You got something to say?" she asked, with her hand on the lid.

"No…" I said.

"Good…now, get in there and watch those brats. There's a pipe out there calling my name."

I climbed out of the trunk and headed into the motel room. She slammed the door behind me. When I looked around, they were all crying.

"Paulie, I'm hungry…" my little brother said.

I looked at the packet of crackers. There were only two inside and six mouths to feed. I broke it into little pieces and gave it to them. When they were done eating the crumbs, I said, "Come on…let's take a nap…it won't hurt so much when we're sleeping."

A couple of days had passed, when she, finally, decided to check on us. When she walked in, she was followed by a big, black, thing with eyes and a rope around its neck. She saw us on the bed. "Get the fuck out of that bed...who the fuck you think you are?" We all scrambled to the floor. She handed the rope to me. "Take care of him. I promised to watch him for somebody..." She walked back outside and when she returned, she was carrying a big bag of dog food. She handed it to me before jumping into the bed. "I better not hear shit from you little bastards..." She yawned and stretched. "This bitch needs her beauty sleep."

I looked at the thing on the other end of the rope and said, "Where's our food?"

"Ask the dog if he would mind sharing his food with you..." She turned her back to us and said, "Goodnight."

I looked at the dog. He began sniffing around the room. He walked over to the side of the bed, lifted his leg, and pissed all along the side of it. When he was done, he began to sniff the bag of dog food. I looked at it. "So, I guess that you're hungry too." I stuck my hand inside of the bag and pulled some out. I placed it on the floor. The dog began to eat. I looked at him, I looked at my brothers and sisters, and then, I looked over at the bed where Betty was sleeping, soundly. I realized that if we didn't eat, we were going to starve to death. I reached inside of the bag and handed each one of them a handful of food. Without thinking or asking questions, they all began to eat, and they continued to do so until they couldn't eat anymore. As I chewed the food, I watched Betty.

The next morning, she was gone again. As I sat up, I, immediately, began to feel ill. If felt like something was trying to claw its way out of my butthole. I ran to the bathroom to find that there was a line of people waiting to get whatever it was out of their systems. I tried waiting, but I couldn't hold it anymore. I ran out of the room and to the office. Without saying "Hello", I said, "I gotta go...please, can I use your bathroom." The woman behind the desk asked, "Which is it? Number 1 or number 2?"

"NUMBER 2!!!" I screamed.

Without blinking, she said, "No..."

Now dancing in the middle of the lobby, I said, "Please...I'm going to boo-boo on myself..."

Without looking at me, she said, "Go ahead...shit on yourself. 'Cause you won't be messing up my bathroom..."

"Please..." I begged.

"No..." she said, again.

I couldn't hold it any longer. Before I knew it, brown liquid filled my pants. The smell of shit filled the room. She jumped up. "You fucker…I can't believe you just did that…where's your mama? She needs to come and clean this shit up."

Embarrassed, I ran out of the office, back to the room, with a trail of shit following behind me. I locked the door.

"Come back here!!!" She followed me to the room and began to bang on the door. "OPEN THIS GAD-DANG DOOR!!!"

All of us ran and cowered in the corner of the room. "OPEN THIS FUCKING DOOR!!!"

She tried turning the knob, but she couldn't get in. For a moment, the noise stopped. I could hear her walking away. A few minutes later, she returned and put a key into the lock. She opened the door. "There you are you little piece of…"

The dog began to growl. Before she could finish her sentence, it'd lunged at her – grabbing her by the throat. He tore at her as she screamed and tried to push it away. Pieces of flesh flew across the room. The more she screamed, the more he ate her. She screamed and screamed until, there was nothing but silence. The dog licked his mouth and laid next to her. I grabbed the kids, took them into the bathroom, and closed the door. A few hours later, we heard someone turning the knob to the door. When it opened, a man said, "There's kids in here." They escorted us out of the room and into the parking lot. As we walked passed, we could see what was left of her. I told my brothers and sisters to cover their eyes, but I kept mine open. For some odd reason, I wanted to see her. I wanted to see what was left of the woman who wouldn't let me use her bathroom. Just then, Betty walked up.

"Oh my, God...my babies..." she cried. "What happened? Are you hurt? Are you okay?"

I wanted to punch her in the throat for pretending to care about us.

"Mam, are these your kids?" the officer asked.

"Yes, what happened?" she asked, acting her ass off. He ignored her question and asked, "Where were you?"

Lying, she said, "Oh, I just left for a second to get us some food. The kids were really hungry..."

He looked at her empty hands and said, "So, where's the food?"

"Oh...ummm...I was almost there, but...ummm..."

He looked at me and said, "One of them is covered in shit...did you know that?"

Grinding her teeth, she said, "Oh, he does that all of the time. He has a little problem...you know...he's special."

The officer looked at me. "When was the last time y'all ate?"

She looked over his shoulder and squinted her eyes. The look on her face said, "You better not say anything..."

I thought about my trip in the trunk of the car, shrugged my shoulders, and said, "We had some dog food last night."

She mouthed, "I'm going to kill you."

I smiled as I watched them handcuff her. They threw her in the back of the police car. I waved "goodbye" as they took her away.

Later, at the police station, my grandparents arrived. They were so happy to see us. When the police officer explained what'd happened and asked would they be willing to take us, they, quickly, gathered us and took us home. All the way there, I couldn't help but think about Betty. She was pissed. Nobody crossed Betty and those who did, lived to regret it, but I was tired of her and if it was a war she wanted, then it was a war she was going to get.

CHAPTER 13

A few days had passed and all was well. My grandparents used the rent money to bail Betty out and for the first few days of her freedom, things were quiet. She remained in her room and away from all of us. This would have been great, if I didn't know Betty. She was plotting something, and Betty fought dirty. She didn't care if it was one of her kids or Jesus who'd crossed her. She was going to get me back – one way or another. What she had up her sleeve? I had no idea, but I could have never imagined that she was capable of this kind of evil.

She waited until the house was empty, one morning, before she put her plan in motion. I was asleep. In my dream, I thought that the house was on fire. I began to smell smoke. I looked for the source of it but couldn't find it. The dream was so real that I began to cough and choke. The coughing and choking became so severe that it woke me up out of my sleep to find Betty, leaning over me, and blowing smoke in my face. She placed her mouth on her pipe and then, blew smoke in my face. I tried pushing her, but the chemicals in the smoke began to take hold. The only way that I can explain how I felt, at that moment, was happy. I was on cloud 9. I was so out of it that I had no idea what she was doing to me. Then, I began to hear something sizzling like someone was cooking bacon and that made me happy, because I loved bacon, but for some odd reason it didn't smell like bacon. It smelled more like burnt hair and burning flesh. It wasn't until the "clouds" began to disappear that I realized that no one was cooking bacon. Betty's crazy ass was cooking me. I jumped-up to find her lighting the crack-pipe and pressing it against my arm. I felt an intense burning of my skin. "Ahhhhhhhh!!!!! I screamed. In my attempt to get away from her, I kicked her onto the floor.

As my skin began to blister, and still somewhat under the influence, I ran out of the room and landed on top of my grandfather – pushing him out of his wheelchair. Betty came running out of the room, behind me, and ran right into my grandmother. My grandmother grabbed her and looked down at her hand. "What are you doing?"

Betty looked at the pipe and then, looked at her. She didn't say anything.

"Why the hell are you coming out of his room with a pipe in your hand?" My grandmother sniffed the air like a bloodhound trying to track its prey. She inhaled and exhaled, again. She looked down at Betty in disgust. She figured out what was going on. She raised her hand and when it came down it landed on the side of Betty's face, so hard that you could see the "taste" leave her mouth, because she'd just slapped it out of her.

Betty fell to the floor.

She turned to me. "What happened, Paul?"

As my skin burned, I turned and looked at Betty. "She blew smoke in my face and she burned me."

My grandmother sighed and began to roll-up her sleeves. She grabbed Betty by the hair. "Daddy, take him in the kitchen and put some butter on his burns…"

"Shiiiiiiiiiiiiiiittttt," He began. "That butter is for my toast."

"OLD MAN, don't make me say it say again!"

He stuck out his hand. "HEEL SATAN…get thee behind me…" He said. "I'm tired of you telling me what to do, old woman…"

"DO IT, DAMNIT!!!!!" She exhaled and lowered her voice. "I need to talk to Betty. Unless, you want to handle this."

"I ain't got shit to say to her crazy ass."

"Well, then…" She began to drag Betty in her room – kicking and screaming. When the door closed we could hear things being thrown around the room.

I looked down at my grandfather who was still lying underneath me.

"Unless you gon' be my Valentine, you need to get the hell up off of me…"

I jumped up and grabbed his hand.

"Get my chair…" he demanded.

I grabbed his chair and helped him get back into it. He rolled down the hall until he was at her bedroom door. "Girl, I ain't got but one good nerve left, and your ass is wearing the lining out of it."

I walked into the kitchen. My grandfather came in behind me. He mumbled. "Got me using my damn butter for some burns when spit works just as good." I sat down at the table and examined the burns.

"Sorry, grand-daddy…"

He grabbed the butter and began to look at my arm. "That motherfucker ain't got shit-else to do. I don't know what the hell is wrong with her. Running around here burning folks…what was she gon' do next? Eat you?"

I shrugged.

"The bitch is crazy…there's no other explanation for this shit. Just crazy…"

"I think she got me high, too, grand-daddy…" I said. My head was killing me. It felt like hamsters were trying to claw their way out of my head.

"That's all we need is another addict in the house."

"Am I going to turn into an addict?"

"No, I think that you'll be fine. I will keep an eye on you, but just know that if you start tweeking and shit, I'mma have to put you down."

I sighed. "Why did she do that, grand-daddy?"

"Shit, I don't know. Do I look like I speak 'crazy?'"

I wanted to say 'yes', but that wouldn't help me.

"I don't know what they're putting in that shit…we did some stuff when I was in the military. Trying to keep the 'demons' at bay, we did some 'shrooms, some herb...a few folks dabbled in coke...the shit killed a few brain cells, we got the munchies, wanted to fuck like the world was coming to an end, but that's it...but this new shit that they got going 'round got folks losing their damn minds...and back in my day, herb smelled like herbs. This shit they got now got folks walking 'round smelling like gad-damn barn animals...like a skunk's ass? If they gon' do that, then why bother paying for the shit when they can just wrap their mouths around a skunk's butthole and inhale."

I had no answer for that. "Well, what can I do, grand-daddy? Why do she hate me so much?"

"'Can't do nothing, 'cause she hates herself...hateful people do hateful shit...that's the only way that I can explain it. Usually, love can fix hate, but what that girl got going on is too 'terminal' to fix. There ain't no cure."

Watching the butter melt down the side of my arm, I said, "She going to get hers...one day, grand-daddy."

"Yep, sadly, she will...and karma is going to make sure that you're right there to see it happen."

CHAPTER 14

I thought that she was finished with me, but she'd only just begun. She was relentless. Every day, it was something new. It was so funny watching her that I actually looked forward to whatever she had planned for me. She messed with me all of the time. She took my stuff and hid it, lied on me, and called me names. After a while, I'd built an immunity to her dumb-shit until she decided to take it to the next level.

I was asleep, one morning, but was awakened to the feeling of warm air brushing against my face. "Wake-up, you little bitch..." Slowly, I opened my eyes to find her face two inches away from mine. As a reflex, I pushed her back away from me. As she went back, I felt something piercing through my underwear and into my foreskin. I looked down to find her holding a pair of scissors against my crotch. I tried to move, but she pressed harder. She leaned back into my face. "Rise and shine, little girl..."
She was high, which was nothing new, but the blade against my penis was. So, I had to be careful about the way that I responded to her or she would definitely cut my "thing" off. So, I tried not to do or say anything that would prompt her to perform

unnecessary surgery on me. I didn't look at her. I kept my eyes on the blade.

"So, you gon' rat somebody out? Don't you know what happens to rats?"

I didn't say anything. Betty was prepared to cut me with more than the scissors. Her words would prove to be a lot sharper and more painful.

"You know that I didn't want to have you. If it wasn't for your grandmother, your black ass would be swirling around somebody's toilet bowl."

Biting my lip, I remained silent.

"I should have aborted you and the rest of those nappy-haired little brats."

I bit my lip so hard that it began to bleed.

She continued to taunt me. "You know…your daddy was a fucking fag. That's why he didn't stick around and you're going to grow-up and be a fag just like him."

I could no longer hold my tongue. "You sure that it didn't have anything to do with you…maybe you turned him into a fag?"

She pressed the blade against my skin. I grimaced in pain.

"What the fuck did you say to me?"

I didn't respond.

"That's what I thought…"

Becoming fed-up, I said, "Why don't you put the scissors down…"

"And what you gon' do? Fight me? Just like a bitch…you would put your hands on a woman…"

DADDY BY DIANE MARTIN 113

"No, I'm not putting my hands on a woman...I'mma put my hands on you."

She began to breathe heavily. She pressed the blade down deeper. "I should cut your dick off and we can see who's the woman then..."

"And it still won't be you..." I reiterated.

She pushed the blade in so deep that I ended-up kicking her clear across the room. I looked down to see the white of my underwear turn dark red. I lunged at her. I tried getting the scissors out of her hand. She screamed, "Help! Help! He's trying to rape me!!!"

My grandmother came running in the room. "What the hell is going on in here?" She pushed me off of her.

"Grandmamma, she's lying," I said, breathing heavily.

My grandmother grabbed her by the hair. "What the hell is wrong with you? Why would you say that about this boy?"

Trying to untangle her hair from her grandmother's fingers, she said, "But he did!!"

"That is a child...that is your son...he don't want your ass...YOU don't want your ass...why would you think that HE would want your ass."

"Cause he's a man...he's no different than the rest of them."

"He's your son. If your butt started acting like a mama, you would stop treating him like some stranger off of the street. What woman looks at her own child and say that he's trying to rape her? That is the sickest shit I've ever heard."

Betty tried to speak, but my grandmother dragged her out of the room. "Get your crazy ass out of here and stop fucking with that boy before I have you put away. You gon' end-up in one of those hospitals with the rest of the nutcases...playing Chess with invisible people... keep on messing with me."

I crawled over to the door.

"But he did..." Betty insisted.

"Keep on, Betty...I swear." My grandmother called out. "Daddy, get this girl..."

"But my game show is on..." he replied.

She looked at me and said, "Go in the bathroom...I'll be in there in a minute."

After putting Betty out of the house, my grandmother stomped down the hall and began to yell at my grandfather. "I asked you to get that damn girl...I get tired of dealing with this shit by myself..."

"What do you expect me to do? Beat her ass? It's too late for that now. That's why she's so messed-up...you should have done that a long time ago..."

"Waaaaaaaaiiiiiiiittttttt, motherfucker...you just wait one gad-damn minute. I KNOW you ain't about to blame this shit on me..."

"Then, whose fault is it? It ain't mine..."

"You need to take some responsibility..."

"Take it where? She ain't in diapers no more. When she was a baby and she shitted on herself, I cleaned it up…she's grown. She shit on herself now and she's capable of wiping her own ass, but chooses not too? Then, that's just gon' be one smelly motherfucker… at some point, their 'shit' is no longer our responsibility. Gotta learn to let them clean it themselves."

"But we need to do something…" she said, sounding defeated.

"She's too damn old. Her ass needs to be up out of here…Go in there and set that damn bed on fire…it'll put an end to all of this shit."

"And where is she going to go?" she asked.

"I don't know, and I don't care, but what I do know is that you can't keep complaining about the problem when you clearly know what the solution is…I know what the fucking solution is…"

"And what is that?"

"Put her ass out and one of three things is going to happen. Number one, she can't buy drugs and try to keep a roof over her head. She can do that shit here because we're providing the roof. Eliminate the roof and you'll eliminate the drugs. Number two, she'll end-up on the streets. It's a terrible place to be, but she's grown. Some motherfuckers like sleeping on the streets. Maybe she's one of them. Let's put her out and find out. Or number three, she'll end-up dead and sadly, I've already come to terms with that already. We'll mourn her and move on…"

"But that's so cold…" she said.

"She's going to end-up cold no matter how you look at it...cold on the streets...cold in the ground..."

"Well, I won't do it..."

"You gon' end-up loving that girl to death... literally."

"I can't help it..."

"Okay...then, shut the fuck up complaining about it. I'm trying to watch my damn game shows. I'm not trying to deal with this. I've been fighting all of my life...fought as a kid, fought in the war, fighting to keep the white man off my back, and now, this shit. I'm tired and I'm tired of being tired. I want to watch my TV shows in peace. PEACE DAMNIT! Can a motherfucker get some damn peace?"

My grandmother walked out of the room and slammed the door.

"And with my peace, I would like a peanut butter and jelly sandwich!" he yelled.

"Fuck you," she mumbled, as she walked down the hall towards the bathroom.

"I heard you...don't make me come out there..."

"Oh, you'll come out here for that, won't you?" She threw the door open and began to pull at my underwear. I grabbed a hold of them. Suddenly, we were in a tug of war.

"Boy, let go so that I can see what she did to you."

"Grandma, I'm fine..."

Still pulling, she said, "Boy, ain't nobody looking at you."

DADDY BY DIANE MARTIN 117

"Ain't you got to look at it to see if there's something wrong with it?"

"I'm gon' look at it, but I ain't gon' look at it…" she confirmed.

"But ain't looking at it the same as looking at it?"

She, stopped, exhaled, and sucked her teeth. "I'mma give you to the count of two and if you don't let go, something else on your body is going to bleed…"

I hesitated for a second and then, let go. I looked away as she pulled my underwear down.

"Tsk, tsk, tsk…that girl. I don't know what she has against you…" She looked around the room and said, "Look up in that cabinet and hand me that brown bottle."

I grabbed one. "This?"

"No, the other one…"

I grabbed the other bottle. "This?"

"Yeah…" she took the bottle from me and said, "This is going to burn."

Before I could object, she was pouring the solution over the wound.

I balled-up my hands as my toes curled. I screamed. "Aaaaaaaahhhhhhhh!!!!"

She pulled my underwear back up. "That'll fix it, but I would hold off on pee'ing for a while."

I was walking out of the bathroom when she grabbed my arm. "I'm sorry…" she said.

I looked at her. She was tired. I could see it all over her face. "You shouldn't be sorry for the stuff that she do…but I promise you, granny…one day, she's going to be sorry. I promise you that."

CHAPTER 15

I'd developed a chip on my shoulder, but I didn't act out because I knew better. My grand-daddy believed that kids should be seen and not heard and had no problem reminding us of it. He didn't hit us or anything because it was hard to whip us from a wheelchair, but he had other ways of getting us back in line on the days that we'd decided to cross it.

One morning, I'd poured myself a bowl of cereal. I'd almost eaten all of it when I noticed something black floating around in the milk. Closely, I looked at it. As I inspected it, I noticed that it had antennas and an egg attached to its back. I didn't have time to scream because as soon as I opened my mouth, everything that I'd eaten up until that point came flying out of my mouth, onto the table, and into my grand-daddy's face and lap.

For a moment, he didn't say anything. Slowly, he began to wipe the vomit from his forehead. When he was able to finally speak, he said, "Get up..."
For a second, I thought that he was going to help me clean up the mess, but instead, he said, "Assume the position..." and pointed towards the door. In my

house, 'assuming the position' meant to 'go stand in the corner' or worse, 'go lie under his bed.'

With vomit all over my clothes, I said, "Grand-daddy I didn't mean to do it…there's a roach in my bowl."

Wiping vomit from his shirt, he said, "You have a choice…"

"But what did I do…I had no control over that…" I said, trying to plead my case.

"Y'all run around here screaming that you're hungry and then as soon as you get some food, you throw it up…"

"But there's a roach…" I said, pointing at the bowl.

"You think that that's the first roach that you've eaten? You've probably eaten a million of 'em."

"WHAT???"

"No, 'what,' boy…stop acting brand-new…the odds of you eating a roach are greater than the odds of me winning the lottery…now, pick one. I ain't got all day."

Stalling, I said, "But I need to clean up…"

"One of these other little liabilities can clean it up…"

"Awwwwwww, man…" they objected.

He looked at them, "You wanna join him?"

"Nope," they all said, together.

I stood there for a minute to think about which punishment would be easier. If I stood in the corner, with my face to the wall, I would have to stand in place all day, but if I was under his bed, I could take a nap, or I could watch TV from under there. So, I decided that it was best to get under his bed. I walked down the hall and 'assumed the position.' I crawled under and with my back pressed against the floor, I waited for him. You see, what made this particular punishment 'interesting' is that he would come and lay on top of the bed while you were under it and that wouldn't be so bad if he didn't weigh three hundred pounds.

As I laid there, I heard the creaking sound of the bedroom door. It swung open and I could see the wheels of if his chair coming through the door. He turned on the TV. It was one of those game shows that he loved to watch. I positioned myself so that I could see it.

"You better not be watching that TV, boy."

"I'm not," I said, lying.

He came close to the bed and then climbed on top of it. The springs, from the mattress, missed my chest by two inches. After he got comfortable, he began to shout answers at the TV screen.

"$5463…"

The contestant said, "$4321…"

"It's $5463…your ass is gon' lose…"

The game-show host said, "Is that your final answer?"

"Yes…" the contestant said.

"You gon' lose, boy…" my grand-daddy said.

The game-show host said, "The answer is $5466…"

"See, I was close…he should have listened to me. I know what I'm talking about because you know the price of shit when you can't afford the price of shit…"

"Grand-daddy…" I said. "He can't hear you."

He jumped up and down on the bed, causing the springs to hit me in the face. "Shut your vomiting-ass up…"

After about an hour, I drifted off to sleep. Soon, I was awakened by the sound of my grand-daddy snoring. When I opened my eyes, I turned to look at the closet. There was something in there. It was big and standing up on two legs. I rubbed the 'sleep' from my eyes and tried to focus. I slid closer to the closet to see what was in there. Still unable to see what it was, I crawled from under the bed and over to the closet. Before I knew it, I was face to face with it. Staring into its beady-eyes, I realized what it was. I screamed, "POSSUM!!!!"

My grand-daddy jumped up and said, "What? What?"

"POSSUM!!!" I said, crawling towards the door.

He climbed out of the bed and onto the floor. He crawled into the closet. "Close the door behind me and don't open it until I tell you to."

"But grand-daddy…" I said.

"Do as I said, boy…" he demanded.

I crawled over and closed the door. I placed my body against it to keep it from opening. I could hear him struggling. Things were being thrown against the door. This went on for a couple of minutes, before I heard a loud scream and then, there was silence.

Suddenly, I heard a quiet knock against the door. Slowly, I opened it.

"Here…"

"Ewwwwwww…what is that?" I said, looking at the bloody rug in his hand.

"Dinner…now, go and get a pot, so I can throw his ass in it."

CHAPTER 16

"Ignorance is bliss" is what she always used to say. I guess she thought that by making me think that no other world existed, then I would learn to accept my lot in life. It wasn't until, one winter, when they'd turned off the heat, again, that I learned how deep the lies went. My uncle John had come to get a few of us to protect us from the cold. We'd never been to his house before, but I didn't expect more than a one room shack – just enough for one man to live comfortably. As we rode through the community, I noticed that the houses didn't look like ours. There were no boards on the windows or doors, there were new cars in the yards, and there were children outside, playing - smiling. They didn't look hungry. Their clothes weren't tattered. They looked happy.

When we pulled into the driveway. There were colorful lights flickering on and off on top of the house. There was a big green wreath on the door. The door opened. A woman stepped out and waved. When we got out, the woman yelled, "Come on in…I made hot chocolate." We looked at each other. *Hot chocolate?* I thought to myself. As I walked across the yard, I noticed a snowman sitting out front. He had a carrot for his nose. My brother ran up and snatched it off of his face. My uncle ran behind him.

"What are you doing?" he asked.

"Food…" my brother said.

My uncle took the carrot from him. "It's okay…there's more inside." As we approached the door, we all looked at each other and began to remove our clothing.

"What are you doing?" he asked.

"Taking our clothes off…Aunt Jasmine makes us take our clothes off."

"Why?" he asked, confused.

Embarrassed, I hesitated before saying, "'Cause of the roaches…"

He frowned. "Are you hiding them in your pocket?"

We all looked at each other. "No…" we said in unison.

"Then, get your butts in here…" My uncle walked in first. We stood outside for a second. He turned to us. "Come on in, you're letting the heat out." We walked in and looked around the room. There was music playing in the background. There was a beautiful tree in the middle of the room – surrounded by boxes that were wrapped in beautiful "shiny" paper and beautiful bright bows. I'd never seen a Christmas Tree before, at least not in real life. I've only seen them on TV. It was exciting to see one with presents underneath it.

We all sat down on the floor. The woman walked into the room and asked, "Who's hungry?"

We didn't hesitate to respond. All at once, we yelled, "Me...me...me...me...!"

She smiled and walked into the kitchen. When she walked back out, she said, "Well, come on..."

We all ran into the room. When I walked into the door, I stopped and rubbed my eyes. There was food, real food, and lots of it. We all ran to the table and began to eat. She stopped us. "You have to bless your food, first."

"Bless?" I asked.

"You know...pray over your food..." she said.

"Why do we need to do that?" I asked.

The woman shrugged. "You've never blessed your food?"

I shook my head. "Never had enough to bless..."

Tears began to form in her eyes. She yelled, "John!!!"

My uncle walked into the room.

Wiping her eyes, she said, "They're not feeding these kids?"

I was about to say something when she turned to me. "Y'all go ahead and eat..."

She didn't have to say that twice. Immediately, we put our faces into our plates. "This is good, lady. What is this? Squirrel? Rat?"

The woman's eyes-widened. Horrified, she said, "John, this is terrible. They're eating rats and squirrels? They don't have food? Why didn't you tell me?"

Embarrassed, my uncle said, "They got food…just not food that you're accustomed to."

"What do you mean by that, John?"

"Look, it's how we all grew-up."

"But these are kids," she said.

"We were kids too…"

"How can this happen? In America?" she asked.

"My parents are from the south…they made do with what they had…plus, what's wrong with eating squirrels and rats…we eat cows and chickens…"

"Cows and chickens are different…"

"How are they different?"

"Cause, they are…they're raised on a farm."

"No, they're not…they are animals too…and you can find rats on a farm…squirrels too, if you look hard enough…don't be opposed to one without opposing the other…"

The woman pointed at us. "Look at these kids…they are licking their plates. When was the last time they ate?"

He scratched his head. "Who knows?"

Frustrated, she said, "WHO KNOWS????!!!!! These are your people…your family…how do you not know???"

"It's complicated," he said.

"Complicated???" she asked.

He grabbed her arm, pulled her out of the room, and down the hall. Their voices were muffled. I left the table and walked down the hall to hear what they were saying. I placed my ear against the door and listened.

"It's their mama…" he said. "She gets assistance for them but converts it into cash…and smokes it."

"Look at those kids, John…"

"I know…I know…"

"Then, why don't your mother become their guardian so that she can get them some food?" she asked.

"She doesn't want to take my sister's rights from her."

"What? Her right to do this?"

"She's hoping that she will get her act together…"

"Hope? Your mama sitting around hoping? She should be ashamed of herself…both your sister and your mama. This is ridiculous. Hoping…there's things that no human being should have to hope for. They shouldn't have to hope for a roof over their heads. They shouldn't have to hope for air. They shouldn't have to hope for food or water…"

He interrupted. "I know…" He paused for a second and continued, "But my sister just keeps making them. My mama told her to stop, but they keep popping up – one after the other. They can't afford to feed her kids and her addiction, but they don't want to see her suffer…they don't want her to die."

"That bitch…" she mumbled.

"Which bitch?"

"Both of them…and this should be a no-brainer…her kids over her. They shouldn't think about it twice."

"My mama has a fucked-up way of dealing with her kids. I would have put Betty out a long time ago, but not mama."

I cracked the door and looked in. The woman frowned. "I can't believe that they are living that way because of Betty...making these kids suffer... because of her addiction..."

"She's draining them dry and what they don't give to her, she takes." My uncle looked over at the door. "Boy, what are you doing in here?"

Trying to process what I'd just heard, I couldn't bring myself to address it with him. I didn't want to cause a disturbance and I didn't want them to take us back home, so I said, "I...I...I just wanted to know if I could have some more food?"

The woman wiped her eyes and said, "Of course...as much as you want." She walked towards me. "Come on...let's get you some more food."

As we walked down the hall towards the kitchen, I began to feel angry and confused. I couldn't understand what I'd just heard. I didn't want to believe that they would be willing to hurt us intentionally for something that my mama did. I didn't want to believe that they would make us suffer. Then suddenly, my anger shifted. For some odd reason, I wasn't mad at them anymore. My thoughts shifted back to the root of all of our pain and suffering. Betty was a disease, eating us all alive, and the only way to survive was to find a cure.

Early, the next morning, we were all awakened to the sound of someone shouting, "HO, HO, HOOOOO! Merry Christmas!"

I was so afraid that I jumped up, ran over, and kicked the man between his legs. "OUCH!!! Son of a bitch!!!"

"Uncle?" I asked.

In a high-pitched voice, he said, "Boy, what the hell is wrong with you?"

I looked at him. "What is wrong with you? You're the one waking folks up, in the middle of the night, dressed like a serial killer."

"I'm not a serial killer..." he insisted.

"Well, I know that now...sorry 'bout your nuts."

He shook his head. Frustrated, he stood, and limped over to the other side of the room. "Get your ass over here. We got y'all some presents."

My eyes lit-up. "Presents?" I turned to my brothers and sisters. "Get up y'all...we got presents..."

They all stood and ran over to where my uncle was sitting. He yelled into the other room. "Baby, could you bring me a drink?"

She looked around the corner. "Yes…you want some ice?"

He looked at me. "Yeah, put it in a bag."

She walked into the room, handed him the glass and the bag. "What do you need the bag for?"

He swallowed the drink with one gulp and then, placed the bag between his legs. He grimaced. "Now, let's open some presents."

He looked at the boxes and then, handed them to us. We looked at it. "Okay…open it." Excitedly, we ripped the boxes open. I received a game, the other boys received race cars, and the girls received dolls. Happily, the kids began to play, but I couldn't.

"What's wrong, boy?" he asked. "Aren't you happy?"

I looked at the game. "Yes, uncle, but…"

"But what?" he asked.

I thought about what he'd said about my grandparents and my mama and as much as I liked the game, I knew that a game wouldn't erase the pain that I was feeling or erase the betrayal. It was a temporary fix for a problem that wasn't going away. At some point, we had to go back home, and I didn't want to. I looked up at him. "Uncle…" I said, hesitating.

"Yes, boy," he said.

"Can I stay here with you and auntie?" I asked.

He removed the bag of ice. "Come here…"

I grabbed the game, walked over, and sat next to him. He sighed. "I know that it's bad, but you have to hang in there. It'll be over soon. I went through the same shit…"

"But didn't you wish that someone would come and rescue you?"

"I did…" His eyes filled with tears. "Believe me, I did."

"Why can't you rescue us?"

He wiped his eyes. "I can't…you kids are the only reason that mama stays with daddy…what would he do if she left?"

"I don't know…"

He placed his hand on my shoulder. "This is just one part of your life…it's dark now, but things will get brighter…I promise."

"And if they don't?"

He didn't respond.

I turned to look at my brothers and sisters. I closed my eyes, trying to save this moment in my memory, because I wasn't sure when or if it would ever happen again.

When we returned home, we didn't find any blinking lights, there was no tree, other than the one in the front yard, and there were no presents underneath it. I asked my grand-daddy, "Why don't we celebrate Christmas?"

Before he could answer, Betty came stumbling through the front door, high as a kite.

Slurring her words, she said, "Ho, ho, hooooooo…Me, me, merry fucking Christmas."

My grand-daddy looked at her and said, "That's why we don't celebrate Christmas."

She came and sat down next to me. "Guess what I got you for Christmas."

I looked at her. Excited, I said, "What?"

"The same thing that I got you last year…and the year before that and the years before that…not a gad-damn thing." She began to laugh, hysterically.

I frowned and stood to leave the room when she grabbed my arm. "There's no such thing as Christmas…no such thing as a fucking Santa Claus…that shit ain't real." She stuck her finger through the hole in my shirt. "This shit...this shit is real..." she began to laugh again. I snatched away from her and ran to my room.

"I'm your fucking Santa Claus...you want to see what I got in my bag for you? Nothing, but this pipe. Ho, ho, ho, you little bitch!!!"

I jumped in my bed, still holding the game that my uncle gave to me and cried myself to sleep.

CHAPTER 17

The next morning, I noticed that things were, unusually, quiet. As I walked down the hall towards the kitchen, I noticed that mostly everyone had gone for the day. It wasn't until I walked into the kitchen that I found him, lying on the floor, next to the refrigerator. I tried turning and leaving the room, but it was too late. He saw me.

"Come here, boy…"

I sighed and walked over. "Yes, grand-daddy…"

"Come down here…" he instructed.

I huffed and dropped down on my knees. He reached up and hit me.

I yelled. "What was that for?"

"Shhhhhh…" He shushed me and said, "You're trying to give away our position?"

"Our what?" I asked, rubbing my arm.

"Our position…" he confirmed.

I looked around the room, hoping that someone would save me, but it didn't happen.

"Shhhhhhh…" He shushed me again. "Come down here and look…"

Slowly, I lowered my head to look under the refrigerator. "What are we looking at, grand-daddy?"

"Do you see it?" he asked, as he pointed under the refrigerator.

Growing impatient, I asked, "See what?"

He grabbed the back of my head and pushed it closer to the floor. "SEE IT?"

The longer I didn't see whatever it was that he wanted me to see, the longer I was going to have to stay on the floor, so I lied to him. "Oh yeah…now, I see it."

Satisfied, he smiled. "Soooooooo, how do you want to kill it?"

I didn't know what to say. I couldn't admit that I didn't see anything, because that would piss him off, but now, he wanted me to help him kill something that didn't exist. I had to think fast. I sat up and started looking around the room. Before I knew it, he'd pulled his gun out of his pants. Without thinking, I grabbed his hand. "Grand-daddy…what are you doing?"

"I'm going to kill that son-of-a bitch…"

Struggling to get his gun out of his hand, I said, "Grand-daddy…wouldn't it be better to kill it with a knife…"

"No, no, no…it's gotta be quick."

We continued to wrestle. "Grand-daddy…" I begged. Suddenly, the front door opened. I could hear my grandmother coming towards us. "What the hell is going on in here?"

All of a sudden, I heard a loud *BANG!* We both stopped to see where the bullet landed. I looked over in grandma's direction. She had this weird look on her face. We all heard something dripping. She looked down to where the sound was coming from. In her hand, was a wounded gallon of milk. Frustrated, she walked over to the sink and sat it down. She pulled me by the shirt. "Get your little ass out of here... messing around with this crazy bastard...you gon' get killed." She looked at my grandfather. "I can't even go to the damn store without coming home and you turning the milk into a casualty. Instead, of picking up this gun why don't you pick up a remote or a gaddamn book or something..." She snatched the gun from his hand. "One day, old man, you gon' kill somebody..."

Later that day, I was sitting on the porch when all hell broke loose. I could hear things being thrown around the house.
"Where is it?" he asked.
"Where is what?" my grandmother said.
"Don't play with me woman...I know you got it."
"Got what?" she said.
I walked in to find her trying to get away from him. "I told you not to put your hands on it."

"I don't know what you're talking about," she proclaimed. "You probably lost it."

"Woman, don't play with me...I wouldn't lose my gun and you know it."

She tried getting away from him, but he was on her heels. "I said, 'that I don't know what you're talking about...'"

"I will tear up everything in this house until I find it...if you think we ain't got shit, now, wait until I'm done...I will burn this motherfucker down. Now, I'm going to count to three...1, 2...2...I'm on my way to 3...don't make me say '3'..."

She stopped and placed her hands on her hips. "You've said it twice..."

"You ain't gon' be happy until I set fire to this shit..."

"You ain't gon' do nothing..."

His eyes widened. "Okay, okay...now, you gon' make a motherfucker show his ass..."

She huffed and walked down the hall to the living room. She sat down in the chair. I walked over and looked at her. "Grandma, ain't you worried?"

"I ain't thinking about his ass...now, go and turn on the TV..."

I was turning on the TV when he yelled from the kitchen. "Boy, go and get me some toilet paper. I ran out of the room and down the hall. Once I had the toilet paper, I headed back towards the kitchen.

"You better not be burning the last of the toilet paper. Your ass is gon' be pissed when you take a shit later on and you ain't got nothing, but your hands to wipe your butt with…"

"Shut up!" He yelled. "I told you what I was gon' do…your ass ain't gon' believe me until you feel the flames under your feet."

He turned towards me. "Hand me that toilet paper…"

"But grand-daddy…"

"Get out of the way…" He turned on the stove, held the roll over the flame, and before I could blink, it was on fire. It burned so fast that it burned his fingers. He dropped it into his lap. I yelled, "Grandma, grand-daddy's on fire!"

Without getting out of her chair, she said, "Throw some water on his ass and then, come in here and change the channel for me."

I ran over to the sink and grabbed a glass of water. I tossed it at him. The smell of smoke and burnt hair filled the room.

He looked so funny, sitting there soaked from the water, with half of his beard singed completely from his face. I couldn't resist. I started laughing.

"Is this shit funny to you?"

I tried holding in the laughter, but I couldn't.

"You think this shit is funny? I wonder how funny that mattress is going to be."

"What? Why am I being punished? I put the fire out."

"It's your fault that there was a fire in the first place…"

No longer laughing, I said, "Wait…you were the one who told me to get the toilet paper and you were the one who set it on fire…:"

"And my beard would still be here if you hadn't of listened to me…this is one of those 'damned, if you did or damned, if you didn't' moments."

"Wait…that's not fair."

"You know where to go…" He pointed down the hall.

"Grandma!!!" I said, hoping that she would help me, but she said, "I told you to stop messing with his crazy ass."

"Awwwww, grandma."

"Oh, before you go. Come and change the channel. My 'stories' are about to come on."

I did as I was told and then, walked down the hall to their bedroom. I climbed under their bed. It was then that I saw it. The item that he was looking for. His gun.

CHAPTER 18

I was a loner and although, there was a lot of us, I spent a lot of time by myself and loneliness can be a strange bedfellow. Most of the time, I would just sit in silence, but soon, the silence would become too loud to ignore, so like most kids, I gave it a voice and then, soon, gave it a name. I called it, Brian. Brian didn't stick around for long like most of the stuff and people in my life, but he arrived at the two most critical points of my life.

He was just like me except, he was white. I don't know why Brian was white. I guess it made my situation more tolerable if, in my imagination, Blacks folks weren't the only ones who had to go through this shit. And it was pure luck that he showed-up, one day. It was after Betty, who was having one of her 'episodes', decided to take it out on me, again, that he became my friend.

She loved torturing me when my grandparents were out. I used to dread watching them leave because I knew that she was somewhere, scheming. I tried avoiding her, but on this day, I was too sick and too weak to run from her.

"Come here…let me check your forehead," my grandmother said. She placed her hand on my head and continued, "Child, your head is hotter than concrete during the summertime…"

My grandfather stared over her shoulder. "The boy looks fine to me. He ain't dead or dying, so he should take his ass to school."

She looked at him and shook her head. "He can't go to school like this. He would infect all of the other children…"

"He ain't gon' be putting his lips on any of them…" He paused for a second and asked, "Are you?"

"Stop talking stupid…you ain't got to kiss nobody to make them sick," she said, pouring something black into a spoon. "Here…take this…"

I looked at it. "What is that?"

"That's the good shit. We paid a whole $1.50 for it," he said. "Make you forget all about being sick…run it right out of you."

I frowned. "Granny, that stuff looks like tar…"

"And it tastes like tar too. That's how you know it's the good shit. The worse it tastes the better it is for you…" he said.

My grandmother was getting tired of holding the spoon. "Come on…I ain't got all day."

"But grandma," I complained.

"You can either volunteer to take it or I can force you…and you don't want me to force you."

Surrendering, I took a deep breath and opened my mouth. She shoved it in – banging the spoon against my teeth. I exhaled and swallowed. My body shook from my toes up through the rest of my body. It was the worst thing that I'd ever tasted. I grabbed on to the bed as it went down. When it was gone, I took the bottom of my shirt and began to scrub my tongue with it.

"Now," she began. "...we're going to make a run. I will check on you when we get back, okay?"

"Okay..." I said, climbing back underneath the blankets. "Can you get some orange juice, granny? I hear that it's good for colds."

He huffed. "Who got money for orange juice? You got money for orange juice?" Before I could answer he responded, "You better close your eyes and dream about orange juice...cause that's the only way you gon' get some."

Standing at the door, my grandmother said, "Bring your ass on here..."

He turned to follow her. "You ain't the boss of me, woman. Don't get your ass kicked."

"You need legs to do that...you old bastard. Now, come on here...always talking about what you gon' do to somebody. You ain't gon' do nothing."

"Fuck you," he said, as he closed the door behind him.

I'd just closed my eyes when I heard Betty moving around in her room. I'd began to doze off when I heard her feet shuffling down the hall towards my bedroom. I pulled the covers over my head hoping that she would look inside of my room, think that I was gone, and just walk away, but I should have known that it wouldn't be that easy.

She walked in and said, "Paul…I need your help."
Pretending to be sleep, I didn't say anything.
She walked over and snatched the blankets off of me.
"Paul, I need your help."
"I don't feel well…" I said.
"It'll only take a second," she said, but something in her eyes told me that she was lying.
"Grandmamma told me to stay in bed…"
"I SAID that it's only going to take a second…"
"NO!" I said, defiantly.
She dropped the blankets on the floor and began pulling at my feet. "NOW!" she demanded.
The next thing I knew, she'd pulled me out of bed and onto the floor. She began dragging me out of the room and down the hall. I tried kicking her, but it didn't work. The whole time, all I could think about was how cold the floor felt against my skin. Before I knew it, I found myself lying in the middle of my grandparent's bedroom.
She let me go. "Get over here and bend over…"
"What?" I asked, confused and angry.
"Get over here…" she demanded as she sat in a chair across the room.
"Why?"
"'Cause I said so…" she said.
"But what did I do?"
"You ain't got to do anything…"

Daddy by Diane Martin 145

"Can I go back to bed? I don't feel well…" I begged.
"You can get your ass over here…that's what you can do."
"But I didn't do anything…"
"I'm going to say it one more time…"
When I stood, my head began to spin. "I don't feel well."
"Guess what? And I don't care."
I stumbled over towards her and kneeled down on the floor. She used her feet to force me to the floor. With her feet on my back, she said, "That's a good doggy…you know why I call you that? 'Cause you're a dog just like the rest of them." She turned on the TV. "Now, be still while I watch my stories."
I was so hot. Sweat poured off of me like rain. I couldn't stay in the position that I was in, so I fell down onto the floor. "Get up!" She yelled. "Get up… with your lazy ass!"
I began to shake, violently. "I don't feel well…please, let me go to bed."
She was screaming so loud that she hadn't heard the front door open. When they came into the room, my grandmother dropped her bags on the floor and ran over to me. "What is going on in here?" she asked.
Nervous, Betty said, "I caught him in here…I think he was stealing something."
"This boy ain't in no condition to steal anything from anybody…you're making it up."
"Are you calling me a liar?"

"Yes...look at him. He can barely stand and what is he going to steal? Huh?" she said, as she lifted me to my feet. "This boy should be in bed. You see that he don't feel well..."

"I was telling him that when I caught him stealing..." she said, grabbing my arm. "Right, Paul? Isn't that what I said? I said, 'Paul, sweetie...what are you doing? Wonderful son of mine..."

I turned towards her.

She dug her nails into my arm. "Right, Paul?"

I didn't answer.

My grandmother snatched me away from her. "I'm going to get him into the cold water before he burns up and leave ashes all over my floor."

Before I could object, I was dragged across the hall. The next thing I knew, I was being forced into the tub. She'd turned on the water. When it hit my skin, it felt like I'd been thrown into a freezer. I screamed. "Noooooooo...noooooo...!!!"

"Hold still, child. It's going to be alright...now, hold still."

"Noooooooo, I gotta pee..."

"Pee in the tub." I heard my grandfather say.

"You better not pee in this tub," she mumbled. "It's almost over."

After a few more minutes, she turned off the water and touched my skin. "Now, that's better...come on...let's change your clothes and you can go back to bed." She wrapped a towel around me.

Dripping wet, I walked down the hall to my bedroom. I was changing my clothes when she walked into the room holding a glass. "Here, drink this?"

Excited, I asked, "Orange juice?"

"Close…" she said.

I looked at the contents of the glass. "What is this, granny?"

"All I could afford was the powdered stuff, but it all taste the same…"

Grateful, I said, "Thanks granny…" as I sipped from the glass.

I climbed back into the bed. She tucked me under my covers and said, "What were you really doing in my room?"

I thought about it for a second and said, "Betty took me in there…she had me on my hands and knees…"

"What she do that for?" she asked.

I shrugged. "She said that I was a dog like all the other men…"

She stood and said, "You get some sleep."

I closed my eyes, but before I could drift off, I heard them arguing. Then, there was a loud thud and suddenly, a door closed. After that, I fell fast asleep.

I was sweating so bad that it woke me up out of my sleep. I was freezing and shaking when I heard his voice for the first time. "Hey Paul…" he said.

"Huh? Who is that?" I asked, looking out into the darkness.

"I'm over here…" he said.

I looked up to find a shadow near my closet door. I asked, "What's your name?"

"I'm whatever you want to call me…"

"What do you want?"

"Well, I'm here because…you're dying, Paul."

"I'm what?" I asked, becoming scared.

"You're dying…" he said, again.

"I'm not dying…"

"If you don't get out of that bed you will…" he confirmed.

"But what am I supposed to do?" I asked.

"You need to get that fever under control or you're going to shake yourself to death…" He came out from the shadows and sat across from me.

Frightened, I jumped back. "Who are you and how did you get in here?"

"We don't have time for that? You need to get up and go back into that bathroom…turn that water on and get that fever under control."

I rolled out of the bed and fell to the floor. Crawling, the rest of the way, I climbed into the shower and turned it on. I began to scream. "Aaaaaaahhhhhh!!!!"

The person came into the bathroom and sat on the toilet across from me. "Good…don't that feel better?"

I didn't respond. A few minutes later, my grandfather came into the room. "What the hell is going on in here?"

I looked over at the toilet. "I was hot, and my friend told me to get in the shower."

My grandfather looked around the room. "What friend?"

"My friend," I said, pointing at the toilet.

He looked over at the toilet. "Your ass is delirious…ain't nobody on the toilet."

"Yes, he is…see…he's right there."

My grandfather looked again. He shook his head before coming over and turning the water off. "Your ass is nuts. Get out of this damn tub…running up my water bill and talking to the damn air…"

"See…see…" I pointed.

He shook his head again. "Y'all kids are going to cause me to drink…I swear. Take your ass to bed."

I changed into my remaining outfit and climbed back into the bed.

Before I drifted off, I heard a voice say, "You're going to be alright now." He sat down next to my bed and placed his hand on my shoulder. "Get your rest…you're gonna need it."

CHAPTER 19

I was a little scrawny kid and it made me the perfect target for kids who didn't have shit else to do, but mess with little scrawny kids. Every day, like flies on shit, they would find and mess with me. It's kind of hard to be the kid with duct tape on his shoes and clothes and not expect to get my ass kicked every day. And what better reason does a bully need to kick your ass? Behind being fat and ugly, being poor is in the top five. And it hurts like hell, as a kid, to have to defend and protect yourself over something that you have absolutely no control over.

If every kid could have their way, they would be rich, but that isn't how the world works. Some of us are just born with the short-end of the stick and society has an excellent way of reminding you of it. It beats you down in every way possible and after you've gotten your ass kicked and your feelings hurt, enough times, you toughen-up. That's when you decide that you're either going to be a victim all of your life or you're going to start kicking folks' asses. For me, the choice was simple.

My first victim's name was Kenny. Kenny was an asshole. I used to think that Kenny spent every night, of his short miserable life, dreaming about ways to get on my damn nerves. We'd had a few run-ins when we were younger that usually resulted in me having my underwear pulled so far up the crack of my ass, you could see the shit stains that covered them. At some point, you would think that folks would get tired of messing with you and move on to mess with somebody else, but not Kenny. I was his special little project and one day, Kenny caught me during one of those moments when I just wasn't in the mood for his mess. All I wanted to do was go to school, do what I had to do, and take my ass home, but Kenny had other plans.

When I approached the front steps of the building, Kenny and his boys were waiting for me. Now, mind you, I was hungry enough to eat an entire cow, but since there wasn't one available, Kenny just had to do.
They started right in on me. "Hey, it's Pee-boy."
"Pee-boy, Pee-boy, Pee-boy…" they all chanted. Their favorite name for me was "Pee-boy." Although, I'd never wet the bed, I understood why they called me that. When your bed is a resting place for every rodent in the neighborhood, it's bound to smell like piss, and shit, and some of everything else. Anyway, I tried ignoring them. They stepped-out in front of me. "Pee-boy, Pee-boy, Pee-boy…" They continued to chant. I tried walking around them, but they wouldn't let me pass.

Then, he stuck his finger in my face. "You hear me talking to you or maybe you just can't afford to hear either…"

Annoyed, I didn't say anything.

"So, Pee-boy…let's see what you got on…looks like your mama's been shopping for your clothes at the hardware store." They all laughed.

I remained silent.

He continued. "And since we're talking about your mama…how's that bitch doing? Or should I say, 'WHO' is that bitch doing?'"

And while 'Mama jokes' might piss some people off, they didn't bother me, because whatever somebody had to say about mine was probably true.

The bell rang and I tried to get around them, again, but instead, he pushed me. When I fell, it ripped the tape that was holding my pants together and because I didn't have any drawers on, which I decided not to wear just in case someone decided to give me a wedgie, the crack of my ass fell out of them. They all began to laugh, hysterically. I was so embarrassed that I couldn't think straight. Everything around me turned red. I became so hot that beads of sweat formed on my head and my hands felt like they were on fire.

He held his hand out to help me up, but then, he quickly retrieved it. "SIKE!!!!" He said, laughing.

I could barely control my breathing. I bit my bottom lip as I balled my hands into fists. He reached out again. This time, he left it extended. I looked at it.

"Come-on, Pee-boy…I got you…"

Suddenly, out of nowhere, Brian arrived. He stood next to me and whispered in my ear. "You gon' let this motherfucker punk you?"

"Huh?" I said.

Confused, Kenny looked at me. "Huh, what?"

Brian continued. "You know that you have to hurt this boy or he'll be messing with you forever…do you want that?"

"No," I said.

"No, what?" Kenny asked.

"He's handing you his hand," Brian continued, "Make him regret it."

I looked at his hand and then, I looked at his friends who were still laughing.

"Come on…we're going to be late," Brian whispered. I looked at him and decided that today was going to be his unlucky day. I opened my mouth and I wrapped it around his fingers until I heard the bones snap inside of my mouth. He began to scream. "Aaaaahhhhhhhhhh…Stop!"

Brian whispered, "Perfect…"

His 'boys' stopped laughing. Two of them ran, while one stayed behind to try and help him. As they pulled, I could feel the flesh tearing from one of his fingertips. Under his screams, I heard a voice in the distance say, "What are you guys doing?"

When she approached, she saw that I had his fingers in his mouth. "Young man, let him go…" she demanded.

I bit into him, one last time, before releasing him. He fell to the ground, looked down at his hand, and began to cry. "He bit off my finger!!!!"

I spit the tip off into in his face and wiped the blood from the corner of my mouth. She looked at me and said, "Go to my office and wait for me." She grabbed Kenny and said, "Come on...let me get you to the nurse's office."

I stood up and walked inside of the school. The kids in the hallway watched as I strolled down the hall, smiling, like a kid who'd just got an award for perfect attendance. When I walked into the office, I sat down and thought about the look on Kenny's face. I was giggling to myself when the woman rushed in. "Young man, follow me..."

I followed her into the room. "What were you thinking? Why would you do something like that?"

I looked at her and calmly, said, "I was hungry."

They were angry when they came to get me. The look on their faces told me that I was going under their bed and I didn't care, because I knew that I deserved it.

Just like Kenny deserved it too. Amazingly, when we walked in, my grandmother went right into the kitchen and began to pour some syrup on a plate. She handed me three pieces of bread, poured me a glass of milk, and then, walked out of the kitchen. I was tearing that food up and licking the plate, when my grand-daddy came in.

"Are we eating people, now, son?"

I stopped long enough to say, "No…but he…"

He put up his hand. "I don't even want to hear it…right now, there's a boy walking around with the tip of his finger missing. His finger ain't gon' never be right again. He ain't gon' be able to dig in his nose. He ain't gon' be able to scratch his ass. People ain't gon' know what the hell he's pointing at. All because of you…"

"But grand-daddy…"

He put up his hand again. "I must have taken a breath and you felt that it was okay to talk…it ain't. Now, I'm sure that that boy did something to you to make you want to take a bite out of his ass, but you gon' have to grow some skin or you're going to be biting motherfuckers for the rest of your life and it ain't safe to be going around biting folks."

I opened my mouth to say something, but then, he gave me a look that indicated that he was done talking about it and he turned and left the room. I was preparing to leave the room, too, when Brian popped-up.

156

Excitedly, I said, "Did you see that? I messed ol' boy up…"

Brian laughed and said, "Yes, you did…got his butt real good…I'm proud of you."

I was so happy. It felt good to hear somebody, even if it was a figment of my imagination, say that. "Thanks man…" I said. Then, suddenly, I heard, "Go and lay your ass down somewhere, boy, and stop talking to yourself…" he yelled from the other room.

I turned to say "goodbye" to Brian, but he was already gone.

CHAPTER 20

After that, the "system" came-in and took all of us away. Somebody must have reported us, because they just showed-up one day, in the middle of the night and snatched us out of our beds. We didn't know what was happening. All we knew was that there were a bunch of strangers standing in the living room telling us that our home was unsafe and that they needed to get us out of there. Then, they dragged us out of the house and placed us in different cars. I remember begging them not to take us, but they assured us that everything would be okay. They lied.

They split us up and placed us into five different homes. I am not sure where the rest of the kids went, but they placed me in a home with a woman who lived with her adult son. From the onset, I knew that something wasn't right with them. For one, when the caseworker dropped me off, the foster mother was all-smiles and giggles, but as soon as the caseworker pulled off, the bitch, immediately, turned into Satan.

The first night that I was there, she told me that she didn't have time to set-up a room for me, so she told me that I had to sleep on the couch. Which was okay by me, but the room was freezing. Now, I was used to being in a cold house, but I thought that they were moving me to a place that was supposed to be better than the one that I'd come from. When I complained, she walked over and stuck her finger in my chest.

"Here's how this is going to work...ummmmm, what is your name again?"

"Paul..." I said.

"Whatever...you are going to lay your little ass down and you're going to shut the fuck up...do you hear me?"

Right then, I knew that this living arrangement was not going to last, but I did what she said, anyway, while spending the whole night thinking about a way to get back home.

The next morning, I awoke to the both of them standing over me. She smiled and leaned over me. "Good morning, Sleepy-head."

I stretched and rubbed my eyes. "Good morning..."

She smiled. "I bought you something to eat."

I smiled and looked around the room. "Where?"

She pointed at the floor. "Right there..."

I looked in the direction that she was pointing in and said, "There's nothing there, but a bowl."

She smiled and said, "Yep..."

Confused, I asked, "So where is my food?"

With one eyebrow raised, she said, "In the bowl..."

Still confused, I asked, "On the table?"

Becoming impatient, she said, "On the floor…now, get to it. You have one minute to eat all that you can. Whatever you don't finish, will be waiting for you after school…"

"Wait…what?" I asked.

She looked at her watch and began counting backwards, "58, 57, 56, 55, 54, 53…"

Realizing that she was serious, I dropped down and crawled over to the bowl. "Am I going to get a spoon or something?"

She continued to count. "47, 46, 45, 44, 43…"

I realized that she was ignoring me. I turned and sniffed it. It smelled and looked like shit. "What is this?" I asked.

She didn't answer my question, she just continued to count. "39, 38, 37, 36, 35…"

I was so hungry, and I knew that if I didn't eat this, I was going to be hungry all day, so I inhaled, held my breath and ate as much as I could. While I ate, her son laughed.

When she got to "1", she shouted, "Stop!"

When I finally exhaled, I had a chance to taste what I was being forced to eat. Without thinking, I began to gag. "What is this?"

"Why? What do you think it is?"

"It tastes like shit…" I said, trying to hold it down.

She laughed and said, "That's because it is shit and you better not throw…"

She couldn't finish her sentence, because I began to vomit all over her floor.

"You little bastard…lick it up," she demanded.

My stomach acids burned my throat and nose. Still gagging, I mumbled, "What?"

"LICK…IT…UP!" she said.

"I'm not doing it…" I insisted.

"Oh, you're not?" she asked.

"Hell no…" I confirmed.

"Look, you little shit…you need to know right now that when I tell you to do something, you better do it."

I stood and began to walk away. "I'm not licking that mess off of that floor…"

She looked at her son and stuck her hand out. Without exchanging any words, he proceeded to remove his belt.

"What are you going to do with that?" I asked.

She came towards me – swinging the leather strap. I looked around the room and ran towards the back of the couch.

"Get him," she ordered.

Her son came towards me. Kicking and screaming, I fought him. "No, don't touch me…don't touch me…"

"Get him and bring him to me," she instructed.

He grabbed me by the feet and dragged me from behind the couch.

She started swinging and in between each swat, she said something. "You…" *Swat* "Gonna…" *Swat* "Learn…" *Swat* "That…" *Swat* "What…" *Swat* "I…" *Swat* "Say…" *Swat* "Goes…"

This went on for several minutes until she finally said, "Throw his ass in the cage."

Frightened, I looked around the room. "No, please don't…"

She laughed. "You should have thought about that before you threw-up all over my floor."

Her son took me in the back room where there was a small cage sitting in the middle of the floor. He opened up the door, threw me inside, and placed a padlock on it.

"Please…I'll clean it up…I'm sorry…please…" I begged.

She shook her head. "You can have it for dinner…nighty-night…" She waved as her son tossed a blanket over the cage.

"No…" I begged. The next thing I heard was them closing the bedroom door. I looked around the cage to see if I could find a way out. I tried shaking the cage, but it was secure and bolted to the floor. I pulled off the blanket, so that I could look around the room. There was nothing in this room, but the cage.

Suddenly, the whips on my skin began to burn. I wanted to cry, but I realized that it was a waste of time. I needed to think – to be quiet and think.

Several hours had passed before the door opened again. When it did, the son walked in, unlocked the cage and placed the dog's bowl on the floor of the cage. "Please, can I get out of here," I begged.

He looked over his shoulder and then looked at me. "Stop…you're never getting out of here. This is your new home."

I heard the floor creak in the hall. She walked in. "What are you two talking about?"

"Nothing, mama..." he said, as he ran out of the room. She kneeled down next to the cage. "Don't fuck with me little boy...now, I had to call that school and tell them that you were sick. I'm not going to make too many of those calls...don't want nosey administrators in my business...you hear me?" She, turned and walked out of the room.

I looked down at the bowl that was full of the vomit that was on the floor. I pushed it to the other side of the cage and sat, thinking about my escape.

The next day, they walked in carrying a buckct. She whispered something in his ear and left the room. He leaned over and unlocked the cage. "Okay, let's go..." He reached out to me. I grabbed his hand and bit him hard. He screamed and fell on the floor. I jumped out of the cage and ran towards the door. He snatched me by the leg. I fell to the floor and we began to wrestle. Somehow, he managed to stand up. Standing over me, he lifted his leg and when his foot came down, it landed in my chest – knocking the air out of me. I grabbed my chest. He lifted his leg again and this time it landed in my face. I could taste the rubber from the sole of his shoe as he stumped me, repeatedly. Soon, everything went black.

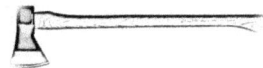

I woke up to find that I was back in the cage and that my clothes were covered in blood. I tried to open my mouth, but it was swollen shut. Suddenly, I could hear someone turning the knob. She walked into the room and unlocked the cage as her son walked in behind her. She turned and nodded at him. He smiled and walked towards me. He opened the door to the cage and pointed at the bucket. "Let's go…"
I was too tired to fight him. As I moved, the pain embraced me. Every part of my body hurt. I moaned in agony. I crawled over to the bucket. I looked at the it and then, back at him. "It's empty…" I mumbled. He smiled. "I know…now, fill it up."
Confused, I looked around the room. "With what?"

He began to pull at my pants. Once they were at my knees, he pointed at the bucket again. "LET'S GO!!!" Understanding what he wanted from me, I stood and leaned over the bucket. I began to relieve myself in it. He smiled. When I was done, he threw me back into the cage.

I refused to eat the vomit, so they continued to bring it to me, every day, until green fuzz grew on top of it. After each refusal, they beat me. Because I hadn't eaten anything for days, I was no longer able to put anything in the bucket. This made her mad. "You are fucking with my money...you have to eat."
I didn't say anything, because I was too weak to do so. She thought that I was ignoring her, and this was unacceptable.
She pulled me out of the cage and tried prying my mouth open. "Eat, you little bastard..."
I held my lips, tightly, shut.
She grabbed my face and began to force it into the bowl. "Eat it!!! EAT IT!!!"
I refused. I looked on the floor to find the lock.
"EAT IT!!!" she demanded.
I reached over and grabbed the lock and with all of the strength that I had left, I swung my arm – hitting her in the side of her head. She fell backwards. Shocked and dazed, she grabbed her face. "I'm going to fucking kill you..." She reached out to grab me, but stumbled instead. "Come here you little-shit..."

Exhausted, I crawled towards her. Before she could say anything else, I was on top of her. I swung the lock, repeatedly.

"Stop!!!" she begged, trying to block the blows to her head. "Stop...please stop...!!!"

I kept swinging until she stopped moving. Soon, I heard footsteps coming down the hall. I looked around the room and saw the bucket. I grabbed it and stood behind the door. When he entered the room, he looked down to find her. "Mama?" he said. When he turned and looked up, he found himself staring at a bucket full of piss and shit. As he opened his mouth to say something, I poured the contents all over him. He fell to the floor. I began to hit him, repeatedly, over the head with the bucket. When he stopped fighting, I ran out of the room and down the hall. I'd made it to the backdoor when I thought about my grand-daddy. Quickly, I turned and ran back down the hall and into the bathroom. I grabbed a roll of toilet paper and ran into the kitchen. I turned on the stove and placed the roll on top of it. I lit the burners and watched it burn. Once the stove and everything around it, caught fire, I ran outside and closed the door.

I waited to see what was going to happen. When I didn't see the fire in the living room, I became worried that my plan had failed and that they would, soon, come after me. So, I walked back to the kitchen door, I began to turn the knob when I heard a loud

BOOM! My body flew into the air and across the yard. When it landed, I hit my head against the ground. Everything turned black.

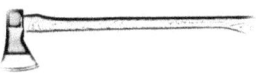

When I came to, I was overcome by the smell of disinfectant. "Are you okay?" I heard someone say. Trying to focus, I looked around the room to find some familiar faces. I jumped up, almost ripping the cords out of my arms. "Grandmamma...granddaddy..."

She kissed me on the forehead.

"Grandmamma, those people..."

She interrupted me. "Don't worry about that. We got you now and we're going to take you home."

As I laid there thinking about the things that'd happened to me, I couldn't help, but feel this overwhelming sense of doom – like something really bad was going to happen and soon.

CHAPTER 21

High school, was the same hell, but with different devils. It was like Hell threw-up and all of the assholes landed smack-dab in the middle of Chicago. At this point, I dreaded going to school. I could think of a million things that were, probably, better than having to go to school – like being run over by a car or being covered in honey and trapped in a beehive, or having my hairs ripped-out from between my legs, one by one, with a pair of rusty pliers. Anything was better than school. I was a little apprehensive about returning, but I knew that I didn't have any choice. High school was another chapter of my life that I had to finish. So, whatever it took, I was going to get through it, but it wouldn't be easy.

Things were a little better for us, now, financially. My grandmother found some programs that were willing to help us. We ate better and I was able to put some meat on my bones. I was taller. Not as tall as a lot of the other kids, but big enough to hold a shadow. We still wore second-hand clothing, but we had more outfits now and our shoes didn't have holes in them.

This made me feel a little better about myself, but I knew that that wasn't going to last for long.

On one particular morning, I woke up and I found my grandmother sitting on the side of the bed. She was smiling. "I got you something."
With sleep still in my eyes, I sat up and looked at her. "What cha' got, grandma?" I asked.
"It's not much…" She reached behind her back and handed the item to me.
My mouth fell open. "Grandma…is that what I think it is?" I said, excitedly.
She smiled.
I grabbed the item. "A book-bag, granny…you got me a book-bag!!!" I threw my arms around her neck and hugged her tightly. "Oh, thank you, grandma… thank you…I won't have to carry my books in a grocery bag anymore." The smile on her face disappeared. My comment saddened her. "I mean…grocery bags aren't bad…it reminded me of groceries."
"Yes, they are…I'm just glad that I was able to get you something else…"
I saw that there were tags still on it. "Is this new?"
"Yes, it is…" she confirmed.
"Oh my, gawd…something new…I got something new…thank you, thank you, thank you…"
She laughed. "You're welcome. Now, let's get up and get out of here…"

"Yes, grandma…" I held the book-bag, tightly. "Thanks again…"

She walked over to the door. "Stop thanking me and get dressed…"

She walked out closing the door behind her. I was smiling so hard that my face began to hurt. "Today, is going to be a good day…" I mumbled to myself. "A good day…"

When I arrived at school, I noticed that everyone had on new clothes except for me. They all looked really nice, but of course, I stuck-out like the only Black kid at an all-White school. Most of the boys had haircuts that were done, professionally. I, on the other hand, arrived looking like a new recruit. That morning, before leaving for school, my grandfather sat me in a chair, placed a bowl on my head, took a razor, and shaved around the bowl. When he lifted the bowl, he slapped some alcohol on my head and told me, "You ain't there to look good…you're there to learn… remember that."

Every eye was on me and for the first time, I didn't care. Sure, my clothes were used, but they were new to me and sure, it looked like I'd got my hair cut by a blind man – I still didn't care. Why? Because I had a book-bag. A brand-new book-bag and I left the tags on it just so that everybody could see that it was new.

I strutted into the school like my shit didn't stink. I thought that nothing could destroy that feeling until "nothing" walked into the school.

His name was Brandon. Brandon was the biggest kid in the ninth grade. He looked like he was being fed a diet of other ninth graders and rocks. I would say that he was butt-ugly, but that would be an insult to all of the butts of the world. He had one eyebrow that went straight across his forehead. His teeth were jacked-up. They were a weird shade of green and yellow and his breath smelled liked death. He had zits everywhere, but on his eyeballs. When God was passing out good looks, Brandon's ass must have been somewhere beating up angels, because he was as ugly as he was mean.

After the bell rang and we were all inside, I could see him coming down the hall – tripping and throwing kids against their lockers. As he approached me, I started thinking about how this was going to go down. He was going to say something to mc and I was going to push his ass in the face, hard. I had it all planned out, but something prevented its execution. Fear crept in. I kept my face towards the wall hoping that if I pretended to be invisible, he wouldn't mess with me and for a moment, I thought that it worked. He didn't stop. He kept going. A wave of relief swept over me until he turned around and began to walk towards me. He tapped me on my shoulder.

"Hey, Pee-boy…"

Shit. I thought to myself. I kept my eyes on the wall. He leaned in – his breath wrapping itself around my face like a pair of dirty gym socks. I began to gag.

Again, he said, "Hey, Pee-boy…"

Realizing that ignoring him wasn't going to get him to walk away, I took a deep breath and turned around. His presence was overwhelming. It felt like I'd just found Big Foot. "Hey, Brandon…" I mumbled.

He pointed at my clothes. "Been shopping at the thrift shop?" He started laughing; hoping to get the other kids to laugh with him.

I didn't respond.

The taunting continued. "And who cut your hair? Ray Charles?" Then, he saw it. "Is that a new book-bag?" He played with the price tags.

"Stop, Brandon…"

He stopped and frowned. "Who you telling to stop?"

Stuttering, I said, "I mean…I'm just saying…"

He leaned into my face. "You're just saying, what?"

I frowned and turned my head because his breath was starting to make my eyes water. "I'm just saying, don't…"

He leaned in closer. "Don't, what?"

I covered my nose. "PLEASE…don't…"

"Don't, what?" he asked, again.

"My grandmother gave me this…"

"Your granny gave you this?" he teased.

"Yes," I confirmed.

He poked out his bottom lip. "The big baby's granny gave him a book-bag."

"Stop, Brandon…"

"Stop, Brandon…" He teased.

This exchange went on for a few more minutes before the bell rang. I exhaled. *Saved by the bell*. It was over, so I thought.

Brandon began to walk away. I turned to close my locker when I felt something tugging at my book-bag. The next thing I heard was a ripping sound. I turned to look at him.

"I took the tags off for you…only lames walk around with price tags on their stuff…"

My eyes widened. He stuffed the tags down my t-shirt. "Lame-o," he called me before walking away.

As the tags worked their way through my shirt, I watched them as they hit the floor. I kneeled down to pick them up. Like pieces of glass, I held them, gently. My heart began to break. I heard a voice say, "Son…you better get to class. You don't want to be late."

With tears in my eyes, I looked up. Without saying a word, I stood and walked down the hall while staring at the price tags. When I walked in, I saw him sitting in the back of the classroom. He smiled at me. Still holding the tags, I walked over to my seat. I heard a voice say, "Paul…Paul?"

I looked up.

"Paul…" she said, touching my shoulder.

I looked down at her hand. "Yes?" I said.

DADDY BY DIANE MARTIN 173

She smiled. "Welcome…are you ready for your first day?" The teacher asked.

I looked down at the tags, looked over at Brandon, and smiled. "Yes, Ma'am…" Even though he'd hurt me by tearing the tags off, I refused to allow him to see my pain.

"Good…" she said, as she walked away.

I couldn't think of anything else. While I was physically there, mentally all I wanted to do was hurt him. I spent the whole day, going through the motions. I knew that Brandon needed to be dealt with. He'd touched something that belonged to me and he had to pay for it, but how? He was 10 times bigger than me. His breath alone could kill me. But it didn't matter. I knew that if I didn't do something, I would be his pet for the rest of my life and if my grandfather found out that I let this boy punk me, he would unload his gun in my ass. Plus, I had to punish him, now, so that he understood why he was being punished. If I waited, I would have to spend the first few minutes beating his ass and trying to remind him why his ass was getting beat. So, it had to happen, today. But how do you take down a giant? I spent the whole day thinking about it and as I twirled my pencil in my hand, it came to me. I walked up to the front of the class and as I sharpened it, I watched him.

When the bell rang, I rushed out of class and to my locker. After retrieving my things, I ran outside, down the street, and I waited for him. When he came upon me, he said, "Hey Pee-boy…what's up?"

Seething, I said, "You touched my book-bag…"

He smiled. "So…"

Rolling the pencil between my fingers, I said, "So? You don't touch my book-bag…my grandma gave me this."

He frowned. "Stop acting like a little bitch…it's a book-bag…"

I frowned. "No, it's not just a book-bag…"

He laughed. "Did you forget to take your meds, Pee-boy? Get out of my face." He tried pushing passed me.

Before I knew it, I'd pushed him back, but he was bigger than me so the force knocked me on the ground. He began to laugh, hysterically.

"Fucking Mama's boy…stay your bitch-ass on the ground before I hurt you." He started to walk away. I reached out and grabbed his foot. He fell on the ground next to me. Shocked, he flipped over and began to kick his feet. Before I could think, I jumped up and crawled on top of him. He started swinging his arms. I held the pencil, tight, between my fingers and with two quick thrusts, he stopped swinging. His eyes widened as he held his throat. "The fuck?" he asked.

I looked down at the blood that was dripping from the lead of the pencil.

Shocked, he said, "I'm bleeding…go and get help, Pee-boy!"

"No…" I mumbled, as I placed my hand over his mouth.

Confused, his eyes widened. He clawed at my hand. I placed my other hand over his nose and squeezed tightly. He continued to struggle. I leaned in close and said, "It's almost over…" He struggled for a moment longer before he realized that this was the end. He blinked one last time before his eyes turned towards the sky. His arm fell limp next to him. I stared at him as I thought about my bag. "And for the record, my name ain't Pee-boy…it's PAUL…BITCH!!!!" I stood and walked away.

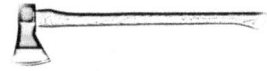

The next day, I woke up to find that my prayers weren't answered. I'd prayed that the world would end, but unfortunately, it hadn't. The realization that I was still alive meant that Brandon was, probably, still dead. I needed a plan. I did everything that I could to stay home from school. I faked the flu by pretending to cough and vomit, but that didn't work. I told them that the school had burned down. I even went as far as pretending to be dying, but they weren't buying it.

"I don't give a shit…die on your way to school," my grand-daddy said.

"But, I'm serious, grand-daddy. I think that I'm going to die," I said.

"Oh, it's not like I don't believe you…I do. I just don't want you to die here. Who wants to be bothered with that shit? Now, take your ass to school."

Bastard. I thought to myself. I grabbed my book-bag and stomped all the way down the hall.

"And you better not slam that damn door…" he yelled.

BAM! I slammed it anyway. As I walked out into the front yard, I'd come to the conclusion that I couldn't run away from what I did. I'd hurt someone and I had to face the music. Normally, I walked fast, because I was looking forward to the free lunches, but not today. I took my time; staring at my feet all the way there. When I arrived at the school, I noticed that there were no police. I thought that maybe they were hiding in the bushes waiting to jump out and snatch me, but nothing happened. When I walked into the hall, everything seemed normal.

I went to my classes and as I watched the clock, beads of sweat formed on my head, but again nothing happened. Every time the door opened, I jumped up – waiting for them to call my name, but, still, nothing happened.

DADDY BY DIANE MARTIN 177

When the end of the day came, I left school and began to walk home when I noticed a crowd of kids gathered by the alley. Nervously, I approached them. I could hear them talking.

One kid said, "Damn…look at him."

Another one asked, "Is he dead?"

I worked my way through the crowd to see what they were looking at.

Another kid responded, "That motherfucker is deader than dead…"

"What's deader than dead?" another kid asked.

"I don't know, but it looks like he came to school and got 'schooled'…"

I jumped back when I saw him. With his cold-dead eyes staring up at me, I noticed that he was still holding his neck where I'd stabbed him. A sense of peace swept over me. I felt relieved; even a little proud of myself.

Another kid said, "We need to tell somebody."

I turned to look at him.

"Nawwww…" he said. "Forget him…he deserved it. He was a butthole."

I turned back towards Brandon. As they continued to talk among themselves, I looked down and noticed two tiny pieces of paper sitting next to him. I kneeled down to see what it was. As I looked at it, I realized what it was. It was the tags from my book-bag. Slowly, I stood up, slid my foot towards him, placed my foot on top of the pieces of paper, and began to slide the pieces close to me. I looked around to see who was looking at me before kneeling down, and pretending to tie my shoe. Once I was on the ground, I slipped my hand under my shoe and grabbed the pieces of paper. I stuffed them into my pocket and slowly walked away.

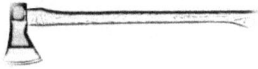

The police never came for me. After the fear subsided, I couldn't help but feel good about what I'd did to him. Of course, it wasn't my intent to kill him. I only wanted to hurt him, but there was something satisfying in knowing that he was gone and that he would never touch my book-bag again.

CHAPTER 22

B ut I couldn't sleep. For days, I tossed and turned all night. His eyes were engrained in my memory – cold, dark, and staring back at me. The way that he looked up at me – like he was blaming me for what happened to him when all I wanted was to be left alone. While, in my head, I was trying to understand and justify what I did and why I did it, I couldn't stop thinking about his eyes – his cold, dead eyes.

The following morning, I was the last one to get up. I'd just climbed out of bed when my grand-daddy came into the room. "Boy, I'm tired of being your alarm clock. You need to learn to get your ass up like everybody else."
I didn't respond. I couldn't get Brandon's face out of my head.
He came closer. "Did you hear me, or do I need to slap the wax out of your ears?"
Tired, I said, "Grand-daddy...I'm not in the mood."
He laughed. "Women got moods...women got feelings...what you got is a grand-daddy who's about to knock the shit out of you. Now, get your ass up before you find your 'mood' and your teeth on the floor." he said.

I walked back over to the bed and sat down. I placed my head into my hands. He pulled at my hands. "What is wrong with you?" he asked.

I snatched my hands from him and covered my face. He snatched my hands again. "What the hell is wrong with you?"

I looked up and said, "Grand-daddy, I did something bad...really bad."

He giggled. "What cha' do, boy...knock somebody up?"

I didn't respond.

Seeing that I was serious, he said, "You didn't knock somebody up did you?"

I sighed. "No, grand-daddy..."

He wiped his brow. "Whew...well, shit, if you didn't knock somebody up, what did you do? Kill somebody?"

I looked out of the window and mumbled, "Yes..."

He leaned in close to me. "Huh? What did you say? Speak up, child..."

I turned towards him. "I think I killed somebody..." He frowned. "You think?"

I exhaled. "No, grand-daddy...I killed somebody."

"You mean like 'kill' as in dead as a doorknob?"

"Yes, grand-daddy..."

He chuckled. "Boy, stop playing...you ain't killed nobody. I can't even get you to kill some of these damn roaches and you killed somebody...get out of here with that bullshit..."

I looked down at my hands. "I did, grand-daddy...I killed him."

"Him?" he asked. "Who is, 'Him?'"

"A boy at my school. His name is...was...Brandon."

"Well, how do you know he's dead?"

"I stabbed him..." I confirmed.

"You stabbed him?" he asked. "With what?"

"My pencil..."

For a moment, he didn't say anything. You could tell, by the look on his face, that he didn't believe me. "Boy, stop playing."

"I'm not..."

"That boy is somewhere alive and laughing at your crazy ass..."

"Naw, I doubt it. If he's alive, he's in that alley doing a bad impersonation of a live person."

Finally realizing that I was serious, he said, "Damn, boy...was it a mistake?" he asked.

I didn't want to lie to him, so I said, "No, it wasn't..."

"What did he do after you stabbed him?"

"Well, he struggled for a moment, but I didn't want to get in trouble, so I placed my hand over his nose and mouth...until he didn't move anymore."

He stared at me for a moment like his brain was having difficulty processing everything. Snapping out of his daze, he said, "Well, follow-thru is important...you don't want to stab someone with a pencil and then leave him alive...wouldn't want him to survive that shit...he would have fucked you up, for sure, when he saw you again."

"I know…"

"Now, tell me, what would make you go and stab somebody?"

I took a deep breath before saying, "He touched my book-bag."

"He broke your book-bag?" he asked.

"No…he touched it. Grandma bought it for me and he snatched the tags off of it. I told him not to do it, but he did it anyway…" I said, nervously.

"Soooooooooo, he didn't break or tear-up your book-bag, right?"

"No…he touched it after I told him not to."

Calmly, he looked at me and said, "Well, you did tell him not to touch it."

His calm demeanor confused me. I was expecting him to go-off, but he didn't. "Grand-daddy?"

"You told him not to touch it, right?"

"Yes…" I confirmed.

"Then, you did all that you could do."

"Huh?" I asked.

"It is not your fault that he ended-up getting stabbed with a pencil."

Confused, I said, "It's not?"

He shook his head. "Naw, boy…you see…those kinds of people deserve to get stabbed with pencils, 'cause they don't listen. When you ASKED him not to touch it, what did he do? He touched it. Now, let's pause and think about that for a moment. What if your book-bag was made of fire and you said don't touch it…"

DADDY BY DIANE MARTIN 183

"Okay?" I said, trying to follow his reasoning.

"And he touched it anyway and got burned. Whose fault is it that he got burned?"

"His…" I confirmed.

"Exactly…except, in this case, he got stabbed. Pencil…fire…whatever…I bet he hear you now…you taught his ass a valuable lesson about cause and effect. Shit, he should thank you…you know, if he wasn't dead and all."

"Huh?"

Getting frustrated, he continued, "Boy, keep up…okay? When I was little, kids like him used to fuck with me all of the time. Then, one of them caught me on Happy Don't Fuck With Your Grand-daddy Day…it's a real holiday…look it up…and one of them walked up on me…talking shit…and I beat the SHIT out of 'em…like he showed-up to celebrate Happy Don't Fuck With Your Grand-daddy Day without a present...and that was the LAST asswhooping that I had to give…I mean, you took yours up a notch with killing that boy…you have to get brownie points for that, but every man has his breaking-point…that's why motherfuckers should keep their hands to themselves…you never know when you're running up on a person who's had enough…if you hadn't of stopped him, he would have been pulling tags off of your book-bags for the rest of your life. You want that shit?" he asked.

"No," I confirmed.

"Well, you definitely ain't got to worry 'bout that anymore…and you know what? I'm grateful that you killed his ass. Those kinds of people grow-up to be serial killers or worse…President of the United States…you saved us, boy."

"So…it's okay?" I asked.

"Ain't nobody gon' miss his ass, but his mama and odds are, she was just like his ass. How many of those motherfuckers do we need running 'round here? It's called, 'Survival of the Fittest,' boy. Nope, I don't see a problem with it…"

"But he's dead…"

"Well, what kind of living was he doing anyway running around messing with people? That ain't living, that's getting on people's nerves. I'm telling ya'…he was already on his way…dead or jail…it was just a matter of time."

"But I can't get him out of my head."

"I don't see why not…it happens. I killed people every day in the war…some good people, some assholes…you learn to process it all the same…" He turned to leave the room. "And, remember, the opposite of wrong is right. He was wrong, so by that alone makes you right…like one plus one…basic Math…So…there you go…now, take your ass to school before your grandmother stabs us, both, with a pencil."

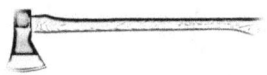

I'd killed someone. All I could think about the entire day was that I'd taken somebody's life. Whether it was right or wrong, justified or not, somebody was dead and it was my fault, but I went the entire day and not one person said two words about it. For a moment, I'd even stopped thinking about it until the teacher told us to take out a pencil and piece of paper so that we could take a test. I fumbled around my pencil case until I found one. When I looked down at it, I noticed that there was dried blood on the lead of the pencil. I was staring at it when the teacher walked up to me and asked, "Is there something wrong?"
I looked back at the empty seat where Brandon used to sit, thought about her question for a second, thought about what my grand-daddy said, and then said, "Nope… everything is right."

CHAPTER 23

I went on with my life, but things weren't easy. Although, for a moment, things had gotten a little better at home, it seemed like now, they were getting worse. Once we started getting more food, tensions in the house began to grow. People began to turn against each other. They were fighting, all of the time, over food. First, they started putting their names on things like boxes of cereal, but then you couldn't open the refrigerator without seeing labels on everything from eggs to apples. I knew things were bad when I came home from school, one day, to find that the refrigerator had a lock on the door.

The only thing that I thought about, all day, was wrapping my lips around a peanut butter and jelly sandwich. When I walked in, I went to the cabinet and grabbed the peanut butter. It had Betty's name on it. I looked at it for a minute. I knew that touching it without her permission was going to start an argument, but I didn't care. I was hungry. I looked around for the jelly and realized that it must be in the refrigerator. I tried to open it, but I couldn't. I looked around the room for the key. I searched the table, the cabinets, and the jars, but couldn't find it. I exhaled and walked throughout the house only to find Betty stretched-out across her bed. I shook her leg to wake her.

"Betty," I said.

She didn't move.

"Betty," I called again.

She began to stir. "Huh? What?"

I hated having to deal with her, but I was hungry. "Betty, where's the key?"

"It's 'mama', boy…" she said, wiping drool from the side of her mouth.

I sighed. "Whatever…anyway, I'm hungry. Why is there a lock on the refrigerator?"

"Cause all y'all do is eat…we got to make the food last until the next month," she said. She sat up and reached over to the table. She grabbed her pipe and began to fill it with something. She lit it, inhaled, held it for a moment and then, exhaled. "Every time I look up you're eating."

I laughed. "Every time you look up? That's funny…"

She inhaled and exhaled. "What's so funny about that?"

Not in the mood for her mess, I said, "Betty…I mean, mama…I'm really hungry. Can I, please, have something to eat?"

"What you gon' do for me?" she asked.

I frowned. "Excuse me?"

"Excuse you? Did you fart or something?" she asked.

"No…" I said, becoming frustrated.

"Well…if you go to the store for me, I will unlock the refrigerator," she said.

I frowned. "Go to the store for what?"

"I need some cigarettes…" she said, putting down the pipe and reaching into her bra for some money.

Confused, I said, "We have to starve to make our food last, but you got money for drugs and cigarettes?"

She paused for a moment and looked at me. "Who are you to ask me anything?" Her 'high' started to kick in. "Shit…I'm a grown-ass woman."

"Well, grown-ass woman…can you get your own cigarettes? I think that there's a law that says that I can't buy them…"

"Fuck the law…I'm your mama…I tell you what to do…not no damn law…"

I shook my head. "You're such a model citizen, Betty. I want to grow-up to be just like you…NOT!!!!!"

She stuffed her money back into her bra. She climbed off of the bed. "Boooooooooyyyyyyyy, who are you talking to?"

I looked around the room and answered, "YOU!!!"

Stumbling, she came towards me. "I am your mother. You need to respect me."

I frowned. "You don't even respect yourself…how do you expect me to respect you?"

"'CAUSE, I SAID SO…" she said.

The sight of her made me sick to my stomach. I was losing my appetite. "Look…give me the money so that I can go to the store and come back…"

She frowned and pushed me. "Who the fuck are you to be telling me what to do?"

"You're high, Betty...can I just go to the store? Let me go and get your cigarettes, so that I can get this over with."

She stuck her finger in my chest. "No...I'm sick of you disrespecting me. I am your mama and if I need to beat the shit out of you to prove it to you, then that's what I'm going to do."

"Yeah, that would really prove it to me...your ability..." I paused and laughed. "I mean, your inability to beat my ass..."

"Did you curse?" she asked.

"Did you curse?" I pushed her hand away. "You get what you give and because you had me don't make you my mama, Betty."

"Then, who is? Your grandmamma? She don't want to be bothered with you no more than she wants to be bothered with me. She just feels sorry for you..."

"You don't think she feels sorry for you? Look at you? You're a mess..."

"You know, boy, I'm sick of your shit..." she began.

"You need to be sick of that pipe..." I turned to leave the room. "That's okay, Betty. I'll just eat the sandwich without the jelly."

She lunged towards me. "Did you touch my peanut butter?"

"Yes, I did, mother, dear and it ain't your peanut butter. You get those stamps because of me."

She grabbed my shirt. "Put it back," she demanded.

I tried pulling away from her. "Get off of me…"

She pushed me. The force pushed her on the floor. As she tried to stand back up, she stumbled, and fell again. Then, out of nowhere, she started crying. "Nobody loves me."

I looked at her.

"Nobody cares about me…nobody loves me," she sobbed.

Watching her cry made me angry. She was trying to get sympathy from a child that she's neglected all of his life. I didn't have any love for her. I couldn't stand her.

"You are just like your fucking daddy…that piece of shit didn't do anything, but use me and when he was done, he went home to his wife. He didn't have a wife when he was fucking me, but as soon as I got pregnant…the motherfucker remembered that he had a bitch at home waiting for him."

"And you're mad at me, why? Because you chose to eat another woman's leftovers and when the plate was empty, he went back home to refill it?"

"You don't know shit…"

"I know he must be smart, because he left your ass…"

Tired of listening to her, I began to walk out of the room. I tried stepping over her, but she grabbed my leg. I snatched my leg away from her and proceeded down the hall. I thought that it was all over until I heard her running behind me. She grabbed me from behind and started shouting. "You can't fuck me and leave me…"

Confused, I said, "What?" I tried prying her hands from around my neck. "Get off of me!!!"

Tightening her grip, she said, "You can't fuck me and leave me..."

Trying to get her off of me, I said, "Bitch, let me go..."

"Oh, I got your bitch..."

Just then, my grandparents walked in. My grandmother ran over to us. "What the hell is going on?"

"He thinks that he can just use me and leave me..."

My grandmother pulled her off of me. "What is she talking about?"

Gasping for air, I said, "She's high..."

She looked at my mother and said, "Take your ass to bed..."

Betty looked confused. "But what about me? Huh? You gon' just let him fuck me..."

"GET THE HELL OUT OF HERE, CRACKHEAD!"

She had a stunned look on her face as she stumbled back to her room. She slammed her door.

Rubbing my neck, I said, "Grandmamma, I didn't touch her."

She shook her head. "I know, child. She's just high. When she comes down, she won't even remember that she said those things."

I sat down at the kitchen table. "Why do y'all put up with that mess?"

My grandmother walked down the hall. When she returned, she unlocked the refrigerator. She saw my sandwich sitting on the table, grabbed the jelly, and began to spread some onto the bread. Then, she grabbed a glass and filled it with milk.

My grandmother smiled. "I'm praying for her. She's going to come out of this. It's just a phase."

I thought about that for a second and said, "No, grandma…it's not. You said the same thing about Uncle Jasmine…I mean, Aunt James…I mean…"

She interrupted, "Prayer can't fix everything or everybody…and you see, God don't make no mistakes. Yet, we got folks running around here trying to erase themselves. What they were, was what God intended them to be. Not this mess that they running around here doing. It's wrong and God has a way of punishing those who do wrong. Look at your grand-daddy…"

"His legs?" I asked.

"His legs are the least of his problems…" she said. Suddenly, my grand-daddy entered the room. Being nosey, he asked, "What y'all talking about?"

"Mind your own business, old man," my grand-mother said, as she left the room.

"Your business IS my business, old woman. Don't forget who you're talking to…"

"I know who the hell I'm talking to…!!!" she shouted.

"Don't make me come in there…!!!" he shouted back.

"Well, roll your old ass in here and see what the hell happens…"

"Bitch…" he mumbled under his breath.

DADDY BY DIANE MARTIN 193

"I heard you, you old stanky-bastard…" she said.

"That motherfucker can hear a fly fart in Egypt…" He turned back to me and asked, "What was y'all talking about?"

I bit into the sandwich and said, "Can't talk…mouth full of food."

Squinting his eyes, he said, "Yeah, right…"

Chapter 24

Until that argument with Betty, I'd stopped thinking about him, but now that I was getting older, I couldn't help but wonder – who is my daddy? There were nights when I lied awake thinking about him - wondering what he looked like, if he was still alive, what he was doing, and if he ever thought about me. I was thinking about this when my grand-daddy approached me.

"What 'cha doing, boy? Why ain't you out there playing?"

"Grand-daddy, I'm too old to be playing…"

"Oh, is that right?" he said.

"Yeah, I'm not a kid any more…time to start thinking about man stuff…"

He giggled. "Man stuff, so you think that you're a man now…"

"Yeah…in a minute, I'll be graduating."

"So?"

"So, that means that I'll be leaving…"

"Where are you going?"

"I don't know…"

"And you say that you're a man…" He shook his head. "A man has a plan…"

"I'm trying to come-up with one…I don't know what I'm going to do…that's why I wish I had a daddy. Somebody to talk to about my future…" I turned and looked at my grand-daddy's face. He looked sad. I touched his hand. "I'm sorry, grand-daddy."

"Don't be sorry, boy. I wish you had a daddy too…would have made my life a whole lot easier."

"We made your life hard?"

He shook his head. "Boy, have you been travelling through life with your eyes closed? Or are you trying to repress your memories because they are that damn painful? If you are, please tell me how to do it…I want to forget this shit too."

For a moment, we just sat and looked out into the street.

"Sometimes, I think about my daddy too. He wasn't there for me either…" he said.

"He wasn't?" I asked.

"Naw…you see, back in the day, not many Black men were allowed to be fathers. Sure, they were allowed to make babies, but they weren't allowed to be fathers or husbands."

"Why not?"

"'Cause, they were slaves…you know about slavery…don't you, son?"

"Yes, we read about it in school."

"And you see some of that shit going on today…can't you?"

"Yeah…I see it. Some girls in my school are pregnant."

"And many of those babies will grow-up without a daddy...it's a sad truth. It's like planting a seed...in the beginning, you give it everything that it could possibly need to grow...sun...water...dirt...but then, what happens when you take the sun away? Sure, that plant may still grow...may not grow as fast as it would have with the sun, but it grows nonetheless...or maybe, it withers-up and die...but if you know that a plant is gon' need the sun, why plant it in the shade...?"

Confused, I said, "Grand-daddy, how did this turn into a conversation about plants?"

"Because kids are like plants and plants need the sun...is all I'm saying."

"But not all plants need the sun to flourish..."

"I'm not talking about house plants, boy...I'm talking about trees...you want to be a tree, or you want to be a house plant?"

"I want to be a tree..."

"Then, stop acting like a gad-damn house plant..."

I shook my head and asked, "Grand-daddy, who's my daddy?"

My grandfather pointed at the street. "Pick one..."

I looked up. "Pick one, what?"

He pointed at the street, again. "It could be any one of them. Your guess would be as good as mine...don't nobody know the truth, but your mama and that brain of hers is so scrambled she probably thinks you fathered yourself."

"But I wanna know..."

"I'm sure that you do, but I can't help you with that…
but if it will give you any peace, then here's what you
do. You can't go back and fix or change anything in
your past. All you have is right now and life is going
to put you in a position to be a father, one day, and
the best way to right the wrong that has happened to
you? Is that when that opportunity arises…for you to
become somebody's daddy…then you be the best
damn daddy that you can be. You hear me, son?"
I smiled. "I hear ya', grand-daddy."
"Now, go out there and get you some sun…" he said,
smiling.
"Okay…" As I walked out onto the sidewalk,
something inside of me told me to turn around. I
looked to find my grand-daddy crying and talking to
himself. When he noticed that I was staring, he wiped
tears from his eyes and said, "Bye, son."

CHAPTER 25

Time flew by so fast. Before I knew it, I was graduating, but instead of being excited, I was depressed. I'd realized that I'd never thought about my future. Maybe, it was because I expected to be dead already, but now, here I am, with a piece of paper in my hand, that some Black men will never see in their lifetime, and I had no clue what to do with it. I, desperately, needed to get my shit together, because I didn't want my future to include another year in their house. I had to find a way to get out.

I set out, one day, just to see what was out there and happened upon a bunch of kids playing basketball. It was hot, and I was just wandering around, so I decided to walk over and watch the game. They had a really good game going. There were people cheering and the crowd seemed really excited. For a moment, I was able to take my mind off of my future. I'd sat through three games when I realized that it was getting dark and that I'd better get home. I was about to leave when a man approached me and said, "Would you like to make a few bucks?"

I looked him up and down before saying, "What do I have to do?"

The man looked around. "Just help me put the balls up and pick up some of this garbage…"

I looked around and said, "Sure, but I got to get home before it gets too late."

The man smiled. "No problem…what's your name?"

Suspicious, I said, "Why do you want to know my name?"

He shrugged. "Hey, if you don't want to give me your name…"

Realizing that I was acting weird, I said, "It's Paul…"

"You 5-0, Paul?" he asked, nervously.

"Naw, man…I'm no cop…"

Whew. He wiped his forehead. "For a moment, I was worried."

"Why?" I asked.

"Oh, nothing…just that a brother has to be careful…you know…"

"I guess…"

He laughed. "Guessing will get you killed, bruh. You better know what world you're living in. You gotta be on high-alert…always looking over your shoulder…"

I thought about what he said, as I cleaned the park. In no time, the park was spotless. I wiped my face with my shirt. "Okay, Mister…I'm done."

The man looked around. "Yes, you are…" He reached into his pocket and removed a few bills. "Here…"

I looked down at it. "Ummmmm…I don't have any change."

The man laughed. "Keep it…that's all for you…"

"Really?" I asked.

"Yes, really…"

Excitedly, I said, "Wow, thank you…"

"No problem and my name is, Jeffrey."

"Okay, Jeffrey…" I was about to walk away when he said, "If you would like to make some more money, come back and see me again, tomorrow…"

"Okay…I will be here." I was walking away when something told me to look back. I turned and found him staring at me. I didn't want to wave because that would be weird, so I just turned and kept walking.

When I got home, my grand-daddy was waiting for me. "Where you been, boy?"

I walked over to the refrigerator.

He stopped me. "Did you wash your hands?"

I frowned. "No, I just walked in."

"Then, wash your damn hands…you bring all of that nasty shit into my house and then touch my bread…touch my lunchmeat. You know how many folks out there scratch their asses and don't wash their hands and you go behind them, bringing their ass-juices into my house…smearing it all over my bread?"

I frowned. "Okay, okay…I will wash my hands."

"Good…"

I was about to turn on the faucet in the kitchen when he said, "Do you think that I want their ass-juices in my kitchen sink?"

I sighed and walked down the hall. After washing my hands, I returned to the kitchen. "Are we good, now?"

"Shit, I don't know…are we?"

I exhaled and walked over to the refrigerator. "The lock, grand-daddy…"

He unlocked the refrigerator. As I removed items from the fridge, I said, "When do you think you'll be removing the lock?"

"When are you moving out?" he asked.

"I don't know," I said.

"Then, I don't know either," he said, twirling the lock in his hand. "Maybe when you start making a contribution, I will give you a key to the lock."

I thought about the money in my pocket and then, I thought about my life. This money was my ticket out of here. All I had to do was save it and I could escape from this place.

I grabbed my food and headed for my room. "Thanks, grand-daddy…goodnight."

"Goodnight, son."

When I got to my room, I ate my sandwich, and sat the plate down on the floor. As I pulled down my pants, the money fell out onto the floor. I picked it up and looked at it. It was more money than I'd ever seen – my whole entire life. I laid back onto the bed, still staring at it, thinking about all of the ways that I wanted to spend it, but then I looked up at the ceiling. I saw a crack that stretched across it and down the wall. I began to visualize a wall without a crack. I was about to slide the money under my mattress when I looked down to find that my plate was covered in roaches. They were fighting for the crumbs that I'd left behind. There were so many of them on my plate that I could no longer see the plate. I thought about killing them, but in that moment, I just couldn't. I was so tired of feeling like I was living in their house. I was so tired of looking at them. It was time for me to leave and get something I could call my own.

The next day, I arrived as promised. After watching another game, I went right to work – cleaning up the park. This time, he gave me twice as much as before. "I can't accept this," I said. "I barely did anything." "That's not the point…I don't pay you for the amount of garbage that you pick up. I pay you, because you're willing to work, and you kept your word." "It ain't like I had nothing else to do," I said, looking around for more garbage. Jeffrey looked pleased. "But that's not the point…the point is, a man is nothing if he can't keep his word." "I try to keep mine…" "That's good…"

"Thanks…" His approval meant a lot to me.

"You did a good job…go home. Believe me, there will be more tomorrow."

"And I will be here to pick it up."

He chuckled and said, "I bet you will…I look forward to it."

CHAPTER 26

I'd been working for him for a few months, now. As time went on, I began to get close to him. I'd never had a man like him take so much interest in me or even bother to help me. I began to trust him like I'd never trusted anyone before - outside of my grandfather. At first, it was about the money, but soon it became about something else, because he gave me what I couldn't get at home.

After the games were over, I watched as he handed out sandwiches and cold drinks to all of the kids in the park. He also provided rides to the kids who had to cross gang-lines to make it home. They all talked to him about the things that were going on in their lives and if he could help them, he did. This was something that I'd never seen before and I wanted it – I needed it.

We were cleaning up, when he asked me, "So, what are your plans?"
"Well, I was thinking of stopping by the store to get some snacks before going home…"
He smiled and interrupted me. "Not plans for today…plans for the future."

I hadn't really thought about it, so I didn't know how to answer his question. So, like a deer caught in headlights, I babbled like an idiot. "I...ummm ...yeah...ummm... about that...ummm..."

He laughed. "Haven't gave it much thought, huh?"

"No, not really," I admitted.

"When do you plan to start thinking about it?"

I shook my head. "Now, that you bring it up..."

"I'm just saying that it's not something that you want to put off...you don't want to be old and trying to get your shit together."

I huffed. "I know..."

He handed me a bottle of water. "Got a girlfriend?"

I frowned. "Who would want to date, Pee-boy?"

"Pee-boy?" he asked.

"Yeah...that's what the kids called me," I said, embarrassed that I'd told him.

"Why did they call you that?" he asked.

"Cause...they said that I smelled like pee..."

He walked up and stood next to me. He inhaled. "You don't smell like pee to me."

Having him that close made me feel funny. I stepped back. "Thanks..."

"You smell like most boys."

I frowned. "Most boys?"

Looking like he'd just got busted, he said, "I mean... guys...we all smell the same, right?"

I thought about it for a second and said, "I guess..."

"Yeah, we do...see...come and smell me."

I stepped back again. "Naw, I'm good. I'm going to have to take your word for it."

He laughed for a second. "I'm not trying to come on to you. I'm just saying that all men kind of smell a like."

"And I'm just saying that I'll have to take your word for it," I told him.

"You know, Paul? You're a good-looking guy…"

"Excuse me?"

"Not in a perverted kind of way…" He laughed, uncomfortably. He reached out and touched my shoulder. "You should be able to get all of the ladies…especially, with those pretty eyes."

I looked down at his hand. He could tell that he was making me feel uncomfortable.

"Come on…it's hot out here…"

Still looking at his hand, I said, "Sure…okay."

We were walking towards the street when his grip tightened across my shoulder. "Paul, I want you to know that if you need anything…ANYTHING… don't you hesitate to reach out to me."

I removed his hand and said, "Thanks…"

When we parted ways, I couldn't help but feel like Jeffrey had a little something "extra" going on. I liked working for him, but that's as far as things were going to go. I had to keep an eye on him.

He was waiting for me. After working all day, I had no energy for him, but there was no way of avoiding him.

"Where ya' been, boy?" he asked.

I grabbed a glass and proceeded to fill it with water. "Grand-daddy, you tell me to get out, I get out and now that I'm 'out', you want to know where I've been. You would think that you would be happy that I'm not looking in your face all-day."

"I just been noticing that you haven't been around..."

"Grand-daddy, there comes a time in every man's life when..."

He started laughing, uncontrollably. "Wow...look at you...went to bed a boy...woke up a man...you get a few hairs on your balls and you start feeling yourself."

I responded, "How you know what I got on my balls?"

He came close to me and before I could react, he had my nuts in his hand. Pulling hard, my knees began to buckle. Tears formed in my eyes. He pulled me close to him. "I know that if you get smart, again, you ain't gon' have no balls." He released them, and I fell to the floor.

Lying in the fetal position, I wanted to tell him that I had a job, just to throw it in his face, but I was in too much pain to do it. As I laid there waiting for the pain to subside, an image of a world without him flashed before my eyes. The thought of leaving all of this behind made me forget all about the pain. I chuckled as I thought about the day that it would all end. I envisioned myself packing, strolling down the hall, and slapping people across the face as I sing, and walk out the door. *Fuck you, motherfuckers, fuck you, motherfuckers... fuck you, fuck you, fuck you...*I wiped tears from my eyes and smiled, coyly. "Soon, grand-daddy…real soon…"

CHAPTER 27

It was late August when it seemed like Summer was at its hottest. I was tired but determined. I'd shown-up every day and did everything that he'd asked me to do – from picking up garbage, to scrubbing graffiti from the walls and sidewalks, to picking up dog poop, everything. I was so desperate to turn my life around that I would have licked chicken grease from his fingertips if it would have gotten me closer to my goal - freedom.

And today it looked like it would be that day. I knew that I'd saved enough to move somewhere. I was so happy that I decided to stop by the local grocery store to purchase a newspaper. I was looking at the classifieds when I found it – my new home.

1 Bedroom

FOR RENT

$550 a month/Utilities Included.
Cable TV Extra

3 Blocks from State Street

Call for an appointment:
(773) 555-5555

I ran all the way home to call them. I ran through the door, ran passed the roaches, ran passed the rats, and looked under my mattress for the rest of my money. As I ran my hand back and forth under the mattress, I realized that there was nothing under there. I lifted the mattress up and threw it on the floor. Nervously, I looked around the room. As my mind raced, frantically, I heard the door open.

"Looking for something," she said.

I turned and looked at her.

"Guess what I found?" she asked – eyes bulging out of her head.

I walked towards her. "You didn't take my money, did you?"

"You mean our money," she said.

DADDY BY DIANE MARTIN 211

My heart began to race. "It wasn't yours...it was mine." I said, balling my hands into a fist.

"How did you get so much money?" she asked.

"I worked for it...now, give it back to me," I said walking towards her.

"I can't," she said.

Afraid, I asked, "Why? What did you do?"

"I needed to use it for something..."

"For what?" I asked, already knowing the answer.

"Well, you see..." she started, but then said, "Wait a minute...I don't have to explain myself to you...you are my child. You owe me...don't I feed you...and ummmmmm, do other stuff...?"

Through clenched teeth, I said, "You took my money 'cause you think I owe you...?"

"That's what kids are supposed to do...take care of their mama..."

"You are not my mama..."

She stopped. Her eyes grew dark and she began to foam at the mouth. Suddenly, she lunged at me. She grabbed my hand and placed it between her legs. "Touch it...you know you want it..."

I couldn't believe what was happening. I pushed her off of me.

"What cha' gon' do, huh?" she spat. "What cha' gon do?"

Something inside of me snapped and she could see it. I began to breathe, heavily. My entire body grew hot. I was done with this shit. *Done.* "You nasty junkie bitch..." I said.

"The fuck you call me?"

"You heard me…did I stutter?"

"No, but you better know who you're talking to…"

"I know who I'm talking to…I'm talking to your triflin' ass…"

"Fuck you, boy…you ain't shit to me."

"And you ain't shit to me either, bitch…" She opened her mouth to say something, but I interrupted her. "You know what? I finally figured some shit out about you and I realize what your problem is…"

"My problem is you…" she confirmed.

"Exactly…and when you see me, you see a part of a man who don't want you and you see a part of yourself that you will never be."

"What are you? You're nothing, Paul…"

"But that's where you're wrong, BETTY…I'm better than you…so much better than you…"

She spit in my face. "Who's better now?"

I wiped my face. "I'm still better than you and you hate it and out of all of your kids, I'm the one you mess with, why? I've never done anything to you…"

She began to breathe, heavily. Her eyes began to fill-up with tears. "You took…" She began. "You took my son away from me."

Suddenly, I remembered that day and I began to replay everything that led up to that moment, in my head, and I began to cry. "You're blaming that on me? I didn't take him. That man took him."

"If you had of just waited for me…"

"For what, Betty? You took your kids from the only two people who loved them and you left us in a building...by ourselves...we were scared and hungry...what was I supposed to do?"

"You should have waited...I was coming back." she murmured. "I loved y'all..."

For a second, I thought that I heard her wrong. For the first time, in my life, she said that she loved us and that she loved me. But, sadly, the moment wouldn't last for long because her hatred for me ran so deep that once she realized that she said it, she took it back. "But I never loved YOU..." she said, smiling.

I'd felt relieved that she said that, because if she did love me, I would have regretted what I was about to do next. I began to walk towards her. When she realized that this was the end, she jumped up and ran into the hallway. On her heels, I grabbed her by the back of her head and threw her onto the floor. "I never loved you, Betty..."

"Get off of me," she said, struggling. "Let me go..."

"You're always accusing me of doing something to you...NOW, I'm going to do something to you." I hit her. Her face swung to the left and when it came back forward, I could see that her mouth was covered with blood. Surprised that I hit her, she stared at me. I paused, for a moment, to look at her. Looking at her was like looking in the mirror. I hit her again. She smiled. I hit her again and again until her face was a bloody mess. I placed my hand around her neck and began to squeeze, hard. Her eyes widened. She began clawing at my hands. She reached up and scratched my face. I moved my head back to avoid her and squeezed tighter. Her neck began to collapse under my fingertips. She coughed and gasped for air. "Paul, please...please...I'm your mama..." Hearing her say that made me squeeze so hard that I heard something snap. Her hands fell to her side as she exhaled for the very last time. I lifted her off of the floor and placed my head against her chest to listen to her heart beat. *Thump...thump...thump...*and then it fell silent. I held her in my arms. I inhaled her scent. She smelled like cigarettes and burnt hair. As I held her in my arms, I realized that this was the first time that I'd hugged her. It was then that I realized that it was, finally, over.

I knew that I couldn't keep her there. If my grandparents walked in and saw her laying on the floor it would kill them, so I picked her up and carried her outside. I looked around until I saw it. I carried her, down the alley, to the first "trap" house on the block. I placed her on the ground and removed one of the wood panels that covered the basement window. I broke the glass, picked her up, and slid her limp body inside. When her body hit the floor, I paused for a moment and said, "Bye, Betty..." I placed the panel back against the window and walked away.

I was walking back to the house to clean up, but as I approached it, I noticed my grand-daddy staring at the blood on the hallway floor. When I walked in, he looked at me. "What happened here?"

I thought about it for a second before saying, "I killed a rat."

My grand-daddy laughed. "What? Must have been a big one...look at this mess."

"It was..." I confirmed.

"What 'cha kill it with?" he asked. He wanted to hear all of the gory details.

"With my bare hands..." I raised them up so that he could see the blood on them.

He looked up at my face. "Damn, boy...never thought that I would see it...I guess you are becoming a man..." He paused to look around the room. "What did you do with it?"

"I threw it out..."

"WHAT!!! You threw out a perfectly good rat?"

"You wouldn't have wanted that one...it had something wrong with it."

"Shit, we could have run some water on it...after your granny get done seasoning it, it would have been fine."

"Not this one, grand-daddy...it came out of Betty's room. I think that it got a hold of some of Betty's stuff..."

He looked relieved. "Then, I'm glad that you killed it. We don't need no rats running around here acting like that girl...matter of fact, where is that girl?"

I paused to think about my answer. "You know that I don't keep up with her..."

"Well, I'm glad that she's gon'…maybe, I can get me some sleep tonight."
I smiled as I wiped the floor. "Finally, maybe, we all can."

They were so used to my mother being messed-up that when she didn't show up nobody thought twice about it – at least, I didn't. They actually looked relieved that she was gone. The one thing that they did notice was that, all of a sudden, we didn't have any rats. For some odd reason, they all flocked to the "trap" house down the street.

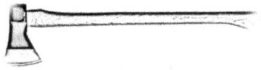

I'd fallen asleep. In my dream, I could see her –
begging me to let her go. I wrapped my hand around
her neck. I screamed, "Die bitch…die, bitch…!!!!"

"Paul…please…"

"Die…bitch…why won't you die…?" We struggled.

"Let me go, boy…what the hell is wrong with you
boy?"

"Mama?" I said, waking up from my dream. When I
opened my eyes, I looked down to find that I had my
grand-daddy in a headlock.

"Let me go, damnit…"

Quickly, I released him and began to apologize. "I'm
sorry, grand-daddy…"

He rubbed his neck. "I come in here to tell you that
your grandmamma made you some breakfast, then
you start calling me a bitch, and the next thing I know,
I'm in a gad-damn chokehold."

"I'm sorry…I guess I was having a bad dream."

"Yeah, and it almost got worst…I was gon' wake you
up by putting a bullet in your ass."

"I'm glad that you didn't do that…" I said, confused.

"Yeah, but I sho' came close…now, what were you
dreaming about?"

"Betty…"

"That's a nightmare and a half…I see why you were
screaming 'Bitch'…but you said that you wanted her
to die."

"I did?"

"Yeah…you did."

"Wow…" I pretended to be surprised.

"Shit, she might be somewhere dead...messing with that shit...it's going to kill her one day."
It already has. I mumbled, as I stood to walk away.

CHAPTER 28

I went to work the next day feeling broken – like I'd lost everything. I worked so hard to save my money and I wanted so bad to get out of there. I wanted to prove that I could do it and, in an instant, it was all gone. All I could think about, was that now, I had to start all over.

I was distracted and thinking about everything that happened when Jeffrey interrupted my thoughts. "What's going on, friend?"

"My money's gone…" I said.

"That's all?" he replied.

"That's all?" I said, angrily. "That was all that I had…"

"Man…don't sweat it…unlike a good woman, money is the only thing, that once you lose it, you can get it back…"

"That's easy for you to say. I had a chance to get out of there…to get away from the bullshit and that bitch took it away from me."

Confused, he said, "Where? And what bitch?"

"My home…my mama…" I answered.

Jeffrey opened a bottle of water and handed it to me. "Things are that bad at home?"

I took it and began to sip from it. "It's hell…and I was going to get my own place…I was going to show them…show her…"

He sat down next to me. "Show them what? Your new place?"

I thought about it for a second and said, "Hell naw…I wanted to show them that…"

He interrupted me. "That you're better than them?"

Stunned, I said, "Why would you say something like that?"

"Well, were you moving, so that you could turn around and go back and help them get out of the place that you're running from? Clearly, it is a bad place…so bad that you will do almost anything to get away from it, right?"

"'No' to your first question and 'yes' to your second…"

"So, why leave them there?"

"Because…"

"Because what?"

"Because, they are a part of it…a big part of it."

"Well, you can change the place, but you can't change the people, that's for damn sure…but don't you feel somewhat bad about leaving them behind?"

"Hell no…"

"They must have really messed over you…"

"No, it was just her…"

"Again…why not take care of the ones who took care of you? Don't they deserve a better life?"

Becoming agitated, I said, "Look, I don't need you trying to get in my head…"

"I'm just curious as to why you, a person who claims that he's living in hell, would leave the people that he loves behind…in hell…you do love them, don't you?"

"I do love them…"

"Well, I'm not trying to tell you what to do, but you gotta do right by the people who's done right by you…you ain't gon' never have shit if the things you obtain doesn't help someone else…that's why I do what I do. I don't owe you or any of those other kids anything, but what if I lived my life thinking like you?"

I thought about what he was saying.

"Someone had to help me, or I wouldn't be able to help you…"

Frustrated, I said, "I'm just ready to move on…I'm sick of this shit."

"And I bet, if you asked them, they would say the same thing…"

"I just need to get away from it for a while…I feel like I'm being smothered to death…"

"That's bad." He took a sip of the water, swallowed, and said, "Well, what if I told you that I could help you with that…"

"How can you help me?" I asked.

"I got a place that you can come to…"

Suddenly, I became angry. I couldn't believe that he was trying to pull this shit on me. "Look man, I told you...I don't play that shit."

Confused, he said, "What?" Then, suddenly, he realized what was happening. "Motherfucker, don't nobody want you. I'm just trying to help you."

"Are you sure?" I asked, giving him the side-eye.

He frowned. "Un-fucking-believable...I don't want to fuck you. If you were the last motherfucker on the planet, I wouldn't fuck you. Shit, I like pussy. Matter of fact, before you pissed me off, I was thinking about pussy..."

Embarrassed, I said, "I'm sorry man...I just thought..."

"Well, you can stop thinking that shit...I don't want your ass no more than I want a dick in my ass. Matter of fact, you can shoot me in my head if I ever...I mean EVER...look at your ass that way...if I'm looking at your ass for more than sixty seconds, I won't you to just kill me..."

I stuck my hands up. Trying to surrender, I said, "Okay...okay...I got it."

"Now, remember it...okay? I don't want to have this conversation with you again."

"Okay...I didn't mean to offend you."

He interrupted me. "You didn't offend me...I know who the fuck I am. The only dick I like is mine. Okay? So, leave that shit alone. I don't want to think about it, again or talk about it, again."

Trying to change the subject, I asked, "Okay, man… so, should I get to work?"

He reached into his pocket and removed a roll of bills. He counted five one hundred-dollar bills and handed it to me. "Take this…"

"I can't do that…" I insisted.

"You want to insult me twice in one day?" He held his hand out in front of me.

I took the bills from him and said, "Thanks…I owe you. I will find a way to pay you back."

He placed the rest on the money back into his pocket. "Money ain't shit to me…you want to do something for me? Find your way out of that place you call 'hell'…"

CHAPTER 29

Eventually, my grandmother went back into her room. For a long time, she hadn't gone in there. She used to stand outside of her door, waiting for her to return, but eventually, she gave up. You could tell by the look on her face that she knew that Betty was dead. She never said it out loud, but the way that she walked around the house, with that "look" on her face said that she'd lost her oldest daughter. It was like someone had turned the light out on the part of her heart that she'd saved just for her. She looked tired. At first, she was tired of dealing with her mess. Now, she was tired of missing her.

For a while, I walked passed the "trap" house where I placed her body. I used to think that I could hear her – calling for me. "Paul, Paul…" I would hear her say, but I knew that, by now, there was nothing left of her, but some bones and a few pieces of flesh that the rodents left behind. I was happy when they finally tore down the house and leveled it to the ground. I watched as they scooped up everything, including her remains, and put it into a city dumpster. My grandmother watched the demolition from the porch. When it was over, she said, "It's about time…that house was nothing but a haven for junkies. It was bad for the community…watching them go in and out of there all times of the night…maybe, now, they'll put something useful over there."

I sat down on the porch and stared at the empty lot. "Yeah…maybe…I'm just glad that it's gone."

"Me too…" she said. She opened the door. "You coming inside?"

"In a minute, grandma…I just want to sit out here and think…"

She walked inside of the house. "What you got to think about?"

"Life, granny and how short it is…"

I was restless, so I decided to walk up to the park. I knew that it probably wasn't the smartest thing to do, but I had nowhere else to go. When I got there, I noticed that he was sitting on the park bench.

"Jeffrey?" I asked. "What are you doing here?"

"I could ask you the same question…" he said.

I laughed. "I guess you could…" I walked over and sat down next to him.

"So, why are you out tonight?" he asked.

"I couldn't sleep…why are you here?"

"I'm working…" he said.

I looked around and said, "There are no kids here…"

"You here, ain't you?"

"Yeah, but you didn't know that I was coming…did you?"

"What if I said, 'yes'?"

"That would be some scary shit…"

He laughed. "Naw, I'm here for something else."

"Aren't you afraid to be in the park at night?" I asked.

"Aren't you?"

"I'm not afraid of much these days…"

"Why is that?" He asked.

"I'm seen some shit…so, no…I ain't scared of shit."

"Well, everybody is scared of somebody," he said.

"Well, I ain't met him yet…"

He huffed, took out a pair of binoculars, and placed them on his face.

"What are those for?"

"I'm bird-watching…"

Those words triggered a painful memory. Something in me snapped. Agitated, I jumped up and stood in front of him.

"Sit your ass down…you're blocking my view." He tried looking around me.

"Say that shit, again…"

"Sit your ass down…" he repeated.

"Not that…what you said about the birds…"

Confused, he said, "What? Bird-watching?"

I grabbed him by his collar. "The fuck you say?" I asked as the memory of my little brother flashed before my eyes.

He dropped the binoculars and grabbed at my hands. "Boy, you better let me go…the fuck is wrong with you?" he asked, as he struggled to free himself.

"Where's my brother?" I asked, preparing to do whatever it took to get the answers that I wanted.

Slowly, he reached into his pocket. When his arm came up, I felt him place something cold against my temple. "Boy, I'm going to say this one time and one time only…I don't know who the fuck your brother is or where the fuck your brother is, but if you don't let me go, something bad…something REAL bad is going to happen to you…and I don't want that. Now, let me go so you can commence to convincing me not to hurt you."

I was ready to die, as long as he told me what I wanted to know first, he could whatever he wanted to. "Pull the trigger…I ain't got nothing to lose…I told you 'bout my life…death would be an upgrade…"

He exhaled and said, "I don't want to kill you…so, at the count of three, I'm going to lower my gun and you're going to let me go and we gon' talk about this…okay?"

Determined to know what happened, I refused to release him.

He began to count. "I, 2, 3…" When he got to three, he realized that I was still holding him. "I didn't come here to kill nobody, tonight…"

"What did you come for? What do you REALLY do with those kids?"

"What?"

He raised the gun up over my head and when it came down, it hit me on the side of my face. I let him go. He pointed the gun at me. "Dude, your ass is crazy...I ain't done nothing with no kids..."

"Then, why are you here?"

"That's my business, but it ain't got nothing to do with no kids. Now, get your ass off of that ground before you draw unnecessary attention to us..."

Rubbing the side of my face, I stood and sat on the bench.

He looked around before putting his gun away. "You know how close you came to dying?"

"Do I look like I care?"

"Obviously not...fucking with me...if you were anybody else, they would be drawing a chalk-line around your ass..."

"You still didn't answer my question..."

"If you ask me again, I swear..." He began to look at his clothes. "What about me, man, says gay...or says pedophile? I ain't down for none of that shit."

"Then, why are you here...at night...by yourself?"

"Motherfucker...YOU'RE HERE TOO!"

What he said was starting to sink in. Trying to slow my breathing, I said, "When you said that..."

He interrupted. "What? About bird-watching?"

"Yeah..."

"Nigga, who raised you? Can a motherfucker watch birds without somebody calling him a freak? Your ass is fucked up. Bird-watching? You 'bout to get killed cause my ass said 'bird-watching?' Something ain't right, dude…seek help."

"No, it was just something that he said…"

"He, who?"

"The man that took my brother…"

"Well, I ain't that man…I ain't that KIND of man…okay? I would never do that…"

"I'm sorry, man…"

"That's twice, dude, that you've tried to 'profile' me…and in both instances, you got the shit wrong…"

"I know and like I said…"

"I know what you said, and you only get one time with me to do something worthy of an apology. After that, we need to start calling your next of kin…"

"You're right…"

"I'm trying to give you a chance, but you're making a brotha' rethink his choice."

For a moment, we sat in silence.

He was frustrated. "Look, I'm going to get the fuck-up out of here…I'll see you tomorrow."

"You want to see me tomorrow?" I asked, concerned that he was going to fire me.

His tone softened. "Well, they say, 'Keep your friends close' and the nutcases even closer…"

I tried to laugh. "After tonight, which one am I?"

"Shit, looks like a little of both…which might come in handy one day."

CHAPTER 30

When I approached the front door, I noticed that the house was completely dark. As I placed my hand on the door-knob, I noticed that it wouldn't turn. I knocked on the door, but no one answered. I went around to the back of house, tapping on all of the windows, but there was still no answer. I sat down on the porch. With my back against the door, I closed my eyes and fell asleep.

The next thing, I knew, I was being awakened by the sun. I looked up at it. Its rays burned my eyes. I shielded my face as I stood and knocked on the door. The door swung open. "Why did you lock the door?" I asked, walking inside.

"We weren't home," she said.

I followed her down the hall. Looking around, I noticed that something was missing. "Where's grand-daddy?" I asked.

She sighed.

It was something about the way that she did that that told me that something wasn't right.

"Is he alright?"

She shrugged her shoulders. "What do you consider 'alright?'"

For a moment, I'd become afraid. "He's...not dead, is he?"

She walked over to the kitchen table and sat down. Wringing her hands, she said, "He's not doing too good."

I sat down next to her. "What do you mean?"

Being evasive, she said, "Your grand-daddy's a proud man..."

"Grandmamma, please...what's going on?" I asked, growing impatient.

She smiled for a second. "We had a lot of good years..."

"Grandma, you're acting like he's dead. Will you tell me what's wrong?"

"He got problems with his head..." she, finally, said.

Concerned, I said, "His head? What's wrong with his head?"

"His brain ain't right..."

Relieved, I sighed. "Is that all? His brain ain't never been right..."

"No, his illness is getting worse..."

"Can't they give him something for it? The PTSD?"

"He's been taking something for it..."

"Really? Are you sure? I don't think it's been working."

She laughed, but quickly, turned serious. "The pills can only do so much...especially, if he's taking them like he's supposed to...which he don't, and he's getting up in age..."

"Is he going to die?"

"We're both going to die…one day."

The thought of them dying saddened me, but she was right. At some point, we're all going to die, but I couldn't imagine a world without them.

She sighed and walked out of the room. When she returned, she had some pictures in her hands. She handed them to me.

"Who is this?"

She chuckled. "That's your grand-daddy."

Looking closely, I said, "It is?"

She took the picture from me and looked at it. "He was one sexy man…especially, in that uniform. I couldn't keep my hands off of him."

I frowned. "You're taking me to a dark place, granny…"

She laughed. "I fell in love with him, immediately."

I smiled and continued to sort through the photos. "Who is this?"

She smiled. "Me and him on our wedding day…"

Shocked, I said, "That's you?"

She frowned. "What are you trying to say?"

I shrugged. "Ummm, nothing…it's just…umm…you look different."

"Living will do that, son…" she sighed, and took the picture from me. "We had a good life. We loved each other…"

"Loved? You say that like you don't love him anymore…"

"Things change...I'm not the woman that I was when I fell in love with him and he ain't the man that he was either..."

"Is it because of his legs..."

She shook her head. "No...no...definitely not. Legs don't make a man..."

"Then, what?"

She paused to think about her answer. "We weathered a lot of storms together...and marriage is like a house in a storm...based on what it's built out of, it can either survive a storm or a storm can destroy it...tear it into little pieces...sadly, this is the piece that we got left."

I reached out and touched her hand. "Why not leave?" I was shocked that I asked that question knowing that if she left us, there would be no one here to take care of us.

She shook her head. "Son, you ever hear folks say that, 'the grass is always greener on the other side'?"

"Yeah, I've heard that..."

"Well, that's bullshit. Somebody else's grass is gon' always look greener if they are taking care of their 'lawn'...you run your happy-ass over there thinking that things gon' get better...not realizing that if you put a little fertilizer on your own 'lawn', your shit would be green too. All you gon' do over there is neglect that lawn like you did your own...No, son...I'mma sit my ass right here...with my lawn and the weeds that come with it and I'm gon' prune...

cut…fertilize…and do whatever I got to do to get mine green again."

Just then, the back door opened. Screaming down the hall, he said, "Y'all ain't gon' be happy until somebody walk in here on ya'…

My grandmother looked at me and said, "Shhhh… okay?"

I nodded 'okay.'

She turned towards the door and said, "And what they gon' do? Come in here, laugh, and then turn around and leave?"

He entered the room. "Daddy's home…"

For a moment, she looked sad. "Yes, he is. Are you hungry?"

"Starving," he said.

"Okay," She walked towards the refrigerator. "Let's get y'all something to eat."

He came over to the table. I was staring at him.

"What's wrong with you, boy?"

"Nothing," I said. "How are you feeling?"

My grandmother stopped what she was doing to hear his answer.

He rubbed his nose. "Why y'all looking at me like I got a damn booger hanging out of my nose?"

"If there was something wrong, would you tell me, grand-daddy?" I asked.

He looked at me for a moment and said, "Yeah, I ain't got shit to hide."

CHAPTER 31

The park was no longer a safe place to hang out. It seemed like, every day, the police were there putting up police tape. In a week's time, several people had been shot – a couple of gang members, a drug dealer, the guy who used to come to the park and stare at the little girls – all gone. For a while, even Jeffrey was gone. I worried that he'd become one of the victims, but then, out of the blue, he showed up.

I was standing outside of a crowd who was looking at a body that was lying on the ground. Jeffrey walked up behind me and said, "What's going on?"

He startled me. "Hey man…what's up?"

He looked around, nervously, and said, "Shhhhhh…"

I frowned. "Why do we have to be quiet?"

He shrugged. "Ummmmm, I don't know…to respect the dead?"

I looked over at the body. "I don't think he cares…"

"So, what happened to him?" he asked.

"Well, I may not be a doctor, but it looks like somebody shot his ass…"

"Yeah…it does." Staring at the police, he said, "What are they saying?"

"They ain't saying nothing…at least, not to any of us."

"Okay, okay…that's good."

Curious, I said, "Why are you acting so weird?"

"Me? Naw, just trying to see what's going on…" he confirmed. We worked our way through the crowd and out onto the street. "Folks are dropping like flies…"

"Ain't a problem when you don't like flies," I said.

Changing the subject, he said, "Anyway…so, what are you up to?"

"Nothing…just hanging out."

"You want to come to my place? We can hang out there…"

"Sure, I ain't doing anything else…"

"Maybe, we could shoot some hoops."

"Now, I'm up for that…it's been a while since I've done something fun."

"Okay, my car's right down there."

As we walked towards the car, a police car drove passed us. Jeffrey stopped to stare at it. When they were down the street and out of sight, he turned to me and said, "I hope that you're ready to get your ass kicked."

I laughed. "Winner buys lunch…"

"Shit, it's a deal…"

We jumped into the car and pulled off. We drove around for about ten minutes, before we found ourselves in front of a beautiful brownstone on the city's eastside. When we pulled into his driveway, we were greeted with the sound of a barking dog. "Don't pay his ass any attention…his bark is worse than his bite."

"I hope so, because I didn't plan on killing a dog today."

He waved. "You ain't gon' kill nobody…you ain't got it in you."

I smiled and said, "You'd be amazed at what I got in me."

He grabbed the dog by the collar, led him to the backyard, and chained him to a tree. "Let me get him some water and then, I can proceed to whooping that butt."

"Or get whooped…" I laughed.

While he was gone, I looked around his yard. It was beautiful. The grass was nice, green, and surrounded by flowers that I'd never seen before.

He walked out and placed a bowl in front of the dog. "Wouldn't want the Animal Activists screaming that I'm abusing my dog…"

"Yeah, you wouldn't want that."

He opened his garage and retrieved a basketball. "Okay…I'll front you ten…"

"I don't need you fronting me anything. I got this…"

He began to bounce the ball between his legs. "Okay, I tried…don't be crying like no baby when I win this game."

"You ain't got to worry about me…worry about yourself."

He tossed the ball into the air for a three-pointer. *Swish*. It was all net.

"So, it's going to be like that?" I asked.

"All day and all night…"

"Alright, let's do this…"

He lifted the ball above his head and tossed it. The ball went in. Shot after shot, it landed, barely touching the rim. He was playing like he took lessons from Mike himself. I was worn out but determined to stay in the game. When he scored twenty-one points, I fell onto the concrete. Exhausted, I tried to catch my breath. He stood over me and teased. "What's that I smell? Smells like defeat."

"Smells like your feet," I joked.

He reached out his hand. "Ha, ha, ha…ready for game two…"

I grabbed his hand. "Let's do this."

He ran circles around me. By the time he was done, my head was spinning. When he scored twenty-one, this time, he began to dance around the driveway. "I'm bad, I'm bad, and you're sad, you're sad…" he sang. "You give up?"

Yeah, man…you're making a fool out of me."

"Good, cause whooping a man's ass can build up a man's appetite."

"Where do you want to eat?" I asked.

He tossed the ball back into the garage. "We don't have to go anywhere…I know that you need your money. Plus, there's food in the house. Come on…let me make you something to eat."

I followed him inside. "Thanks man. It would have been terrible to get my butt kicked and then, have to reward you for doing it."

He laughed and grabbed some paper towels. "Wipe that sweat off of your face. I don't want you dripping DNA all over my kitchen."

I smiled. "Thanks…" I wiped my forehead and said, "You have a nice house."

"Thanks," He pulled food from the refrigerator. "I got some leftover chicken in here…want some."

"Definitely…"

He pulled out a bowl, threw the contents in a pan, and then, placed them in the oven. He opened a can of soda and poured it in a glass. "How's things at home?" he asked.

I took a sip from the glass. "You want the truth or the lie that I tell myself every day?"

"You can tell me the truth…"

"Ain't shit changed…" I asked.

"I'm sorry to hear that…"

"It's cool…I'm saving my money. I'll be free soon."

He checked the chicken and said, "'Free is always good. It's been a long time since I've had to live under somebody else's roof…follow somebody else's rules. That shit is the same as being locked up."

I took another sip from the glass. "So, you been locked-up?"

"You ain't a man unless you've seen the inside of a prison…either voluntary or involuntary…"

"What's it like?" I asked.

"Well, have you ever seen the inside of a box?"

"Yeah…"

"Well, throw a cot in there and a motherfucker who can't wait for you to fall asleep with your ass unprotected and that's prison."

"What you go in there for?"

"That's one question too many…"

"What are you trying to hide?"

"Man, you can't hide nothing…my whole record is on the internet, but if I talk about it, that's bringing up old demons…that ain't my life no more…"

"Yeah…now you hang around kids at the park and watch 'birds 'in the middle of the night."

"First, most companies aren't felon-friendly, so a brotha got to get in where he fits in and second, I'm trying to keep folks out of my ass and out of my business…if you know what I mean?"

"Yeah, I know what you mean."

He pulled the chicken out of the oven and placed it on the counter. He placed a piece on a plate and handed it to me. "Bread?"

"Naw, I'm good…" Then, I thought about the roll of bills that he had in his pocket. "Is that all that you do?"

"Naw, I got a side-gig…I get paid to take out people's garbage."

"Oh, you're a garbage man too?"

"Kind of…"

"Why are you acting so secretive?" I picked up the chicken and took a bite out of it.

"Because what I do is a secret."

"What's so secretive about taking out people's garbage?"

"Because this ain't regular garbage…"

Becoming frustrated, I said, "Jeffrey, if you don't want to tell me what you do, that's cool."

He looked me over and said, "Can you keep a secret?"

I thought about some of the things that I've done and said, "You ain't got to worry about me saying nothing."

He looked around trying to make sure that we were the only two people in the room and said, "I kill people."

Skeptical, I said, "Yeah, right."

"I do…" He had a serious look on his face.

"How do you go from saving lives in the community to taking lives in the community?"

"It's all about balance, son. For every life, there's death and for every death, there's life."

"So, you just go around killing people."

"No, just garbage," he confirmed.

"And how do you decide who's garbage and who's not?"

"I'm not the one deciding. I just take it out…"

"You don't look like a killer…"

"Naw…according to you, I look like a butt-bandit and a perv…" He took a bite out of the chicken and frowned. "This tasted a whole lot better yesterday…"

"I bet it did…" I asked, wishing that I had some hot sauce to pour over it.

He spit the chicken into his hand. "You look like you could kill people."

"Why do you say that?"

"'Cause, it's usually people who've had it the hardest who either rise out of their situation or they take revenge out on the folks who put them there."

I laughed. "You're right…" Since we were being honest with each other, I felt comfortable enough to say, "Yeah, I've killed too."

He started laughing. "Ants don't count, boy."

I huffed. "That's funny…but no, they were bigger than ants."

"And, for some odd reason, I'm not shocked," he said.

"Why you say that?"

"You live in hell, right? They don't put angels in hell…"

"That's not true. The Devil is an angel and He's there."

He was putting the chicken into the dog's bowl when he asked, "Are you the Devil, Paul?"

"I don't know what I am…"

Jeffrey smiled before he walked out the back door. "You know, Paul? There's a reason why you and I've been brought together."

"You think so…"

"Yes, I do. We just have to live long enough to see what it is."

We smiled, but, it was an uncomfortable one. I think that we'd both just realized that our relationship had gone from friends to two admitted murderers. Whether he was being honest or not or whether he believed me or not, things were different now and we both knew it.

CHAPTER 32

S ummer was almost over and fall was, slowly, making an entrance. It was too nice to be at home. So, since, I had some money in my pocket, I decided to do something that I'd never done before. I jumped on the bus and headed downtown. I was walking up and down the street when I saw it – a movie theater. I'd heard a lot about them, but I'd never been in one before. I stood outside of the building – reading the billboards. They had a movie for children, an action flick, and a something that looked like a love story. I decided that I wanted to watch the action flick. I purchased a ticket and walked inside. The smell of hot-buttered popcorn met me at the door. I purchased a bucket, a large soda, and then looked for the room that was playing my movie.

I went inside and looked around for the perfect seat. I walked up the stairs and found a seat in the corner of the theater. They were playing the previews when a couple walked in and sat in front of me. Suddenly, the movie began to play. I was eating the popcorn and enjoying the soda when the young man sitting in front of me wrapped his arm around the girl's shoulder. She placed her head on his arm.

As the movie progressed, the couple began to kiss. Although, the movie was good the real action was going on in front of me. I took my eyes off of the screen and began to watch them. The girl looked around the theater before she placed her hands between the man's legs. His head went back as he began to moan. The girl looked around again before suddenly, her head disappeared into the young man's lap. Her head bobbed up and down like someone had dropped a box of chocolate-covered peanuts in his lap. The young man moaned louder. You could hear it over the loud speakers that were playing in my ears. I was eating the popcorn so fast that I accidentally bit my hand. *Shit.* I didn't have time to feel the pain because I didn't want to miss one second of what was happening. Then, quickly, I began to notice that something was happening to me. I looked down between my legs. I'd become so hard that I could feel my own heartbeat in it. I tried adjusting myself, but the more her head moved, the harder 'it' got. As "it" pressed against my zipper, it started to hurt. Then, I thought to myself, *Nobody's looking. Maybe I can take 'it' out, relieve the pressure, and put 'it' back in. Nobody will notice.* I looked around the theater, and when I realized that no one was looking, I unzipped my pants, and let 'it' out. It almost hit me in the face. It was so happy to be free. I covered both of my hands with the butter from the popcorn and rubbed it around the head of my penis. As soon as I began to stroke it,

I was, quickly, blinded by a light – shining in my face. With one hand on my dick and the other shielding my eyes, I heard them say, "Sir, put 'that' away and come with me."

Shit. I was so hard that I couldn't get 'it' back in. "I'm going to need a minute," I said, fumbling with my clothes.

They pointed the light in my face and then, on the growing "force" between my legs. They turned off the light. "I'll wait…"

I groaned in pain as I tried to move it. I stood up and placed 'it' back inside of my jeans.

"Follow me," they said.

Shit, shit, shit…I'm going to get in trouble. I thought to myself. *They're going to call my grandfather or worse, my grandmother and tell her that her grandson got caught jagging-off in a movie theater. Oh shit, shit, shit…"* Once we were in the light, I saw her face. She looked at mine's. With one eyebrow raised, she said, "You know that you can't be doing that in public, right?"

Trying to deflect the attention off of me, I said, "But what about the people in front of me?"

She sucked her teeth. "I didn't catch them…I caught you." She looked down at my crotch.

There was butter covering my zipper. Embarrassed, I said, "Look…I'm sorry. It's just…it's just…"

"You couldn't control yourself…"

"That's not it…" I said.

"Only animals get to walk around with their penises hanging out…Are you an animal, sir?"

"Look, I'm sorry. I really am…please don't call my grandparents," I begged.

She laughed. "Your grandparents? That explains why you're in a theater, in the middle of the day, with your dick in your hand…"

Looking down, I said, "You're not going to call my grandparents…are you?"

She smiled. "Naw…I'll give you a second chance."

"Thank you, thank you…" I said, gratefully.

"Next time, keep 'it' in your pants…" she said. She turned on the flashlight and pointed it at my zipper. "You might want to get that butter off of your crotch or you're going to attract more than flies."

"Thanks for the advice."

She smiled and walked away.

I noticed that it was starting to get hard again, so I, quickly, left the theater.

When I got home, I ran to the bathroom. I was in there for two seconds before I'd cum all over myself. It felt so damn good. I was so relieved. I washed my hands and washed the stain from the front of the pants. I was walking out of the bathroom when I found myself tripping over his chair.

"What 'cha in there doing, boy?" he asked.

Nervously, I said, "Ummmm…nothing. Why?"

He squinted his eyes. "You were in there playing with yourself, weren't you?"

"No, no, no…why you say that?"

He pointed. "That big-ass wet spot on your pants is a dead giveaway unless you're back to pissing on yourself."

I frowned. "I never pee'd on myself."

"Between your mouth, God's ears, and that yellow-stained mattress in that room…"

Sigh. "I'm good, grand-daddy…" I said, trying to get away from him.

"I bet you are. I hope that you didn't get any of that stuff on your grandmother's good towels."

I shook my head. "Is there something else that I can help you with, grand-daddy?"

He followed behind me. "Did I ever talk to you about sex, boy?"

"Nope and I am so grateful…"

When I got to my room, I tried closing the door, but he blocked it with his chair. He came in. I flopped down onto my bed and covered my face with my pillow. He started talking, but I interrupted him. "If you're in here to talk to me about sex…don't."

"Are you sure that you don't want to talk about sex? I can show you some stuff?"

"Show me?" I began to gag. The thought of him having sex with anybody made me want to throw up. "Naw, I'm good. I think that I can figure it out."

"Are you sure? 'Cause, you only get one chance to get it right…you cannot be acting like an amateur when it comes to sex. You climb on top of some girl…fidgeting around trying to find the 'hole' and you stick it in the wrong spot, you will get your ass kicked. There's a Science to it. You either pass or fail and if you fail, you'll be back in the bathroom getting freaky with the bath towels."

I shook my head. "I think I know where the hole is, grand-dad…"

"You think?" He sighed. "You gon' get your ass kicked a lot. I'll tell your grandmamma to get some more towels." He paused for a second and said, "Are you still a virgin?"

"Why?"

"Don't ask me why…answer the question…"

"Yeah…I am…"

"What are you waiting for?" he asked.

"I don't know…just never had the opportunity."

"Why not?"

"'Cause, I haven't…"

He looked sad. "I've failed you, boy…"

"Why you say that?"

"'Cause as soon as you learned how to tie your shoe, you should've been getting some…"

"I learned how to tie my shoe at age 4…"

"It's never too early to learn…"

"Grand-daddy, I think four is too early and I don't think it's as hard as you make it sound…"

"Says the motherfucker who ain't never had none…"

"That might change…" I smiled. "I met somebody today."

"You did? What's her name?"

"I don't know…" I said.

"Well, looks like you're off to a good start…can you at least tell me where you met her?"

I thought about what happened and said, "The theater…"

"One of those picture show places?"

"Yep..."

"What were you doing in there, boy?"

"Watching a movie…" I said.

He raised one eyebrow and said, "You was in there playing with yourself…wasn't you?"

"Why you say that? Can't a man go to the bathroom and to the movies and not play with himself?"

He shook his head. "Nope…shit, I would be playing with myself, right now, if I wasn't talking to your ass. I can't keep my hands off my dick and can't respect or trust a man who can."

I needed to get the image of his dick out of my head. "She seems really nice…" I said.

"I can hear the church bells ringing already." He shook his head. "Look, here's some advice…if you want her, then, go after her…you can't eat unless you hunt…just let the girl know that you're interested in her. Take it slow, at first, and then…when that opportunity comes…" His eyes widened. "Knock the lining out of those bloomers."

We both started laughing. "Thanks, grand-daddy."

"It's what I do, son."

CHAPTER 33

The next day, I got up early and decided to go to the store. I wanted to make sure that the next time, I saw her, I looked good. Of course, I had no idea what that meant. I'd been wearing the same clothes for so long that I had no idea what was in style. Before, I got there, I decided to stop by the park to see what Jeffrey was up to. When I got there, I noticed that the whole block had been cornered off. The police weren't letting traffic in or out. As I got closer, I could see that they were wheeling someone out on a stretcher. I asked someone in the crowd did they know who it was. They answered. "Just some dealer..."

"You know his name?" I asked, worried that it might be Jeffrey. Even though he hadn't told me that he was dealing, I still had to be sure.

"Yeah, it's Black..."

I didn't know who that was, but it wasn't Jeffrey, so I left the scene and began to walk down the street.

I'd stopped at a bus stop, when I saw a car pull up. I turned and looked at it. "Get in," he said.

I walked over and jumped in. "I was just looking for you."

He sped off.

Trying to get my seatbelt on, I said, "Dude, you are flying. Is everything okay?"

"Everything is fine," he said, looking at his rearview mirror. "Oh, so you went to the park?"

"Yeah, they had it blocked-off…"

"Really? Why?"

"They said that a dealer got shot."

"That's all they said?" he asked. "Nothing else?"

"I wasn't sticking around to get the specifics…it didn't have anything to do with me, so I kept it moving…"

Looking through his rearview mirror, he said, "That's smart…mind your own business. You live longer that way."

"Keeping up with my shit keeps me too busy to worry about anybody else's…"

"You know…that's why I like you, Paul. You're smart…smarter than the others."

"Others?" I asked, still struggling with the seatbelt.

We drove around for a few minutes when suddenly, he stopped the car. "Look…I'm going to have to talk to you tomorrow…okay?"

"But this ain't my stop," I said.

He leaned over and opened the door. With a serious look on his face, he said, "I SAID that I'll talk to you tomorrow…"

Angry and confused, I said, "Damn…okay…" I jumped out and slammed the car door.

"See you at the park," he said, before pulling off.

I stopped to look around. I had no idea where I was. Nothing looked familiar. I was lost. "I cannot believe that that motherfucker dropped me off in the middle of "no man's land." I thought about the ride and remembered that it was a straight-shot. I began to take the road, backwards, hoping that it'll take me back to something familiar. I walked, all alone, thinking, "Where the hell are the payphones?" Pissed and annoyed, I kept walking. Finally, I came upon a woman who was using her cellphone. She was talking loud and her eyes were filled with tears. When she noticed that I was standing in front of her, staring at her, she acknowledged me. "Hold on, girl..." She looked me up and down. "Can I help you?"

Nervous, I said, "I'm sorry, Mrs., but I'm lost...can I borrow your phone, so that I can call for a ride home?"

She wiped tears from her eyes and frowned. "Hell no...you think that I'm going to give you my phone, so that you can run off with it..."

"Mam'...I wouldn't do that...seriously, I'm lost..."

She looked me over and feeling sorry for me, she said, "Girl, I will call you right back..." *Beep.* "What's the number? 'Cause I'm not giving you my phone..."

"Oh, that's fine..." I spouted out the number. She dialed it and waited, impatiently, for someone to answer.

He answered. "Who the hell is this calling me on my phone?"

She looked down at her cellphone and then, decided to hand it to me. "You better take this before his ass get cussed out…"

"Thank you…" I said, taking the phone from her. "Grand-daddy, it's me…"

"Whose number is this? Whose phone are you calling me from?"

"It's a long story…can you, please, come and pick me up?"

"Hell naw, your grandmamma is sleep and I'm not waking her up because your simple-ass got lost. Who the hell gets lost in Chicago, anyway? Find Halsted and walk until your ass can't walk no more…and when you find that you can't walk anymore, make a left, and then walk some damn more…"

"Please, grand-daddy…" I begged.

"Please this." *Beep.* The phone went dead.

Motherfucker. I thought to myself. I handed the phone back to the woman and said, "Thank you…" I reached into my pocket for some money. "Let me pay you for the call…"

Looking at the money in my hand, she said, "Naw…that's okay."

"No, please…take it…" I insisted.

She shook her head. "No, it's okay." She began to punch in some numbers on the phone. "Hello…yeah, girl…I'm back…now, what was I saying?"

I looked up at the street sign and then, walked out onto the curb to see if a bus was coming. The woman watched me. Suddenly, she said, "Hold on, girl…I got me one." She placed the phone on her chest and asked me, "Where are you going young man?"

I hesitated. "Why do you want my address?"

"Didn't I hand you my phone? Trust has to go both ways...and I'm not trying to hurt you..."

I looked her over and said, "Sure...why not..." I gave her my address.

She placed the phone back against her face and said, "Girl, I will call you back..." She turned to me and said, "I'll give you a ride."

"What?" I asked.

"I'll give you a ride," she said. "I'm going that way..."

Trying to be gracious, I said, "I appreciate it, but we were taught not to get in strange folks' cars..."

She frowned.

"Not saying that you're strange, but you just never know..."

Pissed, she said, "Shit...okay...then, you're on your own."

Realizing that I offended her, I said, "Look, I'm sorry...sure, I'll take the ride."

She stuck her mouth out. "You act like you're doing me a favor..."

"I'm sorry...I mean...you know what? How 'bout I just say, 'thank you?'"

"That's a good start..." she said.

For a moment, I hesitated. Something about this wasn't right. It left a weird feeling in the pit of my stomach, but I was desperate.

She began to walk away, but turned back and asked, "You coming?"

"Oh, yeah…" I said. Initially, I was concerned, but considering that she was a woman, I felt that I didn't have to worry about it. If push came to shove, I could overpower her and get away. I followed her to her car. She opened her door and popped the locks. I hesitated for a moment before jumping in. I looked at her.

"Are you getting in or what?"

Apprehensive, I jumped inside and closed the door. I should have followed my first mind, because this would soon prove to be a big mistake.

She adjusted her mirrors and said, "Buckle-up…"

"Okay," I said, as I grabbed the seat-belt.

She began to back up. "What's your name?"

"It's Paul…"

She stopped and extended her hand. "Hi, Paul…I'm Angela."

I shook her hand. "Nice to meet you, Angela."

She pulled off. We'd been riding for a moment before she asked, "So how did you end-up way over here?"

"My friend dropped me off…"

"Did your friend know that you didn't know where you were?"

"I don't know what my friend knows…"

"A friend would take the time to find out…wouldn't you agree?"

I thought about it for a second before saying, "I guess…"

She turned on the radio. "What kind of music do you listen to?"

I shrugged. "I never really paid it much attention..."

"Really? A teenager who doesn't listen to music? I've never heard of that..."

I turned to look out of the window.

Trying to make conversation, she continued, "Do you like to play sports?"

"No..." I said, lying, hoping that it would shut her up.

"A big guy like you?"

"No, never played..."

"Ummmm, okay...well, what do you like to do?"

I turned towards her and said, "Look, I appreciate the ride, but I'm not going to be in your car that long...don't make sense to get to know each other..."

"My car, my rules...plus, you ain't doing shit-else, but looking out of the window. What would it hurt to talk to me? I AM giving you a ride."

"I just got some stuff on my mind."

She threw up her hand. "Okay, okay...whatever you say."

"Thanks..."

She continued to drive, but I started to notice that nothing seemed familiar. "Excuse me...where are we going?" I asked.

"I just need to make a quick stop...I hope that you don't mind...it'll only take a second."

"But I'm trying to get home..."

"I know...I know...but I need to grab something real quick. I promise, it'll only take a second."

Even though her quick detour bothered me, it was only for a second. I enjoyed the drive. Plus, it gave me an opportunity to see a lot of the city that I've never seen before – all of the stores, the beautiful homes, the green lawns – everything was just beautiful – a hell of a lot better than the world I'd come from. I didn't even know that this part of the Chicago even existed until this ride. "Don't sweat it…Angela…I did want to go to the store to get some clothes, but it can wait. Getting lost kinda spoiled that for me."

She paused and looked at me. "Oh, if I'd known that I could have taken you to the shop…"

"The shop?" I asked.

"Yes, I own a few stores…could have set you up right…gave you a discount…"

"Well, if you give me the name of the store, I will come by tomorrow…if that's okay."

"You sure? Looks like you're not good at navigating around the city…"

"I got lost…okay? No big deal…it happens to the best of us…" I said, becoming frustrated."

"The 'best of us' have cellphones that have GPS…you know what GPS is? Right?" she asked, trying to be funny, but failing miserably at it.

I took offense to her question. "Of course, I know what GPS is…just like I know what PMS is…"

She cleared her throat. "Touché…I deserved that." Suddenly, she turned into the driveway of a beautiful house that sat on the corner of the block. "I'll be right back…" She proceeded to get out, but then said, "You look thirsty…would you like to come in for a second for a drink of water or something?"

I was feeling a little 'parched', so I said, "Sure, but I should be getting home."

"Of course, of course…" she said, as she walked towards the house. For a moment, I listened to the *click-clack* sound of her heels hitting the pavement. I got out, taking a moment to look at all of the homes on the block. Angela unlocked the door and walked in. Slowly, I walked in behind her. The smell of roses greeted me at the door. I looked over at the table and saw a dozen of them sitting on the table. "Come on in and sit down…I'll be right back…make yourself comfortable." She tossed her purse on the couch and took off her shoes. She was about to leave the room when she turned and grabbed her purse. "I'm going to need this…"

I frowned. "I wasn't going to take anything from you…"

"That never crossed my mind…I just need to get something out of it…" She walked back into the other room. She was in there for a few minutes before returning with two glasses in her hands. "Here you go…"

I took the glass from her hand. She began to sip from the other one. I examined the glass, closely.

"Drink up…I don't want to keep you too long…"

I examined the glass, again, before taking a sip. It was good. "What is this?" I asked.

"A little something that I put together…just for you."
I took another sip. "It's really good…I've never had anything like this before…"
"I should hope not…" she said. She walked over and sat in a chair across from me.
"You have a beautiful home…" I said, still drinking from the glass.
"Thank you…it really isn't a lot…"
Feeling comfortable, I sat back against the couch. "Do you have any kids? A husband?"
She smiled. "No, it's just me…"
"In this big house?" For some bizarre reason, I took off my shoes.
She smiled. "How are you feeling?"
"I'm gooooooooooood." I felt relaxed.
She smiled. "Would you like another glass?"
I looked at the glass in my hand. As I stared at it, I noticed that the ice cubes were waving at me. I rubbed my eyes, because they were clearly playing tricks on me. "Do you see that?" I asked.
"What?" she said.
"The ice cubes?" I thought that I was going crazy. I looked at the glass again. "You don't see that?"
She giggled. "No, I don't see anything…"
I was tripping. Why? I wasn't sure, but I liked it. It made me feel good, better than I'd felt in a really long time. I said, "Sure…I'll have another…"
She stood, walked over, and took my glass. "I'll be right back…"

I looked around the room as I waited. This time it took her a little longer to return with the glass. She walked in and handed it to me. When she sat in the chair, she put her feet up. "So, do you have a girlfriend?"

This time, I put the glass to my mouth and drank all of its contents in one big gulp. I swallowed, hard and sat the glass down on the table. "GAD-DAMN!!! That's some good shit."

She laughed.

"Naw...I ain't got no girlfriend...the closest I've been to a girl was when one caught me jagging-off to a girl who was giving her boyfriend some head in a theater..."

She laughed. "Did you like that?"

"What? Playing with myself while somebody else was getting all of the action...naw...that was no fun."

The room was spinning.

She sat her glass down. "Soooooooooo, have you ever had sex before?"

"Unless, you count the shit that I do with my hand? No..." For a moment, there were three of her. I blinked, rapidly, trying to get it back to one.

"Would you like to?" she asked.

"Would I like to, what?" I asked.

"Have sex?"

"You're fucking with me, right?" I asked.

She stood and walked over to where I was sitting. She grabbed my hand. "Come on...I want to show you something..."

For some crazy reason, I began to cry. "But I gotta get home…"

"I'm going to take you home, but I want to show you something first…"

I wiped the tears from my eyes. "You want to show me something?"

"Yes…it's back here in the room…"

I smiled and said, "Okay…" As we walked down the hall, I noticed that images were going in and out. I was feeling dizzy. I grabbed her to keep from falling to the floor. She held me up. "We're almost there."

When we walked in, I saw a huge bed sitting in the middle of the room. "Can I lie down for a minute? I don't feel too good…"

She smiled. "Of course, you can…"

As soon as my head hit the pillow, it was lights out. I could feel her doing things to me, but I was too weak to move – too weak to fight her. When I finally woke-up, I noticed that the room was completely black. I tried sitting up, but there was something heavy lying on top of me. I tried pushing it off of me, but it began to mumble, "What are you doing?" Frightened, I jumped up tossing whoever or whatever it was onto the floor. Struggling to understand what was going on, I ran around the room until I found a light. I turned it on. When I looked down, I realized that I wasn't wearing any clothes and across from me was Angela, who wasn't wearing any clothes either. "Come back to bed," she said.

I was scrambling to find my clothes when I immediately felt dizzy. I climbed back into the bed. I felt her place some blankets over me as I fell fast asleep.

When I opened my eyes again, it was morning. I looked over to find Angela sleeping, peacefully, next to me. I tried sitting up, but it felt like I had a two-ton weight sitting on my forehead. She began to stir. She looked up at me.

"Good morning, lover…" she purred.

"What happened?" I asked, rubbing my head.

"You don't remember?" she asked.

"No…"

"You made love to me…all night long…" She sat up and began to kiss me, gently, on my neck.

I flipped around and looked at her. "Made love? We made love?"

She smiled. "Over and over and over and over…"

Scratching my head, I said, "And, where was I?"

She giggled and grabbed my crotch. "Inside of me, silly…"

I looked around the room for my clothing.

"They're in the living room, honey."

Honey? What the fuck? How long have I been here?

I stood to walk out of the room but couldn't. I sat down on the floor next to the bed. "I don't know what the hell happened, but I would remember having sex…"

She crawled over to the edge of the bed. "I'm going to remember...forever...Big Daddy..."

Big Daddy? What the hell is going on? What did I do?
She jumped out of the bed. "Let me run you some bath water and make you some breakfast."

I grabbed my head. "Sure...whatever..."

She ran into the bathroom and turned on the water. "I'm sorry, honey...I should have asked if you would like to take a shower with me..."

Frustrated, I said, "Look...I don't want to do nothing else with you...okay? Nothing..."

She giggled. "You're so silly..." She went back into the bathroom. Suddenly, the water stopped. She walked out into the room. "It's ready...let me go and make you some breakfast."

I watched her as she walked out of the room. As soon as she was gone, I began to search the room for a phone, but there wasn't one. Exhausted and still not feeling good, I walked into the bathroom – hoping that a few splashes of water to the face would wake me up from this nightmare. I walked in and was immediately sucked-in by how beautiful and clean it was. I stared at the bathtub. It was full, all the way to the top, with water. As I stood there, I found myself trying to remember the last time that I'd taken a bath. It had been so long that there were no memories of it. Seduced by it, I climbed in. The hot water felt good against my skin. I took the face towel that was sitting on the tub and dipped it into the water. Without ringing the water out of it, I placed it on my face.

When I removed it, I noticed the bar of soap sitting on the edge of the tub. I picked it up and smelled it. It smelled like flowers or at least, what I thought that flowers smelled like. I placed the bar onto the towel and began to wash myself. I was so immersed in it that I almost forgot why I was in it. Suddenly, the door opened. "Breakfast is ready."

I looked at her. She reached over and grabbed a towel. "Come on...let me help you."

I stepped out of the water and she began to dry me off. When she got to my penis, she stopped and held it in her hand. "You want some more?"

Some more of what? What the hell are you talking about? I thought to myself. "Naw...ummmmm...I think I'm good."

She smiled. "Yes, you are..." She wrapped the towel around my waist. "It's on the bed..."

I walked into the room to find a plate sitting on a tray. Remembering what happened the last time she gave me something, I said, "You know, what? I'm going to pass."

She frowned. "Are you sure?"

My stomach growled as I looked at the plate of bacon, eggs, toast, and bowl of grits. "Yeah...I'm sure."

"Okay...let me get your clothes. I will take you home, now..."

"Thanks," I said.

She went out into the hallway. When she returned, she handed me my clothes. I dropped the towel and began to put on my clothes. She removed her robe and began to get dressed. I looked at her body. For a moment, I had to admit how beautiful she was. She looked up to find me staring at her. She smiled.

After we got dressed, we left. As I sat in the car, staring at her house, I couldn't help but think how ugly it looked to me now. It was no longer beautiful, because something real ugly happened inside of it. What? I wasn't clear about, but from the way that my dick felt, it couldn't have been good.

The entire time that we were in the car, we barely said two words to each other. The only thing that I said to her was my address. When she pulled up in front of my house, she touched my hand, and placed something inside of it. Without looking at it, I placed it in my pocket. She tried talking to me, but I was out of the car before she had a chance to. When I walked into the house, I found that it was empty. I walked to my room and climbed into my bed. I stared at the ceiling, trying to remember what happened the night before, but couldn't. Before I knew it, I'd fallen back to sleep.

CHAPTER 34

I was awakened by the sound of my stomach growling. I got up and walked down the hall to the kitchen. My head was in the cabinet, when suddenly, the kitchen light came on.

"Hey grand-daddy..." I said, grabbing some bread and peanut butter.

"Where you been, boy?"

Confused, I wasn't really sure how to answer his question, so I said, "Out..."

Annoyed, he said, "I know that much, boy...but where you been?"

I sat down at the table, took a bite out of the sandwich, chewed it a little, before saying, "I was at this lady's house..."

With one eyebrow raised, he said, "What lady? And what were you doing at her house?"

I picked the bread out of my teeth before saying, "Grand-daddy...can I ask you something?"

"Sure...after you answer my question..."

"Her name was...is Angela... and I think that we were having sex..."

For a moment, it looked like he'd stopped breathing. I was getting up to check his vitals, when he said, "What did you say?"

"Her name is Angela..."

He interrupted me. "I don't give a fuck about that...what did you say after that?"

"I said 'that I think that we had sex'..."

He studied me for a moment to see if I was lying. When he realized that I wasn't, he said, "I'm going to need you to stop eating and tell me what happened..."

"But grand-daddy...I'm hungry..." I said, holding the sandwich up against my mouth.

With a serious look on his face, he said, "I wonder how you're going to eat it with no teeth...now, I need you to explain why you think that you had sex with this woman..."

"'Cause she says that we did..." I said, placing the sandwich on the table.

"What?" Growing impatient, he tries to relieve some tension by popping his neck. "Boy, I don't have the energy for this shit, so I'm going to need you to start from the beginning and do it fast."

I sighed. "I got lost...a woman offered me a ride...I ended-up at her house...we had something to drink...the next thing I know, I woke up to her laying on top of me...butt-naked."

He slapped his leg. "Gad-damnit, boy...you got you some..."

"I guess..."

"So, you're not sure?"

"I told you…she gave me something to drink. It made me woozy…"

"Sounds like she slipped you a Mickey," he said.

"A who?"

"She spiked your drink…"

For a moment, I'd lost my appetite. "Why would she do something like that?" I asked, confused.

"To get some of that booty, boy…"

"My what?"

"To fuck you, boy…keep up..."

"But why would she do something like that?"

"Shit, why ask why? You got laid, boy. I didn't think that I would see that in my lifetime. Now, I can die knowing that you ain't walking around here with blue balls."

"But if I'd did that to her it would be considered rape…"

"Was she fine?"

"She's pretty, but that don't matter, right?"

"Yes, it matters." He frowned. "It's only rape if she's ugly."

"What?"

He came next to me and slapped me in the back of my head.

My neck was stinging. "Ouch?!!! What was that for?"

"Some pretty woman picked you to have sex with and you talking about rape…pretty women ain't got to rape nobody…it's those ugly ones that'll snatch a person off of the street." He paused for a second and continued, "You know, at first, I was only worried about your brother and his dress-wearing-ass…now, you got me giving you the side-eye…"

"But she took it…that ain't right…"

"She took it…" he laughed. "You should be trying to give it away. What the hell are you saving it for?"

"My girlfriend…my wife…" I said.

He looked around the room. "First, you ain't got neither one of those." He started laughing, hysterically – almost falling out of his wheelchair. He wiped tears from his eyes. "Second, boy, you have to break that 'thang' in before you give it to girlfriend or wife…put some miles on it…it's like a pair of house-shoes…always better after it's been broken-in…"

"Not all of 'us' want to be out there like that…"

He shook his head. "What is wrong with you? Have you looked in the mirror, lately? Ain't nobody lining up to have sex with you…nobody…unless it's an invisible line of folks…" He paused, looked over my shoulder to emphasize his point, and continued, "My question is…why did she feel the need to drug you? That's the real fucking question. She could have had you without drugging you unless she had something to hide…something that she didn't want you to see…" He rubbed his chin. "How's your booty-hole? Is it sore? She didn't have an Adam's-apple, did she?"

I had to think about it for a moment. "No…"

"You gotta ask these days, 'cause motherfuckers be on some sneaky-shit…go down there looking for a peach but find a banana and two kiwis…you'll never look at fruit the same way again."

I sighed.

He rolled closer to me. "Did she kiss it?"

Confused, I asked, "Kiss what?"

"You know…" he began to drill his finger into my crotch. "Kiss…IT…"

Realizing what he was talking about, I said, "I can't remember…"

He smiled. "If she kissed it…you'll remember…"

I grabbed his hand, which was still resting in my lap, and placed it on the arm of his wheelchair.

"Look, I don't understand the problem…you didn't have to take her nowhere first…buy her anything…and she gave you some…the only time that you question a 'gift-horse' is when the gift-horse shows up and it ain't got no gifts…"

"A gift-horse?"

He frowned. "Don't make me hit you again…"

"But I don't remember any of it…"

He smiled. "Sometimes, the best piece of ass is the one you can't remember…"

"Really?"

"Yep…you know how much ass I've gotten in my lifetime?" Before I could answer, he said, "A lot…and 99.9999999999% of that shit I got while either drunk or high as a kite and I'm going to tell you a secret…ain't nothing like drunken sex with a person you barely know."

I shook my head.

"Boy, when I tell you…the shit that you can do to another human being when they are under the influence…"

"Grand-daddy, they have laws against that kind of stuff…you ever heard of 'consent?'"

"Call it what you want…back in the day, you didn't have to worry about all of this 'consent' shit…now, these women got rights…a right to say 'yes'…a right to say 'no'…what they got is a right to suck my…"

"GRAND-DADDY!!!"

"I'm just saying that the shit is out of control, if you ask me…and for the record, if they didn't want to have sex, they shouldn't put themselves in that position…they need to stay their asses at home…instead of in the streets…smelling and looking all good and shit. They're just asking for it."

I couldn't believe what he was saying. "So, you're saying that if a person doesn't want to get raped, they should lock themselves up…away from the world?"

"I'm just saying that when a man is 'thirsty', he's gone drink and he's going to do everything that he can to quench that thirst and if your ass is walking around looking like a cold glass of water…then get ready to be slurped. That's all I'm saying…"

I shook my head in disbelief, but I had to remind myself who I was talking to. My grand-daddy is from a different place and time. Most of the things that he thought, did, and said were considered ancient by today's standards, so instead of judging him, I just listened.

"And let's not ignore the obvious…you got your ass in the car. You gon' throw a tiger a steak and not expect her to eat it? Please…and who in the hell gets in a stranger's car in this day and age…other than a motherfucker who's looking to get raped?"

"But I called you first…"

"And it's a good thing that we didn't come…you would have missed out on all of that sweet booty. You have to love a woman who goes out and takes what she wants…Now, I don't know how much ass she called herself getting from a person whose only sexual experience is the one that he had with my bath towels the other day, but…"

As he spoke, I looked into my pocket for the piece of paper that she handed to me.

"What is that?" he asked.

"It looks like her phone number…"

He snatched it out of my hand. He looked at it and said, "Boy, you must have put it on her…she wants you to call her? She wants to keep in touch? Now, does that sound like a rapist to you?"

"Yes…" I confirmed.

"Do you want me to hit you again?"

"No," I said.

"A woman can't rape no man. That ain't humanly possible. They're too frail and dainty…." He shook his head in disbelief. "That don't even make sense and even if she could…what man would admit that? Huh?"

"I did…" I said.

"That's 'cause you don't have as much sense as a damn doorknob."

I ignored the insult and continued, "I just don't feel right about it..."

"Shit, I don't know why...when you were done, what did she do? Did she kick you out? Did she call you names like limp-dick, little-dick, no-dick?"

"No, she ran me a bath and made me breakfast...then, she gave me a ride home."

His eyes widened. "She offered you breakfast? Boy, she's a motherfucking 'keeper'...you don't realize that you've come up? You have won the pussy lottery. You need to put your name on the back of that ticket, cash it in, enjoy your damn winnings, and stop acting like a little bitch. You can't see that you're blessed? The only time your grandmamma is running my ass a bath full of water is if she's planning to drown my ass in it."

"Who's to say that she didn't want to kill me or something..."

"Believe me...the fact that you're sitting here talking stupid tells me that the odds are that she wants you alive..." He began to tease me. "So, she can get some more of that b-o-o-t-y...but in the future, I would be a little leery about eating and drinking shit at her house and make sure that you're wearing one of those condom things...they got some shit out there that would make your dick swivel-up and fall off..."

I didn't respond – still trying to process the things that he was saying.

"And you definitely don't want to get her pregnant...you see the misfits I got running 'round here."

"Okay..."

"And one more thing...next time, when you're done tearing that ass up...you have to slap her on the ass...REAL HARD..."

"Real hard?" I asked.

"Make her ass scream...let her know who's the boss and then say, 'Now, go and make me a peanut butter and jelly sandwich."

I frowned. "What?"

"Yessssssssss, I'm telling ya'...they love that shit."

"They do?"

"Yes, makes them feel important..."

"You do that to grandmamma?"

"HELL NAW!!! You see how big that woman is? She would beat my ass with my own damn wheelchair. Have you ever been beaten WITH a wheelchair, son? Me neither and I want to keep it that way."

"Oh, okay..."

"...and if I hear you say the word 'rape' one more time...just one more time...I swear, boy...I'm going to cut your balls off and feed 'em to the rats. Do you hear me?"

I hesitated, but said, "Yes..."

"Now, go and call that woman before she remembers how dirty your drawers were and go running in the opposite direction...so you can get you some more ass, and try to remember this time, because I want all of the juicy details."

CHAPTER 35

I spent the whole day staring at the phone number. I was so confused. Everything that I'd learn about this kind of stuff, according to my grandfather, was wrong. I'd been taught that anyone who doesn't give consent to have sex, is considered a victim, but now, I'm being told that that doesn't apply to men. According to him, Angela isn't a predator and she gave me something that every man wants and that I should feel lucky for getting it, but for some odd reason, I didn't feel that way.

But I did what I was told a man should do. I took the phone and I gave her call. She answered on the first ring.

"Hello," she sang.

For some bizarre reason, my heart began to race.

"Ummmmm, hello…" I said.

"Paul? Is that you?" she asked.

"Yes…" I said.

"I didn't think that I would hear from you again…"

"Me neither…"

There was a moment of silence. I was starting to feel like this was a mistake and that instead of calling her, I should have called the police.

She broke the silence. "I'm sorry…"

I didn't expect that. For some odd reason, I wanted to hear her say it again. "What?"

"I'm sorry," she said, again. "I don't know what came over me…"

I didn't respond. I decided to just listen.

"Paul, I can't imagine what is going through your head. I took something from you that I shouldn't have. I had no right to treat you that way…you must think that I'm a monster or something…" She hesitated for a second and said, "Paul…please speak to me…"

I took a moment to think about what she was saying. "I'm not sure what I think…" I said.

"You must know that it was never my intention to hurt you…I just needed some company…"

"If you would have told me the truth, I probably would have hung out with you…"

"But I needed something more, Paul…I was in such a bad place and then, you came along and I…and I…I…"

"You raped me…"

Quickly, her tone changed. "I what?"

"You raped me…" I confirmed.

She laughed. "That's funny…"

"What's funny?" I asked.

"That you think that I raped you…"

"But, you did," I confirmed.

She paused for a moment before saying, "Is that what you think happened?"

"You just admitted to taking something from me...were you talking about my time or were you talking about my..." I felt uncomfortable saying it. "You know..."

She giggled. "Paul...you could have left at any time...I wasn't holding you hostage..."

Angrily, I said, "But I was drugged..."

She became angry. "Really? Is that what you think? I didn't drug you...I gave you something to drink...that's all...or maybe, you gave me something to drink. It's hard to remember. Everything is such a blur."

"What?" I asked. She said it so fast that it left me confused.

"I'm just saying that maybe I could say the same thing about you...I could say that you raped me..."

"But that would be a lie..."

"Yes, no, maybe...memories are funny that way...sex turns into rape...rape turns into sex...same act...conflicting memories...you just never know... and it would be your word against mine and who do you think they would believe?"

"Me..."

"You? That's funny..." she laughed. "A big, black man versus little old me?

"You bitch..." I said.

"What did you say, boy?!" my grandfather shouted from the other room.

I covered the receiver with my hand and responded, "Nothing…" I placed the phone back against my ear. "I see what you're doing…"

"Good, and you're going to be sorry if you refuse to see me again…"

"What? Are you crazy? Why would I want to see you again?"

"Let's just say that it would be in your best interest to see me again."

All of a sudden, it all became clear to me what was going on. "My interest?"

"Yes…in your best interest."

"My best interest?"

"Your best interest," she confirmed.

This sounded like a threat and I didn't like being threatened. I sucked my teeth. "Well, since you put it that way…"

"I got a little time on my hands this evening. How about I pick you up around 8? Be waiting on the curb." *Click*

I found myself staring at the receiver. My grand-daddy came into the room.

"Soooooooooo, are you going to see her again?"

I smiled and said, "I was told that it's in my best interest."

"Well, don't do anything that I wouldn't do…matter of fact, do what I would do and then some more…"

"Oh, I plan to…"

DADDY BY DIANE MARTIN 281

At 8pm, I saw the headlights of a car coming around the corner. She pulled up in front of the house and popped the door locks. As I jumped in, I turned to look at the door to find my grand-daddy smiling and giving me a 'thumbs-up.' Ignoring him, I turned to look at the road in front of me. As she pulled off, she touched my hand. "I'm glad that you decided to see me again."

"You didn't give me much of a choice..." I said, removing her hand.

She huffed. "Think of it this way...this time, we don't have to bother with the foreplay...we can go straight to fucking."

Those words grated my ears like fingernails going across a chalkboard. Everything about her reminded me of my mother. The hatred, for her, began to build inside. I didn't like being and feeling used.

"We're going to have a good time, tonight and we're going to forget all about that rape shit..."

I didn't say anything to her. I knew what needed to be done. I just needed to think about how I was going to do it.

When we arrived at her house, I, immediately, jumped out of the car. Shocked, she said, "Slow down, sweetie…I'm going to give you what you need."

Smiling, I turned and looked at her. "That's funny, 'cause I was just thinking the exact same thing."

"Really? Ooooooooo…" she purred. "I can't wait."

"Me neither…"

We went inside. She said, "Sit down…get comfortable…I'll be right back. You want something to drink?"

I put up my hand. "Naw, I'm good…"

Happily, she ran to the back of the house. I waited, patiently, for her to return. When she came back, she was wearing a long black see-thru negligée. Immediately, I became aroused. She walked over and turned on some music and began to dance around the room. The smell of her perfume filled the air. I watched her, thinking about all of the things that I planned to do to her. She walked over and sat on my lap. "I'm so glad that we met."

I didn't respond.

She began to play with my hair. "What are you thinking about?"

I looked up at her. "You…"

"Me…" she said, as she kissed me. Her lips were so soft and warm against my mouth. I closed my eyes. She stopped and grabbed my hand. As she, gently, kissed the back of my hand, I became confused. I began to want her in a way that I'd never wanted anyone before. I surrendered to her kisses – to her touch. I grabbed her, lifted her, and carried her to the back room. There, I began to remove my clothing. Clumsily, I climbed on top of her. Forcing her legs open, I forced myself inside. Her body tightened, but then relaxed. Each stroke was met with another. Violently, she bit me on my neck and shoulders. I sat up and looked at her. "Hit me," she said. Without hesitating, I slapped her. At first, she looked shocked, but then said, "Hit me again." I held my hand up and then, slapped her as hard as I could. She grabbed her face. "Is that all you got, you little bitch?"

She was ready. I looked at her, but I no longer saw her face. Suddenly, Betty appeared. I rubbed my eyes, but she was there staring back at me.

"Fuck me," she begged.

"No…" I said. The idea that I was stroking my own mother sickened me.

She reached up and slap me. "FUCK ME!!!"

I climbed off of her and flipped her over onto her stomach. I climbed inside of her.

"Yes, yes, yes…" she said. Out of nowhere, I heard her say, "You little bitch…is that all you got?"

I grabbed her by the hair and wrapped my arm around her throat. I began to squeeze. At first, she didn't say anything. She must have thought that it was a part of the "game."

"You're the one on all fours...looks like you're the bitch," I said, taunting her.

She purred. "I like that...call me a bitch." She started barking like a dog. "Woof, woof, woof..."

I thought that this was odd, but I went along with it.

"Yes, give it to me...woof, woof...with your punk ass...woof, woof...squeeze harder...or are you scared?"

I began to squeeze tighter. "The question is, are you?" I took my other hand and grabbed her by the face. She began to struggle. "Paul...you're choking me..."

"I know...isn't that what you wanted?"

She grabbed at my arm. "Paul, I can't breathe..."

"Stop talking...I hear that it helps..."

She began to claw at my arm. "Paul, please...I can't breathe..."

My adrenaline was pumping. I stroked her, harder – pulling tighter. "It's almost over..."

Gasping for air, she said, "Paul...Paul..."

I grabbed her by her head and twisted until I heard a loud popping sound. *Pop!* Her body went limp and I fell on top of her. After several more thrusts, it was all over. I pulled out of her and came all over her back. *I guess, I don't have to worry about you getting pregnant.* I thought to myself. Then, something that my grandfather said came to me. I chuckled and slapped her on the ass and said, "Now, go and make me a peanut butter and jelly sandwich." She didn't respond, so I collapsed on top of her, closed my eyes, and fell fast asleep.

The next morning, I was awakened by the coldness of her skin. I rolled off of her to look at her. I flipped her over to see her face. With her eyes, open, she stared up at me. I pushed her hair from her face. I looked down at her body - cold and rigid, her nipples were still hard. I ran my fingers over them. I placed one into my mouth. That was the first time that I'd tasted one. I ran my tongue over it – trying to get used to its texture. I began to, gently, nibbled at it to see what would happen. I was always told that there was milk in them, but hers didn't have any. No matter how hard I sucked and pulled at them, nothing happened. Then, I ran my hands down her stomach to the big bush of hair that sat between her legs. I began to run my fingers through the hair. This aroused me. I noticed that I was becoming "hard" again. I looked at her and thought, "She wouldn't mind…" I climbed on top of her, and tried pulling at her legs, but they wouldn't give. I didn't know what to do with the growing "problem" between my legs. I looked up at her face and noticed that her mouth was still open. I, hesitated, for a moment, but then climbed up onto her chest. "I promise that this won't take long…" I began to rub the head of my penis, back and forth, across her mouth. I climbed inside. Her teeth were pulling at my skin, but something about that turned me on even more. I grabbed her by the head, and stroked until, I came. I collapsed on top of her head. When I was able to catch my bearings, I stood up, stretched, and walked over to the bathroom. I could see her reflection in the mirror. She looked so peaceful. I smiled, knowing that I gave her that. I stood over the toilet to relieve myself. When I was done, I turned on the water in the tub, filled it with hot water, and went to retrieve her body. Once in the tub, I washed her and afterwards, I dried her skin and placed her back into her bed. I drew her blankets over her.

Still naked, I walked down the hall to the kitchen to see what she had to eat. I looked inside to find some bacon and some eggs. I turned on the stove to cook them when, immediately, there was a knock on the door. At first, I wondered what I should do, but then, suddenly, I didn't care. If it was meant for me to get caught then so be it, but I was lucky that it didn't come to that, because the person at the door would soon end-up just like her.

When I walked into the living room, I looked through the peep-hole to find a woman standing at the door. Still naked, I opened it. Shocked, she examined me and smiled. "Ummmmm, I was looking for Angela, but I can see that she's busy."

I smiled.

"Ummmmmm, could you tell her that I stopped by?" she asked.

"And you are?"

Looking at my penis, she extended her hand. "I'm Stacey."

I realized that I couldn't let Stacey go, but I couldn't snatch her off of the porch without making a scene, so like waving a carrot in a rabbit's face, I began to rub myself. I said, "Stacey, Angela is sleeping. She had a really long night. I'm making breakfast. Would you like some?"

She smiled and sucked her teeth. "I would...if you don't mind."

"Of course, not..." I stepped out of the door so that she could enter.

She inhaled. "Smells like you're burning something..."

I smiled and said, "Why don't you come in the kitchen and help me put the fire out." She giggled and smiled as I closed the door behind her.

CHAPTER 36

Feverishly, I began to pack. I had no idea where I was going, but I knew that I needed to get out of there. Everything I owned was able to fit inside of a plastic grocery bag. I was headed towards the door when I heard him say, "What are you doing?"

I stopped and turned to look at him. "I gotta get out of here, grand-daddy."

"Where are you going?" he asked.

"I don't know…I just need to get away…"

He nodded his head. "I can understand that…"

"You can?"

"Yeah…but before you go, come in here and talk to me for a second."

I looked back at the door. "But grand-daddy, I really need to go."

"It'll only take a second," he said, as he rolled himself into the kitchen.

With freedom only a few steps away, I turned and followed him into the kitchen.

"Sit down," he instructed.

I huffed as I pulled a chair away from the table.

Squinting his eyes, he said, "Soooooooooooo, where are you going?"

Impatiently, I said, "Grand-daddy, I don't have time for this…"

"Really? Why don't you have time?"

Annoyed, I said, "Come on, grand-daddy…" I stood to leave the room.

"If you don't sit your ass down…" he insisted.

"But I really have to go…"

"I know…you said that, but why? You don't like living here?"

I frowned. "Really, grand-daddy…?"

"I know that it ain't the Taj Mahal, but it's been your home…"

Frustrated, I finally said, "I JUST NEED TO FUCKING GO!!!!"

He cleared his throat. "I'm going to give you a minute to fix that, 'cause I don't want to have to come out of this chair and fix it for you…you understand?"

Pissed, I said, "I shouldn't have to explain myself to you. If I want to go then, I should be able to leave…SHIT!!!"

He moved out of the way. "Then, take your Black-ass on…ain't nothing between you and that door, but air and opportunity…and my gun…if you keep talking shit."

I looked at the door. "I don't mean to be disrespectful, but…but…"

"But what?" he asked.

I knew that I'd done some bad things and if the 'heat' came looking for me, I didn't want my grandparents to get swept-up in my shit.

"Look, boy…you gon' have to tell somebody what's going on…me, the police, God…somebody…and you're better off talking to me 'cause I won't send you to jail or send you to hell."

"You won't?" I looked at him. I knew that if anyone would understand, it would be him and once I opened my mouth, the flood-gates were open. Everything from the death of my mother to Angela and Stacey came pouring out of me. As I spoke, the look on his face went from anger to fear. After I was done, he just stared at me.

"Say something, grand-daddy…" I begged.

For several minutes, his eyes bounced back and forth between me and the door. He finally spoke. "So, you killed your mama?"

"Yes…but I didn't mean to. She just wouldn't leave me alone." I felt terrible. Not because I'd killed her and regretted it, because the bitch really needed to die, but I hated disappointing him.

For a while, he didn't say anything. He just looked at me.

"Grand-daddy?"

He, finally, spoke. "That's fucked up…"

That's fucked up? I didn't expect that response.

"That is REALLY fucked up…"

Trying to explain myself, I began, "She took my money and spent it on drugs and…"

He put his finger up. "Stop…give me a minute to process this…" He paused to think about it and then, said, "I get it."

Confused, I said, "You do?"

"As hard as it is for me to say it...I do..." he said. "Not saying that what you did was right, boy...but I can't say that it was wrong either."

Relieved, I said, "I thought that you would be mad at me..."

"I am," he confirmed. "But I understand..." He paused for a second and continued, "She wasn't my baby, anymore. My baby died a lonnnnnnnnng time ago. All you did was take something that we've known for a long time...and make it official." He sighed and continued, "...and a man can only be pushed so far...I probably would have done the same in your situation. She wasn't a nice person. She treated you kids like shit and she took everything from me and your grandmamma. Everything, but the clothes on our backs. While I wished she would have woke-up and got her shit together...the odds weren't working in our favor. She was an 'old' crackhead... been in the shit for too long...It's hard to convince those types to change."

"But she was my mama..."

"Did that cross your mind when you were killing her?"

"No, it didn't..."

"There you have it...she was your enemy. You didn't love her and she damn sure didn't love you."

"It's just that she made me so mad..."

"And you been carrying around that anger since the moment you were born and you have every reason to.

You were angry in the womb...used to kick the shit out of her all of the time, and it served her right, 'cause she used to hit you..."

"Huh?"

"Yep, she used to beat you while you were in the womb. I used to catch her...beating on her stomach – trying to punish you for the shit she did, but you got her ass back and every time she screamed, I used to tell her that that's what she gets...smoking that shit while you were in her belly. It's a wonder that you came out at all..."

I listened, carefully. The more he spoke, the more I hated her. I didn't think that it was possible to hate her more, but I did.

"Sadly, she was your mama...and we can't choose our mamas no more than we can choose our kids." He sighed. "Shit, I wish that we could return fucked-up kids like we can return defective toys. That motherfucker would have been back at the baby-store so fast it would have made the cashier's head spin around and fall off her shoulders."

"I am sorry, grand-daddy..."

"Don't be sorry. You did what you felt that you had to do. The Lord giveth, but you 'tooketh' her away."

"You gon' tell grandma?"

"Naw, it's better that she thinks that the child just hooked-up with some man..."

I paused for a second to think about Angela. Something about the look on my face made him say, "I wouldn't worry about it, boy. If they come knocking, then we'll worry about it. Until then, can you try not to kill anybody else…okay? Can you promise me that?"

I said, "Yes", but I couldn't promise him that. Having that power, right at my fingertips, was an amazing feeling and there were too many people left in the world. I had a lot of life left, and there were too many opportunities for people to piss me the fuck off.

CHAPTER 37

Because he asked me, I didn't go outside for several weeks. It was hard being "locked-up" because that meant that I had to be stuck in the house with him, all day, every day and like I've said before, my grand-daddy is not normal. When I was a kid, I never knew how bad it was, because I had school and bullies preoccupying most of my time, but now, that I was home more, I had a chance to see how bad it was, first-hand, and it was bad, really bad.

I was in my bedroom when I heard someone say, "Attention!!!"
Initially, I didn't move. At first, I thought that it was the TV, but then, I heard a loud popping sound. I sat up and waited. I knew that it wasn't the Fourth of July, so it wasn't firecrackers that I heard, but then, I heard it again. This time the sound was closer, because it came through the door and shattered my bedroom window. I, immediately, fell to the floor and laid there until my door opened up. I looked up to find my grandmother crawling in on all fours. She closed and locked the door behind her.
"Grandmamma, what is going on?"
"Shhhhhhhhhh," she said. "He'll find us."

"Who?" I asked, thinking that it was the police who was finally here to lock me up.

"It's your grand-daddy..." she said, trying to lay as close to the floor as she could.

Pop! Pop! Pop! Pop!

"What is he doing?" I asked.

"He's shooting the enemy..."

Confused, I said, "Who?"

"The enemy...he's shooting the enemy..."

"Rats?" I asked.

"No, the Nazis..."

"The who?"

"He didn't take his medicine this morning..." she said.

All of a sudden, we heard him coming down the hall. When he got to my door, he began to turn the knob. "I know that you're in there, you sneaky bastards...I'm going to kill all of you...if it's the last thing I do...YOU HEAR ME?!!!!!!"

She grabbed me and held me close. When he realized that he couldn't get into the room, he stopped turning the knob. We waited for a second, listening closely to the silence. My grandma looked up at the cracked window. "Look, go out there...see if you can find some help."

As I stood to climb out of the window, I turned to her and said, "Grandma, come with me."

She looked at the window. "I can't get my big ass through that little-bitty window. No, you go...I'm going to try and calm him down." My grandmother stood to walk towards the door. "Grandma, nooooooooo!!!" I said, before I heard it. *Pop! Pop! Pop! Pop!* I saw the bullets coming through the door and into the room. I watched as pieces of wood hit the floor, but then, I looked up and noticed that my grandmother had a weird look on her face. Suddenly, I heard a clicking sound. *Click! Click! Click!* My grandmother grabbed her chest and fell onto the floor. "GRANDMA!!!!"

I ran to her side. She grabbed my arm. "Go help your grand-daddy..."

"But grandmamma..." I said.

"GO! DAMNIT!!!" she demanded. "I will be okay."

Carefully, I opened the door. He was in the hallway, reloading, when I tackled him, throwing him onto the floor.

"BLOOD!!" he shouted. "BLOOD!!! Everywhere... there's BLOOD!!!Do you see it? Do you see it?"

I snatched the gun out of his hand. He looked over to where my grandmother was lying and said, "I got one...take that, you bastard."

I dragged him into their bedroom and placed him on the bed.

"You can't let them get me," he begged. "Please, don't let them get me."

I began to search the dresser for his medication. There were several different bottles sitting on top. I began to read the labels, but was unable to figure out what treated what, so I started grabbing them and pouring the pills into my hand. I walked over to the bed. "Come on, grand-daddy...you have to take this." "But they will get me..." "No, I promise...I will protect you," I said, placing the pills into his mouth. He swallowed. "Let me go and get you some water." I ran to the kitchen and grabbed a glass. After filling it, I ran back down the hall. He took a couple of sips and closed his eyes. I ran out closing the door behind me.

When I returned to my room, I noticed that she was staring at the ceiling. I called out to her, "Grandma", but there was no response. My heart sank into my chest. I called her again. "Grandma..." but she never stopped staring at the ceiling. I fell to my knees, crawled over, and sat next to her. I grabbed her hand. It fell limp into my lap. I became confused. I didn't know what to do. I began to feel anger, sadness, and loneliness all at once. I felt so alone. I was going to call 911, but for what? She was gone and I knew that if I called them, they would take her away from me and I wasn't ready to let her go. I wasn't ready to say "Goodbye." "Grandma..." I whimpered, as I placed my head on her chest. I laid down next to her and wrapped my arms around her. "Grandma..." I said, as I stared out of the cracked window.

For a while after that, I waited for her. It never crossed my mind that I wouldn't see her again and that she was gone forever. I kept expecting for her to walk through the door, kept expecting her to walk into the kitchen and make me some syrup sandwiches, but that moment never came. Then, I thought about him and I began to hate him for taking her away from me. I never thought that I could feel that way about him, but I did. He'd killed my mama, my real mama, and I wanted him to share the same fate.

CHAPTER 38

"Mama, don't leave me...please don't leave me!!!" My aunt Jasmine screamed before passing out.

Only the family attended her funeral. My grandmother didn't have any friends. Her life was spent taking care of her family and sadly, it would be her family who would kill her. It was sad seeing her laying in that box. She didn't look the same. Her skin was no longer bronze, brushed with golden highlights, but an ashy-brown color from all of the makeup that they'd slapped on her face. Her eyes were glued shut and her mouth was covered in bright pink lipstick. She had on her good wig and good dress and they crossed her hands over it – holding her favorite handkerchief.

Everyone in the room was crying except for me and my grandfather. I'm not sure what he was feeling or what he was going through, but I didn't care. He was a grown-ass man who'd killed his wife...that's it. And I didn't cry for my grandmamma because I knew that she was, finally, at peace and away from his crazy-ass. I've heard people say that about their deceased loved-ones, about them being at peace, but

I never really understood it until I saw her lying in that casket. For the first time, she looked like she didn't have a care in the world – that all of the bullshit had, finally, ended. Plus, I knew what happened, so I couldn't cry, because I was too busy being pissed. To think that the only reason why she was laying in that pine box was because he refused to take a few tiny little pills – something so simple. Even though I loved him, I felt like he was more deserving of that box than her.

My grandmother was a good woman who stayed in a relationship where she gave more than she received. She gave birth to and raised a bunch of children who didn't do anything but let her down. The one bright light in her life was her grandchildren and the government took most of them away from her. Then, to top it all off, she gets shot by the man that she'd sacrificed her whole life for – trying to protect her grandson, once again, from the people who were supposed to protect him. She probably left this earth feeling like a failure. I wish that I could have told her that she wasn't, because if it wasn't for her, I would be the one in the box and I wouldn't be sitting here trying to find reasons not to hate the man who killed her. He looked over at me. Emotionless, I turned and looked away.

Impatiently, I waited for it all to be over. After they closed the lid to her coffin, they rolled her out of the church, and into the back of a car. We all followed it to the place where she would sleep eternally. As they lowered her into the ground, I looked at him. Finally, he began to cry. "Louise…I'm so sorry, Louise…" I wanted to run over and push him and his wheelchair into the hole with her, but then, I reminded myself that she was, finally, free. She didn't need his ass following-up behind her.

When we arrived home, I, quickly, noticed that it was quiet. Soon, the entire family came in and sat in the living room. They began to share memories of her. Looking at their fake-asses, pretending like they cared about her made me sick to my stomach. I kept wondering, "Where were you when she needed you?" Frustrated, I walked out of the room and went to my bedroom. Shortly after, my door opened up. My grandfather entered the room. You could tell that he didn't know what to say, so he just sat there in silence. I turned my back to him and fell fast asleep.

The next day, I awakened to him still sitting in the chair next to my bed. I stood and walked passed him. He grabbed my arm. "Can we talk?"
I looked over at the stain on the floor and said, "No…" and walked out of the room. He followed me down the hall. Before I knew it, I turned and shouted, "You should be dead…not her! Why don't you do us all a favor and kill yourself?" As the words flew passed my lips, I, immediately, regretted it, but once

it was said, there was no taking it back. I'd just crossed the line and just wished death on the only man who loved me enough to take care of me. The only man who was there for me.

He looked at me and then, turned to leave the room. We didn't speak again, for a long time, after that. We did everything to avoid each other. Most of the time, I would find him, lying in their bed; staring at photos of her. Through the night, you could hear him crying and calling out for her. "Louise...Louise..." After a while, he stopped taking care of himself. He didn't bathe, he stopped eating, and he stopped taking his medication. He was nothing without her. This house was nothing without her.

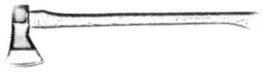

Finally, one day, I got up to leave the house. I walked passed their bedroom to find him sitting his uniform out on the bed. I paused for a moment, when I heard him say, "It's time for me to surrender..."
I knew what this meant. I wanted to turn back and stop him, but instead, I proceeded down the hall,

when I got to the door, I whispered, "Goodbye, grand-daddy."

When I returned home, things were eerily dark and quiet. I didn't call out to him. I'm not sure why, but something inside of me told me that he wouldn't answer. As I approached their bedroom door, I could see the shadow of him sitting in his chair in the middle of the room. I walked passed him to turn on the light. I closed my eyes and when I opened them, I found him, clothed in his uniform. His medals caught the light in the room. In one hand, he held their wedding photo and in the other was his gun. My eyes slowly came to the hole on the right side of his head. For a moment, I stared at him. I walked over to take his gun from him when I noticed that his hand wasn't cold. He was still warm. The one thing that I remembered when my grandmother died was that her body turned cold. Confused, I said, "Grand-daddy? Grand-daddy?" All of a sudden, his eyes rolled around in his head before we found ourselves looking at each other.

He grabbed my hand. Gurgling, he said, "Help me…please, help me."
Panicking, I said, "What do you want me to do?"
He placed my hand on his gun. He led my hand to the middle of his forehead. My hands began to shake. He closed his eyes and whispered, "It's simple…just… pull…the…" *Pop!* I closed my eyes and when I opened them, he was gone. What was left of his head fell backwards, his arm fell limp into his lap, as blood dripped onto the photo in his hand.

The room filled with the smell of blood and gun powder. I sat down on the bed next to him. Still holding the gun, I looked around the room. Their whole life was in that room. They had so little – a bed, a dresser, a couple pair of shoes, and a few pieces of clothing. I stood and placed the gun on the bed. I was about to walk out of the room when I stopped to look in their closet. One of my grandmother's dresses still hung there. I held it in my hands, placed it against my face, and inhaled deeply. It wreaked of Bengay and Oil of Olay. As I placed the dress back into the closet, I noticed a small box on the floor against the wall. Carefully, I removed the box. I sat down on the floor and opened it. Inside, there were several envelopes with all of our names and dates on it. I opened one of the envelopes that had my sister's name on it. I opened it to find a barrette in it. I closed it and opened another one. It had my mother's name on it. I opened it to find two small teeth. I continued to go through the envelopes until I found the one with my name on it. I opened it. There was a lock of hair inside. I smiled and placed the piece of hair back inside. I closed the box and was putting it back in the closet, when I felt something taped to the bottom of it. I held it up to look at it. There was another envelope. I ripped it from the box and opened it. There were several hundred-dollar bills tucked inside of it. I closed the envelope and placed it in my pocket. I stood to leave the room and looked back, before closing the door behind me.

CHAPTER 39

At first things were quiet. I would wake up to nothing, but the sound of my own breathing. At times, I would marvel in the sound of me inhaling and exhaling, and it not being interrupted by the sound of someone screaming. But after a while, that sound was interrupted by the sound of footprints running across the walls and floors. I tried to find the source of the noise, but it would lead me to their bedroom door. I didn't want to go back in there, but I knew that I had to. As I approached it, I placed my ear against the door and listened. The sound of chewing and scratching was almost deafening. I tried covering my ears, but the sound seeped from underneath it. I couldn't ignore it anymore.

Carefully, I placed my hand on the knob and began to turn it. I was, immediately, met with the smell of death. The smell was so overwhelming that I was knocked off of my feet. I slammed the door, sat on the floor next to it, and waited until I was able to catch my breath. As I sat there, roaches crawled from under the door and climbed onto my fingers. I shook them off and ran down the hall to retrieve my shoes. I looked around for the bug spray, but when I found it,

I noticed that the can was empty. I looked around until I found the broom. I walked back to the room and slowly, opened the door. I slid my hand in and turned on the light switch. I could hear them "crunching" underneath my finger-tips as I smashed some of them. I wiped their guts from my hands on my shirt and walked in. I, quickly, covered my nose and mouth to block the smell. The wallpaper came alive and began to move and scatter all over the place. As I surveyed the room, I could feel the rats running across my feet – fighting and trying to get to something. I kicked them to avoid being bitten by them, but it was too many of them. They were hungry and grand-daddy was their dinner.

I ran out of the room and slammed the door. As I stood in the hall, I shook my shirt to remove the roaches who tried escaping from the room. I was smashing them with the broom when the phone rang. I turned to look at it. It rang again. I walked over to it, took a deep breath, before saying, "Hello."
"Hey, Baby-boy…" she said.
Realizing who it was, I said, "Hi, Auntie Jasmine…"
She huffed. "I liked the way that your mama showed-up at the funeral…"
Confused, I said, "Huh?"
"Huh, exactly…" she huffed again. "The bitch couldn't even come to her own mama's funeral…as much as that woman has done for her."
I didn't respond.

"She better not let me see her ass. I'mma beat her ass with that crack-pipe."

I remained silent.

"Anyway, I was calling to check on your grand-daddy. I know that he's probably having a hard time…you know…dealing with mama's death…I just wanted to check on him. How's he doing?"

I looked down the hall and said, "He's…ummm…not feeling too good."

"Really, is he taking his medicine?" she asked.

"Ummmmm, yes…" I said, lying.

Concerned, she asked, "What's wrong?"

I didn't want to lie to her, but I couldn't tell her the truth, so I said, "He's got a headache…"

"Probably from all of the crying…he's not taking things too good, huh?"

"Ummmmm, you can say that…"

"Well, let me talk to him…"

Caught off guard by her request, I said, "I can't…"

"Why not?" she asked.

I thought about it for a second and said, "'Cause he's sleeping…dead asleep."

Satisfied with my explanation, she said, "I bet…well, let him get his rest. I'm sure that he needs it."

"Yep…"

"Well, let him know that I called."

"I will…" I hung up the phone and yelled down the hall, "Auntie Jasmine called…" and walked into the kitchen to make myself something to eat.

The smell of death filled the whole house. I realized that I couldn't ignore this situation any longer and I knew that I wouldn't be able to keep them away. At some point, they were going to come and check on him and when they did, somebody was going to have to answer for this and it wasn't going to be me. So, I had to take care of it – the way that I'd learn to take care of everything else.

So, I waited for a few hours, thinking about how I was going to do it. When I figured out how I was going to accomplish my goal, I walked into his bedroom and I grabbed his gun. I grabbed some ammunition off of the bed and loaded it. I walked out of the room and down the hall to the phone. First, I called my uncle. "Hello," he said.

"Hey Unc...how are you?"

"I'm good...what's up?" he asked.

I paused for a moment and said, "Grand-daddy asked me to call you..."

"Really? Why? What's going on?" he asked, nervously.

I looked down the hall at the door. "He's not feeling too good…he wants you to come and check on him."

Concerned, he asked, "Well, why didn't he call me himself?"

"Ummmmmm, something's wrong with his hands…"

Frightened, he said, "Something's wrong with his hands? What the hell is wrong with his hands?"

"Ummmmmm, he can't move them…"

"Why the hell can't he move his hands?"

"I don't know…I ain't no doctor…"

"Okay…okay…tell him that I'm on my way…dial 911…it might be something serious."

Lying, I said, "Okay, I will…" and then, hung up the phone.

I dialed Aunt Jasmine's number and said the same thing.

"The hell? How long has he been like that?" she asked.

"For a few days…"

"For a few days?" She sighed. "The old man is going to be the death of me…"

"I was just thinking the same thing…" I said.

"Well…tell him that I'm on my way."

"Sure, I'll tell him." I put the phone back on its base and walked into the living room to wait for them.

When they walked in, panicking, they both said, "Where is he?"

I placed the gun behind my back and said, "He's in his room."

They ran down the hall and opened his door. My auntie screamed and ran out of the room. "Oh my, God…oh my, God!!!"

My uncle ran into the room. "What is that? Is that daddy?"

"What's left of him…" I said.

"What is going on here? Why didn't you call us?" he asked.

"I just did…" I walked into the room and Aunt Jasmine followed behind me.

"Paul…what the fuck happened to him? Did you do this?" he asked.

I closed the door behind me and pointed the gun at them. "He killed himself."

My aunt began to gag. "There's nothing left of him."

"He left his gun…" I said.

My uncle looked-up. "Boy, what the hell are you doing?"

"Putting an end to all of this…"

Frightened, he said, "And end to what?"

"To this…it's all over," I said.

My auntie put her hands up. "Please, Paul…don't do this…we can figure this out."

I looked around the room. Roaches were everywhere. Rats ran across our feet. I lowered the gun to look down. My uncle came towards me. I pointed the gun at his face and said, "Feels like home…doesn't it?"

He stepped back. "Paul…"

I thought about my life and said, "Funerals shouldn't be the only time that families come together… wouldn't you agree?"

Neither of them answered.

"Unc, remember when you told me to wait…that things would get better? I did…but it never got better…instead, this is what I got." I pointed at grand-daddy.

Aunt Jasmine began to plead with me. "Paul, let's work this out…in the living room…or somewhere else…" She looked around the room – jumping and trying her best to dodge the rats and roaches that, at this moment, were swarming around the room.

"But this is our home." I paused and shook my head. "Don't y'all miss it?" Then, I became angry. "YOU LEFT US IN THIS RAT-HOLE!!! WHERE THE FUCK WERE YOU?!!"

They couldn't answer.

"Can you hear them? I've been listening to this shit my whole entire life." I said. "I'm tired of listening to it."

"I know, man, but we can fix this…"

I pointed at grand-daddy. "Can you fix that?"

"I'm sure we can…" he said. "Now, come on…put the gun down."

"I can't, Unc. I can't live like this anymore."

"Then, all you have to do is leave…we will take care of this…" he said.

"I could, but you are a part of this…you are as much a part of those rats and roaches as I am."

"But it wasn't my responsibility…you have a mama," Aunt Jasmine said.

"Had…" I said.

"Had?" she asked.

"Yeah…she's dead too."

"She's dead?"

"Now, HER, I did kill," I confessed.

Shocked, they looked at each other.

"I want you to see this as me taking care of you like you took care of me." I cocked the gun. Her eyes widened and before she could say anything else, I pulled the trigger. *Bang!* Her body fell back into the dresser and onto the floor. My uncle screamed, "No!" Then, I turned and shot him. *Bang!* His body hit the floor, but he wasn't dead. He cried out. "Paul…Paul…don't do this…please, I have a family."

I walked up to him and said, "I'm your fucking family…" I walked out of the room and closed the door.

"PAUL…NO!!!!"

I walked to my bedroom and gathered some clothing. I threw the things into a bag and walked down the hall to the kitchen. I fixed myself something to eat. I could still hear him screaming, but I ignored him. When I was done, I grabbed some things from the refrigerator and placed them into a bag. I was on my way out of the kitchen when I saw it. I turned the gas on the stove and left the room. As I walked towards the front door, I heard the bedroom door open. "PAUL!!!"

I looked back and said, "Goodbye, Unc…"

I stood outside and stared at it. As the roaches crawled across the porch and across the lawn, I looked at it for the last time, before striking a match and setting it on fire. "PAUL!!!! PAUL!!!!" I heard him scream.

I walked out onto the sidewalk, walked down the street, and into the darkness.

CHAPTER 40

For the first time in my life, I had nowhere to go. I wandered around the streets for a while until I found myself back in the park. In the middle of the night, things looked different. Things were quiet and very peaceful. It was the perfect setting for someone who'd just killed members of his family. I grabbed a seat on the park's bench to contemplate my next move. While I'd thought about everything else, I hadn't thought about this, but I was already feeling better – already happier, because it was gone and I was free.

I didn't have any "life" skills. They didn't teach me how to survive in school. What I knew about the world came from a book and that wasn't much. I was never taught to be a good person or what it was like to have a good life. All I knew was pain and I felt and watched so much of it. Now, all I wanted was to be happy and if I had to spend a lifetime on a park bench to achieve that, then I was prepared to do it. As I thought about all of this, I saw something crawling out of one of my bags. I let it crawl onto my fingers. I stared at it as its antennas brushed against my fingers. I allowed it to crawl into the palm of my hand

and then I closed it; squeezing, until I felt its body collapse under my fingertips. When I opened my hand, I saw that it was dead. I rubbed his remains on the bottom of the bench and then, laid down to take a nap. I was staring at the stars when, suddenly, my eyes grew heavy. I closed them, but was, immediately, awakened by the sound of gunshots coming from across the street. I looked up to find a shadowy figure running across the park. Curious, I jumped up, grabbed my stuff, and ran behind him.

We dashed across the park, behind bushes, down the alley, and behind a storefront where the shadow disappeared. I was winded. I stopped to catch my breath when I felt something cold being pressed against my back. I dropped my bag and placed my hands in the air. "I don't have anything that's valuable, but you can have everything in my bag."
"Walk…" the voice said.
"Look, I don't want any trouble…"
"Then, don't make me give you any…" the voice said.
"Okay," I said. "Where are we going?"
There was silence.
We continued to walk until we were standing in the moon's light. He lowered his gun. "Paul?" he asked.
"Jeffrey?" I said.
He looked around, nervously. "Let's go…"
"Go? Go where? And what are you doing?"
"Shhhhhhh…follow me…"

I did as I was told. Quietly, we walked until we were standing in front of his car. "Get in…"

I didn't ask any questions. I jumped in. As we pulled off, he leaned over and threw the gun into the glove compartment. We'd driven a few blocks, when he asked, "How much did you see?"

"See? I didn't see anything…"

He stopped the car and pulled over to the side of the road. He drilled his finger into my chest. "You better not be lying to me…"

I pushed his hand out of my chest. "I'm not…"

He leaned into my face.

"Why do you think I'm lying?" I asked.

"Cause niggas lie faster than a cat can lick his ass…"

I tried to imagine a cat licking his ass. Then, I quickly, tried erasing the image from my mind. "What?"

"I'm just saying that niggas know how to lie…"

Sigh. "Well, I'm not lying and for the record, what is it that I'm not supposed to be seeing?"

He looked into his rearview mirror and pulled off. "Don't worry about it. Worry if I find out that your ass is lying to me."

"Dude, I don't need this shit. You can pull over and let me out."

"You ain't going nowhere…"

"What?" I said, becoming angry. "Man, the fuck is wrong with you?"

"Nothing…now, get comfortable before shit gets uncomfortable."

Frustrated, I said, "Man, let me out."

He pulled over to the side of an overpass. He grabbed his gun from the glove compartment and jumped out of the car. He came around to the passenger's door and with his eyes bulging out of his head, he said, "The only way that you're getting out is over this damn bridge. Now, get out…"

Unafraid, I jumped out.

We walked over to the rail. "Jump!!!"

I began to lift my leg over the rail when he said, "Boy, what the fuck is wrong with you? Get your ass back in the car."

I lowered my leg and looked at him.

"Were you really going to jump?"

"Were you, really, going to shoot me if I didn't?"

He looked at me. He'd just been 'bluffed' and lost. "Let's go…" When we got in, he looked at me and said, "I expected you to shit your pants…"

I turned to him and said, "You can't scare a man who ain't got shit to lose…"

"You ain't got shit to lose, Paul?"

"Not a motherfucking thing…"

"Well, damn, who shit in your oatmeal this morning?"

"I just ain't in the mood for games and the next time that you pull a gun on me, be ready to use it."

"Look at you…acting all hard…"

I didn't respond.

"Well, that shit made me hungry. You want to go and get something to eat?"

I turned to face the window.

DADDY BY DIANE MARTIN 319

He pulled into a drive-thru. "Ummmmmm, can I get a number 7 with mayo and onions and…" he punched me in the arm. "Your ass better order something… you know that you're hungry."

I remained silent.

He looked out of the window and said, "Can I get another number 7 with a side of big-ass tits?"

The voice in the speaker asked, "With what?"

"Never-mind," he said. "Just give me two number sevens."

"That'll be $14.97…"

He said, "Okay…" and drove around to the window. He removed some cash from his ashtray and handed it to the girl in the window. She handed him the bags and some change. He was about to pull off when he stopped and said, "Hey…what are you doing later?"

The girl looked at him and smiled. "Who me?"

Jeffrey asked her, again. "Yeah…what are you doing later?"

She said, "Nothing…"

He sat back in his seat and pointed at me. "My boy needs some company…"

I refused to look at the girl who was leaning into the car to look at me.

She looked back at Jeffrey and said, "Fuck you and slammed the window. He began to remove the food from the bag and said, "I tried to get you some pussy to go with your fries, but ol' girl wasn't interested." He pulled off; eating as he drove down the street. We drove around until we were in front of his house. "Get out," he instructed.

I got out and was headed down the street when he said, "Get in here…you know that you don't want to go home."

I turned and walked back towards his house. Once inside, he turned on the lights. He washed his hands and then, walked upstairs. When he returned, he had a blanket and some pillows. "Your 'hard' ass can sleep on the couch." He turned to walk out of the room. "We will talk in the morning."

I waited for him to fall asleep before I stood and began to search the house. When, I came upon his bedroom, I crept inside. He was sleeping peacefully. As I stood over him, I noticed that he had his gun in his hand. I was about to turn and walk out of the room, when he said, "If I were you, I would try, and get some sleep."

CHAPTER 41

But I didn't sleep at all that night. So much had happened the night before. It was hard to process everything. Bits and pieces of the night flashed before my eyes. My thoughts were racing all over the place. Immediately, they were interrupted by the sound of a toilet flushing. He walked into the room wearing nothing but a pair of boxers with his gun stuffed inside of them. "Good morning, beautiful," he said, scratching himself. "You want some coffee?"

Frowning, I stood and followed him into the kitchen. "Look who woke-up on the wrong side of the couch…"

I didn't respond.

"You want some eggs? I could sure use some eggs." He removed the carton and sat it on the counter. "Scrambled or over-easy…"

"Scrambled," I said.

He smiled and continued, "Why were you in the park? Looking to get hooked-up?"

I thought about what'd happened and said, "I needed a place to sleep."

"What happened to your house?" he asked, as he cooked the eggs.

"It burned down…"

"Damn, did anybody get hurt?"

"I don't feel like talking about it…"

"Okay…okay…I understand. Probably was real traumatic for you…"

"No, it wasn't…" I said, smiling.

He placed the eggs on a plate and handed it to me.

"Well, I'm sorry to hear about your house…" He paused for a second and then continued, "And about the bridge…You know that I was just playing, right?"

"I'm too old for games…you are too."

He poured a cup of coffee and walked it over to the table. "Man, when I saw you put your leg up there, I thought to myself, 'Either this motherfucker is bad as hell or crazy as hell…'…I couldn't believe that you were going to do it."

"Why? Because you thought that I was some punk-bitch…"

"No…" He interrupted me. "Look, I don't know why I did that shit. I'd just finished taking care of some foul shit…then, I got caught by you. You could have been the police. I was pissed at you for catching me when I should have been pissed at myself for being caught…"

"And tossing my ass off of a bridge was the best solution for your mistake?"

"You're right? I would have killed an innocent man…"

I took a sip of the coffee and said, "Oh, I wasn't planning on dying."

He squinted his eyes and watched me eat the eggs. "So, what does that mean?"

"It means what it means…" I could feel the tension growing in the room.

We were staring at each other.

He laughed. "You think that you're going to win a staring contest…with me, nigga? Don't you know you can't win a staring contest with no nigga?"

I kept staring.

Realizing that he couldn't intimidate me, he smiled, and looked away.

I guess I win, motherfucker. I thought to myself.

To calm things down, he asked, "So, where are you going?"

"Back to the park…I guess…"

"Well, you can stay here…if you want to." he offered.

I thought about it for a second and said, "And how will I pay you?"

He pulled his gun out of his boxers and placed it on the counter. "I'm sure that we will figure something out."

CHAPTER 42

I needed to clear my head. I asked him to take me to the theater so that I could catch a movie to take my mind off of things.

"Look, I'll be back in three hours. Have your ass right here...don't make me look for you."

"Sure...whatever," I said.

"You need some money?" he asked.

"Sure, dad...can I get some money?" I asked, sarcastically.

He frowned and shoved a twenty in my hand. "I want my change too..."

"Whatever..." I slammed the door behind me. I walked up to the ticket booth and purchased a ticket for whatever was playing and walked inside. I walked down the hall and entered the theater. I'd just sat down when the movie ended. *"The fuck?"* I thought to myself. I stood to exit with everyone else. Once in the lobby, I asked to see the manager. She walked out from behind the concession counter and said, "If it isn't Mr. Hand Job."

Damn. "Look, I purchased a ticket for a movie and it just ended..."

"So?" she said.

"So, I didn't get to see the movie..."

"So?"

"Sooooooo, I want my money back or a ticket to another movie."

"Why? It wasn't long enough for you to finish your business?"

The employees standing next to her began to laugh.

Embarrassed and frustrated, I said, "All I'm trying to do is watch a movie…"

"That's what your mouth says, but your hands say something else…"

They laughed louder.

She continued to tease me. "We don't sell lubricant, but then again…there's always the butter that's left on your hands from the popcorn or maybe some melted chocolate from the candy..." My advice…whichever you choose…make sure to get extra napkins."

Pissed, I said, "Look bitch…"

She twisted her mouth and rolled-up her sleeves; preparing for a fight. "Excuse me?"

"All I want to do is watch a fucking movie…now, you gon' give me my money or what?"

She looked over at one of the employees and signaled for them to give her the phone. "How about I get the police to give you your money?"

Not wanting to see the police, I said, "Fuck you, bitch…keep the damn money." I turned and walked out of the theater. Once outside, I decided to walk across the street to grab some lunch. After ordering my food, I sat at a table and began to eat. When I finished, I walked over to throw out the garbage when I saw her leave the theater. I waited and followed her down the street. I followed her for several blocks until I saw her go inside of a church. I looked around before following her inside. She walked inside of a back room. She was in there for a few minutes before I saw her exit the room. I watched her as she exited the building. I followed her for another block. She walked up a driveway to the back door where she removed her key from her pocket and opened it. She walked inside. I waited a few minutes before walking up the driveway to the back door. I tried the knob. Slowly, I began to turn it. It opened, and I walked inside. I looked around before proceeding down the hall. On the floor, was a trail of clothes that led to the bathroom door. I placed my ear against the door. I could hear the water running. Before going inside, I searched the rest of the house to make sure that we were alone.

I walked back down the hall to the bathroom and began to turn the knob, gently. Once inside, through the steam, I could see the silhouette of her body. Quietly, I watched her. She hummed as she washed herself. When she was done, the humming stopped, and she turned off the water. I crept out into the hall, stood behind a door, and watched her. She stepped out of the shower, grabbed a towel, and began to dry herself. She looked over at the door that was, slightly, open. "Is somebody there?" she asked. She began to walk towards me. "Is somebody there?" I ran down the hall, into a room, and waited behind the door. When there was no response, she turned and walked to a room down the hall. I waited before following her into the room. When I entered, she screamed and fell onto the floor. "Aaaaaaaghhhhh!!!"

"Remember me?" I asked. Slowly, I walked towards her. Kicking and screaming, she begged me to leave, but I couldn't. She owed me something and I was there to get it back. I grabbed and tossed her onto the bed. She cried, "What are you doing here?"

I sat next to her on the bed.

"You took something from me today…"

"What are you talking about? A refund? Is this about the refund?"

I shook my head, "No…this is about more than that…"

"What then? What do you want?"

"You thought that it was funny making fun of me in front of those people…"

"What people?"

"The other employees…" I confirmed, as I remembered their laughter.

She sat up and moved to the back of the bed. "I was just kidding…"

I looked down at my hands. I was wringing them so hard that they began to burn. "Yeah, y'all thought that shit was funny…"

"I'm sorry…look, let's go back to the theater. I will get you another ticket and some free popcorn…a nice cold pop…and some candy. Would you like that?"
I looked back at her. "It's too late for that…"
"I'm sorry," she cried. "I'm sorry…"
"I know…most people usually are at this point, but sadly, that's when it's too late."
I stood and started to get undressed.
"Are you going to rape me?" she asked.
Disgusted, I shook my head. "You think too much of yourself…I'm just trying not to get blood on my clothes."

When he pulled up, I was sitting on the curb. He pushed the door open. Once inside, I closed the door, and pulled the seatbelt across my chest.
"How was the movie?" he asked.
Locking myself in, I said, "It was pretty good…kinda gory, but I like gory."
"Well, I'm glad that you liked it."
"Yeah, me too…"

"I might have to come and check it out…when I got a minute."

"Okay…but spoiler alert…the bitch dies in the end."

CHAPTER 43

"Yeah, that's what I said, motherfucker. You bring your ass over here trying to defend that hoe? I should bust a cap in your ass for being stupid…bringing that shit to my house…you better carry your ass home before you end-up in a body bag!"

I turned the volume down on the TV to hear what was going on.

Jeffrey continued, "Bitch-ass, Nigga…who the fuck does that shit? Find out your girl is doing another nigga and you come over here trying to fight somebody. If anything, you should be whooping that bitch's ass! I didn't violate your trust…she did."

I stood and walked into the kitchen and looked out the back door. Jeffrey was arguing with someone in the driveway.

"You better stay away from my woman…" the man at the end of the driveway said.

"Tell that bitch to stay her ass away from here…I don't have to go looking for that ass…she delivers in 30 minutes or it's free…"

"Man, fuck you…" the other man said.

"Fuck you…sorry-ass, nigga. Shit…she wouldn't have to creep if you were fucking her right…"

"How you know what the fuck I'm doing?"

"I may not know what you're doing, but I do know what you ain't doing and that is satisfying your woman. It's niggas like you that keep niggas like me on speed-dial…"

The man walked towards his car. "Don't let me come back over here."

Jeffrey pulled his gun out. "Anytime motherfucker. I be looking for people to shoot."

The man was pulling off, when Jeffrey yelled, "And when you kiss that hoe again…inhale hard motherfucker…that's the smell of my balls on her upper-lip."

I started laughing. "Who was that?"

"Some punk-ass motherfucker thought that he was gon' come over here and tell me not to fuck his woman…NIGGA, PLEASE…'bout to call that hoe right now…get my dick sucked. You want your dick sucked too?"

I thought about it for a second, but then said, "Naw, man…I'm good…I don't want your crumbs."

"Shit, put enough crumbs together and you got your ass a whole loaf…" He shrugged and walked into the house. "Don't say that I didn't ask you. The girl got skills…make your ass bilingual. I ain't lying…I went to sleep one night after she got a hold of my shit…woke-up, the next day, speaking Spanish… Chúpame la polla, otra vez…sucked the Ebonics right out of my ass." He grabbed his crotch.

Something about the way that he said that made me not want to know what it meant. "Sounds tempting, but I'mma pass…"

"You are a fool. I don't pass-up no pussy. Shit, if I got to wrap my shit up in aluminum foil to tap that ass, I'm tapping…it'll hurt for a few days, but think of the memories and the street-cred you'll get when niggas find out that you fucked a girl wearing aluminum foil on your shit. Talk about being gangster…" He picked up his phone and started dialing some numbers. She answered, immediately. I couldn't hear what she said, but he said, "Your man just left…"

She said something, and he responded, "I was gon' kill his ass, but it's too early in the damn morning to be killing niggas. Now, if he would have come over here around noon, he'd be one dead motherfucker."

She said something and then, he said, "What cha' wearing?"

I'm not sure what she said, but he started to touch himself. "Yeah? Is she wet? Why don't you bring that over here…let me see how wet she is?" She said something, and he laughed, "You should put a 'Caution - Slippery when wet' sign on that ass…with your sexy ass." She said something, again and then, his smile disappeared, "Okay, but you better do something about ol' boy…it'll be noon soon…that's all that I'm saying…" He smiled and said, "Alright…see you later." He hung up the phone and licked his lips. "That bitch right there is gon' get somebody killed."

I sat down at the table and said, "Why would you mess with somebody like that?"

"Like what?"

"All that damn drama...is it worth it?"

He sucked his teeth. "Probably not, but it don't matter...I'm only fucking her to get close to his ass."

Confused, I asked, "What?"

"You don't have to look for motherfuckers who come looking for you...he owes my boy some money. He's been hard to catch-up with until I started fucking with his girl. Now, I got him looking for me."

"Ummmmm, okay...but why didn't you kill him while he was in the driveway?"

"Because it's before noon...too many nosey motherfuckers walking the streets...gotta let them get tired and take their asses to bed...the nighttime...my friend...is the right time."

I laughed.

"You see...there's three things that niggas get killed over...money, drugs, and ass. That nigga is gon' get killed 'cause he owe some MONEY for some DRUGS that he didn't pay for and that 'ASS' is gon' lead him to the grave. That's all three...a triple play."

"You should have done it while you had the opportunity..."

He shook his head. "Look, what fun would that have been? I run out, shoot him, and then, it's over." He pulled a knife from the drawer. "No, I like to catch a nigga off-guard…while he's sitting on the toilet or while he's sleeping or better yet, catch his ass right in the middle of a down-stroke." He jammed the knife into the counter and continued, "Stick this blade into his back and gut his ass like a fish…"

I hung on to his every word. I was drawn-in, excited by what he had to say. He pulled the knife out of the counter and said, "Let's go to the park…I need to do my good deed for the day…gotta keep the kids busy or they'll get into all kinds of shit."

"Like you?"

"What do you mean, 'like you?'"

"I mean…do you think that you should be working with kids?"

He frowned. "What? I don't look like a good role model?"

I thought about it for a second. "Hell naw…"

"And why? Cause I kill people?"

"YES!!!! Cause you kill people…" I confirmed.

"This coming from somebody who claims that he kills people too…"

"I ain't trying to be nobody's role model…"

"Me neither, but you have to admit that it's a damn good cover, ain't it?"

I didn't respond.

"Judges hesitate to lockup a man who volunteers to spend time what kids that society doesn't want to be bothered with…"

I sighed.

"Don't give me that look…somebody is better than nobody…some of those kids don't know what a decent man looks like. Mamas probably got twelve different men coming in and out of their lives. By the time they learn one nigga's name, he's gon' and now, they got to learn another one…Then, I walk in and I give them something to do…keep them encourage…"

"So, that they don't grow up to be like you?" I interrupted.

"Damn right…shit, I ain't ashamed. I know that I'm messed up. If I had a man in my life that handed me a ball instead of a gun, I might have turned out different…"

"Who handed you the gun?"

"My fucked-up ass, daddy…that's who…" he confirmed.

The irony wasn't lost on me. I thought that it was funny that we both became the people that we are because some man put a gun in our hands.

He grabbed his keys. "It can make or break you…"

"What?" I asked.

"The absence of a good man in your life…"

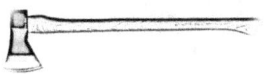

After a few games of twenty-one, we decided to ride around for a while before calling it a night. We didn't say much to each other, at first, but then, out of the blue, he asked, "Soooooooo…who have you killed?" I turned to look at him, but didn't respond.

"I'm just saying…if you've killed someone, maybe I know them…might be a relative…"

Looking out of the window, I responded, "I doubt if you know them…"

"I'm just saying…you killed all of these people…I would just like to know who they are…"

"I SAID that you don't know them…" He was starting to get on my nerves.

There was a moment of silence, then, he laughed. "You know…I think that you were just bullshitting…hyping yourself up…trying to impress a brotha…"

"And why would I need to do that?"

"I don't know…"

The car fell silent, again. We pulled around the corner and parked in front of a house. He turned off the engine and the lights.

"Who lives here?" I asked.

He placed his hands against my lips and said, "Shhhhhhh…"

I pushed his hand. "The fuck, man? Don't put your hands on my mouth…I don't know where your fingers been…"

I was wiping my mouth when, slowly, a car pulled up into a driveway. A man exited the vehicle. Jeffrey leaned over and opened the glove compartment. Something 'shiny' caught the beam coming from the streetlight. He popped the clip, checked to make sure that there was ammo in it, and then, handed it to me.

"I want you to pop that nigga…"

I looked at the gun and then, at the man standing in the driveway. "What? Why?"

"Cause, I told you to…"

"I'm not going to kill that man…" I insisted.

"Why not?"

"Cause, I don't know him, and he's never done anything to me."

"He's never done anything to you…okay…well, what if I told you that he likes to rape little boys?"

Shocked, I said, "No way…"

"Yes…that nigga, right there, rapes little boys."

"Then, why isn't he in jail?"

"Because the wheels of justice all got holes in 'em and it's up to us to fix them."

"So, you want me to just run-up and kill him?"

"Yep…cause he's a fucking ass-thief…a taker of young souls…a wolf among sheep…a cancer on our society…he needs to be put down like all of the other dogs who don't know how to behave themselves…"

Hesitating, I asked, "But why me?"

"Why not you? Who's going to save the children, Paul? WE have to save the children, Paul…you and I…"

"But YOU ain't doing shit, but talking…you want me to kill him…" I looked out into the street.

Tears began to fill his eyes. "What if he did that to your little brother?"

He'd just struck a nerve. My thoughts went back to the man who took my little brother. I popped the lock and walked across the street – holding the gun out in front of me. The man saw me coming and started to run. I chased him into the backyard. With nowhere to go, he threw up his hands.

"Please…take my wallet…take my watch…" He reached into his pockets and continued, "Here, here, take the keys to my car."

His mouth was moving, but I couldn't hear him. I was so full of blind-rage that I couldn't think. I couldn't wrap my mind around the idea of a grown man raping children – let alone, one of my brothers. I pointed the gun and *Pop!* He looked confused, at first, but when his mind realized what was happening to him, he dropped to his knees. I aimed again and said, "This is for all of the little boys." *Pop!*

DADDY BY DIANE MARTIN 339

Not to draw any attention to myself, I walked instead of running back to the car. Just then, the side door, of the house, opened. A little girl was standing in the door. "Daddy...daddy? Have you seen my daddy?"

I paused to look at her, but then continued to the car. Jeffrey was frantic. Standing in the street, he yelled, "Nigga, what did you just do?"

"I killed him like you asked..." We both jumped into the car. I handed him the gun.

"No fucking way..." He looked around for a second and said, "I gotta see this shit..."

"Ain't you worried about the police?" He didn't bother answering. Before I knew it, he was out of the car and across the street. He disappeared into the darkness, but, quickly, returned with a strange look on his face. He jumped in and turned on the ignition. Without looking at me, he said, "I can't believe that you did that shit."

"You told me to kill him and I killed him...remember, the 'Who's going to save the children' speech?"

"I do, but I thought that it would take a little more convincing than a nigga's word of mouth..."

"I can't stand that sick shit...fucking pedophiles."

"I see..." he said, interrupting me.

"Now, he won't be raping no kids no more..."

Jeffrey stopped the car. He put it in park – right in the middle of the street. He started laughing. "Dude, I lied..." he said, through his laughter.

"What?"

"I lied..." he confessed.

"You lied about what?"

"That guy...I...I lied on him..."

"What do you mean that you lied on him?"

"I mean that I don't know that man. I don't know who he's fucking, how he's fucking them, or when he's fucking him...he was just some random nigga that I thought that I could test you with...to see if you're as hard as you say you are...I didn't think that you would actually do it..."

"You put a gun in my hand...tell me that he's a creep and you think that I wouldn't kill him?"

"To be honest...yes..."

"Why would you do that dumb shit?"

"I'm telling you, dude...I didn't think that you would do it. Shit, if you can do that to a motherfucker you don't know...who ain't never did shit to you? I hate to see what you would do to somebody who crosses you...that motherfucker ain't got a fighting chance."

Panicking, I said, "I killed an innocent man?"

"Who says that he's innocent?"

"What?"

"Who says that he's innocent? We are all guilty of something...because he ain't behind bars don't mean that nigga ain't did some shit...it just means he ain't got caught...yet..."

"Yet? The motherfucker is dead...because of me..."

"Yep..." he said, nonchalantly.

"I don't kill innocent people. I kill people who deserve it..."

He frowned. "Really? So, all of the people that you CLAIM that you killed...they all deserved to die?"

I thought about it for a second and said, "Yeah..."

He shook his head. "You said that shit like you gave them a gift...like they all said, 'thank you' for killing me...I ain't never had somebody thank me for taking their life. I mean, what do you say after you put a bullet in a motherfucker? You're welcome? You can keep the bullet? What?"

Ignoring his ranting, I placed my head in my hands. "I killed that little girl's daddy for nothing..."

"Look, if it makes you feel any better...the grave is full of motherfuckers who used to be daddies..."

"But this is wrong, Jeffrey..."

"Right...wrong...it's all relative...and look, I appreciate it...one thing, I can say...that was some gangster shit...straight out of the movies. You jumped out of this car like Denzel. That's some sexy shit...if I was a girl, I would be trying to fuck you right now..."

"What? Man, you are sick..."

"I'm practical...realistic...maybe, even a little insensitive...maybe...but sick? That hurts..."

He sighed and grabbed my shoulder. "He was going to die, one day...whether he was innocent or not...or deserving or not...you just pushed his date up a little bit...cancelled some of his plans..."

In the distance, we could hear some sirens. "We better get out of here before we get caught-up..." He started the car and pulled off.

342

I looked back down the street to the house. In the front yard, I could see the little girl holding her mother's hand. She turned and looked towards us. I will never forget her voice as she called out for her daddy. "Daddy...daddy..." Her sweet little voice.

CHAPTER 44

The next morning, I was thinking about all of the things that I'd experienced over the years and my thoughts kept drifting back to the one man who truly loved and cared for me. I realized that I never mourned for him. It felt weird when I realized that I never took the time to cry. And as I thought about his face, and the pain he must have felt, I couldn't find a reason to feel any sympathy for him. Even in the end, as the rats tore at what was left of him, I didn't see him as human, or as my grandfather. Everything that he'd done to help me, to save me, meant absolutely nothing. He was reduced to a mound of flesh that was left rotting in a wheelchair.

I was thinking of my grandmother when I heard Jeffrey say, "I need you to make a run with me."
Snapping out of my thoughts, I said, "Where are we going?"
"I got work to do and you need to earn your keep..."
"Can I just stay here?" I wasn't in the mood for Jeffrey and his shit. I just needed a moment to process everything.

"You could…but I better not see your ass in that refrigerator…"

Suddenly, a memory of my childhood flashed before my eyes. "So, if I don't go, I can't eat?"

"That's not what I'm saying…what I'm saying is, we have to pay for food and the way to pay for food is through work…no work, no food…Now, I'm going to work, so I get to eat. The motherfucker who lay on the couch all day, and does nothing, gets to watch me eat…you see what I'm saying? It's simple math. 0+0 equals hungry than a motherfucker."

I exhaled and jumped up. "Okay, let's do this."

He smiled and wrapped his arm around my shoulder. "That's the spirit and I promise…you won't have to shoot anybody."

I removed his arm. "Good…cause, I'm not in the mood."

"Oh, ain't that cute. Bet your ass will be in the mood for those steaks that I got in that refrigerator."

"Steaks? Wow…I've never had one of those…what is it like?"

"What's it like?" He opened the car and unlocked the doors. "You ever eat pussy?"

I jumped in and locked the door. "Ummmmmm, no…"

"Then, it's kinda hard to explain…but a perfectly cooked steak kinda reminds me of that…"

"That's a weird comparison…I've never eaten pussy, and I don't know if I would want something on my plate that would remind me of that."

He laughed. "That's 'cause you ain't had it yet. It's delicious…unless you run across some jump-back…"

"Jump-back?" I asked, curiously.

"Yeah…it's some pussy out there that smells so bad that it makes you jump-back…smell like spoiled sardines." He pulled out of the driveway and said, "Make your damn eyes water and, unfortunately, sometimes, you don't find out until you got a nose full of that shit, that you realize that you've gotten hold of a bad one."

"Why not get her checked-out first?" I thought that that was a good question, but the look on his face said that it wasn't.

"Dude, ain't no fun in that…if you stopped to ask every chick about the quality of her pussy and what's going on with it before you stick your thing in it, you'll never get none…I can't imagine getting hot and heavy with some chick…dick all hard, balls all full…and I stop and say, 'When was the last time you had a tune-up?'…and it'll be cool if she says, 'Recently' but what if the answer is 'Never'…now, I'm stuck with a hard dick and some blue balls…I'll have to kill her for the principal of it…and who got time for that?" He started laughing. "Man, please…"

"I don't see anything wrong with that…" I said.

"And that's why you ain't getting none…while you're asking questions, she's giving that ass to the one who ain't."

"I got a weird question for you…" I said.

"What 'cha got?" he asked.

"So, you eat pussy, right?" I asked.

He laughed before answering. "Hell yeah…love that shit."

"Do you eat pork?"

He frowned. "Hell no, that shit will kill you."

"Eating, both, pork and pussy will kill ya'."

"Yeah, but if you die from eating pork, you just one dead motherfucker, but if you die from eating pussy, you gon' die with a smile on your face."

I was about to comment, but I heard a knocking sound coming from under the car. "Hey man, I think you got a flat…"

Listening closely, he said, "Oh…let me turn up the radio…"

Confused, I said, "Turning up the radio ain't gon' fix a flat…"

"Oh, it ain't a flat…" he said.

The thumping sound got louder, so to drown out the sound, he turned the radio up, louder. He drove several miles until we found ourselves near the forest preserve. When he parked the car, I said, "Let me look at the tires…"

"No need…" he said.

We both got out and walked around to the back of the trunk. I thought that we were getting a spare, but when he popped the trunk there was something laying on top of it. It was kicking and trying to get out of the trunk. Without looking at him, I said, "Jeffrey, what is this?"

We both stared into the trunk at the bound body laying inside. "This is Carl...Carl, say 'Hi' to Paul..." The person mumbled something that sounded like "Help me."

"Jeffrey, why is Carl in the trunk of your car?" I asked.

"Carl, doesn't like to pay his bills, so Carl needs to be taught a lesson..."

"You know, Jeffrey...I remember when my grandparents didn't pay their bills. Sometimes, the lights got turned off. Sometimes, they turned the water off. Not once, did they end-up in somebody's trunk," I said.

"But I bet you, if the light company and water company started killing folks who didn't pay their bills, bills would start getting paid...shit, they wouldn't even have to send out reminders. Folks would break their necks to pay their bills."

"Killing? I thought that we weren't killing anybody."

"Nooooooooo, I said that we weren't going to SHOOT anybody..." He pulled a knife from his back pocket. "The person who hired me wants this nice and slow."

Frustrated, I said, "Can I get back in the car?"

"No, I'm going to need you to help me drag Carl into the woods..."

I looked around. "Well, come on...do what you got to do, so that we can go home."

"Okay, okay...but you can't rush things like this..."

Now, pissed, I said, "WILL YOU HURRY THE FUCK UP?!!!"

He shrugged. "Well, Carl...I'm going to have to kill you fast...Paul's in a hurry...we don't want him to miss his cartoons."

I sighed. "I thought you said that you don't kill people in the daytime."

"Carl is the exception...not the rule."

Carl's eyes widened. He began to mumble.

Holding the handle of the knife, tightly, he pulled Carl's body out of the car and threw him on the ground. He began to plunge the knife into Carl. He did this several times before Carl stopped moving. He wiped the knife on Carl's pants and said, "Get his feet..."

I tried not to look at Carl's face, but it was hard not to. Curiosity, led my eyes to the bloody mess that was now his face. Jeffrey caught me staring at him. "Let's go..."

I grabbed his feet while Jeffrey grabbed his arms and we carried him out into the woods. His body grew heavier as we walked. After walking for about fifteen minutes, he looked around and said, "This is a good spot."

I dropped his legs. When they hit the ground, I noticed that one of them moved. I kicked his leg and it moved again. "I don't think he's dead."

Jeffrey looked down. "Why you say that?"

I kicked him, again. "His leg moved."

Jeffrey kicked him. "His leg didn't move..."

I kicked him, again. "His leg moved."

"His leg didn't move," he said, kicking him again.

Annoyed, I said, "His fucking leg moved…"

He handed me the knife. "Okay…then, you finish him…"

"Duuuuuuuuudddddde, I'm not here for that shit. I already helped you carry him."

"If you don't kill that motherfucker, I'm going to kill you."

I frowned. "You gon' kill me…shit, you couldn't even kill him right…Does that make any sense?"

He thought about it for a second, "Yeah, it makes sense…"

"How does it make sense? YOU kill a person who ain't even dead…then, you threaten to kill me…am I supposed to be scared? Man, if that's the case, then kill me…shit…the odds say, I'm going to be good…"

He frowned and kneeled down over Carl. He placed the blade against his throat and slid it from ear to ear. Blood flowed out onto the ground. "I bet he's dead now…"

"Are you sure, Jeffrey? It'll be a shame to do all of that and then we find his ass limping down King Drive looking for a place that'll sell him a spicy two-piece with a side of mashed potatoes…"

He stabbed him twenty more times – until he was bleeding from head to toe. "Are you happy, now?"

I huffed. "I was happy before we got into the car…now, you just gave me some more shit to think about."

"Is that what you were doing?" He wiped his blade on some leaves. "Thinking about this shit?"

"Well, not THIS particular shit, but shit, nonetheless…"

"Dude, I told you…don't let this stuff bother you. Motherfuckers starving on the other side of the world…now, that's some shit to bother you."

I looked down at the lifeless body. "Should we bury him?"

"What the fuck for?" he asked.

"'Cause…that would be the human thing to do…"

"The human thang to do…was not to kill his ass, but we've already missed that boat…anyway, I didn't bring a shovel and unless you plan on digging one with your hands or teeth…"

"Ain't nobody doing that dumbshit…"

"Well, then, shut the fuck up…"

Agitated, I said, "Man, make that your first and last time telling me to shut the fuck up…"

"And what you gon' do?"

I looked at him for a second, thinking about all of the things that I could and would do to him and said, "We better go get in the car." We started back towards the car.

He grabbed my shoulder. "You know what we need? We need to relax…"

"What you got in mind?" I asked.

"Women…alcohol…weed…"

"Naw, I'm good man…"

"Dude, ain't nothing wrong with letting your hair down after a long day's work…"

"But I don't drink…don't smoke…and don't know any women…"

He laughed. "I know a lot of them." He opened the door and jumped in. "…A woman can help take your mind off of this shit…plus, weed and alcohol costs money…I ain't trying to spend any when pussy is free."

"It is? Now, why would I want something that some woman is giving away for free?"

"Air is free and you ain't got no problem taking that shit. Now, do you? Plus, you can't live without it…try holding your breath and see what happens…same applies to pussy…it's free and no man can live without it…now, just like there's bad pussy, there's bad air… pollution…avoid that shit."

"Like the 'jump-back…'" I said, remembering what he'd said about it.

"Yeah, we don't want no jump-back."

CHAPTER 45

He woke-up the next morning singing gospel songs. "Jesus is on the main line...tell him what you want...oh, Jesus is on the main line...tell him what you want...well, Jesus is on the main line...tell him what you want...ohhhhhh, call him up and tell him what you want..."

"You're in a good mood this morning..." I said.

He began to slide across the floor. Still singing, he said, "Call him..." Then, he stopped and looked at me.

He was staring so hard that I asked, "What?"

He said it again. "Call him..." Then, he stopped to look at me, again.

Again, I asked, "What?"

He grabbed a spoon from the drawer and sang into it. "Call him..." Then, he stuck the spoon in my face.

"Call him?" I asked.

He smiled and began to dance around the room. "YES...you better call him..." he sang.

"What's going on Jeffrey?" I asked.

"I'm trying to get in the spirit..." he said.

"For what?"

"We're going to church today..."

"Shit, I ain't going to no damn church…"

"Oh, yes you are…"

"No, I'm not…"

"Oh yes, you, fucking, are…"

I stood and walked out of the room. "Man, fuck that…I ain't never been to church and I ain't gon' start now…"

He followed me into the other room and said, "Church is good for the soul…plus, I got some repenting to do…"

I laughed so hard that I almost pissed on myself. "You what?"

"I gotta repent…"

I waved at him and said, "Get out of here with that bullshit…you want to repent like I want to get shot in the head."

He frowned. "Hey, I'm serious…"

"Yeah, right…"

He started laughing. "You right, nigga…I'm just playing with you. I'm going to get us some hoes…"

"There's hoes in the church?"

"Shiiiiiittttttt, that's the best place to find them. You don't go looking for hoes on the street. Those are the nasty ones…if you want a nice, clean one…you go to church…it's like picking vegetables…would you eat one that you found on the street? Nope, you go to the store to get them, 'cause you know that they'll be nice, fresh, and clean."

"What if I don't like vegetables?" I asked, knowing that it would get on his nerves.

"You better learn to like them, 'cause, like hoes, they keep a nigga nice and strong."

"I ain't never heard of that..."

"You learning a lot of new shit... and you have to think about it...they been in the club all night...working up a sweat...bumping and grinding on some nigga...getting all wet...they go home...ass dreaming about the dick that got away...then, they go to church...shit, the Lord might be able to save their souls, but only the devil can put that fire out between their legs...and that devil is me, nigga."

"And why do you think that they want you?"

"Shit, why wouldn't they? And you got to remember...they can't touch the pastor 'cause his wife and his twelve mistresses ain't gon' have that shit...the deacons are old as fuck...most of them got one foot in the grave and they can't get with the choir director, cause his ass is probably gay...and then, I walk in...looking like the end piece of bread that's left in the bag...they don't want it, but they ain't gon' let it go to waste." He began to strut around the room. "They see my ass and want to sop me up with some gravy..."

"Interesting..."

"Damn straight it's interesting..."

"But I ain't feeling it..."

"You ain't got to feel it...just go in, pick one out, smile, and when she smiles back...you go in for the kill..."

"That's all it takes?"

"That's all it takes…" he confirmed.

"Can you just bring me one back?" I asked.

"Man, I ain't going to the store to buy some damn fruit…I'm trying to help you get laid…I don't know what you want…"

I sat down on the couch and placed my feet on the table. "I'm not going to church…that God-shit is for folks who need it…I don't need it…and I ain't pretending just so I can get some ass…"

"Then, suit yourself…don't be trying to get none of mine…"

"I won't…"

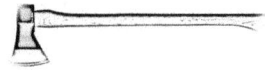

A few hours later, he returned empty-handed. "Where's those desperate church girls you were talking about earlier?"

"The fish weren't biting…but you know a nigga got a Plan B…"

"And what's your Plan B…"

He picked up his phone and started dialing. "Hey, what 'cha doing?" He waited for a response and then, said, "You know that I miss you, baby…" He waited, again and then, said, "Can I see you?" He paused and said, "Okay, I'll be waiting for you...bring somebody with you for my friend." He hung up the phone and said, "I missed that bitch like I miss the 'clap'...but she'll do in a drought."

"Then, why did you lie to her?"

"Cause, that's what Niggas do..."

"What are you? The gad-damn nigga-whisperer?"

"Why you say that?" he asked.

"You always talking about what niggas do and don't do, like you've taken a class on the shit...a class on Nigga-ology...not all niggas act like you..."

"I'm a nigga...born and raised...I've spent my whole life doing nothing, but nigga-shit...so I think I know a nigga when I see one..."

"Well, first, let's clear some shit up...I'm not an expert because you're the only nigga that I know, but what I can say is...there's no two people alike...even niggas."

"So, I'm the only nigga you know..."

"Yep...the only one..."

"Shiitttttt...in every human being there's an undercurrent of nigga...in all of us...just waiting to get out."

Sigh...

"And, unfortunately, there's no cure...a lot of us end-up dying from it...it's called, 'nigga-shit.'"

"That's tragic as hell..."

"Tragic indeed, but it's niggas that make the world go 'round...without us, there wouldn't be anybody left to talk to…but you of course…with your non-nigga ass…" He paused when he heard the doorbell ring. He smiled and yelled, "Pussy's here!!!!" He walked over and opened the door. "Hey sexy…get your ass in here…"

She giggled and walked in. "Hey baby…"

He kissed her and said, "And who's this?"

She looked over in my direction and said, "This in my girl, Janet."

Janet smiled and whistled, "Hi…" Three of her front teeth were missing.

Jeffrey grabbed his girl's hand and proceeded down the hall. "I'm going to leave y'all alone to get to know each other."

I mouthed, "Don't leave me in here with her…"

He ignored me and continued down the hall. Uncomfortable, I said, "You…ummmmm…want something to drink?"

She whistled, "No…I'm good." Spit flew out of her mouth and landed onto the table.

I stepped back to avoid the spray. Trying to figure out what I was going to do with her, I said, "You want to watch TV?"

"Sure," she whistled.

We walked into the living room and sat down. It was only seconds later that we could hear Jeffrey and his girl having sex.

Janet smiled. "They sound like they're having fun…"

I turned on the TV and turned the volume up. She was yelling over the sound. "So, what's your name?"

"Paul," I said, trying to avoid looking at her.

"I like that…your name…it sounds strong…are you strong, Paul?" she asked, spitting in my face from the chair that she was sitting in.

I wiped my face. She was getting on my nerves. "Could you move back a little?"

"Why?" she asked.

Frustrated, I just asked her, "Where the fuck are your teeth?"

She covered her mouth with her hand. "Oh, that…"

"Yeah, that…" I confirmed.

"Well…" she hesitated. "I used to be on that stuff…"

"What stuff?"

Embarrassed, she said, "You know…that stuff…"

"No, I don't know because I don't do that 'stuff'…unless you're talking about toothpaste. Do you know what toothpaste is, Janet?"

She giggled. "No…I'm talking 'bout meth…"

I frowned. "How you get a hold of that shit?"

"My old boyfriend did it…and you know how it is…'when in Rome'…" she spat.

"Naw, I don't know…"

"Well, missing my teeth ain't a bad thing…guys like it…" She slid her tongue back and forth through the hole in her smile.

"How many guys are we talking about?" Suddenly, I began to feel sick to my stomach. I wanted to punch her in the face for making me feel that way.

She waved her hand. "None now…" she smiled.

I turned away to keep from throwing up all over the place. We were watching TV when she decided to come over and sit next to me. She placed her hand on my leg. I looked down at it. It felt like a hundred-pound weight was sitting in my lap. "You want to have fun, Paul?"

I removed her hand. "You don't want to watch TV?"

"TV is so boring...let's do what they're doing..."

"Who? The people on TV?"

"You know who I'm talking about," she purred.

"But you don't even know me," I said, becoming disgusted with her. Something about her seemed so dirty and nasty. I didn't want her next to me.

She began to "walk" her fingers across my chest. "You can tell me all about yourself while you're hitting it from the back."

Gagging.

"Come on, Paul...let's go and have some fun."

I grabbed her hand and began to squeeze it, hard.

"Don't touch me..." I said. The image of my mother flashed before my eyes.

She looked at her hand. "Paul, you're hurting me..."

"So..."

"But it hurts..."

Squinting, I said, "But you said that you want to have fun...let's have some fun."

Her eyes widened. "Paul...you're hurting me..."

"Bitches like you want a man to hurt you...that's why you brought your ass over here...you were ready to give yourself to a complete, fucking, stranger...so,

I'm going to let you have it." I grabbed the remote and turned the volume up. She began to scream. "HELP!!!! HELP!!!!"

Jeffrey yelled down the hall, "That's my boy…tear that ass up."

"No, please, help me!!!" she begged.

I twisted her arm around her back and pulled it up until her fingers were touching the back of her head. She screamed louder. "HELP!!!!"

I pulled her onto the floor and stuffed her face into the seat cushions on the couch and sat on the back of her head. She struggled for several minutes until, finally, she stopped moving. I picked her up, dragged her outside, and placed her inside of the gate. For a moment, there was nothing. Then, the dog ran over and began to sniff her. As if he understood what he needed to do with her, he began to bite at her. I walked back into the house and sat down to watch the TV. Jeffrey walked down the hall wearing nothing but a towel. "What happened to old girl?"

I smiled and said, "She couldn't handle it, so I sent her home."

Jeffrey walked over and gave me a "high-five". "That's what I'm talking about, nigga…" He strutted back down the hall. I laid across the cushion with the imprint of her face in it and fell fast asleep.

The next morning, I got up before Jeffrey. I went into the backyard to see what was left of Janet. Slowly, I opened the gate. I looked around to find pieces of her scattered across the yard. I began to pick some of the pieces up when the dog walked out of his dog house. He stretched and licked his lips. I thought that he was going to growl and bark at me, but instead, he came over and sat next to me. He watched me recover all of the pieces and throw them in the garbage-can. When I was done, I walked over and began to pat him. He licked my hand. When Jeffrey walked out of the house, he saw me. Shocked to see me and the dog getting along so well, he said, "Damn, he don't, usually, let people do that to him…unless, you give him a treat."

I looked down at him, patted his head, and smiled.

CHAPTER 46

While I was grateful that Jeffrey had put a roof over my head, I'd outgrown him. He was getting on my nerves. He was careless and with my history, I had to avoid careless people. I knew that it had to end, but when I told him, he didn't take it like I thought he would.

"Sooooo, you come in here, eat my food, make a little money, and now, you ain't got no use for me."

Grabbing my bag, I said, "Look, it's nothing personal, but I'm a grown man living with another man...it's not a good look. Plus, it's time for me to get my own place."

He cracked his neck and said, "But you know too much about what I do..."

Starting down the hall towards the door, I said, "If you're thinking that I would say something...don't... I got my own skeletons...don't want them falling out of the closet trying to expose yours."

He ran and jumped in front of me. "And I found one of your skeletons in the garbage-can out back."

I stopped and put my bag down on the floor. "What are you talking about?"

"I thought that it was strange when Janet up and left her girl, but when the dog coughed-up a finger...it made me curious. Plus, that dog don't like nobody. Why, all of a sudden, he wants to be your best friend?"

"What makes you think that I had something to do with that? She could have easily gone into the gate...tried to pat him and ended-up being lunch..."

"But he would have barked...he didn't bark...you know why? There was no threat. The threat was already dead and being handed to him on a silver platter..." He folded his arms. "A man knows his dog..."

We were at an impasse. We both had shit on each other, but it was a "bitch" move for him to try to use it against me. So, I thought about it for a second and said, "You know...things are good here. How about I stay a little longer?"

He liked that response. "Yeah, you can help me with a job that I have tonight...it's a big one...a two-man job...pays a lot...I'll split it with you...right down the middle..."

Right down the middle is right, motherfucker...I thought to myself. "That sounds good..."

So, we went about our day like nothing happened. All the while, I was thinking about how I was going to put an end to all of this. As the hours and minutes ticked away, I became anxious. I wanted it all to be over. Later that evening, he walked in the room and said, "It's time…"

I smiled because he didn't know how true his words were. I jumped up and quickly, headed for the car.

"We're taking the truck," he said.

"Why?" I asked.

"We have big cargo that needs to be taken to the pier."

I didn't ask any more questions. I just jumped in the truck and buckled-up. After about an hour, we found ourselves parked in front of a warehouse. He backed in. After throwing the truck in "park", he jumped out and knocked on the overhead door. Slowly, the door went up. Sitting in the middle of the floor was a large crate. He yelled for me to get out. I jumped out and walked over to where he was standing. "Help me get this in the truck."

"What is it?"

"I don't fucking know and I don't fucking care… now, come on."

I bent over to lift the crate. "This is heavy…"

"Lift with your knees…"

I looked at him and frowned.

"Standing there, looking at me, ain't gon' get this shit in the truck."

I huffed and sucked my teeth. I kneeled down and lifted the crate. We dragged it to the back of the truck and put it inside. He closed the door. We jumped back in and pulled off. We drove around for thirty minutes, pulled off of Lake Shore Drive, and waited. He turned off the car and said, "Let's get this over with."

I walked back to the back of the truck. We were pulling it off of the truck when it slipped from my hands and hit the ground. To my surprise, out rolled two kids. They were bound and gagged. The sight of them laying on the ground sent a chill through my body. "What is this?" I asked, angrily.

Nervously, he tried to put the crate back together. "Help me put them back in there…"

I threw my hands in the air. "Hell naw…hell, fucking, naw…I'm not doing that shit…these are kids." The kids did not move. They looked like they were already dead. "I can't believe you would involve me in this shit."

"You think that I knew that there were kids in the box?"

"Hell yeah, you did…you knew that there were kids in there…"

Trying to lift the little girl's body to place her back in the disassembled crate, he said, "I swear that I didn't know…but we have to finish the job or we won't get paid."

"Fuck you and the money…I'm not touching those kids…"

He stopped messing with the crate and began to carry her towards the water. Something in me snapped. I ran up behind him and pushed him so hard that the little girl went flying in the air. When she landed, she began to stir. As he scrambled to get on his feet, he said, "What the fuck is wrong with you?"

Still looking at the little girl, I didn't respond. The next thing I knew, I heard a clicking sound. I turned to look at him. "You pull a gun on me?"

"Don't make me shoot you, Paul…please…just help me finish this…we will get paid and if you want, you can go on your way."

This motherfucker pulled a gun on me. I thought to myself. There was no turning back. I looked over at the little girl who was, slowly, coming to. I walked over and picked her up. Groggily, her eyes began to open. She looked up at me. I leaned over and whispered, "I'm sorry…" I walked over to where Jeffrey was standing and still pointing the gun. Without thinking about what would happen to the little girl, I tossed her at him. Trying to catch her, he dropped the gun. They both landed on the ground. I ran over and grabbed the gun. I pointed it at his head. Breathing heavily, he looked at his watch and smiled. "The nighttime…is the right time…" he laughed.

I placed the gun against his forehead and smiled back. "Yes, it is…my friend…yes, it is." As he took a deep breath and exhaled, his eyes drifted towards the sky. I pulled the trigger. Surprised, he stared at me for a second before his eyes rolled back into his head as his body hit the ground. For a moment, I looked at him. I whispered, "Goodbye" as I dropped the gun next to him. I walked over and untied the little girl. I picked her up and carried her over to the truck. I put her inside and walked over to untie the little boy. He began to stir. "It's okay," I said to him. He rubbed his eyes. I placed him in the truck next to the little girl. I walked back to where Jeffrey was lying and began to drag him to the edge of the pier. I pushed him and the gun in and watched as they, both, sank into the dark murky water. I walked back over to the truck and jumped inside. I'd never driven before and decided that it wouldn't be a good idea to learn on the night that I'd killed a man while in the process of kidnapping and attempting to kill two kids. Instead, I looked down, grabbed his cellphone, and dialed 911. I placed the phone against the little girl's face.

"911…what's your emergency?"

The little girl looked at me. She thought for a second and said, "Me and my brother needs your help…"

"Where are you?" the operator asked.

The little girl said, "I don't know…"

"Don't worry…stay on the line…we will find your location…"

"Okay…"

"Is there anyone else with you?"

She looked at me and then, back at the phone. "No…no one else is here…"

"Okay…sit tight…help is on the way."

With tears in her eyes, she smiled at me, and whispered, "Thank you…" For a moment, I thought about the other little girl whose father I'd killed.

I handed her the phone and walked away. Moments later, I could hear sirens coming our way. I walked down the street – blending into the night.

CHAPTER 47

I was alone, again, with nothing but my thoughts. It's a strange place to find yourself in with nothing and no one, but yourself. It's a lonely place to be, but at least there was finally some silence. It was in that moment that I realized that I'd never been truly alone. Sure, there were moments when I was by myself, but there was always someone with whom I could turn to. But that was all gone now and it was time for me to make my own way.

So, I walked and while I walked, I listened to the sounds of the night – people laughing, kids playing, and the sounds of the cars roaring passed me. No one saw me and no one cared. I was just a person walking the streets – trying to find a place to call my home. After a while, the bottom of my feet began to burn. I needed to sit down. I looked up and found myself standing in front of a restaurant. I grabbed a booth in the back and rested my head. The next thing I knew, I was drifting off to sleep.
"Sir...sir?" a voice said.

Startled, I jumped up and began to look around the room. Wiping drool from my mouth, I asked, "What? Where am I?"

Concerned, she touched my arm. "You're in a restaurant..."

As the light hit her face, she looked like an angel. "We're closing up..." she said.

I stood, but my feet hurt so bad that I began to limp. "I'm sorry...let me get out of here."

"Take your time...I see that you're in pain..."

I turned to look at her. I was taken aback by her kindness. It had been such a long time since someone was nice to me – truly nice to me. It touched me. She could see that I was struggling. She grabbed my arm and wrapped it around her shoulder. "Here...let me help you."

My heart began to feel something that it'd never felt before. As we walked across the room, I watched her. She smiled. "There you go...you want me to call you a cab?"

At first, I didn't know what to say to her, but after a brief pause, I said, "Yes...could you?"

She removed my arm. "Oh, sure...where are you going so that I can tell them?"

I gave her Jeffrey's address and she walked away. She was gone for a couple of minutes before returning and saying, "They will be here in ten minutes."

"Oh...okay...thanks..." I said.

She looked around for a minute and said, "Are you hungry? I can give you some pie. There's some left on the counter. I wasn't going to do anything but throw it away. You can have it, if you want it."

She was beautiful and the more that she spoke, the prettier she got. Humbled, I said, "Yes…"

She walked away and when she returned, she had the pie in her hand and a cup of water. She smiled as she handed it to me. "I hope that water is okay. I can't pass out the pop. These assholes have a way of monitoring how much we sell and drink in a day." Then, she covered her mouth. "Sorry for the foul language, but cursing keeps me from drinking." She giggled.

I smiled and took it from her. "It's no problem and thank you so much for this…"

She waved. "It's no problem…" She looked over my shoulder and said, "It looks like your cab is here."

I looked out towards the street. I turned to her and said, "Thanks again…" For a moment, we didn't do anything, but stare at each other. The silence was broken when the cabby blew his horn. "Well, I better go."

"Okay…it was nice meeting you…ummmmm? I forgot to get your name."

"It's Paul…"

She extended her hand. "Hi Paul…I'm Deidra…"

"Deidra…that's a pretty name…it matches you."

She blushed and giggled. "Well, you have a good night," she said.

"Thank you…I will…" I walked out of the doors but turned back to look at her one more time.

She waved and smiled.

I walked out towards the street and climbed into the backseat of the car. I didn't want to look at her again. As bad as I wanted to, I just couldn't. After all that had happened that night that led me to this moment...that led me to her...for a moment, I felt ashamed.

The cab driver said, "She's still waving..."

I looked up at him and said, "Pull off..."

Once at Jeffrey's, I paid the driver, and walked around the back to see if there was a window open. The dog saw the pie and came towards me. "No! Get away!" I told him. He began to growl. I looked around the yard to see what I could hit him with, but there was nothing. I took off my shoe and waved it at him. He turned and went back into his doghouse. Trying not to drop anything, I carefully placed the container inside of the window. Once inside, I carried the pie to the bathroom, sat it on the back of the toilet and then, turned on the water in the shower. As I removed my clothing, I caught the smell of something sweet on my shirt. She'd left the smell of her perfume on my clothes. I inhaled deeply. I folded the dirty shirt and placed it on top of the toilet. I climbed inside of the shower. As I washed myself, I thought of her. Something inside of me told me that I had to have her – that I needed someone like her in my life and I had to do whatever it took to make her a part of this ugly world that I've created.

372

CHAPTER 48

I went back every day hoping that I would run into her again. I ordered the same thing every day for a week and just when I thought that I would have to eat it again, she walked in. She had the most beautiful smile on her face – like she didn't have a worry in the world. I never believed in 'love at first sight' until I met her, and I was in love. I knew, in that moment, that I wanted to be the reason that she had a smile on her face. I wanted to protect her from all of the evil in the world. I wanted to protect her from men like me.

But why would she want someone like me talking to her? I didn't have shit to offer her other than the money I made working for Jeffrey. I had his house and cars, but for how long? And it would be horrible to assume the possessions of a dead man to try to impress a girl, but if 'things' are what she likes, I will do anything to give it to her. But I didn't know how to approach her. I didn't have much experience with girls, but I figured that it couldn't be that hard if a guy like Jeffrey could get them, so I huffed into my hands to make sure that my breath didn't stink, I smelled under my arms to make sure that I wasn't musty, I straightened my clothes and then, I walked up to her. Just as I approached her, a man walked up and grabbed her into his arms.

"Hey, sweetie…" she said, wrapping her arms around him.

He kissed her. "Hey, beautiful…"

No, I wanted to kiss her and I wanted to call her that. I thought to myself.

They were playing with each other when she looked up and saw me. "Hey…" she said, waving.

I could feel my heart breaking into a thousand pieces. I couldn't look at her. Instead, I walked passed as if I didn't see her.

When I made it back to Jeffrey's, I walked inside and fell down in the middle of the living room floor. I covered my eyes with my arm and I saw her. I saw her kissing him. I saw her kissing him and smiling. I wanted to believe that she was rare and not convenient and that for a moment, she really cared about me. I didn't want to believe that she could be that way with any and every man that crossed her path. But when I saw her smiling for him, the pain in my heart began to turn into something else. It wasn't anger, because I knew what anger felt like. This was something darker. It made my skin hot, my head hurt, and my heart beat fast. The same "heat" that I was feeling when I first saw her was the same "heat" that I was feeling now, just twisted into something else –

something ugly. Then, the images, in my head, no longer contained her face…just his and the more that I saw his face, the more that I wanted it to disappear, completely.

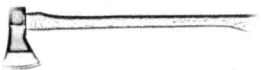

My mission was clear - eliminate the obstacle between me and my future wife. And like I was getting up to go to work, I got up to watch her and it was frustrating because she didn't have a regular schedule. She only worked a couple of days a week and those days differed from week to week, and every day that she was there, he was too. And I watched them kiss and hug like no one was watching them, but I was there, wishing that it was me.

And just when I thought that I couldn't take any more, I arrived one night just in time to see them leaving the building. They walked around the back of the building and jumped inside of a car. They turned it on, but didn't pull off. They sat in park and talked to each other. Then, suddenly, talking turned into kissing. They did that for a while before they jumped out, looked around, before climbing into the backseat. They were back there for so long that I could no longer see inside because of the steam that covered the windows. I wondered if she was okay, so I looked around before walking towards the car. As I got closer, I could hear the moans and cries of passion. I walked around to the back of the car where I could see them better. I could see her on top of him – riding him like she was riding one of the rocking horses in the playground. He had both of his hands on her breasts. She turned towards me and I saw that smile again. But she didn't stop. The sight of me made her ride him harder, made her moan, and scream louder. I was confused. While I watched her make love to another man, instead of wanting to hurt the both of them, I became excited. I began to touch "myself." I began to squeeze until I could feel the circulation being blocked and there was no blood flow. The more that she rode him, the harder I squeezed until her mouth fell open and her eyes rolled into the back of her head. When she opened her eyes, she was no longer smiling. She just stared at me. We watched each other until I walked away.

All the way home, I wondered why she did that. Why would she make love to him right in my face or was it me that she wished that she was making love to. Was that why her eyes never left mine because it was me that she wanted inside of her? I had to know, so I decided that I would ask her the next time I saw her. Until then, I dreamed about her.

CHAPTER 49

I needed to get my thoughts organized, but that wouldn't be easy, because, on that day, the police had other plans for me. As soon as I walked in the house, I heard a knock at the door. I knew that if I hid inside, it would only draw suspicion towards me, so I took a deep breath and prepared to put on the best performance that I knew how. I opened the door. "Ummmmmm, hello?"

"Hello...I'm Detective Majors and this is Detective Wallace..."

"Ummmmm, hi..." I said, casually.

"Can we come in?"

I moved out of the way. "Ummmmmm, sure..." They walked in and I closed the door behind them. "How can I help you detectives?"

"Can we, first, have your name?"

I thought about my answer for a second. Then, I thought about my Aunt Jasmine and how people reacted to and treated her. I figured that if I pretended to act like her, maybe they would just leave me alone. So, in the highest-pitched voice that I could muster-up, I said, "Sure...it's Princess..."

"Okay, Princess…" He twisted his mouth and rolled his eyes in disbelief.

I waved my hand. "That's Prin-cess…emphasis on the 'cess'."

He frowned and said, "Got it…"

"How can I help y'all…Mr. Officer?"

"Well, we found a vehicle belonging to Jeffrey Williams. It was a part of a crime scene…the tags led us here."

I placed my hand over my mouth pretending to be surprised. "Really? Is he okay?"

"Well, we're not sure…when was the last time that you saw him?"

"It was about a week or so ago…"

"Did it bother you that he hadn't returned home?"

I said, "No…first, he's an adult. He can do whatever he wants to do." Then, I placed my hands on my hips. Their tone changed, immediately.

"So, he leaves a lot?"

"Yes, and second, I'm going to be straight with you. Jeffrey and I've been falling out, lately. You see, he's been cheating on me." I poked out my mouth.

"Do you know with who?"

"No, I don't know who the bitch is and I don't want to know." I smacked my lips.

You could tell by the looks on their faces that they weren't going to be here long. "Plus, I think that he was into some other shit…he never told me what he was doing, but I suspected that it was illegal." I batted my eyelashes.

"What makes you say that?"

"Just the way that he acted...always so secretive...you know how you MEN can be..." I said. They looked at each other. Then, Detective Wallace spoke. "Do you mind if I look around?"

"No, go ahead...and don't mind my panties that are hanging up in the bathroom. I was about to take a shower," I said. "You like showers, Mr. Policeman?" He frowned, looked me up and down, before walking down the hall.

Detective Majors continued asking questions. "Did you notice anything else?"

"Well, he had no job, but he was able to afford all of this...and me." I licked my lips.

He adjusted the collar on his shirt. "What else should I know about Jeffrey?"

"Well, he volunteered at the park...helping kids stay out of trouble...I was one of those kids. He helped me find work...put a roof over my head...gave me a bed to sleep in."

"Sounds like a really nice guy..."

"I didn't get much sleep...if you know what I mean..."

Suddenly, the other detective walked back into the room. He nodded at the other detective. "Well, we're not going to take up too much of your time. If you hear from him, could you tell him to give us a call?" I stood to open the door for them. They handed me a card. "Of course...no problem, sir...I'll let him know as soon as I see him…but quick question, is this your personal line…Mr. Detective?"

He had a look on his face like he was trying to put an imaginary lock on his butthole.

They were leaving when one of the detectives walked out into the driveway. I followed behind him. As they got closer to the gate, the dog charged, barking and growling.

They both jumped back. "Damn, what are you feeding that beast?"

I smiled and said, "Bitches…"

They paused and looked at me and as if I'd told them a joke, they began to laugh. I joined them in their laughter.

Detective Majors said, "He'll never go hungry on a diet like that…will he?"

Detective Wallace joked. "He's big…you might want to put him on a low-bitch diet…"

They both began to laugh. "He looks like he could hurt a bitch…"

"Believe me…he can…" I confirmed.

"You better keep him locked-up…" joked, Detective Majors.

"Don't worry…I'll put him to sleep before I let him hurt somebody."

CHAPTER 50

I waited for the perfect time to approach her. Her boyfriend had just left and she was standing by the door, alone. I walked in and stood next to her.

Without looking up, she said, "We're closing."

In a low whisper, I said, "Hi."

She looked up. "Oh hey...how are you?"

She was talking to me as if we didn't have that moment together. "How are you feeling? How's your feet?"

I grabbed her hand. "So, you don't remember what happened..."

Confused, she asked, "No, what?"

I thought that she was just playing with my head, so I said, "I saw you in the car..."

Still confused, she said, "Was I going home?"

Tired of the game that she was playing, I said, "You know what you did..."

She smiled, but then began to laugh, loudly. "No, I don't..."

Humiliated, I said, "But I watched you...you watched me..."

She shook her head. "What are you talking about?"

"The night that you were in the car with your boyfriend…in the back…"

She interrupted me. Embarrassed, she said, "Oh shit…you saw me? Fuck, fuck, fuck…" She began to wring her hands and pace back and forth. She continued, "That was you? I saw someone, but I didn't know that it was you…it was dark, and the windows were all fogged up…really, I didn't know that was you…I'm sorry…"

Angry, I asked, "How could you do that to me?"

"Do what?"

"Don't play stupid, Deidra…it was you and me."

She rubbed her forehead. "I'm not sure what you're talking about."

"That moment that we shared…"

Scratching her head, she said, "I don't know what your malfunction is, but I have no idea what's going on and I'm so sorry that you had to see that, but we…you and I…we shared no moment."

I felt deflated – like a fool. "Look, I need to go…" I said, walking towards the door.

"No, wait…don't go…"

"Naw, I need to get out of here."

"Look, I shouldn't have done that back there, but you know how it is…don't you?"

"No…I don't."

"I'm really sorry, Paul, but…could you, please, not say anything about this? I could lose my job."

I didn't want her to see how hurt I was. "Sure."

"Thank you, Paul...but I hope that we can still be friends."

"Friends?" I knew what it meant when a woman called you a friend. Either you were too ugly to date, they thought you were gay, or they thought that you were a loser, so they throw the "friend-shit" at you to keep you from feeling sorry for yourself.

"And you promise that you won't tell?"

"I said that 'I won't'..."

"Good..." She paused and looked around the lobby. "Would you like some more pie? My treat..."

I looked at her mouth as she tried to bribe me with food. "No, thanks."

"You can have anything that you want..."

"I'mma hold you to that..." I said, as I walked out of the building.

For a while, I didn't go back. Instead, I decided to distract myself. I needed to better myself and become a productive member of society. So, I looked for a job, and obtained one at a local grocery store stocking shelves, I went to the DMV to learn how to drive and to get my driver's license, and I opened a savings account and deposited every check that I earned into it. All the while, I never stopped thinking about her.

I'd never had a job before, so I wasn't sure what to expect. All of the employees seemed really nice, but I stayed to myself. I knew that once I opened myself up to conversation, people would start asking questions that I didn't want to answer. Plus, I wasn't really interested in getting to know people. I just wanted to make my "bank" and get the hell up out of there, but that wouldn't be easy. I had a manger whose biggest mission in life was to become everybody's homie. Every time I looked up, I was looking in his face.

On the surface, he seemed nice, but you could tell that there was something not right with him. He used to spark-up conversations about random shit, just so he could have a reason to talk to you. It wouldn't have been so bad, but he had a heavy accent and I could barely understand half of what he was saying. The other employees found him amusing while I just thought that he was an asshole. At the time, I couldn't understand why I couldn't "stand" this man, but like with most assholes, they could only hide their shit for so long, and when it finally exposed itself, it stunk to high-hell. In the end, it's what got him killed.

One day, while working overtime, he approached me.
"Paaaauuuullll..." Farrad said.

I hated when he said my name. He was always ending it with his tongue hanging out of his mouth. I used to try to get him to see how annoying it was by saying his name the same way. "Faaarrraaadd ..." But he just laughed it off.

"Paaaauuuullll..."

Sigh. "What's up, Faaarrraaadd...?"

"You know, I started-off just like you..."

"Really? You started off as a Black man too?" I said, zoning and stocking shelves.

It took him a second, but when he caught on to the joke, he said, "Oh...that's very funny. Mr. Funny Paul..." He placed his hands on his hips, proudly. "No, no, no...I was saying that I stocked shelves too."

"Great..." I tried to keep my responses short hoping that he would go away.

"Yes, my family traveled many miles to get here..."

"That's wonderful..."

"It was not easy..." he said.

"I bet..."

"Yes, but look at us now...we come here with nothing and now, we own several grocery stores."

"That's great..."

"Do your family have grocery stores, Paaaauuuullll?"

Annoyed, I said, "If they did, would I be here counting cans of peas and talking to you?"

He laughed. "That's funny..."

386

"Yeah, I bet…" I said, not laughing. He could tell that I was annoyed, so he decided to walk away.

When I was done stocking the shelves and throwing away my garbage, I went in to tell him that I was leaving when I noticed that he was doing something "strange" to the milk. I walked closer to see what he was doing.

"What are you doing?" I asked.

Startled, he jumped and hid something behind his back. "Paul? I thought that you were gone."

"I bet…"

"Can I tell you a secret?" he asked, nervously.

"No, you can tell me what you're doing to that milk."

"But you'll like this secret…"

He was trying to divert my attention, but I wasn't having it. I would play his game for a minute, but he was going to answer my question. One way or another. I said, "Okay…what's the secret?"

"I'm doing inventory…" he said.

"Inventory? That's the secret?" I asked, suspiciously.

"Ummmmm, yeah…that's it. So, you can just go home now…and remember, I'm just doing inventory."

Angry, I said, "Dude, don't insult my intelligence with that bullshit. Now, tell me what you're hiding behind your back."

Stuttering, he said, "It's…it's…it's…it's nothing."

"People don't hide 'nothing'…"

His tone changed. "Look, I don't have to explain myself to you. You work for me. Now, go home or find yourself without a job."

I pushed him out of the way and walked over to look at the milk. The containers all looked sealed, but I noticed that the ink from the expiration date was running down the side of the plastic container. I touched it and looked at my fingers.

Busted, he said, "I was just fixing it…"

"Fixing it?" I asked.

"Yeah…you see it running…" He pulled the thing that he was hiding behind his back. "I was just putting the date back on it."

"Really?"

"Yeah, that's all…"

I smiled and said, "Okay…" I was about to walk away when something said, "This motherfucker is lying to you." I reached into my pocket and said, "I want to buy one."

Thrown-off by my request, he said, "Look…these are not for sale…"

"They're not for sale?"

"Well, they are, but not right now. The store is closed. I can't give you your change."

"I don't want any change…just give me the milk."

He adjusted his collar. "Look, I'm not selling this milk to you…you need to go home."

I looked up to see the cameras sticking out of the ceiling. "Damn, and you do this shit in front of the cameras?"

"Those cameras don't work...just like you."

"Just like me?" I asked.

"Yeah...you're fired..."

"So, I'm fired?"

"Are you slow? You won't me to spell it for you, Paaaauuulll..." he confirmed. "Now, go fuck yourself...homie."

Homie? I laughed to myself. I was unfazed. The moment that he said that I was "fired", I knew what I needed to do. Everything from this point on was just foreplay. Somebody was getting "fucked" tonight and it wasn't me. "You want me to go and fuck myself?" I asked.

"Yes...fuck yourself..."

"Alright...I'll go 'fuck' myself...but I want my last paycheck...first."

"I'll mail it to you...now, go."

I didn't respond. I just walked out. From the street, I watched him change the date on the rest of the milk and then stack it back into the cooler. When I saw him walk to the back of the building, I ran around and then knocked on the door. He answered it. "What?"

"I left my keys inside..." I said, lying.

He looked me up and down and said, "Where did you leave them?"

I patted my pockets. "I must've left them over in the vegetable aisle."

He looked around and said, "Wait right here...I'll be right back."

As he turned to go back in, I stuck my foot in the door and waited for him to go down the hall. When he disappeared down the hall, I entered the building. Quietly, I approached him. Startled, he jumped.

"What are you doing in here?"

"I wanted to help you look..."

"I don't need your help..." he searched the floor. "There are no keys here...now, leave."

I scratched my head. "Are you sure? They must be here..."

Frustrated, he said, "There are no keys...you leave...you leave NOW!!!"

I threw up my hands. "Okay...okay..." I looked around and said, "Maybe they're in the back by the freezer...can I look there? I promise...if they aren't there then, I would leave you alone..."

Suspicious, he looked at me. He wanted me to leave, but said, "Okay...okay...this is it...then, you go..."

"Thanks, man..." I said, walking towards the back. He was on my heels.

"I need you to hurry up..."

"Why? So, you can sell that spoiled milk to my people?"

He ignored my question.

We passed by the meat department on the way to the freezer. I stopped and said, "You know what? I think that they might be in there."

"No, no, no...you said freezer. Now, get out before I call the police."

"Maybe you should call them…I bet they would love to hear about you changing the dates on that milk…what else are you changing the dates on…" I ran into the meat department. "Are you changing the dates on the meat too, Faaarrrraadd?"

He ran in behind me. "Bring your ass out of here…I've had enough of this…"

I walked over to the one of the cutters. I pretended to look around on the floor. "Damn, where are my keys?" I began to search my pockets. "Shit…" I pulled them out of my pocket.

He folded his arms. "They were never lost…were they?"

"What was the clue, Sherlock?" I asked.

"I need you to leave and never come back…"

I walked up and hit his ass so hard, his sandals flew across the room. He lay unconscious on the floor. I walked out back and grabbed a Butcher's coat and some glasses. I was looking around for some knives when I saw it – a butcher's ax. I walked back into the room and turned the cutter on. I began to remove his clothing. I took the ax, held it over my head, and when it landed, I noticed that I'd cut his foot off. He bolted upwards and began to scream. "Ahhhhhhhh!!! My foot! My Foot!!!" I grabbed his foot and stuffed it into his mouth.

"Shut up…shut the fuck up…"

He swung his head back and forth – spitting teeth out of his mouth and onto the floor. "Oh God…please don't…please don't…" he begged.

I rammed it harder into his mouth.

He gagged and choked. He grabbed me. He tried to struggle but couldn't. His grasped tightened around my arms before he closed his eyes, exhaled, and his arms fell limp onto the floor. I stared at him. "Things are going to get messy..." I mumbled to myself. I started cutting him up and placing pieces of him into the grinder. I'd gotten all the way down to his head when the grinder jammed. I turned off the machine and looked inside. I began to pull pieces of him out of the grinder until I saw what was jammed into the bottom of it. I looked closely and found something "shiny" in the bottom of the machine. I stuck my hand in to remove the object. When I pulled it out, I wiped it clean to look at it. It was his wedding ring. I stuck it into my pocket and placed his head into the grinder. When I was done, I found myself stuck with a table full of ground "Farrad" on it. I grabbed some packaging and began to wrap and label them. When I was done, I placed all of the packages in the freezer.

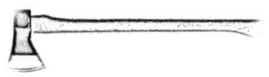

I arrived to work the next day at my scheduled time. Everyone was asking about Farrad. When they approached me, I said, "I saw him last night..."

"Oh..." a customer said. "I'm so used to seeing him here. He opens and closes this place. I used to think that he lived here, because he never went home."

"Well...maybe he's sick." I suggested.

"Yeah...maybe..." she said. "Well, let me get the stuff that I came in here for...you have a good day."

"Thanks." I opened a box of beans and began to place them on the shelf. "Oh, and don't buy the milk or the meat...they're both expired."

CHAPTER 51

B ut there was still that other problem that I needed to solve. So, after I had everything in place, I went back to see her. I felt proud because I'd driven one of Jeffrey's cars to the restaurant. As I felt the road underneath me, I thought about this phase of my life. I had a place to stay. I had a car. The only thing missing was somebody to share it with, but the one I had my eye on had her eye on somebody else and if I wanted her to see me, I had to get rid of the 'somebody else.'

For several weeks, I watched him until the moment presented itself. I'd followed him for several miles until I saw him pull up in front of a house. The porch light came on and a woman wearing a robe answered the door. He jumped out and ran inside. I turned off the car and waited until all of the lights went out. While I waited, I thought about the woman. I didn't expect him to have someone waiting at home for him. I hadn't considered the fact that after spending so much time with Deidra, that he was coming home to somebody else. I hadn't planned for this, but this was war and in war, there would be casualties.

When the lights on the house went out, I exited Jeffrey's car holding my grand-daddy's gun. I looked around the house; checking all of the windows and doors. When I approached the patio door, I turned the knob. It opened. I removed my shoes and walked inside. Walking through the dining room, I saw two plates and a baby's bottle sitting on the table. *There's a baby.* I thought to myself. *You need to go home. Do this on another day...but it's too late. You're here now...just don't hurt anyone and everything is going to be okay. You're just here to talk some sense into him. Expose and embarrass him and he would leave Deidra alone.* I saw a cellphone sitting on the table. I picked it up and carried it into the kitchen. I pressed the power button and his name popped-up on the screen. It was password protected. Frustrated, I looked over at the counter and saw several knives sitting on it. *Remember...you just want to talk, but if things get out of hand, don't use the gun. You don't want to wake the baby.* I thought to myself. I picked through them until I found the right one. Quietly, I proceeded down the hall.

In one room, there was an infant sleeping, peacefully, in his crib. I continued, pass, until I found myself in front of the door to the master's bedroom. Gently, I turned the knob to find them both asleep wrapped in each other's arms. I walked in and stood over him. I opened the camera from the locked screen and began to take several pictures. The flash woke him up.

"The fuck are you doing here…what do you want?"
The woman jumped up. "What is going on?" She
grabbed for the phone on the nightstand.
"Don't do that." I held the knife up and said, "I came
here to talk." I sat down on the bed next to them.
"About what?" he asked.
"Do you know him?" she asked, him.
I interrupted them. "I'm a friend of your husband's
girlfriend."
She frowned and pulled the blanket up to her neck.
"His what?"
He tried to turn on the light. "Turn that light on and
I'm going to go down the hall and grab that cute little
baby of yours."
"No, please…" she begged.
He lowered his arm.
"Good boy…" I said. "I stopped by to tell your wife
what you've been doing at the restaurant…"
"Did she put you up to this?" he asked.
She began to cry. "Who?"
"He knows who? Now, tell your wife so that she
knows too…"
"Fuck you," he said.
I shook my head. "So, you want to fuck me and
Deidra?"
"Deidra?" she asked, wiping tears from her eyes.
"Look, you better get out of my house…" he
demanded.
I snatched the covers back. He crawled away from his
wife, trying to protect himself. I snatched him by the

leg and pulled him close to me. I placed the knife between his legs. "Stop moving…"

He threw up his hands. "Okay…okay…"

I, gently, ran the blade against his inner-thigh. Blood began to stream down his leg. He flinched and said, "What do you want?"

"I want you to leave her alone…" I said.

"Who the fuck are you and why do you care about what I'm doing?"

"Because what you're doing is wrong…"

He frowned. "Is that bitch fucking you too?"

His wife stopped crying. Her face turned pale as if all of the blood had been drained from her body.

I moved the blade, closer, until it sat between his legs. He tried to move away from it, but there was nowhere else to go. I handed the phone to him. "Unlock this…"

"Fuck you…"

I stuck the knife in deeper. This time he yelped like a wounded dog.

She whispered. "It's our baby's birthday." We both looked over at her. "I know what he's been doing…" she admitted. "It's 061317…" she said.

I sat back down next to him. I entered the password and opened the phone. I was scrolling through the photos, when I saw her, naked laying across their bed. I looked around the room. "Wow…this one was taken in here."

His wife began to cry, again. He reached out to her. "I'm sorry…"

"Fuck you…" she said.

I turned the camera towards her. "Have you seen this one? Is that a mole or a birthmark on his ass?"

The woman began to sob, uncontrollably. "I told you to leave that girl alone, but noooooooooooo…and look at this shit. You fucked her in my bed…in my house…and you got this motherfucker in here waking me up out of my gad-damn sleep in the middle of the night…" She paused and looked at me. "I'm sorry…"

I shrugged. "I'm good…continue…"

"I tried to ignore this shit, look the other way, but look what you've done."

"She didn't mean anything to me…" he said.

Her eyes grew dark. "She didn't mean anything? You don't waste time and energy on shit that don't mean shit…you don't lie and sneak around for some shit that don't mean shit…you don't bring some shit that don't mean shit into our bed…so don't give me that bullshit."

"Look, I'm going to leave her alone…this time…I promise."

"You know how many times you've said that shit? I loved you…married your broke-ass…gave you a baby, and you know what you gave me?"

He didn't respond.

"You gave me debt, bad credit, and fucking Chlamydia…" She stood and wrapped the blanket around herself. "I could have married somebody else. You think that you're the only nigga in the world with a dick? Newsflash you piece of shit…you're not. Shit, he's got a dick." She pointed at me.

I smiled and allowed her to have her moment.

She continued. "With that fucking crooked-ass dick of yours…can't tell what direction that motherfucker is going in? Need a map just to find my pussy."

I began to laugh.

He became angry. "My dick could find it if you didn't have all of that fucking hair down there…like trying to find a cave in the fucking wilderness."

"Fuck you… and look at his balls. They look like two dried-up prunes with a dick the size of a AA battery stuck between them…I'm surprised that he can get somebody else to fuck him. The hoe must be blind or desperate." Then a weird look came over her face. "You would fuck a blind, desperate bitch…wouldn't you?"

"I wouldn't have to fuck somebody else if your ass didn't get your period every other day…how much bleeding can one motherfucker do without dying?" he said.

She frowned. "I would rather have a tampon stuck up my ass then that thing that you call a dick."

"Fuck you, bitch…" he said.

I laughed because watching this shit was funny.

"I GOT YOUR BITCH!!!! FUCK YOU!!!" She paused and turned to me. "You know what? KILL HIS ASS!!!!" she screamed.

The man waved his arms. "Wait a minute…wait one fucking minute…"

"NO! I mean it…I got insurance on his ass. He's worth more to me dead than alive, anyway…he ain't doing me no good...causing me all of this damn grief."

"What the fuck are you saying?" he asked.

She walked up to me. "I will tell the police that somebody broke in here and killed him and it wouldn't be a lie...would it?"

"Wait a minute, baby...please, let's talk about this." He begged.

"We just talked...you piece-of-shit."

Suddenly, we heard the baby crying. She began to walk towards the door. "When I come back, I want his ass chopped-up in tiny little pieces..."

"FUCK YOU, BITCH!!!!" he screamed.

"Looks like you're going to be the one getting fucked, BITCH!" She was walking out the door when she turned and said, "Make sure that you take the cash. He just cashed his $2 paycheck...it's in his wallet. I have a grand in my purse...make a real mess and I'll take care of the rest." She closed the door behind her. I turned back and looked at him. "This is awkward..."

"Look, I won't say anything..." he said.

"You heard your wife..."

"Fuck that bitch..." he spat. "You don't have to do this..."

"I don't, but you heard the lady..."

"You can have that bitch..."

"What your wife?"

"Either bitch...shit, I don't give a fuck."

I bit into my bottom lip. "You know...Mike...I just realized something. My mama..."

"I didn't fuck your mama..." he said, interrupting me. I continued. "I just realized that it's niggas like you that turn a woman like that into my mama..."

Confused, he said, "What are you talking about?"

I was done talking. I took the knife and plunged it into his chest. He grabbed onto my hand and held it. He stared at me. I twisted the handle like I was turning down the volume on a radio until he didn't make a sound.

When I was finished, I walked out of the room and down the hall. The woman was feeding her baby. She looked up at me. "Is it done?"

I looked back down the hall and then, back at her. "Yep...it's done."

"Did you get the money?"

"Naw, keep that for the baby..."

"Well, how am I going to explain what happened?"

"Just tell them the truth...show them his phone...tell them that your husband ain't shit and a nigga who knew it came and killed his ass."

CHAPTER 52

S he looked so sad. For days, I watched her trying to move on with her life. Each day, she looked up and down the street – waiting for his arrival, but he never came and of course, he wouldn't. I knew it, but she didn't and even though she wasn't aware of it, I felt that it was time for her to let go and move on. And I knew that it was lowdown to try to brush up on her when she was grieving for another man, but I'd killed a man for her and it was time to claim my prize.

So, I decided that it was time to approach her. She had exited the building, and was looking for someone, when I pretended to be lost. "Hey…" I said.
She looked like she'd been crying. Her eyes were sunken-in and there were dark-circles underneath them. "Hi," she mumbled.
I looked around. "Looking for someone?"
She took a deep breath and said, "I was hoping…"
"Hoping for what?" I said, interrupting her.
"Nothing…" she said.
I kept walking, but she stopped me and said, "I'm getting off in a minute…want to watch a movie?"

I turned back. "Let's do something different..."

"Okay...what do you want to do?"

"Whatever you want to do..."

She thought about it for a moment, before saying, "You want to go downtown?"

"I said, 'whatever you want to do'..."

She tried to smile but couldn't. She looked around one last time before saying, "Let me go and fix myself up...I'll meet you out here."

I smiled out of the corner of my mouth. "I'll be waiting right here..."

After spending the afternoon, walking around, we decided to walk down to one of the local fast food restaurants in the neighborhood. We ordered some food and sat down in one of the corner booths. She didn't touch her food. She spent the whole time staring out of the window.

"Your food is getting cold," I said, filling my mouth with French fries.

Still looking out of the window, she said, "I'm not really hungry."

"Why didn't you tell me? I could have picked another place for us to hang out..."

"It's not that..." She paused and sighed. "I lost someone..."

Trying to be funny, I said, "Did you check the lost and found?"

She barely cracked a smile. "Men are so fucking stupid..." she blurted out. "No offense...'

"Do you want to talk about it?" I asked.

"No, it's not fair to dump this off on you…"

"I ain't doing nothing else…dump away…"

"I just…" she paused to wipe tears from her eyes. "I loved him and just like that, he just walked away…without even saying why…or good-bye."

"Who?"

"This guy that I've been dating…"

"That's terrible…" I said, lying. "Do you think that he's with somebody else?"

She wiped her eyes, again. "He has a wife…"

This confession bothered me. "And you knew that and you still wanted to be with him?" I asked. I was confused. Why would a girl like her settle for a man like him?

"Paul, when you love somebody…just love them. The heart is fucked-up that way. You think that I wanted to mess with a married man? Destroy his family? I didn't, but the heart wants what it wants and mine wanted him…"

I understood what she was saying, because I felt the same way about her.

"And Paul, you would do almost anything for that kind of love, because it only comes around once in your lifetime…"

"You believe that?"

"I believe that it would be foolish to walk around thinking that it could happen more than once. We don't have long in this world…you have to embrace everything and every moment like it's your last, because it could be…and I didn't blame or judge him for being married."

I chuckled. "You say that like you were with a man who was born with a disability or something. The man made a conscious decision to commit his life to another woman. I'm sure that he didn't make that decision lightly…"

"We all make mistakes, Paul."

"So, you think that his marriage was a mistake?"

"Had to be or he wouldn't be with me…"

Without thinking, I said, "Well…looks like he didn't feel the same way…"

Her tone changed. "Thanks, Paul, for reminding me that I'm a fucking fool…"

"No, Deidra…that's not what I was saying. I'm saying that while you're focused on a man who's willing to cheat on his wife…you might miss a man who could truly love you…the way that you deserve to be loved…"

"I'm done with men, Paul…I'm never giving my heart to another man…"

"Don't say that…it hurts to hear you say that…"

"I'm serious…I'm done with this shit."

I knew that I needed to, carefully, think about what I said next. She was in a fragile state and I didn't want to make things worse, so I thought about it for a second and said, "Deidra…you may see this as an ending, but it may be the beginning of something truly special…sometimes, people are put in our lives to prime us...prepare us for the next level of our lives..."

She looked at me and smiled. "Where did you get that shit from...a fortune cookie...?"

I smiled. "No, but it made you smile..."

"Yes, it did..." She giggled and began to eat her fries. I took them from her. "Let me go and get you some fresh fries..."

She grabbed my hand. "No, Paul...I'll eat those..."

"Naw...you deserve better than that..."

We'd sat there, talking and laughing until they began to lock the doors. We were walking back to her job when I asked her, "How are you getting home?"

She shrugged. "He usually gives me a ride home...I guess now, I'm back to riding a bus."

Seeing this as an opportunity to spend more time with her, I said, "I could give you a ride..."

She stopped and looked up at me. "That's probably not a good idea..."

"Why? You think that I would hurt you?"

"No, I'm just in a bad place, right now...I don't want to spoil the rest of your evening."

"I'm fine...I don't have anything else to do."

"You don't have a girlfriend out there waiting for you?"

"I'm single, right now..."

She touched my hand. "Well...I think I'm just going to get a cab. I don't want to impose..."

"You could, but what did I say about what you deserve..."

She looked around us. She knew that it was late and getting a cab at this time of the night would be hard and riding the bus was dangerous.

"You can take a chance with me or with the unknown..."

"You're the unknown too, Paul..."

"True, but your ex was an unknown too...you took a chance on him?"

"True, but he turned out to be a piece of shit..."

"I might be a piece of shit, too...I guess you will have to take a chance and see..."

We both laughed.

Surrendering, she joked, "I guess if you wanted to do something bad to me, you would have already done it..."

Yes, I would have. I thought to myself.

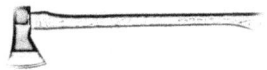

After being in the car for five minutes, she could tell that I wasn't a professional driver. Every time we approached a stop sign, she shouted, "STOP SIGN!!!"

Her shouting scared the shit out of me. It became so annoying that I said, "You want to drive?"

Holding on to the door, she said, "No, I want to make it home in one piece…"

"You'll make it home…"

"How long have you been driving?"

"Not long," I confessed.

"Clearly…" she teased.

"You know that I could have let you ride the bus…" I joked.

"Not sounding like a bad idea…at this point…"

After driving for another ten minutes, she said, "That's my apartment, right up there…"

I parked in front of the building. There was an uncomfortable moment of silence. "You want me to walk you to the door…"

Opening the car door, she said, "Naw, I got it from here. I'm just worried about you…"

"Why?"

"Not knowing how to drive will bring on the same amount of attention as drunk driving and a brother, driving around like he's drunk might get him shot…"

"I got my license…"

"Don't mean nothing when they pull you over…"

"So, what do you recommend?" I asked. "You think that I should leave the car here? I did make it to the restaurant and I got you home without getting hurt…"

She thought about it for a second and said, "How about this? And I don't usually do this, but I really don't want to be alone...you can stay here, tonight and in the morning, I can take you around...help you improve your driving."

I tried to hide my excitement. "Okay...as long as you don't rape or try to kill me..."

She laughed. "You ain't got to worry about that."

I followed her inside. She walked in the back and then, returned shortly carrying a pillow and a blanket. "You can sleep on the couch."

"Not a problem..."

She handed me the remote control and said, "Please keep the volume low...I have a room-mate and they complain about everything..."

"Would she mind me being here?"

"Don't worry about that...and it's a 'he'...I'll take care of it if he says something. He probably has somebody in his room and no telling what they're doing...the bathroom's down the hall to the left...if you need to go." She yawned and stretched. "I'm going to turn in..."

Disappointed that she was going to bed, I said, "But I thought that you wanted to talk..."

"I did, but it's late...we can talk in the morning... goodnight." She turned and walked out of the room.

I wanted to know which room hers was, so I made up an excuse to follow her down the hall. "Where's the bathroom?"

She motioned for me to follow her. "Right this way…"

When we got to the door, she said, "Here you go…"

"Thanks…" I walked in, but closed the door, slowly. I watched her enter a room. When she turned on the light, I closed the door and proceeded to wash my hands. I looked in the mirror. Realizing how lucky I was, in that moment, I wanted to scream, but didn't. Instead, I flushed the toilet to give the impression that I 'went' and left the room. I walked back down the hall and back into the living room. I placed the blanket across the couch, took off my shoes, and laid down. As I laid there, I wondered what she was doing. I wondered if she was crying over him or if she was at peace enough to fall fast asleep. I wanted to make sure that she was okay, so I waited until I thought that everyone was asleep and walked down the hall. Gently, I turned the knob. I looked in and saw that she was sleeping. She was wearing plaid pajamas as she embraced a teddy bear. There were dried tears on her face. I wanted so badly to wipe her face, but I couldn't. As I was leaving the room, I noticed a pair of her underwear lying on the floor. I kneeled down and picked them up. I placed them against my face and inhaled, deeply. She smelled so good. Curious, I wanted to know what she tasted like, so I took my tongue and began to lick the crotch of her panties. I wanted to keep them, so bad, but she may look for them in the morning, so I placed them back on the floor. My desire for her began to grow stronger. I felt the urge to hold her, to touch her, but I couldn't. For now, the scent of her body, on my face, would just have to do.

CHAPTER 53

The next morning, bright and early, I was awakened to the smell of her perfume. She was standing over me with a bowl in her hand. She smiled. I hope that you like oatmeal. I haven't had a chance to do any shopping…"

I wiped crust from my eyes and reached out for the bowl. "You didn't have to do this…"

"It's the least that I could do…you know…for you not killing me and all…" she joked.

"Killing you?" I asked, confused. Maybe I said something that I wasn't supposed to in my sleep.

"You know? With your non-driving ass…"

"Ohhhhhhhhh," I said, relieved. I took the spoon and placed some of the oatmeal in my mouth. I couldn't tell if it was my breath bouncing off of the oatmeal or maybe, it was the oatmeal, but something smelled like feet.

"Come on…now, eat up…I would like to hit the streets early…while folks are still in bed. Don't want you running into anybody…"

I tried forcing the food down my throat, but it stuck in my esophagus like I was trying to swallow a brick. When I finally got it down, I said, "I can drive…"

She laughed. "And I can make oatmeal…looks like we're both in denial…"

We both laughed as I tried to finish the food. Finally, I couldn't take it anymore. "How about we stop to get something to eat?"

She grabbed the bowl and said, "Sure…"

And she was right. The roads were completely empty. We jumped in and pulled off. "You have the basics down, but it's the execution that you're struggling with."

"I 'execute' just fine…"

She motioned for me to turn down a road and said, "Your turns are just a little choppy and you have to remember that they put traffic signals up for a…" Then, suddenly, she stopped. "Paul…pull over…"

"Huh?"

"Pull over…I think that I'm going to be sick…"

I thought that she was joking. "Come on, now, my driving ain't that bad…"

"Pull over or your dashboard is going to be covered in oatmeal."

I, immediately, stopped the car. She jumped out and before she could find the sidewalk, she was on her knees. I parked the car and ran around to see if I could help, but she stuck her hand up. She held her stomach as she heaved and wretched. I waited for her to finish and reached out my hand. She wiped her mouth with her hand and then extended it to me. I looked at it for a second and then grabbed it. "Thanks…"

"No problem…"

We both jumped back into the car. I waited a second before pulling off – watching her to make sure that she had nothing left. She touched my hand and said, "I'm good…"

We were driving along, when I decided that it would be a good idea to stop by Jeffrey's house to get some things, but as I got close, I noticed several cars parked out front. I stopped and parked.

"What are we doing, Paul?"

"I just need to see something…"

"What?" she asked, as she watched the men walk in and out of the house, carrying boxes of stuff. "Do you know who lives there?"

"I do…" I said, wondering what they'd found in the house.

"Is that the police?"

"I think so…"

"Are you in trouble?" she asked.

I hope not. I thought to myself. "No, they're looking for my boy, Jeffrey…"

"Why? Is he into some illegal stuff?"

"He was…" I said.

"He was?"

"He's dead now…"

"Oh, I'm so sorry to hear that?"

As I looked on, I said, "Don't be…it's what happens when you mess with the wrong people…"

"Oh, he must have really pissed somebody off…"

"Yeah…he did…"
"So, what are you going to do now?"
"I guess I have to find me another place to stay…"

That night, after dropping her off, I went back to Jeffrey's house to gather whatever I could find to take with me. When I went in, I noticed that the house had been ransacked. They went through everything. I wasn't sure what they were looking for, but if they decided to come back, I wanted to make sure that my ass was nowhere to be seen.

Clothes and papers were thrown all over the place. Underneath my feet, I could feel broken glass being crushed beneath them. I went down the hall into his bedroom and began searching through all of the remains. I turned on the light to find that his bed had been turned over and they'd gone through all of his drawers. There was nothing left. I was about to leave the room when I, accidentally, knocked his TV onto the floor. The back fell off. I tried to ignore it, but something told me to look inside. I pulled the back off and inside was a vanilla envelope. I began to open it when something told me that something about this scene wasn't right. I've never been in a situation like this, but I couldn't believe that the police would search a person's home and leave it in this condition. Whoever those men were, they were looking for something important and maybe, I was holding it in my hand.

As I thought about the situation, I heard the dog barking. He'd been going at it for a minute or so when suddenly, there was a loud yelp and then, silence. Afraid to move, I waited, but then I heard glass being broken. I crawled over and turned off the light. *Oh shit...shit, shit, shit, shit, shit...*I thought as I tried looking around the room in the dark. Across the room, I noticed a pile of clothes sitting in the corner. I crawled over and climbed underneath them.

"It's gotta be here...somewhere," the male voice said.
"We looked everywhere..." the other male voice said.
"But you heard what he said...we better not come back empty-handed or he's going to kill us..."
"I know...I know..."
One of them began to pace back and forth across the room. He walked over to the pile of clothes and stood next to them. He was so close to my face that I could smell the shoe polish bouncing off of the leather on his shoes. "Where do you think that he put it?"

"If I knew that, would we be standing here?" the other voice said, becoming frustrated.

"Keep on and you won't have to wait for him to kill your ass…I'mma do it for him."

"Look, we need to do what we came in here to do…"

"Or we could wait until the hospital releases his ass…"

Who? I thought to myself.

"That is one lucky-ass bastard…who gets shot, thrown into a pier, and survives that shit?"

"Holy shit…" I mouthed.

"They ain't releasing his ass anytime soon…that motherfucker's brains are mush. They gon' pull the plug on his ass any day now…that's why we need to get that shit before they come here…trying to find a suit to bury his ass in…and stumble upon it. You know how many motherfuckers will end-up in jail if that shit ends-up in the wrong hands?"

I looked down at the envelope.

"Come on…we searched through this shit already…"

"But what about the boss?"

"We'll tell him that Jeffrey swallowed the shit, so that he can send somebody over to the hospital to drill a hole in his ass to find it. If he ain't dead already, he will be after that."

CHAPTER 54

I couldn't knock on her door. Instead, I sat out in front of her apartment, in Jeffrey's car, staring at the contents of the envelope. As I held the flash-drives in my hand, I wondered what was on them. I was still looking at them when there was a knock on the window.

"What are you doing?" she asked.

I rolled down the window. "Good morning…"

"Why are you here?" she asked.

Embarrassed, I said, "I don't have anywhere else to go."

She motioned for me to get out of the car. "Come inside…"

I closed the envelope, followed her inside, and sat down on the couch.

"What is that?" she asked.

Feeling like I could trust her, I said, "Something that I found at the house…"

She reached out her hand. "Can I see?"

I hesitated for a second, but then handed it to her. She looked inside. "What's on them?"

I shrugged. "I don't know…"

She stood and said, "Let's go and see…"

I followed her into another room. In the middle of a desk, sat a computer. She turned it on. After logging in, she inserted one of the drives. It opened up and we began to scan through its contents. At first, there wasn't much to see. There were some documents that contained some names and numbers. She kept clicking on files until we came across a folder that held pictures. The first few were too dark to make out, but the next one was clear – very clear. She paused. She placed her hand over her mouth. With tears in her eyes, she looked up at me. "What is this?"

I stared at the image. I knew what she was looking at. It was clear that it was a picture of a person who'd been stabbed to death. But she was asking what it was because she wanted me to convince her that it wasn't real - that maybe her eyes were playing tricks on her. I didn't respond. She "clicked" the mouse again. Another disturbing image popped-up and each time that she "clicked", one, more disturbing than the other appeared on the screen.

Finally, she couldn't take it anymore. She turned off the computer and removed the drive. She stared at it. "Did you do any of this?"

Although I did help him kill people, none of the murders were captured on a camera. "No…"

"So, what are you going to do about this?"

I took the drives from her hand. "Nothing…that's what I'm going to do…"

I turned to leave the room. On my heels, she followed behind me. "But you have to tell somebody…"

"Naw…I can't do that…"

"But you have to…"

I turned, abruptly – causing her to run into me. "Deidra, do you know what happens to people who talk? They end-up with their tongues and throats cut out…"

"But you can't hold on to something like this…"

"Yes, I can…"

I turned to walk away.

"No, Paul…" She stopped and fell to her knees. She groaned as she held her stomach.

I turned to help her. "Are you okay?"

She grabbed my hand. "Yeah…I just haven't been feeling well, lately…"

"Have you gone to the doctor?" I asked, helping her to her feet.

"Naw…it's just a 'bug' going around. I should be okay…"

I helped her to the couch. After she regained her composure, she said, "Paul, if you hold on to that…it's going to always be hanging over your head…our heads."

"Our heads?" I asked.

"Yes, Paul…whoever those people were…I'm sure that they were looking for this…which means that they are, now, looking for you and guess where you're at?"

I hadn't thought about it, but she was right. In my attempt to avoid getting involved in Jeffrey's bullshit, I may have inadvertently, gotten us both involved. So,

I thought about it for a second. I needed to protect us just in case those people decided to come after one of us. "Okay, how about this...let's make a copy and hold on to it...for insurance. We can mail this to the police...anonymously..."

"Okay..." she tried standing, but then fell back onto the couch. "Give me a second..." She covered her eyes.

"You want some water or something?" I asked.

"Could you, please?"

"Yes...yes...of course..."

"Thank you..."

I went into the kitchen to find a glass. After finding one, I filled it with water and ran back into the room. She was stretched-out across the couch. One of her legs was propped-up on top of the couch. The other was laying along its side. Her legs were wide open revealing what lied between them. She'd shaven all of her hair off exposing her "lips". I was staring at "it" and "it" was staring back at me. Quietly, I approached her – trying to see all of it. Feeling my presence, she tried to hide "it". She jumped up and covered herself. "I'm sorry...I'm so, so, sorry..."

With the image branded across my mind, I said, "It's okay..."

"Damn, you must think that I'm a slut..."

I handed her the glass. "No, I don't...it's beautiful..."

She paused for a second and said, "You think so?"

"Yeah...I do..." I smiled. "I think that you're beautiful."

She looked away from the glass and looked up at me. Looking into my eyes, she said, "You have some beautiful eyes, Paul…you know that they say 'that the eyes are the windows to the soul…"

"These 'windows' have seen a lot of things…" I said. "Maybe one day you can tell me about it…"

I looked down at the floor. "Naw…'cause what's hidden behind these 'windows' need to stay behind these windows."

Chapter 55

After discussing my current situation with her roommate, she decided to let me move into the room that they used as their office. I was so truly grateful for the invitation, because while I'd been out on my own for some time now, I was still trying to navigate the life of being an adult. It looked easy on television, but the truth of the matter is, that it wasn't. And this way, it gave me a reason to be close to her and I was very close to her. She didn't know it, but I was. I used to watch her as she slept, smell her clothing after she removed them, I drank from the same glass that she drank from, and I even brushed my teeth with her toothbrush just to know what her mouth tasted like. I dreamed about her every minute of the day. Thoughts of her consumed me and that's why watching her, in her current state, was so hard to bear.

I did everything that I could to try to get her to forget him, but nothing that I did seemed to work. She loved him even though he'd betrayed her. She couldn't let him go. And while I did everything that I could to show her that I loved her, she didn't want that from me. What she wanted from me was a shoulder to cry on, so I decided to be that shoulder, but I still held hope for the day that she would look at me through the same eyes that she looked at him and see that I really loved her too.

So, while I waited for that to happen, I tried to fit in. Coming from the world that I was born and raised in, trying to fit in wasn't easy. Deidra and her roommate weren't normal, but they were more normal than I was accustomed to. Now, their neighbors were a different story. They were the oddest group of people that I'd ever come across, and considering the folks in my family, that was saying a whole lot.

When you walk out of her apartment, to your left, you would find an apartment that had about thirty people living in it which wouldn't be a problem if it wasn't a two-bedroom apartment. Every time I looked-up, there was somebody new moving in. I don't think any one of them had a job unless they were getting paid to sit on their asses. Across the hall was an old lady who was nosey as hell. She knew everything about anything that happened in the complex and if she didn't know, she had no problem finding out. Then, down the hall was our neighborhood pharmacist. He wasn't a licensed drug-dealer like the ones at our local pharmacy, but he sold as many drugs as they did, if not more. He was open 24 hours a day, 7 days a week, and even on holidays. He had more locks on his door than Fort Knox and the only people that he opened it up for was either doing business with him or looking for an ass-whooping. I never went over there because I didn't want or need either.

I used to walk the block just to see what was around there. The neighborhood was nice compared to where I'd come from, but like most areas of Chicago, it wasn't without its issues. Back in the day, this was probably a really nice place to live, but it had become a hostage to gangs. People were afraid to leave their homes. You saw people leave for work and school in the morning and you saw them return home later in the evening, but for the most part that was it. The sounds of the streets were loud music and gunfire. I'd resigned myself to just work and go home, because I didn't want to get caught-up in any of the mess that was going on around there.

As I thought about this new chapter in my life, I couldn't help, but think about all of the lives I'd taken. I knew that at some point my past was going to catch up with me. While I wasn't spending my life looking over my shoulder, I would soon find out that I didn't have to, because someone else was doing it for me.

CHAPTER 56

Each day, more and more, it seemed like her health was declining. I knew that I hadn't been in her life long enough to tell her what to do, but it was starting to concern me. She'd been throwing up so much and she'd lost so much weight, I was starting to think that maybe she wouldn't be around long enough for me to love her. So, the next morning, when I heard her crying behind the bathroom door, I said, "Deidra...how are you feeling?"

"Like shit, Paul...like fucking shit."

"Is there something that I can get for you?"

"Do you have a gun to put me out of my damn misery?"

"No..."

"Then, you can't help me..."

"You don't want to do that..."

She opened the door and with breath that indicated that she'd been throwing up, she said, "Yes, I do...I want to die, Paul."

"Don't say that..."

She opened her mouth to say something else when a strange look swept across her face. She kneeled over the toilet. In between breaths, she said, "Get a knife and kill me…"

I walked over and began to rub her back. "Have you been to the doctor?"

She wiped her mouth and said, "No…"

"Let me take you to the doctor so that we can find out what's going on?"

She pushed me back and spat. "I'm not doing that shit…"

Stumbling, I fell against the wall. "Why did you do that?"

"Because I don't want to hear that…look at me…I may be dying. I don't want to know why or what I'm dying from. If I'm going to leave this world, I just want to close my eyes and leave this bitch in my rearview mirror…"

"Deidra…that doesn't make any sense."

She sat back against the wall. "To you it don't…you ain't the one walking around here throwing up shit all day every day…losing weight…" She began to cry, again. "Look at me…I'm a fucking stick-figure…"

"You're not that bad…" I said, lying. She looked horrible.

"Are you blind? I'm wasting away, and I don't know why…"

I knew that what I was going to ask next might piss her off, but I needed to know. "Do you think that you have…you know?"

She frowned. "What are you trying to say?"

Being, real, careful about what I was saying, I continued, "Well, they taught us about STDs in school…"

She stuck her hand up. "Don't be wishing that bullshit on me…"

"I'm just saying, Deidra…"

"I ain't got no damn STD and if I do, I'm going to kill the motherfucker who gave it to me…"

"I don't think that you have to worry about that…"

Confused, she said, "Why?"

"I'm just saying…if he got one of the 'bad' ones, he may already be dead…again, I'm just saying."

"Well, I better not have that shit…I swear fo' God…I better not have that shit."

I extended my hand. "There's only one way to find out."

She looked at my hand, for a moment, and said, "Okay…let's go."

It felt like we'd been in the emergency room for days. I was starting to think that maybe we should have packed a lunch or something. My ass was starting to go numb when all of a sudden, they called her name. She raised her hand and began to follow them down the hall. The nurse turned and looked at me. "Aren't you coming?"

I pointed at myself.

Deidra looked back. "Oh no…he's not my husband."

The nurse said, "Okay…"

They disappeared behind the double doors. I closed my eyes and began to settle in for a long wait.

About an hour had passed, when I felt someone touching my arm. Startled, I jumped up. "Wha...what?"

She looked at me. "Hey stranger..."

"Shit..." I said. "What are you doing here?"

"I work here," she said. She looked around the room. "Who are you with?"

I looked over at the doors and said, "I'm just here...with a friend."

She smiled. "Well, I hope that they are okay."

"Me too..." Becoming nervous, I glanced at the doors again.

She leaned in and whispered in my ear. "Thanks for taking care of that little problem that we had..."

"Ummmmm....no problem."

"He'd still be alive if he learned how to keep his dick in his pants..."

"Yeah...dick in his pants..." I said, becoming agitated.

"If you want to call it a dick..." she began to laugh when the doors opened.

Deidra walked out with a look on her face that looked like she'd seen a ghost. I looked up to find that the woman standing next to me had the same look on her face. It was clear that Deidra had no idea that the woman standing next to her was her late lover's wife, but the look on the woman's face confirmed that she knew all about Deidra. I stood to intervene when Deidra blurted out. "I'm pregnant, Paul. I'm not going to die. I'm fucking pregnant…"

The woman looked at her. Biting her tongue, she said, "Well, congratulations…Paul…"

"Thanks…" I said, pulling at Deidra's arm.

Deidra snatched away and asked, "Who are you?"

"I'm a friend of your boyfriend…" she said, as she patted my shoulder.

Deidra laughed. "Oh no, he and I are just friends…"

I felt deflated, but in that moment, my ego was the least of my concerns. I had to get her out of there.

"Sooooooooooo, if he's not your boyfriend. Then, who's the lucky father." She looked like someone had stuck a stick of dynamite up her butt and any minute now, she was going to explode.

Squinting her eyes, Deidra said, "And how are you two friends?"

I interrupted. "We went to school together."

Deidra frowned. "Was she your teacher or something…?"

She didn't like Deidra's jab at her age. She was about to take off her earrings and turn the waiting-room into a boxing ring when Deidra said, "Well, if you must know…"

"I must…" the woman said.

"It's my EX-boyfriend's baby," she said, grinning from ear-to-ear.

Oh shit…I thought to myself. Trying to get her out of the emergency room, before we both ended-up needing a hospital bed, I said, "I need to get you home…"

The woman looked like someone had just kicked her in the chest. Deidra had just confirmed the woman's worst nightmare, but she wanted more evidence. "And what is your ex-boyfriend's name?"

"I prefer not to say…it's over and I'm afraid that if I say his name, he might pop-up like the freakin' Candy-man and I don't want that."

The woman wasn't done. She had to confirm her worse suspicion. "Oh…I'm just curious…you know…how about I try to guess his name?"

Deidra frowned. "Why do you care who my baby's father is?"

Pretending not to care, she said, "I don't…but I'm just curious."

Entertaining her, Deidra said, "Go ahead…guess…"

I said, "Deidra…we're double-parked…we need to get out of here before we get a ticket."

The woman placed her finger on her chin, pretending to think about it, before saying, "Ummmmm, Mike?" She smiled. "Wow, that's right…how did you guess?"

The woman didn't laugh. She began to breathe heavily. "It was an unlucky guess…"

"Unlucky?" Deidra asked.

She balled her hands into a fist. "Very…fucking… unlucky."

I grabbed Deidra's hand. "Let's go…"

Pulling away, Deidra said, "I know why it was unlucky, but why do you say that it was unlucky? Do you know him?"

She had an evil look on her face. "Do YOU know him? That's the fucking million-dollar question...isn't it, Paul?"

Deidra was becoming annoyed. "You know...I don't like your tone."

The woman's eyes widened. "My tone? You don't like my tone...YOU DON'T LIKE MY TONE? Bitch, my tone is the last thing you need to worry about."

I jumped in the middle of them.

"Did she call me a bitch? Why would you call me a bitch? You don't even know me..." Deidra said.

She balled-up her fist. "Oh...I know some shit, bitch and in a minute, you gon' find out EXACTLY what I know..."

I stood in her face. "Now, you don't want to do that...do you? As a FRIEND, you know that that wouldn't be a good idea, right? Considering that you're at work...remember?"

She sucked her teeth. "You're right...but we'll be talking about this, again, later...FRIEND."

Deidra was mad. "You called me a bitch...I want to see your supervisor."

I looked at her. "Come on...let's not make any trouble for her. She's having a hard time because she just lost her husband."

Deidra stopped. She began to feel sorry for the woman and extended her hand to her. "I'm sorry to hear that, but you shouldn't take your anger out on strangers."

The woman didn't take her hand. Instead, she laughed. "You can take your advice and stick it up your..."

I grabbed Deidra's arm before she had a chance to finish her sentence. I dragged her out of the building. When we were in the car, she said, "You need better friends, Paul. That bitch has an attitude problem..."

As I started the car, I said, "Yeah...and that's not her only problem."

CHAPTER 57

"So, what are you going to do? I asked her.

"Well, now that I know what's wrong with me, I have to admit, I've been too shocked to think about it."

"Well, you know that you have to…"

"I know, I know…"

"Are you ready to be the mother of a married man's baby?"

"I'm not ready to be anybody's mama…shit, I had sex…I wasn't thinking about no baby. During the 'heat of the moment', your thoughts are on the 'heat' not the 'moment.' You don't start thinking about the 'moment' until the 'heat' subsides and dumbshit like this happens." She paused for a moment and said, "I don't know what to do and who's going to show me? My mama is dead…"

"Oh, I'm sorry to hear that…"

"Thanks, but I never really knew her. She died when I was six…and how much can a six-year old remember?"

"My mom's dead too…"

"Oh, I'm sorry to hear that…me and you both…no mama…when did she die?"

"It's been a minute…"

"Was she sick?"

"Yeah, she was sick..." I confirmed.

"What? Cancer? Heart Attack?"

"No, stupidity..."

"Stupidity killed her?" Deidra chuckled as she rubbed her stomach. "I didn't know that that was a disease..."

"And yet, many people die from it..."

"I take it you didn't like your mama..."

"No, I didn't..."

"I'm sorry to hear that...I can see that this is a sore-spot for you..."

"It's not sore anymore...she did her job..."

"Which was?"

"She brought me into this world..."

"That's it?"

"That's it..."

"I think a mama's job is more than that..."

"For Betty, it was the one thing that she was good at...and she did it...well...beyond that, she didn't know her ass from a hole in the wall..."

"Wow...that's harsh..."

"That's Betty..."

"Well, it's hard living without my mama...not having a mama put me in a lot of difficult and scary situations. Shit, if she'd been around, I probably wouldn't have dealt with a married man."

"I thought that women who did that had some type of daddy-issue..."

"Or maybe, they end-up there because they don't have a woman to teach them their worth or to help them understand what a woman should and should not do…her absence put me in a lot of compromising positions…this being one of them…"

I didn't want to ask her this question, but like the elephant in the room, it couldn't be ignored. "So, you gon' tell the daddy?"

"No, I would never do that…I wouldn't want to hurt his family."

"So, you gon' try to raise the baby alone?" I asked, knowing that it would be hard for the father to send child support payments from the "great beyond."

"Why? Are you volunteering?" She pushed me in the arm and began to laugh, but she could see that the look on my face indicated that I didn't find it funny.

Insulted, I asked, "Why couldn't I help you? I'm here…"

"But we're not in a relationship, Paul. Why would you want to dedicate your life to raising another man's baby?"

"Men do it all of the time…you don't have to share blood to be someone's father…"

"But…" She looked away for a second and then continued, "You're talking like a godfather, right?"

I was becoming frustrated. I couldn't understand why she couldn't see that I loved her and I didn't understand why she didn't love me. "Why? Would it be so fucking horrible to have someone like me in your life?"

"What is wrong with you, Paul? You are in my life…"

I jumped up and began to pace around the room. "NO! I'm talking about something else, Deidra. I've been here, and I watched you cry over a man who fucked you and another woman…"

"Paul…" she said.

"No, that's bullshit. You need to hear this shit. I never understood why you would settle for a man who would go home after he's rolled off of you just to roll his ass on top of another…when there is a good man right here who wants to love you…you and only you."

"You?" she said, again.

"Why the fuck not? Am I not good enough for you?"

"I never said that, Paul…"

"Well, what are you saying, Deidra? What the fuck are you saying?"

She reached out and grabbed my hand. "Paul, please…sit down."

"I don't need to sit down to hear bullshit. My ears can hear it over here…"

She begged. "Paul…please…"

I exhaled and plopped down next to her. "Go ahead…"

"Why would you want somebody like me?"

"Wait…what?"

"I mean, you think that I think that you're not good enough, but what if it's me?"

"What are you saying, Deidra?"

"Look at me, Paul…I'm a fucking mess. I'm pregnant by a married man. What kind of 'amateur' bullshit is that? It would be one thing, if I didn't know that he was married and got caught-up, but I knew that he was married…this type of shit only happens when you're not careful. He's married. I should have been more careful."

"Amateur? Is your goal to become a pro?"

"No…no…that's not what I meant."

"Well, did you do it on purpose?"

She hesitated to answer the question.

"Well, did you?"

"No…not really…"

"Not really?"

"Well…" She looked confused. "I guess I could have done more…to be careful."

"Yeah, by not fucking somebody else's man…"

"It happened, shit. There's nothing that I can do about it now."

I gave her a 'look.'

"No, no…I know what you're thinking and I will never do that…kill my baby? No, hell no…"

"Well, this is definitely a sucker's move…nobody wins."

"Shit, I know. I'm not delusional, Paul. I'm stupid. There's a big difference and I know that all he wanted to do was fuck me and I gave it to him…willingly. I fell in love and he used that to use me…"

"And, now, you're sitting here acting like being with me after being with him would be like going from sugar to shit...I wouldn't shed a tear for his ass."

"And I wouldn't expect you to...just like I don't expect you to understand. Yeah, he ain't shit, but he just..." She looked away. She wiped her face and continued. "He makes me feel so good. It's hard to explain."

"Yeah, AND he's gone now...and I'm here..."

"You're right, Paul, but as fucked-up as he is, he's a part of me...more, now, than ever before."

"Well, I'm here for you...even if you think that I'm not good enough."

She grabbed my face with her other hand and kissed me on the cheek. She stopped and looked at me. "Okay, Paul...but if he does come back, if he wants to, I'm going to let him be a part of this child's life."

I huffed and said, "Yeah, that's IF he comes back."

Chapter 58

I was being given a second chance to have something special. I felt like, even though, I'd done some bad things in my life, I, almost, felt worthy of this opportunity. But as badly as I wanted this, something about it didn't seem right. Maybe, my judgement was clouded because I was so desperate not to be alone, again and I wanted, for once in my life, to know what a normal family is. Maybe, I was willing to take on this challenge because I was looking for the one thing that I never had as a child and I'd already committed myself to her. She started to depend on me, so I didn't want to let her down, but I would soon find out that she would be the one letting me down – one, deep, secret at a time.

Each day, we were getting a little closer, but I still hadn't graduated from friend to lover – at least, not to her. I still loved her and being in her life was as close as a relationship that I've ever had, but that left me in an odd position, because in my eyes, she was mine and that baby was mine. I just needed for her to see it, but my 'game' kept getting delayed because of all of the skeletons in her closet.

She and I were sitting on the couch when her roommate walked in with two girls, one on each arm. He told them to wait in his bedroom. He walked into the kitchen and returned with some spoons, a bottle of water, and some paper towels. He walked into his room. Deidra and I were talking when the door to his room opened up. He walked out, butt-ass naked, and said, "You want to get in on this?"

Caught off guard, I asked, "Who the fuck you talking to?"

"I'm talking to Deidra..." he confirmed.

I looked at her. "What is he talking about?"

She squinted in his direction. "Nothing...he ain't talking about nothing."

"Are you sure? 'Cause he looks like he's talking about something..."

"I said that he ain't talking about nothing..." she confirmed.

"Suit yourself, but if you change your mind, there's room for two more..." He scratched his ass and walked back into the room.

I scratched my chin. "For that motherfucker to be talking about nothing...he sho' looks like he's talking about something, Deidra..."

"I told you that he's not talking about nothing..."

"A minute ago, you was all like 'let's be honest' and shit, but when a motherfucker walk out here with his dick hanging out...I'd expect you to flinch...cover your eyes...do something...but you looked at it like dicks swinging in the wind is a normal occurrence around here…like the rising of the sun."

She stood to leave the room. "Paul, you're being silly."

"Again, with the silly shit…I was a little uncomfortable, but not you…you looked real comfortable."

She opened the refrigerator and stuck her head inside. "Did you drink the last of the orange juice?" She asked.

"Do you think that I give a shit about some damn orange juice? Are you trying to change the subject?"

"No…I just, really, want some orange juice…" she said, rubbing her stomach.

I began to breathe heavily.

She sighed. "Okay…I've seen him naked before…"

"Naked walking to the bathroom or naked laying on top of you."

She sighed again and then, confessed "Naked laying on top of me…"

I grabbed my ear and leaned close to her. "What did you say? I didn't hear you."

"It happened once, Paul…a long time ago…I was lonely…he was lonely…one thing led to another…"

"Once…?"

"Well, maybe twice…"

"Maybe? Two is not a hard number to remember."

"Well, like I said…it was a long time ago…"

"That motherfucker is acting like this is some new shit…fresh…recent…like he'd-just-popped-the-cap-on-this-shit-kinda new."

"Well, I can't help what he thinks or feels…"

Frustrated, I said, "Damn, this seems to be the story of your life…" I turned to leave the room.

The roommate's door opened. "Did you change your mind?"

"NO!!!!" we both said.

He slammed the door.

I walked over to the table and grabbed my keys.

On my heels, she said, "Paul, where are you going?"

I placed my hand on the doorknob and began to turn it. "I need to get some air."

"Paul, don't leave like this…let's talk about it."

I looked over her shoulder. "When I get back, that motherfucker, his dick, and his hoes better be gon'…"

"Or what?" she asked.

I smiled. "Or nothing…you know, like you say, 'nothing'…"

CHAPTER 59

S he wasn't taking me seriously and his disrespect for me and our 'situationship' began to cause a rift between us. We started to argue about him and it wasn't because I was jealous or feeling insecure, but this motherfucker was out of control and needed to be checked. It was hard to get her to understand that unless you're in a locker room or you're fucking, a man should not be comfortable with having conversations with another man with his dick hanging out and it was on a daily basis. If I didn't' know any better, I swear that he didn't own any underwear and I didn't want to see that mess. It was inappropriate, not to mention weird as fuck. I wasn't going to allow him to punk me. I've been there before and the person who punked me ended-up with a pencil in his neck and this guy was about to meet a similar fate.

I was getting ready for work, when I heard someone arguing down the hall. I cracked the door to hear what was going on. I looked out to find a naked woman standing in the hall.

"I don't have time for that 'think I can, I think I can,' bullshit…when you climb up in this pussy, you better KNOW you can…" she said, smacking her lips.

"Look, we've been fucking all night…can a man have a moment? I'm not a machine, damnit," he said.

She frowned. "Is that what we were doing? Fucking? You should have told me."

"Bitch, don't act new…you knew what we were doing and you were enjoying it. I saw the look on your face."

"I was passing gas, fool…I wasn't cumming."

He looked down the hall and noticed that our door was cracked.

He snatched her by the arm and said, "Get in here."

She snatched her arm back and said, "I don't have time for this shit. Plus, my husband is waiting on me to get home."

He snatched her again. "You will go home when we're done."

She snatched her arm again and looked down at the limp flesh that sat between his legs. "You must be kidding. Unless you got a spare for that flat tire, I'm going home."

He looked down the hall at the cracked door, again. "Get in here!!!"

"No," she said.

They began to struggle. I walked out of the room hoping that when he saw me, he would let the woman go home, but, instead, the woman saw this as an opportunity to draw me into their mess. She looked me up and down. "Hey," she said.

Trying not to look at her, I responded. "Hey."

This pissed the roommate off. "Hey…she likes what she sees. You want to tag-team this…"

She laughed. "What you gon' do? Watch? 'Cause you ain't tagging shit with that thang. You are all tagged-out."

"Fuck you, hoe," he spat.

"There you go again…talking about shit you can't do," she teased.

I kept walking until he said, "You can have her…I'm done with her ass."

"Who you talking to?" I asked.

She turned to him and said, "You done with me? I'm done with you…with your tired ass and I do mean 'tired'."

Before I could say anything else, he'd waved his hand and when it came down it landed against the side of her face. Her head swung backwards and when she was able to regain her composure, she swung back, so hard that he let out a loud *Yelp!* The next thing, I knew they were exchanging blows. I jumped in the middle to stop the fight. Standing between them, the woman walked into his room, grabbed her purse, and stormed passed us. "Forget my number, asshole."

"Already forgotten, bitch," he said.

When the woman was out of the apartment, I began to walk away. He placed his hand upon my shoulder. "Now, about you getting into my business."

I looked down at his hand before saying, "Move it or lose it…"

He didn't remove it, so I assumed he chose the option to lose it. I grabbed his hand and twisted it until his hand was facing towards me. I pushed him into his bedroom and closed the door. His eyes widened. He tried to get away from me, but it was too late. I grabbed on to the first finger. I held it as I stared into his eyes. I smiled. "When I was a kid, my grandmamma used to play this game with us called, 'The five little piggies…ever heard of it?'" For a moment, he had a confused look on his face. Looking at the first finger, I said, "This little piggy has a limp dick…" I pushed it back until I heard it snap. His mouth fell open. He tried to scream, but nothing came out but air. I grabbed the next finger. He struggled to release his hand, but I held on, tighter. "This little piggy hates the truth about his limp dick." I pushed the second finger back until it snapped. His knees began to buckle and he fell to his knees. I grabbed the third finger. "This little piggy like to beat-up on women who tells him the truth about his limp dick." I pushed the third finger back until it snapped. This time, he let out a sound that I was unfamiliar with. I stopped and said, "Are you okay? You don't sound too good…"

He began to whimper. "I'm…I'm sorry."

I grabbed on to his fourth finger and said, "I know, but I like this game and we're almost done. Now, where was I? Oh, that's right. This little piggy…"

He held up his other hand. "Look...look...look... what I said about your girl...look, I didn't mean it."

I stopped and looked at him. "Oh, I almost forgot about that..." I pushed the fourth finger back until it touched the back of his hand. He let out a loud scream. "Aaaaaaahhhhhh!!!"

"Now, for the last piggy. This little piggy decided to fuck with the wrong motherfucker today." I pushed it back until it snapped. I let his hand go. He grabbed his hand and held it close to him. I extended my hand. "No harm done...let's shake...oh, that's right... maybe, some dap?" I laughed and began to walk away. "I have to go to work...you try to have a good day."

He ran over to his bed and when he returned, he was holding a gun. I looked at him. "When I woke-up this morning, and got dressed, I had no idea that I was going to die today. If I'd known, I would have put on my good underwear."

He frowned. "You think this shit is funny?"

"No, what's funny is your dumbass. What do you think you gon' do with that?"

He pointed it at my head.

I walked up to it and pushed the barrel against my head. "Don't pull a gun on a man unless you plan to use it."

He smiled. Then, I heard a *click* and then a loud *pop!* There was a wisp of smoke as the smell of gun powder filled the air. At first, I was unclear what'd happened, but then suddenly, there was a loud ringing in my ears. The sound was so loud that it was the only thing that I could hear. I felt something warm drip down the side of my face. I looked down to find red stains covering my shirt. I touched the side of my face. When I looked at my hand, I noticed that it was covered with blood. I looked up to find him laughing as if someone had said something funny. His mouth began to move, but I was unable to hear what he was saying. With all of the strength that I had left, I lunged at him. We struggled. He was blinded by the blood that was dripping from my head. I hit him several times until everything went black.

The next thing that I remember was a loud beeping sound. I tried opening my eyes, but my eyelids were too heavy to move. I felt something warm lying on top of my hand. A voice said, "Paul?"
"Deidra?"
"I'm right here..."
"Deidra?" I mumbled.
"I'm here...I'm right here..."
"Where is he?"

"He's dead, Paul," she confirmed.
I closed my eyes and fell fast asleep.

CHAPTER 60

We tried to move on, but Deidra's past wouldn't let us. The baby in her stomach was the only thing that kept her connected to me and to the man that I murdered. I'd tried to forget that it belonged to someone else and that when it came into the world, it won't look like me. And although it won't have my blood flowing through its veins, by law, it would be mine and I would love it like I was the one making love to her on the night that it was conceived. And I have to admit that I was excited; probably more than she was, because I had a chance to have someone who will love me, for the first time, unconditionally.

The whole apartment was converted into a baby's room. Everywhere I turned, there was something to remind me that it was on its way, and while we prepared for its arrival, we were unaware that there was somebody else who was waiting for it too, but she wasn't as happy as we were. She wanted the baby out of the picture and she was on a mission to make that happen, so much so, that the woman was crazy enough to show-up at Deidra's baby shower. I wasn't there when she arrived, but when I walked in, I saw her sitting in my living room, laughing and talking like she was Deidra's best friend.

"Look who's here, Paul..." Deidra said, pointing at the woman sitting next to her. "Tiff, stopped by to deliver a gift for the baby."

"Tiff?" I asked.

Deidra smiled and wrapped her arm around her. "Yeah, she apologized for the way that she acted at the hospital...why didn't you tell me that y'all dated in high school?"

I thought that I was having an 'out-of-body' experience. I walked out of the apartment, looked at the address to make sure that I was in the right place, then turned, and went back in. "Excuse me...we did what?" I asked, trying to figure out what the hell was going on.

Tiff walked up and grabbed my arm. "I told her that she had nothing to worry about, but seeing y'all together at the hospital...well, it just reminded me of that night that we shared together...you remember that night, don't you?" She dug her nails into my arm. Through clinched teeth, I said, "No, I don't." I pried her hands from my arm.

"Now, you gon' hurt my feelings. You were my first...remember? I'd never experienced anything like that...left blood all over my sheets. Remember baby?" She sucked her teeth and smiled.

I adjusted the collar on my shirt. "Ummmmm.... Tiff...you're...ummmmm...embarrassing me." I looked around the room and noticed that everyone was staring at us, especially Deidra.

I turned back to Tiff. I narrowed my eyes. "It happened a long time ago...now, let it go."

She giggled. "You're right...you've moved on and now, she's having our..." She stopped and cleared her throat. "I mean...she's having your baby? Right...she's having your baby?"

I grabbed her arm, tightly. "Ain't you got somewhere to go?"

"Yes...now, that you mention it."

I walked her to the door and down the stairs. When we were at the bottom, I said, "What the hell are you doing?"

"She doesn't deserve that thing growing inside of her. It's his, so that makes it mine..."

"You sound insane...you do realize that when he fucked her, he didn't have you in mind..."

Without hesitating, she said, "Well, if I can't have it, neither should she..."

"What are you saying?"

"I'm saying that that baby has to die."

I grabbed her arm and dragged her to the curb. "Ain't nobody killing no babies..."

"You didn't have a problem killing its daddy," she said.

"I'm its daddy and your husband was a cheating-piece of shit...I did the world a favor..."

"Well, do the world another favor and kill his offspring."

"You want me to come to your house and kill your son?" I asked.

Realizing that I was serious, she said, "Of course, not."

"Then choose your words wisely...offspring includes the one that you got at home."

"You know that's not what I meant..."

I looked over my shoulder to find Deidra peeking out of the curtain. "Look, don't come back over here."

She stuck her finger in my chest. "No, you look. I can make shit real uncomfortable for you. I could tell that cute little home-wrecking-baby-making machine, up there, that her boyfriend is a murderer and then, after they lock you up, I can fight for shared custody of my husband's baby."

"First, I'm not worried about you telling anybody since it was your idea to do it. The police would find it real interesting to find out why I came in, killed him, but left you and your child alive and second, you can't fight for custody of another woman's baby..." I confirmed.

"Probably not, but I will receive some joy after I prove that she's an unfit mother and they come and snatch it and stick it in a foster home while they investigate the charges...and while some of the foster homes are good...there's a few horrible ones...you don't want to roll the dice and hope that the baby gets a good one...now, do you?"

I was about to snap her neck right there on the curb when I heard Deidra say, "Paul, come on...I want you to see the cute little outfits that my friends got for the baby…" She paused and waved at Tiff. "Bye Tiff…" "Bye, bitch…and my name is Tiffany, you fucking side-piece..." She mumbled under her breath as she waved. "She gon' make me come back over here and carve my name in that stomach of hers…she don't want that…believe me."

CHAPTER 61

I watched over her like a hawk. I barely slept at night for fear of Tiffany coming to harm her and the baby. The only time that I couldn't be there for her was when we were both at work, but beyond that, I never let her out of my sight. At home, she couldn't even use the toilet without me standing outside of the bathroom door. She never knew of the danger she was in and it was my goal to make sure that she didn't. But the shooting left me with headaches that were debilitating. Sometimes, the pain was so bad that I had to take something to ease it and with me not sleeping, when I did fall asleep, I was gone. Even the last Resurrection of the Lord couldn't wake me up and on this particular night, that would prove, almost, deadly.

We'd gone to bed. Before we laid down, I went through the checklist. "Okay, Deidra...you have to go to the bathroom?"
"Nope," she said.
"You're hungry?" I asked.
She rubbed her stomach and pretended like she was having a conversation with the baby. "Are you

hungry?" She leaned towards her stomach and then responded, "Nope…we're good." She giggled.

"Okay…I'm turning off the light. We're good?"

"We're good…" she confirmed.

I locked the door and climbed in the bed beside her.

"Goodnight, Paul."

"Goodnight, Deidra…" I said.

My thoughts drifted to my grandmother. I really missed her. I wondered if she would have been happy to become a grandmother again. As I imagined her reaction to the news, my eyelids grew heavy. I tried forcing them open, but sleep was a stronger opponent. Soon, I lost the fight and fell fast asleep. When I opened them again it was to the sound of someone banging on the door. Startled, I looked down and noticed that she was gone. I, immediately, thought that she'd locked herself out, so I didn't even bother to put on any clothes. When I opened it, I said, "I thought that we agreed that you would stay in bed."

The man at the door looked me up and down before saying, "Sir, are you Paul?"

Confused, I asked. "Yeah…what's wrong?" Looking at his uniform, I realized that something terrible had happened. I ran back into the apartment – running from room to room, I screamed out her name. "Deidra! Deidra!"

The man at the door, said, "Sir! Sir!"

Running through the house, I grabbed a pair of pants off of the floor and threw them on.

"Sir…that's why I'm here."

I ran passed him to find them hauling her away. I ran down the stairs to catch-up with the stretcher. "Deidra! Speak to me…"

The man caught-up with me and said, "Sir, let them take her to the hospital."

I flipped around and said, "What happened?"

"She fell down the stairs…" he said.

"How did she fall down the stairs?" I asked.

"Look, I don't know…a neighbor found her at the bottom of the stairs. That's all of the information that we have for now. We're taking her to the hospital." He ran to get on the ambulance. "You can meet us there…"

As I watched him walk towards the street, I saw Tiff standing on the sidewalk. I ran across the street towards her. "What did you do? What did you do?!!!!"

"I fixed our little problem…"

"You what?!!! Bitch, I will kill you."

"Smile, Paul…your neighbors are watching…"

I turned to look at the crowd that was forming in front of the building. I walked away from her. "Bitch, I swear, if something happens to her…something is going to happen to you."

She placed her hand against her ear. "What was that? Could you say that louder? They didn't hear you."

"Go home to your son…hug him…while you can."

"Is that a threat?"

"No, just some advice."

I ran back to the apartment, changed my clothes, and grabbed my keys. I was on my way out of the door when I noticed a teddy bear sitting in her favorite chair. I ran back and grabbed it before closing and locking the door behind me.

When I arrived at the hospital, I asked the guard, who was standing at the door, where I could find her. He scrolled through some papers before saying, "She's in ICU…"
"What?" I asked, nervously.
"Yeah…take the elevator to the sixth floor…stop at the nurse's desk and they will take you to her room."
I caught the elevator before its door closed. I jammed my finger into the button several times trying to force the door to close. When it did, I began to dance, nervously, in the middle of the floor. I watched the numbers until it reached the sixth floor. As soon as the door opened, I raced out and ran towards the desk. "Hi…I'm looking for Deidra…" I didn't get to finish my sentence before the woman asked, "How are you two related?"
I thought about it for a second before saying, "I'm the baby's father."
She stood and said, "Right this way…"
I followed her down the hall and stood in front of the room. From the door, I could see her. There were tubes attached to her arm. She had bandages wrapped around her head. I was about to walk in when the nurse said, "Sir, she really needs her rest."

I stopped and asked her what happened. "We're not sure...she was unconscious when she arrived, but it looks like she sustained a blow to the back of her head."

"Did it happen because of the fall?"

"No, we think that the blow caused the fall...someone hit her from behind."

I thought about Tiff. "Is she going to be okay?"

"Yes...we stopped the bleeding..."

"And the baby?" I asked, afraid of her answer.

"The baby is fine...the fall caused some bleeding, but we were able to stop that, as well...we're going to keep monitoring her. We think that it would be best to keep her here until she delivers since she is so close to her due date..." She touched my hand. "She's really lucky..."

A tear fell from my eye. I looked down at the teddy bear. "Can I give this to her?"

"Sure, but she won't know that you're in the room."

"That's okay...I won't stay, but a minute...I have something that I need to take care of."

"Okay, but don't be long..."

She stood in the door and watched me. I placed the teddy bear on the table next to the bed and leaned over and kissed her on the forehead. "It's going to be okay...I promise." I touched her hand and walked out of the room. I walked over to the elevator. I was waiting for it, but began to grow impatient, so I decided to take the stairs instead. As I proceeded down the stairs, I thought about what my life would be like if I'd lost her. What it would have been like if something had happened to the baby? Then, I thought about Tiffany. I began to feel guilty, because if I'd dealt with her when she made the first threat, Deidra and the baby would be at home and not lying up in some hospital. My "hesitation" almost hurt my future. Now, it was time that I tied-up some loose-ends.

When I left the hospital, all I could think about was how I was going to do it. I couldn't use my grandfather's gun because it was loud and the bullets would probably trace it back to him which would, eventually, trace it back to me. I could stab her to death, but I wanted something that would have a greater impact – something that would make her really regret fucking with me. So, I stopped by the hardware store. As I walked up and down the aisles, I became excited. There were so many things to choose from that would fix my problem. I was like a kid in a candy store. My mouth salivated as I picked up saws, axes, knives, and box cutters. I saw a nail gun, but decided to keep it simple, so I purchased an ax. I held it in my hand. As the light bounced off of the blade, I knew that I'd made the perfect choice.

I decided to change my clothes before going to visit her. As I walked back towards the apartment, I saw the pool of blood lying on the bottom of the steps. The sight of it confirmed what I needed to do. I walked back into the apartment, changed my clothes, and set-out to find her. I drove around until I found myself parked out in front of her house. The entire time that I sat there, I thought about Deidra and the baby. I grew more incensed by the minute. I couldn't wait to see Tiff.

I waited until the neighborhood grew quiet. When all of the houses grew dark, I, slowly, got out of my car and looked around before crossing the street. I held my car keys in one hand and the ax in the other. I knocked on her door. She looked through the blinds before opening it. She cracked the door. "What do you want?"

I stepped back and kicked the door in, pushing her onto the floor. I walked in and slammed it behind me. "Have you lost your damn mind?" she said, crawling across the floor.

I grabbed her and dragged her into her living room. "I told you not to fuck with her."

She scrambled to the couch. "I told you what was going to happen."

Looking around the room, I said, "Well, your plan backfired…she's fine and so is the baby."

"Damn." She looked disappointed. "Well, you know what they say? When the hoe doesn't die the first time…try and try again."

"It's over, Tiff…"

"Paul, didn't your parents ever tell you not to leave the table until you finished your food?"

"What does food have to do with this?"

"Nothing, but it taught me the importance of finishing what I've started. So, I'm sorry, Paul…your little Ms. Homewrecker has a date with death and the invitation is for her plus one…" She looked down at my hand. "What are you going to do with that?"

I grabbed her by the arm and began to drag her down the hall to the bathroom. "Stop…let me go," she begged, trying to get away from me.

When we arrived at the door of the bathroom, she placed her hands against the door-frame. "No, stop!" I pushed her inside and closed the door behind us. I threw her into the tub. I pointed the ax at her head and said, "Don't move."

She began to cry. "I'm a mother…you wouldn't take my baby's mother from him? Would you?"

I laughed. "Of course, I would…you weren't trying to kill Deidra to protect your son. You were trying to kill Deidra, because you're hurt that your man didn't find you adequate enough to make and keep him happy."

"But I…it's just that…you will never understand."

"You're probably right, but what I do know is that you almost killed somebody for your own selfish needs…your husband is dead. You could have moved the fuck on…"

"But I couldn't…not while that baby is alive…"

"And that's why you got to go…that baby will never be safe as long as you're alive." As I sat there, my mother's face flashed across my eyes. I raised the ax as she raised her hand. "Look...wait...I'm sorry...I just..."

I swung the ax. "This is for the best..."

She screamed for a second, but became quiet. When I looked down at the blade of the ax, I realized why she was silent. As I pulled the blade back, her head rolled down into her lap. Her body twitched several times before it came to a complete stop. I sat down on the toilet and watched as blood streamed down into the drain. I stood and walked down the hall to the kitchen, grabbed several garbage bags, and walked back to the bathroom. I stood over her and began to swing the ax until she was nothing but a bunch of puzzle pieces. I threw her into several bags and began to clean up the bathroom. Once there were no more traces of her in the tub, I began to drag the bags down the hall and out the back door. When I'd gathered the last of the bags, I heard a light whimpering coming from the baby's room. I walked into the room to find the baby lying in his bed. I stood over him. I didn't know what to do with him. I couldn't leave him, because by the time someone found him, he would be dead. I couldn't drop him off anywhere, because I didn't want anyone to see me taking him out of my car. I'd already decided that Jeffrey's car was going to be her tomb, so I didn't want to get caught driving it with the baby of a dead woman in the trunk of my car, and I definitely couldn't leave the baby in a car with a rotting corpse. And as I struggled to figure out what I was going to do with him, the baby did something that helped me make my decision. He reached out his hands for me to pick him up. He cried, "Mommy," as he placed his little hands over my mouth. I kissed his fingers and placed his head against my chest. I placed my nose into his neck and inhaled his scent. "I can't be your mommy, but I'm going to love being your daddy."

CHAPTER 62

As I walked to work the next few days, I realized that she didn't love me. The cruel realization had just come to me that I've dedicated this part of my life to a woman that did not love me and to a child that wasn't mine. Sure, she cared about me, but I knew that she didn't love me. Deidra, right now, was like a woman caught in a thunderstorm. Mike, her ex, was like her favorite umbrella – she would hold on to it even if it was broken. Me, on the other hand, I was the brother, who she saw as a piece of newspaper. Not prepared for that storm, she picks me up one day, she uses me, and when the storm passes, she's going to toss my ass to the side like all of the other pieces of old newspaper in her life. The funny thing is, is that after I found out who she really was, I no longer wanted to be the "umbrella" in her life. I just wanted to be the one who kept her baby safe, warm, and dry. But why?

I could not understand why I wanted to be that child's father or why I felt like I HAD to be that child's father. I wasn't really invested in either one of them and yet, I couldn't walk away. For some odd reason, I felt obligated to stay. Maybe it had something to do with the fact that I was a fatherless child and didn't want this for that baby, but why should I even care? Then it came to me, once again – my mother – and I never needed to ask myself that question again.

For the next few weeks, I busted my ass. I worked overtime sticking around at the store trying to find other things to do that would help put a little extra cash in my pocket and my hard work, began, to pay off. The store manager promoted me to supervisor over produce and with the raise and the money that I'd put to the side, I was able to purchase a new car. It wasn't much, but it was mine. That car meant everything to me. It was a symbol of my accomplishment and I took care of it. I washed and shined it to the point where you could see your reflection in the rubber mats on the floor. I loved that car so much and had no problem hurting someone over it.

I'd just washed it and walked back into the apartment to get the little boy when I returned to find some boys leaning up against it. When I approached them, I, politely, asked them to get off of my car. I'd seen these kids around the neighborhood and while I didn't know them personally, I knew of their reputation. They were gang-bangers who were known for terrorizing the people in the community, but, at that moment, I didn't give a shit about them or their reputation. I wanted their asses off of my car.

I tried being diplomatic – trying to appeal to them – from one brother to another.

"Excuse me, bruh..." I said, as I opened the passenger's door and placing the baby inside.

"You're excused..." he said. His friends began to laugh.

Still not trying to start anything with them, I said, "I need to get in my car."

"Get in, shit...I'm not stopping you," he said.

It was clear that he was the "nigga in charge", so I said, "Look, I don't want any problems..."

"Then, take your bitch-ass on, shit...'cause problems are what you're going to have if you don't get out of my face," he said.

I looked into the car and saw the baby playing in the backseat. I looked at the boys, smiled, and tried to get into the car, but the boy wouldn't move. I said, "Excuse me," again.

"Did you forget to say something?"

I knew what he wanted and as much as I didn't want to give it to him, my goal was to keep my nose clean and stay out of trouble. I swallowed, hard, and said, "Please..."

He smiled. "Please, what?"

"Could you PLEASE excuse me?" I said, trying not to choke the shit out of him.

Slowly the boy began to peel his ass off of the driver's side door. "You see, boys...that's how you do it. You demand your respect...don't let these niggas get away with nothing."

468

When he said that, I couldn't help, but stop.

"Did you forget something?" he asked.

The baby began to say, "Da, da, da, da, da..."

I turned and said, "Back in the day, kids got their asses kicked for this type of shit..." I climbed in.

He stuck in hand in the door, preventing me from closing it. He turned around and raised-up the back of his shirt to show me the handle of his gun. "Here's my ass...kick it."

I was so tempted to snatch his gun out of those dirty-ass drawers that he had on and beat the hell out of him, but I knew that if he was carrying, his boys, probably were too. I had no plans to die in a gunfight that day and I didn't want to get the baby hurt, so I decided to let it go – to let him have his moment, because one thing I've learned is that the universe will give me my moment. I'll just wait for it, but until then, I let his stupid-ass walk away thinking that he got the best of me. I was pulling off when he said, "You better get that kid a car-seat before they pull your dumbass over." I pulled away from the curb leaving them in my rearview mirror.

I went about my day like the incident hadn't happened. I stopped by the store and purchased two car-seats and picked-up some other baby stuff. I was paying for everything when the cashier said, "Awwwwwwww, he's so cute."

I looked at the little boy and said, "Yes, I guess he is."

She smiled and began to play with him. "Of course, he is…look at those big cheeks."

I turned and looked at him, again, and wondered if the baby in Deidra's stomach was going to look like him. The baby smiled and reached-out to her. She touched his hand. "Wow…he looks just like you."

Offended I said, "Why? 'Cause, we're both Black?"

She took the money from my hand, reached into the drawer for the change, and grabbed the receipt. "Have a good day…" she frowned.

I took the items and the baby and left the store. When we got to the car, I took one of the car seats out of the box and began to read the instructions. I leaned inside of the car and began to install the seat. When I climbed back out, I noticed that the cart wasn't where I left it. Nervously, I looked around for it until I found it sitting across the parking lot. Panicking, I ran over and snatched him out of the cart. Crying, I embraced him. "Shit…shit…shit…I'm so sorry little man. So sorry…" I was holding him and kissing him – so happy that he wasn't hurt. "Please forgive me, man…I'm so sorry." The baby smiled and touched my face. He wrapped his little arms around me and placed his head on my chest. I kissed the top of his head and carried him over to the car. After I placed him in his seat, I wiped tears from my eyes. "Damn, that was some scary shit…wasn't it?"

The baby smiled and clapped his hands. I began to feel something that I'd only felt when I first met

Deidra. Was I falling in love with this kid? I wasn't sure, but I knew that I liked the feeling.

After spending a whole day out with him, I could tell that he was tired of being in the car, so I decided that it was time to take him back. When we pulled-up in front of the apartment building, I noticed that the streets were, extremely, quiet. In Chicago, there were only three reasons why the streets would be quiet. One, because everybody was sleep, two, because there's a heavy police presence, or three, heavy gang activity, so when I pulled in to park, I waited to see what was going on before jumping out. Everything seem to be okay, so I proceeded to get out. As I walked around to the other side of the car, I saw one of the kids, that I ran into, walking down the street, alone. When he walked passed me, he nodded. I took the baby out of his seat and walked upstairs to the apartment. Once inside, I changed him, fed him, and laid him down to sleep. I'd sat down to watch some TV when I realized that I still needed to get the stuff out of the car. I turned the lights off in the apartment and looked out of the patio door before walking out. When I got to the car, I was leaning into the trunk when a voice said, "I didn't get to tell you how much I like your car."

Startled, I flipped around and found myself staring in the eyes of the boy who'd gave me some "lip" earlier. It pissed me off that he was bothering me. "Go on about your life, boy…I don't have time for your shit." I turned my back to him to get the stuff out of the trunk. I felt something being jammed into my back. "I said, 'that I like your car.'"

"Look kid…" I turned to look at him.

"I ain't your fucking kid…now, give me the keys," he said, pointing the gun at me.

"Look…I just got this car…I need it…I have to pick-up my baby…"

"Not my fucking problem…" Growing impatient, he continued, "If you don't want to die over this shit, you better give me the damn keys." He began to look around, nervously.

I knew that I wasn't going to give him my car. I wasn't sure how I was going to keep him from taking it, but I knew that I wasn't going to just let him drive off with something that I'd worked so hard for, so I lied to him. "Look, I got some money…"

He frowned. "Did I ask you for some damn money? This is what I want."

Trying to think fast, I said, "I know, but I got a large chunk of change upstairs in my apartment…if you let me go and get it…"

"You must think I'm stupid? Give me the damn keys…"

"Look, I swear…you can come with me…I'll give you the money…you can buy another car with it."

Interested, he asked, "It's that much?"

"More…" I confirmed.

Suddenly, his tone changed. "I swear, man…if you're lying to me, I'm going to kill you and then, I'm going to put a bullet through that baby's head."

"I swear…I wouldn't lie to you. I wouldn't want you to hurt me or my baby."

He scratched his head and said, "Let's go…"

I picked the stuff up, closed the trunk, and began to walk towards the building. I looked back to find that he was still pointing the gun at me. My adrenaline was pumping and my thoughts were racing. I hadn't thought this through. I knew that I couldn't take him to our apartment and put the baby at risk and I knew that if I didn't get him the "money", he was going to shoot me. Then, I remembered the guy down the hall. I had no idea how this was going to work-out, but I knew that I had to take a chance. When I got to his apartment, I tried putting my key into the lock knowing that it wouldn't fit. He opened his door. "What the fuck do you want?"

Before I could answer, the boy who was still pointing the gun at my back, said, "Who the fuck is this and where is my money?"

The guy at the door looked at my face and then, back at the boy. He could see that some bullshit was taking place, so he said, "My mistake...the money's in here."

He stepped to the side to let us in. We walked inside. I placed the baby stuff on the floor. When the boy walked in, I heard the door slam shut behind us. When I turned, I saw that the man had a gun placed up against the boy's head. "Drop it..." he instructed.

The boy frowned before he dropped his gun on the floor. He looked at me. "Go home...I'mma teach this little motherfucker some manners."

I picked-up the stuff and walked out into the hall. The door slammed shut behind me.

I never saw that kid again.

CHAPTER 63

I t'd been a month before they released her, but before letting her go, they induced her labor and brought into the world our beautiful baby girl. We named her Imani. When they handed her to me, I fumbled – almost dropping her on the floor. I'd never held a baby before, but after a few minutes, it felt like I was born for this moment. I placed my nose against her face. She smelled like, what I thought, Heaven would smell like if it had a smell. Everything about her seemed perfect. She was mine and I'd fallen, deeply, in love with her.

I was so caught-up in the moment that I'd completely forgotten to tell Deidra that we had company. When we arrived at the apartment, I paid the young girl who did some babysitting in our apartment complex a few dollars for keeping an eye on our little friend and she left. When Deidra walked in and saw the little boy, I'm sure she wondered who he was, but she seemed too tired to care at that moment. She just walked in, went straight to the bedroom, fed the baby, laid her on the side of her, and fell asleep.

In the few months that he'd been staying with me, we built a bond. Of course, he cried a lot at first because he missed his mother, but he soon realized that she was never coming back. He learned to trust me and being a parent to him wasn't as hard as I thought it would be, maybe because he was a little older. Although, still in diapers, I didn't have to deal with all of the 'newness' that came with parenting. He was already starting to walk. He enjoyed eating food from my plate. He began to say words like "ma-ma and "da-da". I wasn't really sure how old he was, but I figured that he had to be at least a year old, because it had been that long since I'd killed his daddy. Plus, I remembered what my brothers and sisters were like at this age. So, I decided that I would tell people that he was a year old.

And when Deidra awakened from her nap and asked me who he was, I said, "He's mine."
Confused, she looked at me like I was crazy. "When did you have time to make a baby and where is his mama?"
"She got caught-up with some dude…called me…said that she didn't want him and left."
Imani began to stir. She pointed to the other side of the room. "Please hand me a diaper and some wipes…"
I got what she needed and then sat down next to her. She looked at me. "You want to change her?" She began to remove Imani's diaper.

I saw her little vagina. Embarrassed, I said, "Naw...I'll let you handle that."

"Soooooo, just like that...she just up and left him?"

"You say that like you've never heard of that before. Folks leave babies all of the time..."

"What I'm trying to figure out is when you had time to make one..." Then, all of a sudden, a weird look swept over her face. "Hold up...hold the fuck up..." She paused, looked at the kids, apologized for cursing, and then said, "You got a lot of damn nerves."

"What do you mean?"

"Didn't you and I just go through some shit over my ex and my roommate? God bless his soul..."

"The dude was walking around with his 'shit' hanging out...I didn't want to see that..."

"But your 'tripping' went beyond that...you were upset that we, once, slept together..."

"Part of it was...I will admit that, but he was gross and not to mention the fact that the dude shot me...did you forget about that?"

"That happened afterwards..."

"Before...after...doesn't matter...I still got shot and you seem to be jealous...are you jealous, Deidra? Your eyes are looking a little green..." I asked, hoping that she would say 'yes.'

"I'm not sure how I feel about it..." She leaned over and looked at him, closely. "He don't even look like you."

"That's because he looks like his mother."

"Well, what's his name?"

Her question caught me off-guard. While I'd thought of everything else, I hadn't thought about a name for him. She could tell that I was struggling.

"Paul?" she asked.

"Oh…" Trying to think of a quick lie, the only name that came to me at that moment was the name of my bully. "His name is Brandon."

"Brandon? Why did it take you so long to say his name? Brandon isn't a name that's that hard to forget…"

"Believe me…I've tried."

"Now, why would you want to forget the baby's name?"

I looked away and said, "Because it brings back bad memories…"

"Why? He seems like such a good little boy."

"He is…I knew another Brandon…he was an asshole."

"Well, this one seems to be a sweetie…" She smiled and called him, "Brandon…hi Brandon…" She waved her hand, but the little boy didn't respond.

"He needs to get to know you…" I walked over and picked him up.

"So, when is she coming to get him?"

"Ummmmm…she's not. You know how it is…you create a permanent problem while caught-up in a temporary situation…you should know all about that."

She frowned. "Damn, she just left him? Just like that? That's horrible." she asked, pulling down the sleeve of her gown and placing Imani's face to her breast.

"She didn't have much of a choice," I said.

"Wow…I couldn't just give my baby away like that. What kind of mother just leaves her baby?"

I thought about it for a second before saying, "The decision wasn't an easy one…she struggled with it all the way to the end. Plus, he's better off with me, anyway. His mama had a lot of issues…"

"Had?" she asked.

"Yeah…had…but she don't have to worry about this one anymore."

CHAPTER 64

There was something different about her. They say that babies bring people together, but this only pushed us further apart. We disagreed about everything. If I said that it was up, she said that it was down. If I said left, she argued for right. I knew that I couldn't be wrong all of the time, but according to her, I was. She was on my back like a bad case of acne. All I wanted to do was help her, but she was determined to create a divide between me and the kids. At first, I thought that it was because she knew that I was inexperienced, but that was not the case and she made it known that that wasn't the case. I tried to be patient, but I couldn't help but think that there was something more going on - like she had an agenda.

Brandon was crying, one day, and I saw that she was in the shower, so I decided to pick him up and hold him until she came out when, suddenly, I heard the water stop. It was weird, because both actions happened simultaneously – like she had a pair of eyes in the kids' bedroom. I looked at Brandon and said, "Did you see that? I swear she's watching me." Brandon cooed as I searched the room for a video camera.

Immediately, she ran out of the bathroom, agitated. With her eyes bulging out of her head, she screamed and dropped her towel. "Why aren't you at work?" Feeling the need to defend myself, I said, "He was crying. I couldn't just leave him here crying..."

Naked, she walked up to me. "Give him here..."

I frowned. "I can hold him while you put your clothes on. You got stuff hanging-out...all over the place."

"He's a baby. He doesn't care about my stuff like that. Plus, it wasn't too long ago that he crawled out of your baby-mama's vagina...remember your baby mama?"

"Yeah, but that's her vagina...he's a kid. He don't need to be looking at strange vaginas."

"I'm not going to show him my vagina and even if I did, he's a boy...he's going to be looking at a lot of them soon."

"He don't need to be looking at yours. Now, go and put on some clothes," I insisted.

She began to tug at him. "Give him here...and you go to work."

I tugged back. "I can take care of him and go to work..."

She tugged again. "I need you to work, Paul...now, give him here."

"But he's my baby...how are you going to keep me from holding him?" I'd been saying that so much, lately, that it started to become the truth.

"Are we gon' play the 'that's my baby' game? And I'm sure that your baby's-mama would be happy knowing that I'm in her son's life…"

No, she wouldn't. I thought to myself.

Back and forth we tugged at him when he began to cry. I let him go. When he climbed in her arms, he reached down and grabbed her by the nipple. She giggled and carried him away. I was leaving when I decided to stop by and check on Imani. Imani was resting, peacefully – swaddled in her blankets. I leaned over to kiss her. I was thinking how much I hated that she wrapped Imani in her blankets. It just didn't make sense to me, so I began to unravel her. "Let me get you out of this straight-jacket. She got you tied up like a damn mental patient…" Imani stretched like she was happy to be set free from the restraints. Suddenly, I heard, "Paul, ain't you got somewhere to go." I grimaced, because the sound of her voice grated against my nerves. The sight of Imani smiling in her sleep brought me back from my "dark" place. I kissed her again and left the room. As I approached the door, I began to feel guilty that we were fighting. I did appreciate that she was willing to take care of Brandon, so I decided to apologize. I didn't want to leave on a sour-note. So, I turned to go back to the room. As I got closer, I could hear her talking to him. At first, she was making baby noises as the baby giggled. Then, she said something that threw me completely off.

"You know…you look a lot like my baby's-daddy…"

I felt, both, surprised and stupid. It never crossed my mind how much Brandon looked like her ex.

"You are so fine, little boy and you're going to break a lot of women's hearts…"

I walked up and peeked around the corner. Brandon saw me and pointed. "Da-da…"

Deidra kissed him and placed one of her breasts inside of his mouth. He began to suck, loudly.

She looked down at him and said, "Yeah…we'll see about that."

CHAPTER 65

Being a father was such a life-changing experience for me. It was the only thing that mattered to me. I loved them more than I loved myself. Everything that they did excited me – from their learning to talk, learning to walk, just everything. And then they learned to call me, "Daddy." It was the greatest title that anyone could have given me. What could be more important than taking care of two people who called me daddy? They were, completely, dependent on me to do my job as their father and I took it seriously. Everything that I did from that moment on was for them. I realized how much those kids needed me and how much I needed them. I dropped them off and picked them up from school. I helped them with their homework. I made their lunches and learned how to do Imani's hair. I did everything. And as the years, passed, Deidra and her love for me didn't matter anymore. Matter of fact, Deidra didn't matter anymore, and she knew it. She didn't hide her disdain for me and I didn't mind showing her mine.

My dream of having a beautiful life with her and the kids had, quickly, become a nightmare. Imani looked so much like her father that Deidra was unable to move on like she thought she could. Her desire to have Mike as a part of Imani's life became the only thing that she thought about. The problem that I had with all of this, is that she was willing to destroy that man's marriage. At first, she was completely against it, but now, it was her only mission. It didn't matter that I was here standing in the gap for a dead man – what mattered was that I wasn't her first choice. She would always crave for that man even though she knew that he wasn't good for her.

She tried reaching out to him, but there was no response. Instead of moving on, she saw this as a rejection and became more desperate to find him. It was worse that she thought the he'd left her, but he would not ignore her daughter. She even hired a lawyer and filed for child support and when they couldn't find him, she used my money to hire an investigator. Her desperate need to find him was beginning to threaten my peace of mind. I had to do something about it. But what? I had no idea.

I needed to talk to her about this without revealing my motives for her to let this go. I had to find a way that it was in Imani's best interest that she walked away from this, because the "real" truth was going to hurt her more than me. She'd just gotten off of the phone with the investigator when she said, "I think that we're close…"

"Close to what?"

"Finding him," she said, happily.

"I doubt that," I said, walking over to the cabinet to find a snack.

"Why do you say shit like that, Paul? You act like you know where he is…"

Lying, I said, "I don't, but I ain't running around trying to find a man that, clearly, don't want to be found. Just let sleeping dogs lie, Deidra. What do you plan to gain from bringing that man into our lives?"

"Not our lives, Paul. Imani's…"

"How can he be in her life without trampling over ours?"

"Paul, your jealously is showing and it is not attractive." She stuck her mouth out and left the room. I followed her out of the room.

"What's not attractive is you taking my money and looking for another man…"

"Our money, Paul. I work too."

"Really? That's amazing…" I paused for a moment because I thought that I'd heard something but was too immersed in this argument to go and see what was going on.

"Paul, don't start. I'm those kids' mother. That's my job."

"Okay, the next time that the car note needs to get paid, I will send them the money that you make from being their mommy."

"Paul, that was mean…now, you would think that someone who was raised without his father would do everything he could to make sure that his daughter had hers."

"Do you hear yourself? I need to record some of the dumbshit that you say and replay it back to you. 'Cause what you just said don't make no damn sense. Imani has a father."

"Paul…"

"What those kids needed WAS a man who would step-up and I've done that. I'm real tired of trying to get you to respect my presence…respect my role in their lives."

"I respect you, Paul…"

Angry and frustrated, I interrupted her. "You can't be…you know how much thought goes into trying to find somebody and how much energy it will take to make him do what he ain't volunteering to do now? What makes you think that he's going to be happy that you expose a baby that he made while he was dipping-out on his wife?"

"But he has to take responsibility for his child…"

"But does his wife have to take responsibility for what he's done and what he's done with you?"

"What do you mean, Paul?"

"That piece-of shit fucked you…"

"You don't have to be so crude, Paul…"

"Oh…sorry…y'all made love…"

She frowned.

"He did what he did to you…not her…and the real-life evidence of that affair is running around here in lip gloss…she will have to suffer for some shit

Y'ALL decided to do. Then, you want to get Imani involved in that. You think that she's going to respect the fact that she is the physical reminder of a sin that you committed. That's not fair to that girl and you know it and you're so damn selfish that you can't even see it."

"I'm not being selfish…"

"You're too damn selfish to see that you're too damn selfish…" She was making me so mad that I couldn't think straight. "Shit, you're chasing his ass and he might be dead somewhere…"

She pushed me in the chest. "Don't say that, Paul…don't say that…"

I grabbed her hands. "That's a whole lot of emotion for somebody you ain't seen in a while." Pissed, I said, "I don't know who the hell do you think I am? I know bullshit when I see it…this ain't about that girl…that girl has a daddy. This is about you…you running around here thinking that he's still holding a candle for your ass…newsflash…he ain't." Seeing her act this way over him made me do something that I said I would never do to her. Before I knew it, I pushed her back. She flew back into the dresser. Startled, she screamed, "You pushed me…did you push me?"

"Are you on the floor?" I said, breathing heavily.

"I'm going to kick your ass…" she jumped up and ran towards me.

I pushed her again. This time, she landed on top of the bed. "Stay where you are, Deidra...you don't want none of this...not right now...not ever."

She, quickly, realized that she was no match for me in stature, so she tried to hurt me with her words. "You can't hurt me, Paul...I would have to care about you for you to hurt me."

I couldn't see anything, but fire and the only way that I knew to put it out was to put a pillow over it and smothered it until it went out. I was walking towards her when over my shoulder, I heard someone crying. I looked back to see who it was. It was Imani. With tears in her eyes, she said, "You're not my daddy?" Everything around me fell silent. The only thing that I could hear were her tears as they fell on her cheek. I walked up to her and wrapped my arms around her. I looked over at Deidra and then, kissed Imani on her forehead. "Ask your mama..." I walked out of the room and went outside to wait in my car.

A few hours later, the front door opened, and Imani walked out. She opened the door on the passenger's side and climbed in. She looked out towards the house. We sat, quietly, for a few minutes and then, she broke the silence. "She told me the truth..."

I laughed. "Of course, she did...I wouldn't expect nothing else from that woman."

She continued. "I don't want to know that man..."

"Why wouldn't you want to know your real father?"
I asked, knowing that unless somebody had an Ouija
board that was never going to happen.

"He's been gone this long…if he wanted to see me,
she wouldn't have to look for him…he would have
come looking for me."

"That's true…"

"And what do I look like forgiving a man who left his
mistake for another man to fix…"

"You're not a mistake…"

"Clearly, I wasn't planned either. How can you be
planned when the parties involved are already
scheduled to be somebody else's husband…
somebody else's father? Who wants a part-time
daddy when I got one who wants to be my daddy full-
time?" She touched my hand. "I don't want to be like
her and disrespect you after all that you've done for
me."

"Thanks, baby-girl…"

"Why 'thank' me? I didn't do anything…you did and
I hate that she tried to hurt you…you don't deserve
that." She shook her head. "One day, she's going to
get what's coming to her…"

"Don't wish nothing bad on your mama…"

"Sadly, I don't have to. She's going to bring it on
herself."

"You think so?"

"I know so…that's life, daddy. You do bad things.
You have to get punished…she messes with people's

lives and one day, somebody is going to return the favor."

"And how would that make you feel?"

She shrugged. "I don't know…I just want my daddy back...you. You should hear the stuff that she says and what she does when you're not around."

"I think I do…"

With fear in her eyes, she said, "No, you don't, daddy. I just want it all to end."

I opened my arms and she collapsed inside of them.

"You know that I love you, right?"

"I know, daddy…I know…"

"And you know that I'm going to fix this, right?"

"I know, daddy…I know…"

As I held her, I looked-up to find that Deidra was watching us. Her attempt to hurt me and to divide us failed, but there is a price that has to be paid for trying, because if she's capable of this, she's capable of anything.

CHAPTER 66

I refused to forgive her, but I tried to keep things "normal". Whatever that meant and for a while, things were normal. We got married, not because we loved each other, but because it was the right thing to do for the children. We didn't have a honeymoon. We didn't consummate the marriage. Matter of fact, when the Justice of the Peace said, "I, now, pronounce you man and wife," and I slipped that ring on her finger, she got out of there so fast, she left heel-marks on the marble flooring. I went home to be with the kids and where she went, I don't know, but they must have been giving away free hickeys because when I saw her again, she had a neck full of them.

We moved to a different neighborhood and tried to live normal lives. I got a new job working in the mailroom at the Board of Trade and it wasn't long after that that I landed a job in sales and was making a lot of money. We were doing extremely well, but my job was very demanding and extremely stressful. The trade-off was knowing that my family never wanted for anything. I didn't want them to have the life that I had, growing up. I didn't want them to know what 'struggle' meant and they were grateful for how hard I worked. All of them, except for one.

She saw me as the man who paid the bills and she wasn't shy about letting me know it. So, while my family walked around like somebody had won the damn lottery, I remained the poor boy who had four outfits to his name. I packed my lunches every day and to save money on gas, I drove two days a week and rode the bus the other three. I held on to one pair of shoes until the lining fell out of them and I never kept more than five dollars in my pocket. The only debt that I had was the one that Deidra created for me.

While she loved the kids, their needs became secondary to hers. The kids and I became a part of a plan to get her ex back and when she couldn't find him, she spent most of her time trying to find the love that she'd lost in him. I couldn't replace him and I stopped trying a long time ago, but there was a hole in her heart, and she went searching to fill it in the streets.

Sometimes, I looked at her to try to find the girl that I once fell in love with. I tried to remember the girl who used to work at the restaurant; beautiful, brown, tall and had the prettiest smile that I'd ever seen. The girl who cared about me and for a moment, wanted to make sure that I was alright. Then, overnight she became something else. I didn't know this woman and every day that I spent with her, the less I wanted to know her. She was an asshole. And, of course, I'm not a saint. I've left a trail of dead bodies in my past, but killing somebody doesn't make me an asshole. Beyond killing people, I can say that I'm the nicest person on the planet, but Deidra had being an asshole on lock-down and she was, also, starting to tap back into her inner-hoe.

Now, I consider myself a good father. Sure, I've made some mistakes. Nobody's perfect, but we survived. And I thought that I was a good husband, but clearly, when you refuse to touch somebody with a ten-foot pole, they'll run out to find a nigga with a ten-foot pole. So, that left me with working hard and taking care of my kids and that left her with a whole lot of free-time on her hands and a reason to get them into a lot of shit that they shouldn't have been into.

The first time that I caught her ass, I felt something inside of me die. It wasn't like before that moment, I had much of a soul, but the little that I did have, left, never to return. Now, first I must tell you that I'm not a jealous man. Even after all that we've been through, I just found it hard to develop a close bond with her, so when it went down, I didn't even react. At least, not in the way that I should have.

I'd just worked a twelve-hour shift and she'd been complaining that I wasn't spending any time with her, so I decided to surprise her. I stopped by the store, picked-up a dozen roses and picked-up some dinner. I was so hungry all I could think about was eating, so I was annoyed when I pulled up to find that there was a car parked in the driveway. I'd checked my watch. It was late; too late for someone to be parked in my driveway. I grabbed my cellphone. At first, I was going to call her to see what she was doing, but somehow, I already knew. I'd seen it with my mama, so I didn't expect much more from her. I took a deep breath, backed my car up to make sure that the piece of shit had an escape route, grabbed my food and walked in.

I placed everything on the counter, washed my hands, and sat down to eat before I walked upstairs. When I was done, I washed everything, before I went up to check on my kids. I opened their doors to find them, both, sleeping peacefully in their beds. As I approached our bedroom door, I could hear the sound of the headboard banging against the wall. Gently, I turned the knob. They were so into what they were doing that they hadn't even noticed that I entered the room. At first, I thought that it would be good to go ballistic on both of their asses, and beat the shit out of them, but I remembered that my kids were in their rooms, so I decided not to. I was walking out of the room when I saw the man's pants lying on the floor at the end of the bed. I crawled over to them, reached into his pocket, grabbed his wallet, and crawled back out of the room. When I was in the hall, I looked through his wallet to find his Driver's License. I stared at it and as their moans seeped from behind my bedroom door, I knew what I wanted to do.

I walked back downstairs. I put the flowers in a vase and sat them in the middle of the kitchen table before I left the house, because I wanted her ass to know that I'd been here. I jumped into my car, plugged his address into my GPS, and decided to see how he was living. When I pulled up in front of his house, I noticed that there were lights on. I turned on my radio and waited. I was dozing-off when I saw someone turn into his driveway. He was getting out of his car when I ran up behind him. "Hey…you got a minute?" He turned and looked at me. "Who are you?"

I stuck out my hand. "Let me introduce myself…you just finished fucking my wife…and don't try lying. I'm too fucking tired."

Scared, he said, "What do you want?"

"I just want to talk…"

"Are you sure?"

"Well, if I wanted you dead…you and everybody in that house would already be dead…but why? Over some ass? Please…" I looked over at my car. "Let's talk in my car…"

Nervous, he said, "Why? We can talk right here…"

Annoyed, I said, "Or we can talk in your house…"

He looked around before closing his car door. "Ummmm…okay…"

I opened my door and then, signaled for him to get in on the other side. I sighed, heavily. "You know…I've tried to do right by her…"

He opened his mouth to say something.

I interrupted him. "Don't talk…I don't give a shit about anything that you have to say…"

He closed his mouth.

I continued. "I just want you to know that I don't care…" I looked at his Driver's License, again, before handing it to him.

He opened his mouth, again, but thought it best to remain silent.

"Earl…I, once, loved that woman…but now, I'm just so tired of her and her shit…you want to fuck her…be my guest…" I paused and looked out of the window. I felt so diminished. I'd given everything to that woman and this is how she paid me back. "I'm not going to hurt you over her…it just isn't worth it…I know that that may surprise you. I mean, at some point, you must have considered that I might find out and what would happen if I found out and you didn't care…she didn't care…and why get myself worked-up over two motherfuckers who just don't care? What my problem is, y'all trifling asses did that shit while my kids were in the house. Now, see that's an issue for me." I paused for a second and then, asked, "You got a family?"

He was afraid to speak.

"You can answer…and again, don't lie, 'cause it won't be nothing for me to knock on that door…"

"Yes…" he said.

"You got kids? How many?"

"Three…" he said.

"How would you feel if you found some nigga riding your wife while your babies were in the house?"

"I would be pissed…" he said.

"Well, now that you know how I feel…here's how we gon' do this…I don't care what you do and I don't care who you do it to, but if I catch your ass in or around my house or my kids, again, I'm going to pour gasoline all over you and I'm going to set your ass on fire and I'm going to do this in front of your kids. And after you burn to death, I'm going to do the same thing to the rest of your family…I wouldn't want to leave any witnesses behind. You understand, right?" I smiled, but quickly frowned. "Have you ever been set on fire, Earl?"

"Ummmm…no…" he stammered.

"I bet that shit hurts like a hell…what do you think…Earl?"

Looking like he was fighting back tears, he shrugged.

"Would you like for me to do that to you…Earl?"

Shaking, he could barely speak. "N…n…no…"

"Just know that I'm not playing with you and if she comes-up pregnant, I'm going to kill the both of you…slowly and painfully…but mostly painfully… 'cause I'm not taking care of one more motherfucker's baby. Do you understand…Earl?"

He nodded his head, "Yes…"

I leaned over him and opened the door. "Now, get the fuck out of my car and remember to practice safe sex…"

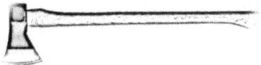

Sadly, he wasn't the first. It had gotten to the point where I'd expected to be number 2 or 3 or 4, in her life, but bringing them in my house is a level of disrespect that I won't tolerate. My home is my sanctuary – the only piece of 'normal' in my life and she was wrecking that. I needed to convince her to change her ways before her dumbshit started to rub-off on my kids.

Chapter 67

She's been showing her ass – in more ways than one.

B lindly, I reached over to turn it off. I'd been turning the alarm off every day at the exact same time for the past seven years, but for the first time, today, it felt weird. Usually, it would prompt me to spring out of my bed, jump into the shower, throw on some clothes, say "hello" and "good-bye" to my babies and I would head-out to fight traffic for two hours to work for a company that I thought cared about me and valued me, but I was wrong and today, as I reached over to turn it off, I was faced with the realization that those motherfuckers didn't give a shit about me. After all of those years of loyalty, dedication, and sacrifice, those bastards let me go.

As I stared at the ceiling, I was reminded of all of the special occasions that were ignored because I had to work – the ball games, the birthday parties, the PTA meetings, all of the special occasions – all ignored because I wanted to provide them with the life that I'd promised them – the life that they'd deserved. The lies and excuses for the times that I could not spend with them. And now, here I am staring at the wall trying to figure out what I'm going to do and how I was going to tell them. For the past two weeks, I'd gotten up, did the same shit that I did daily, so that no one was aware that I'd lost my job. I don't know why, but maybe I thought that I could find another one before they started shutting the lights off, but that didn't happen.

I looked over at the other side of the bed. For the first time, in a long time, I had a chance to look at her – to see her. For a moment, I didn't recognize her. It'd been so long since I'd seen this face – untouched, natural, as tears and drool dried along the side of her cheeks. She was beautiful. We'd been through so much, that I forgotten that. I began to remember how much I, once, loved her. I leaned over to brush her hair out of her face. She stirred. I was about to kiss her on the cheek, when she jumped up and screamed, "Stop that! What are you doing? You know that I don't have on my make-up!!!" I reached out to her, but before I could touch her, she was out of the room and into the bathroom. She, immediately, turned on the shower to mask the sounds coming from the toilet.

I sat up and threw my feet onto the floor. I took a deep breath and decided that today was the day that I was going to tell her. Sure, she would be pissed, but I hoped that she would comfort me, reassure me that everything would be okay, and that she would support me like a good wife is supposed to. I hoped that we could get through this like we've done so many other times and we will come out stronger and better this time. Why? Because even though we didn't have a 'traditional' husband and wife relationship, we did promise to be there for each other - "for better or for worse." I just hoped that things got better before they got any worse. I just had to tell her.

As I stepped out into the hall, I was embraced by the silence. Normally, the kids were up, getting ready for school, but they weren't. I walked into Brandon's room. I sat down next to him and rubbed his back.
"What dad?" he said, pulling the cover over his head.
"Get up, son…you have to get ready for school," I said.
"Awwwww man…come on…can I skip a day?"
"No…now, get up…"
"But I feel like I'm getting sick or something…"
I reached over and touched his forehead. "You're not hot…"
"It's one of those diseases without fever…"
Raising one of my eyebrows, I said, "Really?"
"Yeah, folks are getting sick all over the place…dropping like flies…"
"Sounds serious…"
"It is and you better get out of here before you catch it…"

Shaking my head, I said, "This wouldn't have anything to do with that final exam that you have in math?"

"Naw…of course not…I'm just sick…" he said, covering his face.

I stood and calling his bluff, I said, "Sure…I will take you to the doctor."

He threw the blanket back and said, "I don't need to go to the doctor. Just give me some pain-killers and let me sleep it off…"

"No, son, that would be irresponsible…I'm going to call the doctor and make an appointment…maybe they have a shot that'll fix it…"

His eyes widened. "A SHOT!?"

Trying to keep a straight face, I said, "Yes, a shot…fix you right up…one with a long needle…right in the ass…you'll feel better in no time."

He grabbed my hand. "You know what? I'm starting to feel better…"

Looking at his hand, I said, "Really? Already?"

"Yep, it's a miracle…see what prayer can do?" he said, sitting up.

"Who prayed?" I asked, confused.

Searching his floor for a pair of pants, he said, "I did…last night…won't He do it?"

Unable to contain my composure, I laughed and said, "Get your ass ready for school…"

Walking out of his room, I could hear the water running in the other room. I tapped on the door.

Imani yelled, "Good morning, daddy…"
"Good morning, sweetie!" I yelled back.

I walked into the kitchen and sat down. I was staring out of the window when I heard the phone ring. I was going to answer it, but I didn't feel like it. I had too much shit on my mind. I walked over to the counter and grabbed the coffee pot. I began to fill it with water when she came storming in the room.

"The fuck, Paul?!!" She screamed, waving the receiver in the air.

She knows. I thought to myself. I turned to look at her. Shocked and frightened, I stumbled backwards; almost dropping the coffee pot. "Shit, what is that on your face?!!"

"It's a mask, Paul and what is it this I'm hearing? You lost your job?"

Regaining my composure, I said, "You need to warn a brother when you put your 'ugly' on…"

"I asked you a question…"

"I'm sorry…I can't get passed the shit on your face…Now, what did you ask me?"

"Did you lose your damn job?"

I frowned. "Who told you that?"

"Doesn't matter…is it true?"

"Who told you that?" I insisted.

"Cindy…" she confirmed.

"Who the fuck is Cindy?"

"Doesn't matter, because we are not talking about her…we are talking about you…"

I frowned. "You need to stop talking to Cindy..."

"Why? Is she lying?"

"No, but the bitch needs to stay out of my fucking business..."

"She's not a bitch..."

"Oh, she's a bitch, alright...who ain't got shit else to do, but stick her nose in other folks' business and instigate some shit..."

"Paul..." she began.

I poured water into the pot, walked over to the counter, grabbed a couple of slices of bread, and then placed them into the toaster. I turned my back to her to keep from looking at her face.

Her voice grew deep. "I asked you a question, Paul..."

"And, clearly, Cindy provided the answer..."

"I'm talking to you, now..."

"You can't be talking to me."

"Then, who else am I talking to?"

"I don't know, but if you're talking to me, you better take some of that bass out of your voice...ain't but one man in this room and that's me."

She took a deep breath and began, "Paul..."

Pop! I removed the pieces of toast and placed them on the counter. "Look, I was going to tell you..." I pulled-out one of the drawers to remove a fork but couldn't find one. I looked for a spoon but couldn't find one of those either. "The fuck y'all doing? Eating with your hands?"

She walked over to the sink, grabbed a spoon, and proceeded to wash it. "Since you're going to have some extra time on your hands, you can wash some dishes."

"That's funny…when you wash that green shit off of your face, you should look into becoming a comedian. Matter of fact, you should keep it on. Isn't that what clowns are wearing these days?" I frowned and walked over to the refrigerator to grab some butter and jelly to spread on top of the bread.

"Ha, ha, ha…" She frowned. "Now, you were going to tell me what, Paul…that you are unemployed? That you're trying to ruin my life."

"'My'? Don't you have some kids too?" I began to spread butter on top of the bread. "Look, I was going to tell you a couple of weeks ago, but…" I grabbed everything and walked over to the table and sat down. I took a bite from one of the slices of toast. "But…"

My admission left her dazed and confused. She shook her head like someone had just punched her in the face. "Wait a minute…what? A couple of weeks?"

I continued. "Let's not get caught-up with specifics. Now, we have some savings…we will get through this…"

"A couple of weeks? Wait a minute…your ass has been getting up, every day, and getting dressed like you got a job…where have you been going? What have you been doing?"

I wanted to tell her that I'd been watching her nasty-ass, but my kids were in the house and as much as exposing her would make me extremely happy, I didn't want that nasty shit in my house – either by action or by conversation. "I hate to point out the obvious, but I think that you just answered your own question. I was pretending that I had a damn job..."

Suddenly, the kids walked into the room. She turned and looked at them. "Go to your rooms..." she demanded.

"What?" They both asked.

"GO TO YOUR DAMN ROOMS!!!!!" she yelled.

"Okay...okay..." Brandon mumbled as he threw up his hands. "First, you want us to get ready for school and now, you want me to go back to my room...make up your damn mind..."

She scowled in his direction. "What did you say?"

"Damn is not a bad word...look it up...it's in the Bible..."

"I'mma 'look' this DAMN jar of jelly up against your DAMN head...how about that?" She scoffed.

I turned to her. "Don't talk to the kids like that..."

With her mouth turned-up, she said, "What did you say?"

"I SAID, DON'T TALK TO THE KIDS LIKE THAT." I huffed. "Did you hear me that time?"

"I HEARD YOU THE FIRST TIME. I just don't think that you should be telling me how to raise MY kids."

"YOUR KIDS?"

"That's what I said, Paul...did you hear me?"

"Oh, I heard you, but I know you ain't talking to me."

"There's no one else in the room, but me and you."
The kids raised their hands.
She turned to them and said, "Go to your GAD-DAMN rooms!!!"
They didn't move.
"So, you wanna play that game?" I asked.
"No, game, Paul...I spend the most time with them..."
"Sooooooooooo, that's what you're basing that shit on? I work all day, but based on your logic, that bread, over there..." I paused and pointed across the room. "...even though I was the one who worked and paid for it...it's yours because you have more time to look at it, everyday...or because you have more time to eat more of it, because I'm at work, or because a piece of paper gives you a right to make it yours even though you have no idea what it took to get it in this house or what it took to get it on the table..."
"I know what it took to get it on the table, 'cause I picked it up from the store..."
"WITH MY DAMN MONEY!!!!" I yelled, trying to remind her.
She looked back and forth between me and the kids. Trying to decide which fire to put out first. She decided to direct her attention back to me. "You've got a lot of nerves..."
"Me?"
"Where's the money going to come from now? You lying son-of-a-bitch..." she spat.

Tired of hearing her disrespect me in front of the kids, I said, "Go to your rooms."

Brandon mumbled as he left the room. "She gon' get mad because I said 'damn' and she's in there throwing 'son-of-a-bitches' around like daggers…"

She turned towards the hallway. "Don't make me come in there!!!!" She, quickly, turned back to me. "You lying…"

I shook my head. "You don't want to go there…believe me." *Bitch lie so much, she lie in her sleep.* I thought to myself. "Plus, I didn't lie to you. I perpetrated. There's a difference."

"Really, Paul?"

"Yes, you never asked me where I was going every day. You just assumed that I was going to work. I can't be held accountable for the shit that you assume. I perpetrated the act of going to work, but you wake up every day with a face full of lies…have you looked at yourself, lately?" I pointed at all of the shit she had on her face. "And I paid for that shit too."

"Don't be trying to pull that Jedi-Mind Trick shit on me."

"Mind-trick? Really? That's interesting…when I do it, it's a lie and when you do it, it's just a part of you getting ready for your day…"

"You know what I'm talking about, asshole…"

I stopped chewing and looked up. "Asshole?" I asked.

"Yes, asshole. You know what the fuck you're doing…"

"What I do know is that Cindy can't be a bitch, but the man who has given his life to you, come home every day to take care of HIS kids, provides for you…is, now, a fucking asshole…"

"I didn't say 'fucking' asshole…I said, 'asshole'…"

"And the difference between the two is that one is fucking and the other one isn't? One is me and the other is you…"

"Which one is me, Paul?"

"Pick one, Deidra…you know yourself better than me."

She could tell that I wanted to get some other stuff off of my chest, but she couldn't do that because that would put a kink in her strategy to defeat me, because she knew that if that 'door' was opened, right now, in the middle of this argument, she would end-up on the other side of it. She needed to maintain her "angel" status even if it was a perceived one. So, she treaded lightly.

I exhaled. "You know, Deidra…shit is bad enough between us, but would it have hurt you to show me some compassion. Instead, you bring your ass in here looking like the 'Creature from the Black Lagoon'…talking shit…"

"I asked you what happened, first, Paul?"

"I couldn't hear it over all of that fire coming out of your mouth…I'm not your fucking kid or your asshole."

"I know…but you're SUPPOSED to be my husband."

"Damn…it's interesting that you brought that up. You want to talk about that, Deidra? I was trying to avoid it, but since a nigga wanna remind a motherfucker of his role…let's talk about that, then we can talk about what your role is supposed to be." I said, reminding her.

"I am your wife…you should have told me…"

"Wife…wife…damn, I saw that on a piece of paper that was in that drawer the other day…under the instruction manual for the lawnmower and some leftover ketchup packages."

"You know what else Cindy said?"

"Why the hell would I care about what Cindy has to say? That bitch is your friend…not mine…"

"I asked you not to call her that and Cindy noticed how much the kids look alike…"

I began to cough – choking on air. "Why would she say that?"

"Because…they kinda do…why would she say that, Paul?"

"Because that's what bitches do…plant seeds of doubt in a head full of nothing but dirt…"

"Like I said…you're an asshole, Paul."

Through clenched teeth, I said, "Ease-up on the name calling before I tell you about yourself."

She put her hands on her hips and said, "You want to tell me something, then go ahead and tell me…shit, I don't care."

"You've never cared, Deidra…"

"I did care…"

"When? I would like to know when?"

"I married you...doesn't that say anything?"

"It says that you're a joke and this conversation is a joke...I'm going to do what I need to do to take care of mine's."

"And what is yours, Paul?"

Not your trifling-ass. That's for damn sure. I thought to myself.

She continued. "I can't buy groceries with hopes and dreams, Paul."

"Why don't you take that pretty little mouth of yours and..." I paused and sucked my teeth.

"And do what with it, Paul. What would you like for me to do with it?"

"You can start by shutting the fuck up and if you can find time between getting on my damn nerves and using your mouth for all of the other shit that you do during the day...maybe you can kiss my ass too?" I shrugged my shoulders. "You did ask."

She was pissed. "How dare you?"

"No, Deidra...how dare you?"

"This ain't about me...this is about you and you are useless without a job."

I huffed. "Damn, is that so?" It took everything in me to keep from jumping across the table and choking the shit out of her. "So, that's all I'm good for?"

"You're not giving me nothing else, Paul..."

"What I want to give you, Deidra, a motherfucker can end-up behind bars for..."

"Did you just threaten me?"

"Naw…I'm just thinking out loud…"

"Well, you better remember that I'm their mother…"

"That's just like you to try to one-up somebody…like being a father ain't important too, but the difference is, my job requires that I actually bring in a paycheck…that I not only do some of the shit that you do, but, pay some damn bills too."

"Damn-right and if I didn't have a husband, I would get a job, but I got one…you…and you need to get on your shit." she said, rolling her neck and smacking her lips. "We had an understanding…"

Disgusted by her behavior, I said, "I understand that it don't take much for a motherfucker to unleash their ghetto-side…does it? Money sho' make a nigga messy."

She huffed. "And I need you to hear me…I'm not going to move back to the 'hood' and you will not embarrass me by having my Benz repo'ed…I would leave your ass before I let that shit happen. You hear me?" She stormed out of the kitchen. "Kids!!!"

Then, leave, bitch!!! I thought to myself. I took another bite from the slice of toast as she walked out of the room. I thought about what she said and I thought about her reaction to 'our' crisis. I didn't love her and I no longer liked her. I stayed with her for the sake of the kids, but the gloves were off. She was making it real easy for me to hurt her. It was just a matter of time. One more 'asshole' or 'son-of-a-bitch or one more fuck-up and I'm going to have to show her what an asshole is capable of.

CHAPTER 68

S he spent the whole night thinking about what she was going to do next. Until that moment, I'd done all that I could to hold this "family" together, but I guess losing my job was her last straw. She'd been looking for a reason to go, but clearly, she hadn't considered the consequences of her actions and sadly, there would be consequences.

I'd awakened out of my sleep to find her standing over me. I stretched and said, "Are you lost?"
She motioned for me to move over and said, "Paul, it's over."
I stared at her, blankly.
She waved her hand in my face. "Paul...did you hear me?"
When I snapped out of my daze, I began to laugh, hysterically. "What?"
"It's over, Paul..."
"When did it begin?" I asked, holding my side to keep from splitting it from laughing so hard.
"Paul, it's just not working..."
"No...no...I'm not working, right?"
"I just...I just have to think of the kids..."

She told me exactly what I needed to hear and all niceties were out the door, it was now on and crack-a-lackin'. "Bitch, you ain't thinking about nobody, but yourself. If you cared about the kids, you would leave me the hell alone."

"Bitch? Bitch? I got your bitch…" she asked, shocked that I'd called her out of her name.

"I bet you do…"

"You know what, Paul? I've had it with this shit…"

"You've had it? Bitch, please…"

"That's the second bitch that you've said…I ain't gon' be too many more bitches today…you hear me?"

"And what you gon' do? Fuck me or are you saving that for somebody else?" I'd struck a nerve.

"That's why I never loved you…"

"Boo-hoo," I pretended to cry. "Boo-hoo, Deidra's whore-ish ass has never loved me. My heart is breaking…boo-hoo…but I bet if I was married when you met me, I could have got some ass…"

"I'm not arguing with you anymore. 'Cause I don't have to…" She paused to roll her neck and her eyes. "You know what? Get your shit and go…"

"Shit, you ain't got no job either…how are you going to take care of those kids?"

"I got a Plan B…"

"Knowing your triflin' ass, you probably got a B, C, and D…" I grabbed my blanket and pulled it over my head. "You better gon' on about your life, Deidra…I paid for everything in here…even the clothes on your back. You better stop fucking with me before you find yourself sitting on the front porch wearing nothing but air…"

She stood over me. "No, I want you out…"

"And I wanted a woman who could act like a damn wife, but instead, I ended-up with you. Guess we can't have everything that we want."

When she realized that I wasn't taking her seriously, she said, "I'm going to call the police."

"And tell them what? That your crazy-ass woke me up out of my sleep talking shit? Go ahead…be my guest."

She folded her arms and said, "No, I'm going to tell them that you hit me."

"How are you going to prove it without bruises?" I fluffed-up my pillow and drew the blanket up around my neck. I'd just closed my eyes when I heard something crash against the floor. I jumped up and found her laying on top of a broken glass table. "What is wrong with you?" I reached out my hand to help her up.

She laughed and said, "Ain't nothing wrong with me, but that's not what I'm going to tell the police. I want you gone, Paul…and NOW!"

I frowned. "I'm not leaving…"

"Then, prepare to go to jail."

The noise had awakened the kids. Rubbing his eyes, Brandon said, "What is going on?"

Deidra looked at me and said, "You have five minutes before this go from my "bad" to 'yo' ass'…"

Imani said, "Daddy, did you do this?"

"You know that I wouldn't do this," I insisted.

"Go to your room, kids…" she instructed.

"But daddy…" Imani said.

Deidra wiped blood from the corner of her mouth. "That ain't your daddy…"

Her words cut me like a knife. I climbed on top of her. I was about to hit her when Imani screamed. "DADDY NOOOOOOO!"

She smiled and said, "Come on, daddy…show the kids what you got."

I climbed off of her.

"The clock is ticking."

I turned to the kids and said, "Daddy, loves you…"

"Tick-tock…tick-tock…" she said. "Say goodbye, kids."

With tears in their eyes, they said, "Bye, daddy."

To keep from upsetting them any further, I grabbed my shoes, keys, and left the house.

CHAPTER 69

The line in the sand had been drawn. We were enemies and at a point of no return. I expected the worst from Deidra, but I never expected this. I'd given her everything that I had and this is how she thanked me for it. This wouldn't be an issue, if she hadn't taken my kids away from me. They were the only thing that kept me alive. Now, I had to do everything that I could to get them back.

With the few dollars that I had left in my wallet, I got a room at a motel that was not too far away from the house. I, immediately, found another job at a telemarketing company as a supervisor. I wasn't making the type of money that I was making before, but after a few months, I was able to get me an apartment. Even though, we were no longer together, I still stopped by, every payday, to give her money for the kids. This went on for several months until one day, I pulled up to find all of my belongings sitting on the front lawn. I knocked on the door and a man answered the door.

"What do you want?" he asked.

I sucked my teeth and asked, "Where's Deidra?"

"She told me to tell you that she don't want anything from you…"

I yelled over his shoulder. "Kids! Kids! Kids!"

He stepped in front of me and said, "She told me that those kids ain't yours…"

It felt like someone had cut off my oxygen. It took a minute for me to catch my breath. When I did, I said, "What?"

"Yeah…they got a new daddy now…" he said.

"Is that so?" I asked, and before he could answer, I'd hit him so hard that one of his teeth found a home in the back of my hand. "What did you say to me, punk?"

The man didn't respond. He was sleeping, quietly, on the floor. I threw his tooth at him. "Bitch-ass, nigga…you gon' die and the bitch that you're fucking is gon' die too."

I walked out onto the lawn, grabbed my stuff, and began to throw it in the car. When I was done, I looked up to find Deidra running towards the car. "Roll down this window!" she screamed.

I rolled it down.

"What did you do to him?" she asked.

"I knocked his ass the fuck out. That's what I did. How can you do this, Deidra? I was good to you and those kids. You know how much I love my babies."

"Paul, it wasn't working and I found someone who loves me."

"DEIDRA, I LOVED YOU!!!"

"Paul...please...just don't come back over here. Okay, don't come back..."

"You gon' learn today, Deidra...you gon' learn." I rolled the window up and pulled off.

I was fuming. My hands were shaking so bad that I had to pull over and scream. "AHHHHHHHH!!!!!!" I jumped out of my car and was pacing back and forth when a stranger approached me. "Hey man, are you okay?"

Through clenched teeth, I said, "Get the fuck out of my face."

He threw his hands up and said, "I'm sorry...I was just trying to help."

"Did I ask for some damn help?" I asked.

The man turned and walked away.

I jumped back into my car, pulled off, and raced to my apartment.

Once inside, I threw my keys on the counter and began to pace. "THIS IS IT!!!" I said, pacing back and forth across my apartment's floor. "THEY'RE DEAD!!!! THEY ARE BOTH DEAD!!!!"

I walked into my bedroom and leaning against the wall of my closet, I found what I needed to make all of this right. I held it up and as the light bounced off of its blade, I smiled. "Nice and quiet..." I mumbled to myself. I didn't even wait until it was dark. I was ready to end this no matter the price. I put the weapon in my left hand, grabbed my keys, and left the apartment. I jumped back into my car and repeated the same thing over and over until I found myself parked in front of the house. "THEY'RE DEAD!!!! THEY ARE BOTH DEAD!!!!" I jumped out and ran to the door. I banged on the door.

Pissed, he answered it. "Nigga..." he began. I swung like I was trying to hit a home run. The blade wedged itself into his chest. He fell to the floor and looked down at his chest.

"Where's Deidra?" I asked. When she entered the room, I said, "Thanks, I see her." I used my foot to dislodge it and swung again. This time, it landed right in the middle of his forehead. I pulled it out.

She ran to his side. "Oh my, Gawd..." She tried to stop his bleeding by placing her hand over the hole in his chest. I pointed it at her. When I lifted it over my head, she looked up. "Paul...what are you doing?" I swung and missed her. She crawled over to the couch. "Paul...Paul...wait...ummmm...I was wrong...let's be together...you know, like a family. I'm sorry... you hear me? I'm sorry..."

I walked towards her and stood over her. She stuck her hand up in the air. I kneeled down next to her. I placed the blade against her head and slid it down her cheek. "Never come between a man and his kids."

"Paul...PLEASE!!!"

""Now, you say goodbye, Deidra..." I stood up and lowered the ax into the top of her head. She grabbed the blade. I watched as the blood dripped down her forehead and into her eyes. I kneeled down and kissed her on the cheek.

DADDY BY DIANE MARTIN 521

Her head dropped towards her chest, as she took her last breath. I removed the ax from her head and walked upstairs to the kids' rooms. I found them, both, playing video games, unaware of the carnage that was waiting for them in the living room. I placed the ax behind my back.

"Daddy?" Imani said.

"Daddy?" Brandon said.

"DADDY!!!!" They both said, extremely excited to see me. They ran up to me and wrapped their arms around me.

Imani found the ax. "What's this, daddy?"

"I have some bad news…" I said, "I killed your mother…and her boyfriend."

They looked at each other. They didn't have much of a reaction. I thought that maybe they hadn't heard me, so I said it again. "Your mama is dead…"

Still, there was no reaction. "You should probably call 911…" I suggested.

They just looked at each other. I started to think that maybe they were in shock. "Did you hear me?" I asked.

Imani took the ax from my hand and then, looked at Brandon. "We should, probably, start cleaning up," she said.

"What?" I asked.

Brandon nodded in agreement. "Let me get a shovel…it'll only take me a minute."

Confused, I stared as he walked out of the room.

"And I'll get a mop," she said, as she skipped, happily, towards the door – swinging the ax behind her. "I'm so happy to see you, daddy…welcome home."

EPILOGUE

We left the state and never looked back. Imani and Brandon went on to graduate from high school and were preparing for college. In my search for any sense of normalcy, I found a woman who, truly, loved and cared for me. We, eventually, had a child together and everything was wonderful, until they came knocking on the door. I should have known that at some point they would come looking for me. I could only run so far and for so long. The weirdest thing is, is that it wasn't for what I thought it would be. Out of all of the terrible shit that I've done, the only murder that they tracked me down for was the attempted murder of the one motherfucker who deserved to die – Jeffrey's ass.

If it's true that the "good die young" then that explains why his ass is sitting in a cell down the hall from me instead of taking an eternal dirt nap. He's half the man that he used to be, and the wheelchair put an end to his murdering career, but he still had enough evil left in him to point the finger at my ass when they started asking his ass questions. Of course, he wouldn't go down by himself, because evil likes company.

And as I sit here, I can't help but think how ironic all of this is. I said that I never wanted to go to jail, but did shit that would, eventually, land me here. The good thing is, the state knew that I was only an accomplice to some of his bullshit and having those kids testify on my behavior was the difference between life and me ever seeing my family again. Not to mention, that I held on to those flash-drives. They came in handy and helped save my ass. So, I'll do five years, get out early for good behavior, and then, I'll be home with the family that I love.

I'm sure you're asking yourself, "Will he kill again?" I can't say that I will, and I won't say that I won't. But if someone messes with me or one of mine, I'm going to have to introduce them to the real Paul.

Other Books by Diane Martin

1. Never What it Seems
2. Autumn Leaves
3. Fallen Angel
4. Never What it Seems II – A Mother's Love
5. Somebody Else's Baby
6. Somebody Else's Baby – The Screenplay
7. Kiss My Ass – This is Not Your Typical Self-Help Book
8. Born-Again Hustler – From Pimping to the Pulpit
9. Peaches – Always Kiss Your Baby Goodnight
10. Dead Ringers – Peaches II
11. Officer Friendly

Website: dianemartin.weebly.com

Daddy by Diane Martin 527

www.ingramcontent.com/pod-product-compliance
Lightning Source LLC
Chambersburg PA
CBHW051932020726
47501CB00001B/97